THE SABOTEUR

Also by Andrew Gross

The One Man
One Mile Under
Everything to Lose
No Way Back
15 Seconds
Eyes Wide Open
Reckless
Don't Look Twice
The Dark Tide
The Blue Zone

Novels by Andrew Gross and James Patterson

Judge & Jury
Lifeguard
3rd Degree
The Jester
2nd Chance

ANDREW GROSS

THE SABOTEUR

MACMILLAN

First published 2017 by Minotaur Books

First published in the UK 2017 by Macmillan
an imprint of Pan Macmillan
20 New Wharf Road, London N1 9RR
Associated companies throughout the world
www.panmacmillan.com

ISBN 978-1-5098-3157-9

1 3 5 7 9 8 6 4 2

A CIP catalogue record for this book is available from the British Library.

Typeset by Palimpsest Book Production Ltd, Falkirk, Stirlingshire
Printed and bound by CPI Group (UK) Ltd, Croydon, CR0 4YY

Visit **www.panmacmillan.com** to read more about all our books
and to buy them. You will also find features, author interviews and
news of any author events, and you can sign up for e-newsletters
so that you're always first to hear about our new releases.

THE SABOTEUR

PROLOGUE

In the years leading up to 1943, British and American intelligence in WWII focused on the possibility that the Nazis were creating sophisticated and potentially decisive weapons, weapons powerful enough that they could potentially alter the war, including the possibility that the Germans were making progress on what the Allies saw as their *own* decisive weapon—the atomic bomb. British intelligence networks undertook a vigorous campaign to determine the extent of the Nazis' progress in this area.

As far back as 1939, it was determined that the Germans were engaged in atomic research, built around the use of deuterium oxide (D_2O), or "heavy water," which acted as a moderator for the crucial step of isotope separation, essential to the creation of an atomic bomb. D_2O required enormous amounts of electrical power to produce, power not available in Germany. But D_2O was being produced and synthesized in smaller quantities for the end use of ammonia fertilizer at the Norsk Hydro plant at Vemork, Norway. This remote plant was tucked into a narrow gorge under the Hardanger vidda, or plateau, one of the most desolate and inhospitable mountainous regions in Europe.

In October 1941, these worries grew even more dire. British intelligence received a report from the Danish underground detailing a meeting between the Nobel laureate physicist Niels Bohr and Germany's leading atomic scientist, Werner Heisenberg, director of the Kaiser Wilhelm Institute in Berlin. Their conversation alarmed Bohr enough to send an immediate warning to London that he was convinced the Nazis were on the verge of obtaining a devastating weapon based on the heavy water experiments in Vemork.

On both sides of the Atlantic, Churchill and Roosevelt gave the matter their highest attention. In England, a secret committee was formed to deal with the issue, part of an organization known as the Special Operations Executive, or SOE, that only a handful of people even knew existed.

What follows is the story of how only a few brave men put an end to that threat.

PART ONE

1

March 1942

The old, creaking ferry steamed across the sun-dappled mountain lake. The *Telemark Sun* was a serviceable ship, built in 1915, coal-fired, and at around 490 tons, it could still make the thirty-kilometer jaunt across Lake Tinnsjo from Tinnoset to Mael in just under an hour and a half. It held about sixty passengers that day, as well as two empty railway wagons in the bow, heading back to the Norsk Hydro plant at Vemork after loading their cargo onto the train to Oslo at the railway depot across the lake.

Kurt Nordstrum had taken the boat across the lake a hundred times, but not in the two years since the Germans had occupied his country.

He had grown up in this region, known as the Telemark, in southeastern Norway—a place of lush, green valleys in summer and endless expanses of snow and ice in winter—between the town of Rjukan and the tiny hamlet of Vigne at the western edge of Lake Mosvatn. Like most Northmen, Nordstrum had learned to ski these mountains before he even rode a bike. He grew up hunting and fishing, in the way boys in other places kicked footballs around. To this day, the network of huts and cabins that dotted the Hardanger vidda were as familiar to him as were the lines on his own hands. His father still lived in Rjukan, though Nordstrum dared not visit him now. At least, not directly. Nordstrum was known to be one of those who had escaped to the hills and

3

continued the fight against the Nazis. It was common knowledge that the Nasjonal Samling police kept an eye on the family members of known resistance fighters in the hope of tracking them down. The Hirden of the NS party were everywhere, as feared in their tactics as the Gestapo. Followers of the puppet dictator Vidkun Quisling, they had forsaken their country and king to do the Nazis' bidding. It had been two years since Nordstrum had seen his father, and it was unlikely he would see him on this trip.

On the aft deck, dressed in workman's clothes and carrying a satchel of carpentry tools, but with a Browning .45 in his belt, Nordstrum sat back as the boat came within sight of the familiar mountains of his youth ringing the Tinnsjo. It felt good to be back in his valley. He let his face soak up the sun. He hadn't seen much of the sun lately. Since April 1940, when he'd left the university in his second year of engineering school to make his way up to Narvik and join the British trying to blockade the Nazi invaders, the blue skies of Norway had seemed under a perpetual leaden cloud. At first they'd managed to hold them off. The Germans focused their blitzkrieg on the cities. First Trondheim, then Bergen and Oslo fell in a week. Then the king took flight, first to Nybergsund, and then on to Elverum, near the Swedish border, and people knelt in the street and wept. Nordstrum had seen his share of fighting— in Honefoss and Klekko and the Gudbrandsdalen valley. A year ago in Tonneson he hooked up with what was left of a militia unit—a small group of men in tattered uniforms who would not give up. "*Here,*" they said, and put a Krag in his hand with only thirty rounds of ammunition. "That's all you get, I'm afraid," the captain said apologetically. "Better make them count." Boys, that was all they were, with rifles and Molotov cocktails to

4

make them men, and down to a single cannon taken out of mothballs from the last war. No one knew how to wage a fight. Still, they'd left their mark on the bastards. They blew up bridges, disrupted supply lines and motorcades, ambushed a couple of high-ranking SS officers; they'd put an end to a few Quisling traitors as well. At Haugsbygda, the fighting became close in. Knives and bayonets when the bullets ran out. Until they were no longer going up against soldiers and machine guns, but tanks and artillery and nose-diving fighters unloading bombs. Fifty-millimeter shells rained in from a mile away and blew their trenches into the sky.

"You're a sergeant," they told him. Mainly because Nordstrum, who'd grown up a hunter, could shoot with the best. And because he'd seen his share of bloodshed. He was tall and well built, with a high forehead and short, light hair, and a kind of purposefulness in his gray, deep-set eyes that from his youth people seemed willing to follow. His looks had hardened now. Two years of watching limbs blown in the air and a man next to you dropped by one to the forehead had made him appear ten years older.

But somehow, he was still alive. His ranks had long since splintered; most of his friends were dead. Now it was simply do whatever he could do. The king had made it to London. Nordstrum had heard they were forming some kind of Free Norwegian Army there. *England* . . . Maybe in '40, it might have been possible to find your way there—250 kilometers across the vidda through blistering storms to Sweden and then hop a neutral ship. Today, it might as well be China. He'd made the trek to Sweden once, after fleeing Narvik, but, finding little support there, came back to resume the fight. And even if you made it all the way to England, and weren't sunk to the bottom of the North Sea or handed back over by the Swedish police to the wrong people, yes, you could join up. *And then what . . . ?* Sit the war out and train. *The Free Norwegian Army . . .* He had to admit, it had a nice ring. He knew there'd be a new front one day, the real one. In time, the Allies would invade. With its endless jagged coastline that in all of Europe was the hardest to defend, Norway actually made good military sense. And Nordstrum's only remaining hope was to stick around long enough to be a part of it. To take his country back. In the distance, through the glare of the sun off the water, he spotted the port of Mael. He'd left Rjukan for the university some six years ago, still a boy. He wasn't sure what he had come back as.

"Take a look." Nordstrum elbowed his friend, Jens, a fellow fighter who was from the region as well, pointing toward the ring of familiar mountains. "Like an old friend, no?"

"An old friend if we were actually coming back to live," Jens replied. "Now it's more like some beautiful woman that you can't have, who's teasing us."

He'd known Jens from their days in school. He was from Rauland, just to the north. Their fathers had been friends. As school kids they played football against each other; hunted and skinned deer together. Skied the same mountains.

"You sound like an old man," Nordstrum said reprovingly. "You're twenty-five. Enjoy the view."

"Well, two years of war will do that to you." Though through it all, Jens had somehow maintained his boyish looks. "I look forward to one day coming back here with no one shooting after me and—"

"Jens." Nordstrum cut his friend off in mid-sentence. "Look over there." This time, he indicated an officer in full gray Hirden uniform who had stepped out on deck like some preening rooster, as if the ribbons on his chest came from battlefield valor instead of from some political appointment. The Quislings were in control now, National Socialists who took over after the king had fled, and who happily had become the Nazis' puppets. Traitors, collaborators, they stayed at home, spying on their townsfolk, making secret arrests, spouting propaganda on the radio, while all the brave ones fought in the mountains and died. Enough of Nordstrum's friends had been put up against a wall and shot on information squeezed from informants by the Quisling police to make his stomach tighten in a knot at the sight of the traitor.

The officer sauntered toward them. He had a pinched-in face like an owl and beady, self-important eyes under his peaked officer's cap, his chest puffed out by his meaningless rank. National Unity party, it was called. *Unity in hell*. Nordstrum would have gladly spat at his feet as he went by, if his journey here didn't have some real importance attached to it.

"I see him," said Jens. The Hird had a pistol in his belt, but they had a Bren at the bottom of their tool bag, and the will to use it. They'd taken care of many such traitors over the past year. "Just give me the word."

"Why do you need *my* word?" Nordstrum said under his breath, nodding pleasantly to the officer as he approached. "Good day to you, sir."

"Good day to you. Heil Hitler." The Quisling raised his hand and nodded back.

Jens, who looked like he barely shaved, but had killed as many Germans as Nordstrum, merely shrugged as the man strode by. "Because you're the sergeant."

Sergeant. . . Nordstrum laughed to himself. Anyway, their outfit was now dispersed. His rank was meaningless, though Jens never failed to bring it up every chance he could.

7

"Because we promised to meet up with Einar," Nordstrum said. "There's a reason, if we're looking for one." He held back his friend's arm.

"You're right, that *is* a reason," Jens acknowledged with a sigh of disappointment. "Though not much of one." They followed the Quisling as he made his way down the deck. "There'll be other times."

Einar Skinnarland had gotten word to Nordstrum in the mountains near Lillehammer that he needed to see him on a matter of the highest urgency. He couldn't tell Nordstrum just what it was, but Nordstrum's friend was not one to trifle with when he claimed something was urgent. Nordstrum had known him from youth as well, and they both had gone on to engineering school in Oslo, though Einar, two years older, had graduated before the war and now had a good job on the Mosvatn Dam, as well as a wife and son. *Please come,* the message read, so Nordstrum did. No questions asked. At considerable risk. They were to meet at a café on the wharf in Mael on the east end of the Tinnsjo, near where the ferry docked.

From there he and Jens had no idea where they would head. Likely search for some unit up in the mountains to join up with. He had some names to contact. One had to be very careful today about what one did. The Nazis had adopted a forty-to-one policy for all acts of sabotage, rounding up and shooting forty innocent townsfolk for every German killed. Protecting the home folk was vital to Nordstrum, as to all true Norwegians. What else were they fighting for? What did it really matter if it was forty soldiers killed in an effort to retake their country or forty innocents lined up against a wall and shot? Forty dead was forty dead. Nordstrum had seen this policy carried out firsthand, and still carried around the pain in his heart. He didn't want to be the cause of it to others. It didn't put them out of business; it only changed the rules a bit. And it made him loathe the bastards even more. They just had to be careful about what they did.

Farther down the deck, the Quisling came up to a young woman with a child by her side. She had dark hair and a swarthy complexion, and hid her eyes as the officer went by, which was like milk to a cat to these weasels.

"May I see your papers, please?" The officer stopped at her, putting out his hand.

"Sir?"

"Your papers," the Hird said again, his fingers beckoning impatiently.

Frightened, the woman held the child with one arm while she fumbled through her bag with the other, finally producing her ID card.

"*Kominic* . . ." The Quisling looked at the picture on it and then back at her. "What kind of a name is that? Gypsy? Jewish?"

"It is Slav," the woman declared in Norwegian. "But you can see, I'm from Oslo. I'm just taking my son to his father, who's been working in Rauland."

"Your Norwegian is quite good, madame," the Quisling said. "But it is clear you are not of Norwegian blood. So what is it then?"

"It should be good, sir, I've lived in Norway my whole life," she replied, an edge of nerves in her voice. "I'm as Norwegian as you, I swear."

"Yes, well, we will have to verify this when we get to Mael." The Quisling looked again at her ID card. "Do not disembark until you see me, madame. Otherwise I have no choice but to turn you and your child over to the authorities there."

Fear sprang up in her eyes. Her boy, sensing his mother's agitation, began to whimper. "Please, sir, we're not meaning anyone harm. I only beg you to—"

"Your child appears sick, madame. Perhaps you should keep him separate from the other passengers."

"He's fine. You're just scaring him, that's all."

"If you have nothing to hide, then there is nothing to be afraid of, I assure you." The Hird handed her back the card. "We are only interested that the law is followed and all Jews and non-purebloods must be registered as such with the state. Now, I insist you take your son and wait for me inside. We'll settle this little matter in Mael."

Clearly upset, the woman struggled to pick up her belongings, and, grabbing her son's hand, led him to the third-class seating. A nearby man got up and helped her gather her things. But it was hard not to notice the agitation that had taken over her face. Her papers were likely correct. She could be a Jew or a Gypsy. Nordstrum had heard they'd begun to round up those people and send them to places like Grini, a guarded camp outside Oslo, and some of them shipped even farther to places in Europe, to who knows where? Maybe she was fleeing into the mountains with her son to hide. Maybe she had someone there to take them in. Whatever, they were no bother to anyone. Nordstrum looked toward the shoreline. They were about three-quarters through the crossing. Another half hour or so to go. The tiny ferry stop at Mael, tucked underneath the mountains, was now visible in the distance off the port side.

"*Fucker.*" Jens gritted his teeth in disgust. "Using his power to terrorize an innocent woman." He looked toward

Nordstrum with a kind of conspiratorial gleam in his eye, a silent communication they both instantly understood. *Are you up for it?*

And Nordstrum, angered by the Quisling as well, looked back with resignation, as if unable to stop what would happen next. "Why not? Let's go."

Jens grinned. "Now you're talking."

Nordstrum stood up. He got the officer's attention with a wave, motioning the man toward him.

He and Jens stepped back toward the stern, where there were no passengers around.

The Hird came up to him. "Yes?"

"You were asking about that woman?" Nordstrum said. "I know her. If you want, I can fill you in."

"There are rewards for good citizens as yourselves." The Quisling's eyes grew bright, likely thinking of the favor he would receive for uncovering and turning in an escaped Gypsy or Jew.

"Over here, then." Nordstrum motioned him to the railing, Jens a step behind. "Not everyone feels the same way. I don't want anyone to hear."

The breeze whipped off the lake, sharp and chilling. Most passengers were either inside having a coffee or lining the deck amidships in the sun. One couple was having a cigarette on the second deck by the rear smokestack, the gusting wind flapping their hair.

"We're workmen. We've seen her in Oslo, as she says." Nordstrum leaned close.

The Quisling sidled up to him. "Go on . . ."

The two on the second deck had now turned and were pointing toward the mountains. Nordstrum caught Jens's eye, and then leaned close to the Quisling. "Well, you see, it's like this . . ."

From behind, Jens lifted the officer in the air. There was barely time for him to realize what was happening. "What the hell—"

"Here's *your* reward," Nordstrum said, seizing the man's legs. "Enjoy your swim."

They carried him to the rail, the Hird kicking against them now with a shout that was muffled by the whipping wind, and then hoisted him, his arms cycling frantically and his face twisted in shock and fear, over the side and into the icy lake.

The Quisling's scream was drowned out by the heavily churning engines as the *Telemark Sun,* chugging at ten knots per hour, pulled farther away.

"Heil Hitler to you, as well!" Jens called after him, extending his arm.

There was barely a noise as he hit the water.

But someone must have seen him from the decks. Suddenly there were shouts. "*Man overboard! Someone in the water!*"

On the top deck, people ran to the railing, pointing. The alarm began to sound, a big booming *whorl, whorl.* Passengers rushed out to see what was happening.

The frigid March waters were probably no more than thirty-five or -six degrees, Nordstrum figured, and, coupled with the weight of the Quisling's now water-sodden coat dragging the struggling man down, even the strongest of swimmers wouldn't last more than a couple of minutes before he succumbed.

People were shouting now, gesturing toward the water. "*Save him!*" Two of the crew ran to the stern, one of them holding a life preserver and untying a coil of rope. Bravely, he climbed onto the rail, readying himself to throw it. "Hold on!" he called to the drowning man. But it was pointless to hurl it now; they were too far away.

The boat's engines slowed as the ship gradually came about. People streamed to the lower deck, passengers and crew, pointing toward the water as the Quisling struggled and flailed, the weight of his jacket and medals dragging him under.

"Someone do something!" a woman yelled. "Help him!"

"It's the Quisling," another said.

"Oh. Let the bastard swim then."

One member of the crew gamely removed his jacket, about to dive in. Nordstrum held the man back. "Let him be."

"Let him be, sir?" The crewman looked aghast. "The man's drowning."

"He's not drowning." Nordstrum shrugged. "He's swimming." And when the puzzled seaman looked back in confusion, Nordstrum told him again, "Just let him be."

In the minutes it took for the ferry to make a sweeping turn and come around, the Quisling had disappeared. All that was left was his gray, billed officer's cap, bobbing on the surface.

A woman crossed herself. "He's gone."

The captain, a gray-bearded man in a thick sweater, finally made his way down from the bridge. "What the hell's happened here?"

Nordstrum shrugged and met the seaman's gaze. "He wanted to take a swim. Who were we to hold him back?"

"Take a swim . . . ?" The captain glared accusingly. "There'll be hell to pay when we make land."

"He was a fucking Quisling," Nordstrum said. "Any problem with it?"

People huddled around, on the main deck and on the deck above, staring.

The captain's eyes slowly drifted to the place in the water where the officer's body had gone down. Then he looked back at Nordstrum and spat into the lake. "No problem at all."

No one uttered a sound.

"Full speed ahead," he shouted up to the bridge. "We've got a schedule to maintain."

2

An hour later, at a café called The Gunwale along the wharf in the tiny village of Mael, Nordstrum, Jens, and Einar Skinnarland sat at a table having beers. The town was barely larger than a few docks and a rail depot, where cargo from the Norsk Hydro chemical factory in Vemork was carted down the mountain and loaded onto the ferries.

Nursing his Carlsberg, Nordstrum noticed the surprising number of Germans in town, which made him uneasy. Up to now, any Germans he encountered this close, he usually killed.

"You have to get used to it," Einar said. "Things have changed since you've last been here."

"I hope I never get used to it," Nordstrum said, his eyes roaming to the Germans milling about freely.

"Before we start, I just wanted to say, Marte and I were very sorry to hear about Anna-Lisette." Einar gave him a nod.

"It's war." Nordstrum shrugged. "Things like that happen. But thank you. Tell Marte the same for me."

"It may be war, but it's still a fucking shame. And what's the word on your father?" Einar asked.

"Not well, from what I hear." Nordstrum's father had been a train mechanic for twenty years, and now ran the small farm on the edge of town where Nordstrum had grown up. "Working around all that coal has finally gotten the better of him."

"I'm sorry to hear."

"Maybe you can get word to him for me. Let him know I'm okay."

"How long has it been since you've seen him?"

Nordstrum took a swig of beer. "Not since the war. Two years."

"Two years . . . A lot's changed in two years. I'll see what I can do."

"I'd be in your debt," said Nordstrum. "But, more important, tell me, how is your son?" Karl was merely a baby when Nordstrum had seen him last.

"Booming." Einar's face lit up with pride. "He's going on three now. His vocabulary's already larger than mine."

"Now that's not much of a surprise," Nordstrum said with a grin, and took another sip of beer.

Einar laughed obligingly. "And we already have him up on skis."

"Of course. Like any Northman. He'll be beating you down the Hawk's Nest before you know it. And then, he'll—" Nordstrum stopped mid-sentence as his gaze shifted to two SS officers who took seats at a table at the opposite end of the café. They were polite and removed their caps. The proprietor of the place hurried over to them with napkins and silverware. "Look over there."

"Relax." Einar shrugged. "You don't have to worry about them. They're far too busy to care about us. It's the stinking Quisling militia you've got to worry about. They've got their noses in everything now."

"Well, we know one less you'll have to pay attention to." Jens sniffed, pushing a blond curl off his forehead.

"How do you mean?"

"There was one on the ferry putting the fear of God into some woman and her boy, probably a poor Jew on the run,"

Nordstrum explained. "Anyway, he had this sudden urge for a swim."

"*A swim?* It's freezing in the lake this time of year."

"You know these Quislings. . . ." Nordstrum's face barely twitched. "Hard to stop them when they get their minds set on something."

"*Jesus . . . !*" Einar's eyes went wide and he said under his breath, "You sent him over the side. What are you trying to do, hang a sign around your neck, 'Come and get me—I'm right here'?"

"Couldn't be helped," Nordstrum said with a glance toward the Germans.

"These bastards . . ." Einar sipped his beer with an eye to the soldiers as well. "They're all over, like fucking crickets in June. Rjukan's overrun with them."

"*Rjukan?*" Rjukan was Nordstrum's home, about as unstrategic a place as could be. "Why here?"

"The Norsk Hydro plant. Up in Vemork. They've got something big going on up there."

"Norsk Hydro? I thought all they made up there was fertilizer," Jens chimed in.

"Ammonium nitrate." Einar nodded. "But that's all small potatoes now. These days it's run by the Germans." Nordstrum gave him a look of surprise. "All very top secret. It's actually why I asked you here."

He reached into his pocket and took out something, careful to conceal it from the German officers on the other side of the café, who had ordered sardines and beer.

It was a toothpaste tube, halfway rolled up.

"Trying to tell me something, Einar?" Nordstrum said. "I know I've been up in the hills a long time."

"Perhaps. But this one's likely the most important tube of

toothpaste in all of Europe. It was smuggled to me by Jomar Brun. He's the chief engineer at Norsk Hydro. There's something inside it." Einar took a cautionary glance at the Germans, who were trying to gain the waiter's attention for two more glasses of beer. "Microfilm."

"Microfilm?" Chief engineer was an important job, Nordstrum thought, and the Norsk Hydro factory was one of the largest operations in all of Norway. It was built into the narrow gorge a mile up the valley, since the rivers and cataracts that came down from the vidda were an excellent source of hydroelectric power. Truth was, the Norsk Hydro plant was the only reason Rjukan even existed as a town in the first place.

"He says we have to get it into the hands of Leif Tronstad, Kurt. That it's a matter of the highest importance."

"*Tronstad?*" The name got Nordstrum's complete attention. "Tronstad's in England, is he not?" Leif Tronstad was a world-renowned scientist whose name was known to most Norwegians. In fact, he had run the Norsk Hydro plant years earlier, before he escaped to London. Word was, he was a leader in the Free Norwegian Army there now. Nordstrum inspected the tube. If Tronstad needed to see this, one could be sure it *was* of the utmost importance. He handed it back to Einar. "Microfilm, huh? Of what?"

"Brun would only say that it was vital to get it safely into Tronstad's hands in the fastest possible way. He knew I had contacts." He put the tube back into his pocket.

"Getting to England isn't exactly an easy thing, Einar." Nordstrum took a pencil and sketched a map on his napkin. "Sweden would be the best route. But that's not an easy journey. The sun may be shining here, but in the mountains it's still winter. And even if you make it there, through the storms and German patrols, there's still no guarantee."

"That's why I contacted you, Kurt. You know the way. You're at your best up there on the vidda. I'm hoping you'll come with me."

"With *you?* You're an engineer, Einar, not an agent. You belong in the field, checking for cracks on dams, not playing with guns. Besides, you have a family to take care of. It's two hundred and fifty kilometers to Charlottenberg." The town closest to the Swedish border. "You're truly willing to take this on?'

"I can hold my own as well as any in the mountains, Kurt. Brun said it was vital. And besides . . ." He trailed off.

"Besides, *what* . . . ?" Nordstrum took another sip of beer.

"Besides," Einar gave him a smile, "I already took my full vacation allotment to do this. Twelve days. If I can make it back by then, they'll never even know I was gone."

"Twelve days . . ." Nordstrum shook his head. "Even if you do make it, I can promise it won't be much of a vacation. Does Marte know?"

Nordstrum knew her from back in school. Pretty and no pushover. His friend had chosen well in that department.

"The country needs this, Kurt. Maybe the world needs this. So yes, I am prepared. But I'd be a damn sight happier if I had you along with me. And, of course, you too, Jens, if you're game?"

Jens shrugged. "I'm game for whatever the sergeant here says. . . ." He took a swig of beer, leaving a foam mustache on his lip.

"Sergeant?" Einar widened his eyes. "I'm not surprised."

"All it means is that I can point a rifle and pull the trigger." Nordstrum waved it off.

19

"Still, I'm sure you've seen some things." Einar's eyes grew serious and Nordstrum knew exactly what he meant.

"We've all seen some things, Einar." He nodded grimly. "But getting across the vidda is no easy feat. You know the difficulties. Storms, German patrols. It surely won't be twelve days, no matter how we ski."

The weather on the vidda could change in an instant. There would be days when travel would be next to impossible. They'd have to arrange food, clothing. "And even if we get to Sweden," Nordstrum took a sip of beer, "what do we do, just put out a hand and hail a taxi to England?"

"Brun felt certain he could arrange transport for us through the British embassy in Stockholm," Einar said.

"He felt certain, did he? You know if you're caught by the militia there they just ship you right back. And there are Germans waiting with big smiles and their hands out on the other side of the border to pick you up. It's what almost happened to me."

"I know all that," Einar said. "But I'm still going. With you or not."

Nordstrum shook his head and sniffed, as if it were folly. He knew his name was on a list of fighters in the resistance. Lately, it was getting far too dangerous here. It was only a matter of time before he and Jens ended up shot or handed over to the wrong side. And *Tronstad* . . . A true hero. A man the whole country admired. And it would be good to join up with the Free Norwegian Army there and one day return to take his country back for good. As part of a real fighting force. That was the true new front in this war, the way to make a real difference.

"The fastest way, you said . . . ," said Nordstrum, thinking.

Einar smiled, his hope rising. "Yes."

Nordstrum tapped his index finger against the table. "And you're one hundred percent willing to put your life at risk and take this on? Who knows when you'll be able to make it back?"

"In my view, the importance far outweighs the risk," the engineer said. "So, yes."

"And you're in as well, I assume?" Nordstrum turned to Jens. "Though in your case, I know I hardly need to ask."

"I don't exactly have a vacation to devote to it," Jens said. "But my dance card is surprisingly free."

"All right then . . . In that case, the fastest way to England would be by ship," Nordstrum said, turning to Einar.

"*Ship* . . . ? Across the North Sea? That's crazier than the vidda." Then, as he ran the thought in his head, his eyes grew brighter. "It would certainly have to be a large one." He seemed to be warming to the idea.

"So what did you tell them at your job that you'd be doing while on vacation?" Nordstrum drained the last of his beer.

"A few days of skiing . . . Helping out a bit with the kids . . ."

"Maybe instead you should have told them you were thinking of going on a cruise.

"Three more!" Nordstrum called to the proprietor with a friendly wave toward the table of Germans, who raised their mugs back to him. "We're Vikings, aren't we?" His gaze drifted to the wharf. "For Vikings there are always ships."

3

The road out of Rjukan toward Vigne was usually quiet after dark. Nordstrum huddled in the shadow of the stone wall that ran from the church to the border of his father's farm. The old *stabbur* wooden farmhouse, situated on four hectares, that Nordstrum grew up in was built in the traditional Norwegian style: a narrow first floor suitable for storing grain and hanging meat, and larger living quarters situated on top. Tonight, the house was dark. The room Nordstrum had as a boy was over the front door and faced the street. His father still kept a couple of Telemark cows on the property and a few hens, which his mother had tended when she was alive. After she died, when Nordstrum was only twelve, his father took his pension from the railway company and retired to the farm. In his tastes, Alois Nordstrum was a simple man, but in action, he was as large as anyone Nordstrum knew. A man who could sustain himself for weeks alone on the vidda in winter with only his hands and his wits. He taught Nordstrum how to shoot, how to make a shelter, how to make a fire with only dried vegetation in all that snow, how to melt water. When Nordstrum was eleven, his father took him into the mountains in the dead of winter to a hut above Mosvatn, fifteen kilometers from town. "If you are to be a man you must find your way back," his father said to him. "Otherwise, you are still a boy." Then, leaving only a rifle and a few liters of water, his father skied away.

It took Nordstrum six hours to make it back down. A squall picked up on the way and he had to ski through snow so thick and blinding he could barely see his hand in front of his face. If it hadn't blown through quickly, he would have had to shoot his own food and make a camp to survive. Hours later, in darkness, Nordstrum finally trudged back to the house—exhausted, frozen, so spent and cold his skis just fell out of his hands and he collapsed to his knees inside the door. Furious, his mother scolded his father for what he had done, but the old man just told her to shush and waved to Nordstrum. "Come here, Kurt." Wet and famished, and a little angry too, Nordstrum did. His father picked him up and held Nordstrum's blue face close to his chest and said, "'In the Northlands, a true man goes on until he can go no further—and then he goes twice as far.' Remember that, boy. One day, you may be called on to give a lot more than you think you have. Now you know you have it in you. In the meantime . . ." He put Nordstrum back on his feet and mussed his hair. "Tonight, you sit here." He lifted Nordstrum into his own chair at the head of the table. "You've earned it." As the biting wind cut through him on his miserable journey home, Nordstrum had cursed his father the whole way, but now he felt proud and knew the old man was right. He *had* been called on to do more. More than he knew he could. And while other children doubted themselves as they grew into men, Nordstrum always had this strength he could count on. He knew what he had inside, and others felt it.

On the road now, a beer truck clattered by, carrying Ringnes to the taverns in Rjukan. And shortly after, two Germans zoomed by on motorcycles. It was March and the wind was still sharp and brisk, and Nordstrum watched the house in his woolen jacket, huddled against the chill. He knew it wasn't wise to go inside—he was a known conspirator and the NS could easily be watching—but as it grew dark he thought, *What the hell,* and looped around back from the neighbor's property, through the fence, past the cow sheds and tractor stall, and snuck inside through the storage room door, which they always kept unlocked. He knew his father had been sick, though he was helpless to do much for him. This might well be the last time he would see him for a while. Perhaps for good. In the hearth, the fire was low. He saw his father's reading glasses on a table by a book. *The Master Builder,* by Ibsen. Nordstrum smiled. The drama was one of his favorites. His father always saw himself as kind of an uncompromising figure himself. Growing up, Nordstrum had heard about the hubris of Halvard Solness and the wanderings of Peer Gynt a hundred times.

"*Father!*" he called out in the empty house.

No one replied.

Nordstrum knew that sometimes after work his father would head off to the Ox and Wheel in town for a couple of beers and a game of checkers. He picked up a photo on the table: his parents in front of the Royal Palace in Oslo, before Nordstrum was even born. And there was also one of him and his sister, Kristin, with whom Nordstrum had shared a room until he was twelve. She had married a professor and was living in Trondheim now. There was the familiar smell of tobacco about, his father's pipe left in its ashtray, a smell from his youth that brought his childhood back as soon as it met his nostrils, and made him visualize his father as if he was sitting in his chair with a book on his lap, or sanding down wood for a sled, his pipe clenched between his teeth. Nordstrum opened the Ibsen, placing the ashtray on the book's spine to spread it wide. He placed something in it, something that would let his father know he had been here.

Then, knowing the more time he spent here the more

dangerous it became, he headed back out through the storage room and left.

From across the street, he kept an eye out until it grew late and cold. His father had never wanted Nordstrum to go off and fight. He wanted him to come back to Rjukan, to the farm, and wait out the storm here. His old man wasn't a political person in any way; he thought the whole thing would all blow over quickly. "A fuss about nothing," he insisted at first. "What do we even have here but snow and ice? By winter, the bastards will all have numb fingers and leave." By then, Nordstrum was in his second year in engineering school in Oslo. Watching the house, his mind drifted to Anna-Lisette, his fiancée, in her last year of economics, with a face like a picture of the Sognefjord in May but a will of steel. In Oslo, many of the students donned the blue and yellow colors of the king. Patriotism raged like wildfire. Many looked to Nordstrum, who was strong and could handle himself in a fight and so was regarded as a kind of leader. "What about you, Kurt?" his fellow students asked. "You'll be joining up as well, won't you?"

"I don't know," he would reply. "Have you ever even shot a gun? Don't be so quick to jump into uniform."

Then the German flagship *Blucher* was sunk in the Oslofjord, and what was merely a threat became a full-out war.

Anna-Lisette went back to her home up north in Lillehammer. The Nazis weren't anywhere near there yet. Nordstrum took her as far as he could on the train on his way to Narvik to fight.

"Please be safe, Kurt." She held him close. "And smart. You always put others before yourself. In a war, that'll only get you killed."

"I promise," Nordstrum said, making a little fun of her. "I will let the others do all the fighting for me."

"I mean it, Kurt," she said reprovingly, in her red and green reindeer sweater, her blond hair in braids. The Nazis had run easily through Poland, France, and the Netherlands. No one knew what was ahead of them. A ring of worry pooled in her blue eyes.

"Anna-Lisette, don't be afraid." Nordstrum brushed his hand against her cheek, more serious. "You don't have to worry about me."

"It's not just me," she said. She leaned over and kissed him, and pressed the baptism cross she wore around her neck into his hand. And then she was off the train at Lillehammer and he went on, leaning out between the cars and waving to her from the hand rail as it took him away, like some red-cheeked boy heading off to a soccer match, not to war. "I'll be back for you!" he shouted, holding up her gift. They exchanged a few letters. By June she said the fighting was coming close to her; already there were Germans in the Gudbrandsdalen valley. It was August when he got word that a gruppenfuhrer's car had been blown up on the road into town. Anna-Lisette was at the market when the German truck troop pulled up in the square. Soldiers jumped out, selecting townspeople at random. "You there! And you. Yes, miss, you." Until they numbered forty. A proclamation was read aloud, then Anna-Lisette was put against a wall and shot, alongside thirty-nine of her townspeople. It was part of the new response to acts of sabotage against the Reich. And this time it was an act Nordstrum's own unit had set up. He only found out what had happened much later.

Now, back on the road from Rjukan, Nordstrum saw lights coming toward him and then weave to the other side of the road. His father's truck—the coughing old Opel that somehow continued to run, for even in war, it defied imagination how something so beat up could still be moving. Nordstrum's heart sped up. The truck slowed, and Nordstrum almost made a move to follow it. It turned through his father's gate and bounced along the rutted, unpaved road to the house.

From far away, Nordstrum watched the old man climb out. He looked older, of course, stooped a bit, maybe a bit wayward from the beer. In two years, he looked as if he'd aged ten. A man who once could ski thirty kilometers with barely a stop for water, and who could drop a reindeer from a hundred meters with a single shot. Nordstrum watched him collect some wood and load it into a kindling strap, push with his shoulder against the heavy wooden door to their house, which stuck for a moment as it always had, and head inside.

The coast seemed clear. Nordstrum stepped out of the shadows of his hiding place, about to cross the street.

But before he fully stepped into the light, a bolt of caution grabbed him and he ducked back against the wall.

A car came alive from down the road near the church and crept toward him. The crest of the Quisling NS party on its door. It slowed as it came up to his father's road, and then stopped. His father was upstairs now; a light was on in the house. The shades were open and you could see him making his way around, dropping off the collected wood at the hearth, kneeling, stoking the flame. Two men stepped out of the car. The streetlight showed them in dark suits, the uniform of the Quisling police.

Nordstrum's fists clenched into a ball.

They waited for a while, looking down toward the house.

One of them whispered something to the other. The heavier one headed down the street, his footsteps clacking on the stone. The other remained by the car. Nordstrum's hand found the Browning in his belt. He could take them both, he knew. No doubt of it. But his father would be the first casualty. And after his meeting today with Einar and what lay ahead for them both, that would not be wise.

So he remained huddled against the church. The one who had gone around the side came back and conferred a bit with his colleague watching the house. Nothing to report, they must have decided. They climbed back into their car and started the engine. Slowly, they passed the house, and, as if satisfied nothing was afoot, drove on.

Only then did Nordstrum remove his hand from his gun.

Inside, he saw a figure at the window. He was either watching the NS car—the old fox likely knew they were there—or, as he looked out, beyond them, to the street, something else.

On the Ibsen that he'd laid open on his father's table, Nordstrum had left his school ring.

His father stood there, looking out, knowing exactly what it meant. As if he knew Nordstrum was still there. He made a brief wave with his hand; not so much a greeting, with any affection, merely enough to convey *Move on, Kurt. It's not safe here for you now.*

Not now.

Then, with the slightest nod, he closed the shades.

Who knew what lay ahead? Nordstrum would be gone in the morning. He didn't know if he would ever see the old man again. War came with that risk. Truth was, he didn't even know if he would survive the next days himself.

He put up his collar and headed away from the wall,

taking the long way back toward town, around the rectory, away from the road, through fields of snow. The biting wind knifed through his jacket. In his mind, Nordstrum felt the strangest sensation of being lifted up, a child again in his father's arms, feeling the safety of his grip, then being put down into the large chair that was his father's seat at the end of the table.

"*A true man goes on until he can go no further, Kurt*," he heard his father say proudly, "*and then he goes twice as far. Remember that.*"

And he had.

4

Two days later, in the town of Flekkefjord in southern Norway, the D/S *Galtesund* pulled away from the dock with three loud blasts of its horn.

On the wharf, in this quiet fishing village where the war seemed yet to have visited, people waved as the coastal steamer drifted into the fjord and came around. For thirty-five years, the *Galtesund,* at 620 tons, had chugged along at a max of thirteen knots, with a single smokestack and a crew of twenty. Like an old dog that knew its way home, it slowly chugged its way up Norway's western coast to Kristiansand, Bergen, Trondheim, and Tromso, all the way to Hammerfest in the north, if the ice was free, and then reversed its route and made the long slog back to Oslo. It was a kind of maritime bus, dropping off vital supplies, businessmen, and families, a lifeline along the coast. There were two classes onboard, and twelve small staterooms for any willing to make a longer trip of it. Not exactly the *Queen Mary,* even the captain knew. But it damn well got there.

A few fishing vessels got out of its wake as it chugged up the narrow fjord.

Stavanger, the next stop. Four hours.

On the aft deck, Nordstrum, Einar, and Jens, along with two other men known to Einar, Odd and Lars, smoked in the freezing drizzle, waiting for the ship to clear the sight of land.

They had on everyday workmen's clothes, as if heading to their jobs at the boatyards of Bergen or the gunnite mines of Tromso. They carried heavy satchels, which to anyone's eye would appear to be their tools, a common practice in Norway; tools were passed on from father to son. In reality, the bags contained two Bren submachine guns with ammunition clips, several handguns, and a handheld radio. Despite the Occupation, there were still large parts of Norway that went on as if the war had not touched them. And this was one. The boat was filled with happy families and regular folk just traveling up the coast. No sign of soldiers or police onboard. Just the crew.

"So far so good." Einar gave a nod to Nordstrum, a glimmer of hope in his eyes.

Nordstrum flicked his cigarette into the water. "Let's hope it continues."

An hour later, they had cleared the mouth of the fjord and were steaming up the coast at thirteen knots, barely in sight of land. Nordstrum had sized up the crew. A few young merchantmen just going about their jobs. Nothing to worry about. A few more were grizzled veterans. Family men. And the captain. Nordstrum watched him as they readied for sea. Smoking a pipe in his blue uniform with a gray beard and weathered blue eyes. Nordstrum pegged him as the type who would not roll over easily. Happily, they hadn't seen sight of anyone military on board. If they had, they would have had to dispose of them. But you never knew; knew how far someone would go to protect the passengers. Or—be it with Quisling or the king—where their sympathies lay?

An hour out of Stavanger, they chugged along, as much in the North Sea as along the southwest coast.

It was time.

The men looked to Nordstrum, who flicked another cigarette into the sea. "Let's go, boys."

Jens opened his tool bag and hid a Bren under his pea-coat. He slipped another to Lars. Nordstrum took his Browning. They kicked the bags beneath a bench. Lars went to the third-class cafeteria, where the bulk of the passengers gathered. Nordstrum and Einar climbed to the foredeck and headed to the bridge. Jens and Odd slipped inside a poop door and headed to the engine room.

On the bridge deck, Nordstrum and Einar took one last, quick glance at each other, then opened the side door and went in. The captain was drinking a coffee and looked up, surprised. The first mate was plotting the course. A third officer, who handled the radio, was scribbling at some kind of word puzzle.

"We have a request, Captain," Nordstrum said.

"No passengers on the bridge." The captain waved them off. The radioman quickly leaped up to bar their way. "We're behind in time. We have a schedule to maintain."

"We understand you have a schedule. It's just, I'm afraid you're about to be delayed even further," Nordstrum said.

They removed their guns from underneath their jackets. Einar stepped back and pointed the Bren at all of them. Nordstrum announced, "In the name of the king, we're seizing control of your ship."

"*My ship* . . . ?" The captain put down his mug and stood up defiantly. "What do you mean, seizing control?"

"I'm afraid we won't be stopping at Stavanger any longer. We're diverting. Navigator, please put in a new destination."

"New destination?" The captain glared back. "What in hell are you talking about? New destination where?"

"A bit off your regular headings," Nordstrum said. "Due west. Aberdeen."

"*Aberdeen?*" The captain's eyes bolted wide. "Aberdeen's

in Scotland! Are you mad? That's a two-day journey. We barely have enough fuel aboard to make Trondheim. Besides, when the Germans get wind of our course they'll blow us out of the sea. Even if we could make twice our speed, we won't make it halfway."

"May I use the radio then?" Einar asked the befuddled radioman, who glanced toward the captain.

"Radio?" the captain said. "The frequencies are monitored by the Germans day and night. Isn't that right, Svorson?"

"It is, sir," the seaman in headsets answered.

"Well, let me have a try then. Who knows, my frequencies may bring better luck. We'll have an escort as soon as we clear Norwegian waters."

"An escort? In the name of the king, you say . . . ?"

"You're a patriot, aren't you?" Nordstrum asked. "You're not a Quisling?"

"Quisling?" The captain's bushy eyebrows rose. "I fought in the last war with the Danes against the Huns. I'm no collaborator. But king be damned" —he glared— "this is still piracy. If we're caught, you'll all be hanged. If we're not blown apart first."

Nordstrum leveled his gun, a sign for the radioman to get up from his chair. "There's no time to argue, Captain. It's Knudson, right?"

The captain nodded tentatively. "Aye. Knudson."

"Well, Captain Knudson, either take the wheel, or you can spend the rest of the journey in your quarters. With your crew locked in their mess."

"There's a hundred and forty passengers on this ship to worry about, and keep safe." He refused to budge.

"And we intend no harm to any of them," Nordstrum

assured him. "Or the crew." He picked up the intercom and went to hand it to him. "Change of course, Captain. Tell the engine room full speed ahead. Due west."

"They won't accept it. I promise you." He didn't move.

"And I think they will, sir. In fact, two of my men are down there persuading them right now."

Eyeing him defiantly, Knudson took the handset from Nordstrum and muttered under his breath, "You realize we'll all be dead by nightfall. . . ." He pressed the intercom button and contacted the engine room. "Sven, this is the captain. You have a visitor down there?"

"Aye, Captain. Two. And armed. What's going on?"

"They say we're to go full speed ahead with a change of course." The captain read them their new bearings, his hard, sea-gray eyes locked on Nordstrum, as if telling him, *This will end in disaster. You'll see.* The engineer in the engine room seemed to question him at first, then finally responded, "Did you say due *west*, Captain?"

"Aye. West." He spat. "And with all you have." He put the handset back in its place.

"I'm afraid, sir, the crew will have to be kept under lock," Nordstrum said. "Other than what it takes to man the engine room, and those in food service, of course. For the comfort of the passengers. I'm sure you understand. Now take the wheel." Nordstrum directed him to it.

The captain didn't move.

"Take the wheel, sir." Nordstrum pulled back the hammer on his gun. "Or you can be certain, I will."

Slowly, with a kind of gruff but helpless glance that read, *I hope to God you know what the hell you're doing,* Knudson put his hand around the ship's wheel and spun it left. The

Galtesund, with a loud start from its engines, made a sweeping turn away from the mainland.

Maybe a few people on deck noticed the change.

"One more thing," Nordstrum said to the captain. "It will make the rest of the voyage far more relaxing on everyone's part. . . ."

"And what is that?"

"I believe the ship's weapons are in your quarters, kept under lock and key. I'm sure you'll entrust the keys to my colleague here. And now," he handed the captain the handset, "if you would make an announcement to the passengers to let them know what is going on."

Knudson took the handset and gave Nordstrum a defiant glare. "They're never going to let us leave, you know. That *you* can be certain of."

5

The next day. German Coastal Command,
Bergen, Norway.

Artillery Major Klaus Freyn was relieving himself in his private bathroom at the Norwegian Air Defenses when he heard the knock on his office door. "A minute, please," he called out, squeezing the last from his aching bladder. Whatever condition he'd been suffering from these past six weeks had not improved a bit with these useless antibiotics they had prescribed for him. This was the fifth time he'd had to go today, and it was only 2 P.M. He winced as pain knifed through his groin. "Just be patient. I'll be right there."

As the officer in charge of the coastal command, Freyn's job was to oversee the radar and coastal reconnaissance network on the North Sea sector, sweeping for enemy aircraft on potential bombing missions or the first signs of coastal assault—an impossible task, he knew, since the coastline of this frigid country was as irregular and unrelenting as his kidneys. His job was to identify any intrusion and scramble the Luftwaffe or a destroyer to repel the threat. Or, if the urgency was greater, alert German Military Control in Oslo. To this point, other than twice for a drill, in the year he had had this job Freyn had not had to make a single call.

He flushed, ran tap water over his hands, straightened his fly, and stepped out of the toilet. Lieutenant Holm, who oversaw the radar room, stood at Freyn's desk.

"I am sorry, Herr Major," the lieutenant said, "but it's urgent."

"Nature, my apologies, Lieutenant," Freyn grunted, even though he was well aware his staff privately laughed about how much time he spent occupied. He motioned with his fingers for the report. "What do you have?"

"One of our planes has spotted a ship, apparently a Norwegian coastal steamer," the aide announced. "The *Galtesund*. It was due in Stavanger yesterday afternoon, but never arrived."

"The *Galtesund*." Freyn took a seat at his desk. "Spotted where, you say?" He looked over the paper routinely. *A coastal steamer, urgent? Who in their right mind even cared?*

"Fifty-six point five longitude north, three point five latitude east . . ." The lieutenant read off the coordinates.

"And that would put it . . . ?" Freyn glanced toward the map, sucking in his bladder and wincing.

"That would put it precisely *here*." The lieutenant placed his finger on a spot. "Directly in the middle of the North Sea, sir."

"*The North Sea?*" Freyn stood up.

"That is correct, Major. And heading due west, according to our plane. At thirteen knots. To this point, they've ignored all radio warnings to turn around. By the looks of it, it appears to be making a run for it."

"A run for it . . . ?" The lieutenant had Freyn's attention now and he turned to the map on the wall. "A run for where?"

"The only possible answer is for England, I believe, Major."

A knot rose up in Freyn's gut, the irritation in his bladder suddenly a million kilometers away. He took hold of his phone.

"Give me German Military Command. General Graebner's office. In Oslo."

"General Graebner, sir?" the attendant replied with surprise.

"Graebner, yes, and quickly, Corporal!" He turned back to Lieutenant Holm. "What is the weather in the North Sea at those bearings?"

Holm paged through his report. "Clouds at two thousand meters, it appears. But weather is approaching fast."

"And do we have any ships in the area that can intercept?"

"I am told no, Herr Major. The closest destroyer is the Z32. And it is over three hundred nautical kilometers to the south."

Freyn looked again at the map. He plotted the approximate position of the coastal steamer. And then the destroyer. It was 560 nautical kilometers from Bergen to Scotland. If Freyn was anything, he was prepared. At fifteen knots, England was only a day and a half away. They'd never catch it. He pushed back the pain. *What would a coastal passenger steamer be doing in the middle of the North Sea?*

From outside his office, his attendant called, "General Graebner on the line, sir."

Freyn picked up. Graebner was in charge of all Norwegian air defenses. "Herr General, good day to you. We seem to have an event here, a civilian coastal steamer that is making a run for, of all places, England . . ." He explained the situation, as well as the likelihood that it could never be caught. "I don't know, sir. I have no idea why a coastal passenger ship would be making a dash for England."

The senior officer quickly barked his commands in Freyn's ear.

Freyn drew back at the command. "You are certain, sir?" he asked, and just as quickly, the order was confirmed. "Then it will be done, Herr General. I will inform you as soon as I have news." He put down the phone, ashen, staring blankly past Holm to the map.

"Sink it," he said to his lieutenant.

"*Sink it*, sir?" The junior officer looked dumbfounded.

"You heard me, Lieutenant. Call Luftwaffe command in Bergen on my orders and order the ship to be sunk."

"Herr Major, may I remind you the *Galtesund* is a civilian vessel and likely filled with nonmilitary passengers. Whoever has commandeered it, may I suggest we at least give it proper warning and then—"

"Did you not understand my orders, Lieutenant?" Freyn shot back. Personally, he didn't give a shit if the ship made it all the way to fucking *America*. His only real care was that the pain in his bladder would soon give him some relief. But orders were orders. And he had covered himself appropriately. "Radio our planes to sink the ship." Freyn handed back the report.

"Yes, Herr Major." The lieutenant reluctantly nodded and headed for the door.

"And Holm . . ."

The junior officer turned at the door.

"Make no attempt to rescue any passengers on board."

6

Somewhere in the North Sea. Second day at sea.

The first night on the ship passed uneventfully, as did the following morning. Nordstrum and his co-conspirators sequestered most of the crew belowdecks, allowing only those roles that the captain insisted were essential to the running of the ship to be performed. The passengers were in a state of distress, of course. Afraid. Angry. There were business appointments that had been missed, families that were expecting them at Stavanger and Bergen who were now without word, not to mention the extreme danger they were being put in. The whispering among the passengers was that there was no way the Germans would allow them to go without force. That resistance fighters, however justified in their cause, were putting everyone at risk, even children, families, to make their own escape.

But what other choice was there? Nordstrum asked himself. Explain to everyone on board that there was a purpose to what he and his men were doing that was far more critical to the war than all their private concerns?

No, there was no other way, he knew. Or any reasonable alternative. They had done what needed to be done. This was war. They had to get this film to England. He felt certain that the Germans would allow the boat to return once he and his men had left.

He pressed the captain to push his speed to twenty knots.

"*Twenty knots?* We'll run out of coal before we get half-way."

That morning, two planes were spotted in the eastern sky, black war crosses unmistakable on their wings. People pointed in alarm. "They've found us! You'll kill us all," they appealed to anyone with a gun. One or two stopped Nordstrum on deck. "You know what will happen. The Germans will never let us leave."

"There are families on board," others protested worriedly, "not soldiers. What of them?"

Einar kept at it on the radio to England, begging for air support, constantly transmitting their position. But scrambling a squadron of planes to escort a civilian ship required approval from higher-ups, and that took time. Even with a cargo as important as theirs was, which could not be explained over the radio.

"So where is your escort now?" the captain spat accusingly, with a nervous eye to the German planes as well. They kept their gazes peeled as, high above them, the fighters circled the ship not once, but twice.

Then, as if by some miracle, they disappeared.

People cheered. Maybe the Nazis had let them go after all. But Aberdeen was still close to 300 kilometers away. And every one of them would be fraught with danger.

Hours passed. The skies remained clear. "How are we on fuel?" Nordstrum asked the captain on the bridge.

"You see these seas . . ." the captain replied. Indeed, they had grown heavier. Waves now crashed against the *Galtesund*'s sides. "And the winds are coming from the northwest. Right into our faces. They're up to twenty knots. We're not equipped for this. We're down to less than half fuel."

Less than half. . . Nordstrum did his own calculations and realized, at their present speed, they'd better get into the safety of English waters soon or they would be sitting ducks. And they certainly weren't about to outrace anyone, if it came to such a thing.

"Keep radioing," he said to Einar. "Tell them it's imperative we get an escort."

"You think you're all heroes, don't you?" The captain glared at them, brimming with contempt. "But it's not so heroic, if you ask me, putting innocent lives at risk, so you can do what, flee the Nazis and avoid capture?"

"That's not at all what this is about." Nordstrum defended his actions as best he could. But he could not tell the captain any more. "And in war, innocents are all at risk."

"Then what is it, mind you? Don't get me wrong, we all respect those who stood up and fought the Nazis. But in my thinking, true Norwegians go out of their way to protect their fellow countrymen's lives. Not put them in peril. That's what separates us from *these* . . ." The word he held on the tip of his tongue, but did not say, was "savages." Nordstrum could feel it. "That's what makes us Norwegian."

"We're carrying something that needs to be put into the right hands," Nordstrum finally said, as much as he was prepared to divulge. "Something very important to the war. And those hands are in England, unfortunately."

"Well, if it ends up on the bottom of the North Sea courtesy of a German dive-bomber, I don't exactly see how you fulfilled your job." The captain poured out two coffees and slid one to Nordstrum. "You can see there are women and children on this ship. Many of my own crew have their own families back home. . . . Do you have a wife, sir?" The cap-

42

tain softened his tone. "Here we are in the midst of all this and I don't even know your name."

"Better that way," Nordstrum said. "And no, no wife. But once . . ." He was about to tell of Anna-Lisette, but then stopped. Why? To make himself appear more human? To show what he had given up? *Why even get into it?* he decided.

But the captain kept his gaze trained on him. "Then you can't really see, can you?"

Nordstrum took a gulp of coffee and thought of Anna-Lisette before looking away. "I can see."

Suddenly he heard a high-pitched wail from high in the sky. He looked up, shielding his eyes against the sun. *Damn.* He pointed to the gleam. "Messerschmitts! Two of them at one o'clock."

"*Three!*" Jens shouted back from out on deck.

The three German fighters completed a high circle of the ship. Then they dropped down, one by one, seemingly preparing to dive.

"See?" The captain glared, alarm stamped on his face. "I told you they'd come for us. Where is your precious escort now? We're a defenseless target out here. Sound the alarm!" He grabbed the intercom and barked over the loudspeaker. "*Emergency!* This is your captain. Everyone off the decks. Quickly get inside or stay in your berths away from the windows and get on the floor immediately!"

They looked toward the stern, and whoever was on deck grabbed their loved ones in panic and hurried under cover. Anxious shouts and wails could be heard everywhere. The German fighters descended in a sharp dive and picked up speed until they were no more than fifty feet above them, and suddenly strafed the decks, bullets tearing up the planking of the old ship, windows shattering, their engines screaming a high-pitched, deafening whine.

"We're a goddamn sitting duck!" the captain shouted above the rattle of bullets tearing into his ship. "We're not built to fight. We can't stand much of this. What do you plan to do, shoot them down with your tommies and pistols? We have to turn around."

The fighters shrieked past them and then arced back up in the sky, seeming to prepare for another pass. Nordstrum followed them with his binoculars, unsure of what to do.

"If we move to turn around, maybe they'll just let us go back," the captain appealed to him. "Otherwise, next time around, they'll drop their bombs and sink us for sure."

"If we turn around, we're as good as dead anyway," Nordstrum said, keeping his gun on the captain, though now, neither of them thought he would use it. "Keep course."

"You, maybe, but there's a hundred and forty passengers on this boat. Are you prepared to take them all to the grave with you?"

They followed the fighters as they turned around, their silver sides gleaming in the sun.

"*Are* you?" The captain kept his eyes on Nordstrum with an unrelenting glare.

"Keep the course."

Nordstrum sought out Einar. He knew what they had to put in Tronstad's hands was of the highest importance and might well save lives, thousands of them, down the line. But right now they were faced with 140 lives on this boat. Norwegian lives. What happened to him and his friends was not important. They'd end up in some Gestapo dungeon, or more likely shot as soon as they stepped foot on shore. *But the microfilm...* That's what mattered. That was why they did this.

"They're coming back around!" Jens shouted from out on the deck.

"We're sunk." The captain shook his head with a tragic certainty, fixing on the planes.

"We can take a shot at them on their way in," said Jens, pulling back the bolt on his Bren. Not exactly a weapon that could bring down a plane. It would seem pointless, but maybe it would disrupt them. In the Songvaln, they'd fought with less.

"All right." Nordstrum finally nodded to the captain. "Turn it around."

Einar looked at him. "Kurt, no. We can't."

"What hope is there, Einar? We've families on board. Turn it around." He wasn't prepared to take 140 lives to the bottom of the sea. All of them innocent. Children among them. He turned to the captain and put his Colt on the table. "Bring the ship around now, Captain. Fast as you can."

"Now you're finally talking some sense." The grizzled captain twisted the wheel sharply, sending those on the bridge, and likely anyone standing on the ship, scrambling to the right.

At full speed the old boat quickly responded. Even on the bridge, they had to grab on to remain on their feet. From the air, the German fighters would have to spot their wake. They'd won now; maybe they'd call it off.

But as they came down from the sky, their engines whining, still they didn't break off their descent. Instead they headed directly for them in a terrifying dive. Each plane was armed with hundred-pound bombs that could blow an old crate like this right out of the sea.

"Sonovabitch, they're going to sink us anyway," the captain said, looking straight into their approach. "Well, not if I have anything to do with it!" He jerked hard on the wheel, back to the left. The ship veered starboard. With a chilling whine, the planes bore down on them. One dropped two bombs as it passed overhead. They exploded in the sea, narrowly missing the ship's stern.

"The next one will hit us for sure," the captain said.

The second plane lined up to make the next pass.

Einar looked at Nordstrum with a faint smile that read: *Sorry, Kurt. We're done for now. I wish I hadn't dragged you into this.*

Suddenly Jens pointed to the sky. "Jesus, Kurt, look!"

To the west, several gleaming shapes could be seen coming out of the clouds. At first they were no more than sharp reflections in the sun. But as they dove, in tight formation, who they were became clear.

Spitfires. British.

Six of them.

Quicker and lighter than their German counterparts, who, spotting them on their tails in the midst of their attack and suddenly realizing they were now at a clear disadvantage, pulled off the attack and angled sharply up as the Brits swept down on them, pairing off two to a German plane. Outnumbered and outflanked, the Messerschmitts climbed back up into the clouds and continued away from the ship toward the horizon.

"*See!* So what do you think of my escort now?" Einar shouted to the captain with an ecstatic whoop, shaking the old seaman by the shoulders. The Germans gone, the Brits streamed directly over their bow and dipped their wings.

Passengers rushed back out on deck, waving their arms in triumph, cheering.

The captain looked at Nordstrum with a relieved, bewildered smile, the color slowly returning to his face, a pallor that spoke of just how close they'd come to their graves. "You were damn lucky, son, whatever your name is."

"It's Nordstrum." It hardly seemed to matter now. "Tell me, Captain, is there any champagne on board?"

"*Champagne?* You must be joking. We're a coastal steamer, not the *Queen Mary*. Aquavit, maybe."

"Then break it out." The color returned to Nordstrum's face as well. "I think we've earned a toast."

"To the Brits," Einar said with a gleam in his eye. A gleam of their good fortune.

Nordstrum picked his Colt back up. "Yes, to the Brits. Reverse course, Captain. Due west, once more, in case you've forgotten," he said, patting the old seaman on the back. "The same rules apply."

It would be clear sailing all the way to Scotland now.

7

At the office of the Nasjonal Samling police in Rjukan, Captain Dieter Lund paged through the police report.

Two days ago, a fellow NS officer named Oleg Rand had disappeared between the ferry terminals of Tinnoset and Mael, on his way to Rauland. Not just an NS officer, Lund was quick to note. A fellow Hird like himself, one of the Quisling government's most trusted brigade. As NS prefect over the Telemark region, under the local Gestapo, it was Lund's job to investigate the disappearance, since the missing person was of Norwegian origin. Rand was last seen by the ticket master in Tinnoset as he boarded the ferry there. Then it was as if he had simply vanished into thin air. The missing officer was a decorated lieutenant in an elite guard, on a personal mission from General Amundson in Oslo, hardly someone who would suddenly abandon his duties on a whim or go AWOL. Clearly something had happened. But two days had passed and still no one was talking. Not any of the ferry passengers Lund had been able to round up after the ship landed, nor the crew. In fact, to his amazement (and his deep suspicion, as well), no one seemed to recall even seeing the man. A conspicuous figure in a gray Hirden uniform, by all accounts a committed and decorated officer. Lund knew, of course, no one liked helping the NS, who were looked at as turncoats who had knuckled under and were happily doing the bidding of the Nazis, traitors to the king. But still, he had his ways. Double the ration card of a soul in need or arrange for the procurement of needed medication. Assist a citizen whose wife's cousin had perhaps run into a bit of trouble with the law. And in spite of the held-in disdain that Lund felt every day, from the eyes of those in this region he had grown up with and who he'd known for close to thirty years, a good policeman always knew ways to pierce the public silence.

Surely Lund had his.

One of the crew, whose cousin was in jail on a petty vandalism charge, finally admitted under questioning that the NS officer had indeed been on the boat and had drowned on the crossing.

"Drowned?" Lund finally felt he was getting somewhere. "How?"

"They said he had gone in for a swim. But it was clear. They threw him. Over the side."

"What are you saying?" Lund's blood snapped to attention. This was murder. A crime against the state. "Who?" he demanded.

"Two of the passengers." The crewman gave a hapless shrug. "Dressed as workers. But they surely didn't act the part."

"*Workers* . . . ?" There were not many workers with the nerve to do something that brazen and rebellious. "I have some photos I'd like you to take a look at," Lund said. He opened his desk drawer and took out a file.

The crewman muttered that that was all he could say now and had to go. He got up to leave.

"Of course. I understand your hesitation completely." Lund nodded, feigning sympathy for the crewman's position and placing the album of photographs pointlessly on his desk. "Unless, of course, you want your cousin to be taken out and put against a wall and shot, for simply smashing a store window while drunk. That would be a shame. It's almost out of my hands."

His color blanching, it was like the strength went out of the crewman's legs and he sat back down.

"Good." Lund opened the book of photographs. "Please take your time."

Ashen, the man leafed slowly through the pages of faces. It was clear he was going against all his inner conviction in betraying a countryman. No matter, he was here. One that he seemed to pause on just a moment too long was a boyish-looking fellow from Vigne, a nearby village, who was known to be among those who had joined the Free Army. Strollman was the rebel's name. *Jens.* Lund stopped the crewman, putting a hand on his arm when he saw the man's hesitation, his eyes beading on him sharply as if to say: *Was it him? This one?*

The crewman finally lifted his gaze slowly. "That's one."

Lund's blood surged. He had him. "And now the other . . . ?" He put the file back in front of the ferry crewman. The other could be anyone, he knew. Any of a thousand who fought with this man in the resistance. Not even necessarily from around here. But as the man looked on, Lund already had framed an idea.

If one was this Strollman, the other might well have been a friend of his. There was one Lund knew who was known to have been among the fighters. The two had grown up together. Lund went to his drawer and dug through his files. He came back with another photo, an old one. Taken from their school yearbook, the only one he had of the man. He pointed to the face. "Look here," he said to the seaman. And waited.

Slowly, the crewman let out a breath and shrugged almost imperceptibly. "Yes. Him too."

"The two of them only?"

Another breath out of the crewman's nostrils. "Yes. Them only."

"Thank you." Lund closed the book and smiled. "I think the evidence against your cousin has been misplaced somewhere."

Kurt Nordstrum.

Lund had known him as well. Lund had been a year older in school, but in the classrooms here, small as they were, one knew everyone. Even those you watched from the back of the room and secretly despised. Nordstrum and his friends were known to have fought with the king's army, or what was left of it. A ragtag resistance. At first, they had created a lot of mischief for the Germans in the mountains, as far away as Lillehammer and Voss. Lund stared at the ruggedly handsome face. He was always the ringleader, he recalled. The kind that everyone admired. Catching a slippery eel like that could easily mean another bar on his lapel.

In school, Lund had always sat in the back of the class and watched all the girls and the attention go to people like this, people who skied effortlessly and were quick with the answers. To people like Nordstrum, everything seemed to come easily and naturally. Still, they had no understanding of what it was like to have to earn what they had. To have had to hunger for it. That was how it was for Lund, for whom nothing had ever come effortlessly or without careful plotting.

Years ago, he was convinced the path he had taken was a way to rescue Norway from the trap of liberalism and debt. He knew that he served a puppet government that simply did the bidding of the Nazis. He knew he was despised by most of his fellow countrymen; even those who fed him information were usually paid off or merely collected some favor, as the ferry crewman just had. Trudi, his plump, ambitious wife, had always pushed him in that direction. "You'll amount to nothing in this war. The Germans will win, you'll see." She'd made this case from the start. "They have the will to fight. And they'll look around for the ones who have similar backbone. Who have helped them, Dieter. And what will you be doing when this all happens?" She cast her eyes on him with a knifing disdain. "Stamping identity papers and processing visas. For once, Dieter, you have to be on the side that triumphs. Do you understand?" Then she would soften her tone and lovingly stroke his scalp, and place his head softly to her breast, and his dick would get hard. "Otherwise, what is the point of all this?" she would say. "All this terrible bloodshed. It will lead to no good end."

But now, all the lofty ideas that were there at the beginning had long since faded. Instead, he was sucked into a maelstrom of dark deeds: young men, boys really, taken from their homes in the middle of the night; interrogations in which the normal procedures were not effective; incarcerations that ended up at the concentration camp at Grini, where no one was ever heard from again. Lund couldn't help but notice the averted eyes and spiteful glances he received when he walked the streets of his hometown. Though in truth, no one had ever even noticed him before, not until he put on his gray Hirden uniform. "Someone must keep the order," he would say to those who questioned why he served them. "No matter, ultimately, whom it is for."

But now, two years into the war, things were slipping away. Trudi had been wrong—the Germans were not winning. It seemed they were losing their grip. They were having a hard time holding on to the territory they had seized. Both here and in the east, they heard, where things were going badly. Yet in spite of it all, Rjukan, it turned out, contained a silver lining. "The golden goose," it was called by his Gestapo overseer, Muggenthaler. "The goose that will win us the war. In spite of how things progress on the ground." Whatever they were producing at the Norsk Hydro plant up on the mountain, Lund knew it must be defended and protected at all costs. That was the one path still open for him. How he would turn this whole ugly enterprise to his and Trudi's gain.

And it had fallen right into his lap, in this remote pinprick on a map where he had had to grow up in the shadows. Now he was put in charge. In truth, he had no idea exactly what was going on up there—at the plant. Only that it was whispered to have the highest military value. And he had made his bed in life, and now his career depended on maintaining that magic elixir's orderly production. Otherwise, he'd be dragged out and shot himself one day—if not by the Germans, surely by his fellow townspeople if the Allies were allowed to win.

The very people this Kurt Nordstrum and Jens Strollman were helping to succeed.

Lund placed the two photos on his desk, side by side. This wasn't just the murder of a fellow officer. A crime against the state. For Lund, it was a matter of self-preservation. It challenged the most clear and precious commitment he had made with his life.

But what were these two even doing back here? After two years of war.

Perhaps Nordstrum had come to see his father? The old

man still lived here, alone, though his men kept a watch on him and it was known he was not in the best of health. The attack on the Hird on the ferry was likely not something they had planned, only a temptation that presented itself, one they could not resist. And that was the weakness in these men. They were reckless. Their actions were not tempered with control. That was what would one day bring them down.

No, Lund began to feel sure, if they had come back here, to this place with its hidden significance, it was far more likely it had something to do with what was going on up at the plant.

Yesterday a report had crossed his desk of a coastal steamer that had been hijacked on its way to Stavanger and which he heard was now in the open sea. Presumed to be making a beeline for England, it was reported. An act of piracy, Lund first said to himself, but not without some bravery as well, he had to admit. And will. It took a certain type to possess that kind of boldness.

And now he was certain he knew the two behind it.

He would take his findings down the hall to Muggenthaler. Along with the two photographs. The parts all fit. *But why . . . ?* A coastal steamer. Why the need to take such an audacious risk?

To flee to England. That had to be why.

Maybe Nordstrum was lost to him for now. But he'd be back for sure. A man like that always came back. Not just because there was a fight to wage and he had the will. But because a man like that always believed in his heart in what was right, not simply prudent. And what drove them wasn't the urge for self-preservation or to get others to notice their actions. Lund chuckled; that was for people like *him*.

What drove men like them was duty. The sense that they

believed in something they imagined to be larger than themselves. The very thing that would also entrap them one day. You could be sure.

A romantic. A fool.

Lund put the photos into a file and stamped it OFFICIAL. NS SECURITY MATTERS ONLY, and put it on the side of his desk.

Nordstrum, he was always the fucking ringleader. Just like back then.

Next time Lund would be on them, like a bee to honey.

Next time, you could count on it—*he'd* be the one throwing *them* over the rail.

8

Two days later, Nordstrum, Einar, and Jens and their mates stepped onto the dock in Scotland, as the *Galtesund*—in the company of a British destroyer and a fleet of curious fishing boats, and near its last shovelful of coal—put ashore in Aberdeen Harbor. The passengers lined the decks in nervous anticipation, not sure what to expect. They'd intended to land on the Norwegian coast, not the coast of Britain.

Leif Tronstad, in military khakis and a red beret, with three stars on his lapels, went onto the dock to greet them. He was accompanied by a civilian in a dark overcoat and black bowler and a ruddy-faced British officer in full dress uniform. Nordstrum and Einar bid the captain farewell.

Tronstad was a highly respected figure back in Norway, a renowned scientific mind who studied in Berlin with Bothe and Strassmann at the forefront of the *uranverein* research, then went on to become a lecturer in inorganic chemistry at the university in Trondheim, only to have to flee the Germans after passing along secrets on their V-3 weaponry and make his way through Sweden to London. Now he had the rank of major in the Free Norwegian Army. He had wiry, light hair, sharp blue eyes, and a ready smile, which seemed particularly wide today. And a pipe that he carried with him always.

"Thanks for the escort," Einar said, embracing him warmly as he stepped onto the dock. "And you have no idea how timely it was. Without it, we'd be at the bottom of the sea." He introduced the other members of the team. Nordstrum felt honored to meet such an esteemed national hero. They all shook hands.

"I'm only sorry it took so long," the scientist turned intelligence agent replied in English. "And with such need for the dramatic. But scrambling a squadron of Spitfires for a Norwegian coastal steamer was no easy feat."

"Better late than not at all, as we say," said the Brit in the overcoat, whose name was Gubbins, and who was introduced as part of some outfit named SOE. "In any event, we're glad you all made it here successfully. Very clever feat."

"Which I hope to God was worth it," Einar replied, digging into his trouser pocket. He came out with the rolled-up tube of toothpaste, the purpose of this whole affair. "Here. It almost ended up on the ocean floor."

Tronstad grinned. "You went to all this trouble on a matter of personal hygiene. Kind of you, my friend, but sad to say, they have ample toothpaste here in Scotland. Even in the war."

"It's from Jomar Brun. Of the Norsk Hydro plant in Vemork. You know him, I think."

"As I should." The scientist pulled on his pipe. "I hired him."

"Well, I think you'll find something quite valuable inside it. He said it was vital to get it into the right hands."

"Well, you've done that, boys." Tronstad nodded at the five grimy men who stood before him in workmen's clothes. "And I know if it was Brun that pushed you to do this, I have no doubt that what you have here was worth what it took."

"What's going on up there in Vemork, if you don't mind?" Nordstrum asked. "It seems there are more Germans around Rjukan these days than in Berlin."

"Business. Very nasty business," was all the scientist said. "But well worth the effort it took to bring this here." He put the toothpaste tube in his jacket pocket. "For now, I'm sure you'd all like to get cleaned up and maybe into some new clothes. Say, military issue, if you'd be up for it?"

For two years they'd been fighting in tattered sweaters and skins, whatever kept them warm and dry. The thought of real uniforms sent a glow through each of them. "Yes, we would." They nodded heartily.

"So who was it who engineered this little escapade of yours, if I may ask?" the British officer, a colonel by the name of Wilson, enquired. He was introduced as being in charge of the Special Operations Unit of the Free Norwegian Army.

"I guess that would be me, sir." Nordstrum shrugged, not sure whether he was about to be commended or upbraided for putting so many of their countrymen at risk. "Kurt Nordstrum." He wasn't sure whether to salute or shake hands.

"You've seen action, soldier?" the colonel asked.

"We have." Nordstrum nodded, pleased to be addressed as such after so many months now without a clear chain of command. "At Narvik and Tonneson and the Gudbrands-dalen valley. And more."

"Tonneson?" Tronstad said with a grim nod. "Tonneson was rough, I heard."

"It was," Nordstrum said. "But we held for as long as we were able."

"And you want to continue the fight, do you not?"

"Continue? Until the Germans are out of Norway, and not a day less. I think we all feel that way, sir, if I can speak for the men. That's why we're here."

"Good. And so what rank were you, son," the British colonel asked, "in your regiment back at home?"

"*Rank?*" Nordstrum shrugged. "We had no ranks at the end. We only served the king."

"He was a sergeant," Jens spoke up. "And the best we had."

"A sergeant, you say?" The colonel stood in front of him.

"Only because I could shoot straight, sir," Nordstrum said, glancing at Jens in a rebuking way.

"Well, you'll serve the king as a lieutenant now, if that's all right with you. Welcome to the Linge Company, officer. And congratulations!"

"*Lieutenant!*" Einar's eyes went wide. He rubbed his knuckles against his chest as if he were shining a medal, and went to salute.

"Don't bother, soldier. You're now one as well."

"Two lieutenants!" Jens exclaimed. "The army must clearly be short of officers here. If you're giving away bars, you know, I was part of it too."

"Well, we'll have to leave something to work up to for the rest of you," the colonel said. "But there could be stripes in your future."

"Stripes will do just fine, sir." Jens grinned widely.

"So what exactly is the Linge Company, sir?" Nordstrum asked the colonel. "If I might ask?"

"Oh, we do this and that." He smiled evasively. "You'll find out soon enough. Judging from what I've seen already, I believe you'll be a good fit."

"The three of you will indeed be a good fit!" Tronstad chimed in approvingly. "But now I think we should let these men set foot on the British Isles," he said to the man with the bowler. He clutched the toothpaste tube. "And we'll get on to taking a look at just what you've brought us."

9

Colonel Jack Wilson went down a narrow alley at 82 Baker Street in London, just a few miles from Whitehall itself, one of six men who arrived, one by one, wearing dark business suits and carrying briefcases, and entered the drab brownstone building once owned by the retailer Marks & Spencer. He gave a series of three rings, then two, unlocking the iron-grated side door that only opened for the correct series of rings and led to the home of British intelligence's most secretive wartime unit, named SOE.

The Special Operations Executive was a little-known and highly independent organization directed by the Ministry of Economic Warfare of the High Command. Its stated purpose was to promote "disaffection and, if possible, revolt in all enemy and occupied territories; to hamper the enemy's war effort by means of sabotage and partisan warfare." Their mission was to field and train agents to create as much havoc as possible in their home territories and, ultimately, disrupt the enemy in as many ways as possible.

They were so effective at their craft the Germans even came up with a term for them: "the international school of gangsters."

Of the five other men who went upstairs and took seats around the third-floor conference table once used for making purchasing decisions on men's suits and ties, two represented Whitehall: Lord Arthur Brooks, of Combined Operations, and Dr. Brant Kelch, a professor of applied sciences at Cambridge and an adviser to Churchill himself on scientific matters. The rest were military, though not in uniform that day: Major General Colin Gubbins, the ranking officer in SOE; Leif Tronstad, the onetime scientist and now a major in the Free Norwegian Army; and Lieutenant Commander Henneker, an ex–Royal Highlander and an operations planner in SOE. Wilson was in the company of the highly placed men from Whitehall for the first time. Two years ago, when Wilson had put in for this type of work, Gubbins, who he knew from university days, told him, "I think there's a place for you, Jack. Head of the Norwegian section."

"Norway?" Wilson replied with palpable disappointment. He was forty-five, cool in judgment but quick to act, but a good ten years past many of the officers who held the plum jobs, and this was his last go of it at something important. And Scandinavia was as close to the front lines of the war then as London was to Edinburgh.

"Be patient, Jack," Gubbins told him. "You'll see, the game will come to you."

And now it had.

"So you've had a chance to analyze the film?" Lord Brooks, who had the ear of Mountbatten and the prime minister, looked at Gubbins expectantly.

"We have, sir," the SOE chief replied. "Major Tronstad, I think you'd be best to describe our response."

"Thank you, Major General." The Norwegian stood up. He took a pointer and nodded to an aide, then went to the projector screen as several photos of the Norsk Hydro factory at Vemork appeared on the screen. "What you're seeing, gentlemen, is the plant where the deuterium oxide is being produced."

The sight of the building itself produced an audible grunt from those in the room who had not seen it before.

"It looks more like Edinburgh Castle," Lord Brooks interjected, speaking of the massive seven-story building made of solid concrete, set high above the river valley on a perilous shelf of rock.

"Yes, you can see how it's tucked into what is basically an impenetrable gorge," Tronstad said, "in one of the most treacherous and hard-to-access locations in Europe. The cliffs above it are virtually unscalable. Only a single suspension bridge"—the Norwegian chemist tapped an aerial photo with his pointer— "allows access by car or truck, and it's guarded day and night, of course. The gorge itself is so deep and precipitous that even in the height of summer the sun never fully reaches the valley floor. In fact, workers at the plant are sent up the mountain by tram just to get their minimum doses of daily sunlight."

"Cheery," Brant Kelch, the scientific adviser, remarked with a snort of sarcasm.

"My sentiments as well," Tronstad said. "Though for four years I did have the pleasure of working there. The heavy water electrolysis compressors are located in the basement of the main building. You'll see that in this next photograph . . ."

He nodded to the aide and a new image came on the screen: two rows of nine stainless steel compressors with networks of wires, tubes, hoses, and gauges coming from them, and each with a canister underneath to capture the precious drips of fortified water. "The best access to it would be through the basement. There's a door on the side of the building. Chief Engineer Brun, who we are secretly in touch with at the plant, says the place is regularly defended by a force of twenty to thirty guards. There are gun towers here"—he pointed again, this time to an aerial photo of the surrounding grounds— "and here, by the bridge. There are hourly inspections inside by the guards. As you can see, the entire facility is surrounded by wire fencing. They have also begun to mine the rear of the plant, around the giant water turbines where access from the valley floor is easiest, and where the Germans imagine any attack would have to originate from. Rappelling down these cliffs"—Tronstad dragged the pointer down the steep cliffs above the plant that led from the vidda— "would be virtually impossible at night, even for the most experienced climbers, forgetting the weapons and loads of explosives that would have to be on the backs of any saboteurs. While the defenses at the plant are not overpowering, they believe—and it's not unreasonable to feel this way—that the isolation of the location, and indeed Nature herself, is the best defense for the facility."

"Can't we just bomb the place?" Lord Brooks proposed, looking around the table for support. "We have our Halifaxes and Sterlings that can make the round trip. The Yanks now have their new B-17s. I'm told they've been gearing up for pinpoint daytime bombing."

"I'm afraid that's not as much of an option as it might first seem," Major General Gubbins said. "Geographically, the gorge itself is far too narrow for our planes to get in that close. From higher up, the accuracy of such a strike would be highly in doubt—the plant is made of solid concrete and far too well protected by the cliffs. Not to mention the weather, which is a perpetual challenge, and seems to change hourly. And anyway, Major Tronstad here has other objections to such a raid."

"Any bombing would be completely haphazard, and the damage to the nearby town of Rjukan would be totally unacceptable. Under such conditions stray bombs would likely strike the plant's liquid ammonia tanks, endangering the entire community. I can promise, not a single Norwegian would knowingly assist you in this endeavor."

"Even at what we've established as the cost of *not* doing so?" Lord Brooks, the Home Office minister, enquired.

"To Norwegians," Tronstad said, "you must understand that the mountains and the sea are our nation's body. But our fellow countrymen are its blood." He rested his pointer on the stand. "Not a single one, I can say for sure."

"All right." Lord Brooks nodded and turned back to Gubbins. "So do I assume you and your men think you can get someone in?"

"Commander . . ." The head of the SOE deferred to Henneker, his chief mission planner and one who Wilson knew played by the book.

"Not someone," the ex–Royal Highlander said. "A team. Though it would have to be large enough to overpower the guards, and nimble enough to get out once their work is done. Let us chew it around. We'll come up with something."

"So to be clear, then," Lord Brooks scanned the faces at the table, "we're all aligned on the science?" He looked toward Kelch, the professor. "This heavy water . . . I wouldn't know it from lemonade myself, but we agree, it's essential that its production not be allowed to continue."

"We've run it by General Groves and the Metallurgy Committee in the States, as it's called there," Kelch said. "He's in total agreement. Such a weapon, if it were allowed to progress, would have unimaginable consequences. Destroying the German heavy water stockpiles and their capacity to increase their stocks is the only way to stop its development."

"And as far as the War Command is concerned," Lord Brooks cast a glance around the table, "it's safe to say the prime minister has come to the same assessment." He motioned to the screen. "This Chief Engineer Brun, on the inside, he took these photos?"

"The interior ones." Tronstad tapped out his pipe. "Yes."

"Then he seems to have done us quite a service."

"Indeed, he has." Tronstad nodded appreciatively. "But the most troubling part is what he has passed along in his notes." He took out a sheet of paper and passed it around. On the top, it read in German: *Top Secret. Office of Economic Warfare. Uranverein Project.* The key parts were highlighted: *On orders from German High Command, June 25, D_2O capacity is ordered to be increased from 3,200 to 10,000 pounds annually.*

"Ten thousand pounds . . . ?" Brooks raised his white eyebrows. "I thought three thousand was sufficient."

"Which is precisely what's so troubling," Tronstad said. "With that amount, it is not a stretch to believe it is conceivable the Germans could be testing such a weapon within a year."

Brooks took the paper and read it through himself. "Then it seems we'd better get on it, gentlemen. I'm speaking for the prime minister and the entire War Command when I say the heavy water threat is too severe to let stand. Something must be done about it." He went from eye to eye around the table. "We're all agreed?"

"We are." Brant Kelch nodded, wiping his spectacles.

65

"For me as well," said Tronstad.

Henneker and Wilson nodded too.

"So there we are," Brooks said to Gubbins. "See that you put your heads to it. And quick." The Home Office lord from Whitehall stood up, placed his files back in his briefcase, and locked the clasp.

"Of course, sir." Gubbins stood up as well, with an eye toward Henneker and Wilson. "We'll be on it right away."

"And Major General . . ." The man from Whitehall picked up his bowler, tapping it contemplatively against the table's edge. "Just so we all understand . . . we require complete and total secrecy on this matter. Not a word comes out about what we're really after. Not even to the poor men who will ultimately carry it out, God protect their souls."

"Of course, sir," Gubbins said with a look down the table toward Wilson. "That is how we do things here."

Jack Wilson knew the war had finally come to him.

10

For the next few months, Nordstrum and Jens trained as part of the Linge Company, named for Captain Martin Linge, a member of the Free Norwegian Army who was killed by a German sniper during a commando landing in 1941. They remained far from the action.

The outfit's real purpose soon became clear.

SOE had established sixty special training schools (STSs), each with a different specialty, scattered at secure locations throughout the British Isles. Linge Company's training was about as far from marching in step or learning to clean one's weapon as it could be. Company members were taught the arts of close-combat fighting and silent killing; how to set up and operate a radio; the ins and outs of industrial sabotage and explosives; how to recruit an agent and maintain them in the field; how to recognize surveillance; and how to survive in the most hostile conditions, for months, if necessary. The regimen was thorough and never-endingly intensive. Nordstrum's company trained and trained and then trained some more, until they were in the topmost physical condition they could possibly be.

Many of the men were fellow resistance fighters Nordstrum had fought side by side with back in Norway. Soldiers who had made it to England against considerable odds to continue the fight were surely men of courage and determined spirit, but after being put through the rigorous SOE training programs they emerged soldiers of the highest calibcr. All they awaited was the reason and opportunity to be sent back into the field.

The Norwegian section of SOE was known as STS 26. It was based at Druminoul and Glenmore, shooting lodges in the Cairngorms in the Scottish Highlands, the most approximate terrain in the UK to their Norwegian homeland. The unit was under the direction of Colonel Jack Wilson. These lodges were so secluded that often the surrounding townspeople had no idea what took place in them. At Druminoul, near a loch teeming with trout and salmon and woods that were abundant with pheasant and deer, the men felt right at home, supplementing their rations, as when growing up, with fish and game caught that very day.

Jens was still there, alongside some of the most capable "hill men" Nordstrum had ever met. But early on, Einar had been removed from the group. Word was he was being given different training at another location, a shortened version of the same skills. But after a couple of weeks, when Nordstrum enquired about his friend, the colonel only told him he was gone.

"Gone . . . ?"

"He's back in Norway. I'm afraid his 'vacation' has ended," Wilson said with a wry smile. He told Nordstrum his friend had been secretly dropped by parachute onto the Hardanger vidda the week before and was now back in Vigne with his wife and kids and a secret radio.

"Dropped in? By parachute?" Nordstrum said with surprise. "Einar can barely jump off a fence without closing his eyes."

"Well, he's got a bit more expertise in it now. He's an invaluable asset there for us. The company he was on leave from never even had the slightest idea he was gone."

Nordstrum felt his blood burn with envy. Einar had taken a risk to be here, just as they all had. But he did have a family and a well-placed job that could be of use to them down the line. Still, to be back in action! In Norway. Striking a blow against the enemy. That was the dream of all of them there.

"Don't worry, son." Wilson gave Nordstrum an amiable slap on the back. "Your chance will come soon enough."

But "soon enough" didn't come as quickly as Nordstrum or anyone hoped. Throughout the summer the company continued to sharpen their skills, while back home, the long days and high visibility made flying in low and landing a team on the vidda far too dangerous. Word filtered down through the ranks that the people upstairs were planning something big. But *when*, they all wondered, eager to test their skills.

So they continued to train: nighttime parachute practice in the Highlands; wilderness survival; how to best blow up a bridge or a factory; how to detonate explosives in a matter of seconds. They were timed and retimed until they could thread wires to a fuse and trigger an explosive mechanism in the time it would take some to light a match. Then they did it again, all to shave off precious seconds.

At a castle in the New Forest they learned the arts of coding, radio transmission, and microphotography. Near Manchester, they went over the preparation of drop zones and how to avoid capture and withstand interrogation. They knew this specific work was being drummed into them for some purpose, but even as summer turned into autumn, what that was never became clear. Separated from their home by the expanse of the North Sea, one thought burned in Nordstrum's mind each night before sleep: that the Nazis had tightened their yoke on his homeland, and that those who remained there must be wondering, agonizing: *Where are our boys who left to continue the fight? Who is left to stand up to the Nazis?*

Word reached them that several of their fellow resistance fighters had been captured or killed in the fighting. Nordstrum's own thoughts never strayed far from his father. No doubt they'd be keeping their eye on him—by now those Hirden bastards surely knew who had hijacked the ship. He'd already seen once in this war what the Gestapo and their NS underlings did to those whose family had resisted.

It only made his will to get home even firmer.

11

In late September, the purpose of all their training finally became clear. Nordstrum was asked to the trophy room of the lodge in Glenmore. Several others he knew from the company were there too, including Jens. No one had any idea why.

Colonel Wilson stepped in, accompanied by a stout, mustached Scottish commander named Henneker, and told the group that they'd been chosen as the advance party for a very important mission.

Advance party . . . Nordstrum caught Jens's eye with excitement.

Wilson said, "You've all been singled out for your physical abilities and mental toughness, your various technical skills, and your nerves under duress. What we have in mind will be demanding, but you should know it will have as critical an importance as any mission that will be conducted in this war."

This was it! At last, they were getting their chance to prove their worth.

"You called us the 'advance' party?" a tall, lean fighter named Poulsson asked the colonel. "Can I ask, in advance of what?"

The ex–Royal Highlander clasped his hands behind his back. "You'll be informed. Right now it's our job to get you ready to be sent back."

"*Ready*," Jens said defiantly. "What have we been training for all these months if we're not ready?"

"Yes, I admit you're skilled," Wilson agreed. "From this point on, though, your training will become a bit more . . . technical."

Sent back. The words surged through Nordstrum just as surely as if he'd swallowed a shot of aged Scotch. Each man looked around with anticipation. These were the precise words they all longed to hear.

In addition to him and Jens, there was Claus Helberg; Knut Haugland; Joachim Ronneberg; Arne Kjelstrup; a fellow Rjukan native, Joaquim Poulsson; and an American everyone was curious about.

Poulsson was a man that commanded all their respect. He was tall and gaunt with sharp blue eyes, as experienced an outdoors-man as Nordstrum had ever met, as at home in the wilds of the vidda as in his own family yard. His journey from Norway to England alone told the story of his determination and character: north through Finland to the Soviet Union, then down the Dnieper to Turkey, on to Syria, Lebanon, then Palestine and Egypt, where he boarded a cargo ship to India that took him across the Atlantic to the isle of Trinidad, where he hopped a flight to Canada, and finally rode on one of the supply convoys back across the Atlantic to England.

And all only for the chance to continue the fight against the Nazis.

Claus Helberg was a member of the Norwegian Mountaineering Club, and had been captured by the Germans north of Oslo and sent to a prisoner-of-war camp. Escaping, he fled to Stockholm. At a time when there was no wireless transmission setup, it became Helberg's job to smuggle messages back across the border to Sweden so they could be passed on to London.

Knut Haugland had been a radio operator on a merchant marine ship before the war, and was as skilled at W/T transmission as anyone in the group. Quickly transferring messages into code and ensuring timely transmission under stressful conditions was a vital skill in the field. Communications had to be quick and concise; the German W/T units monitoring them were a constant threat. The longer one transmitted, the greater the chance of being fixed upon and caught. Even the act of changing batteries in the frozen wild was no easy task: both hands and batteries froze quickly, not to mention the need to always lug around thirty pounds of weight. The job took nerves, dexterity, and a knack for quick thinking—qualities Haugland possessed abundantly.

Joachim Ronneberg was tall and thin and as unflappable under pressure as they came. He'd been training with the Linge Company since '41, after he'd commandeered a small fishing vessel and crossed the North Sea.

Rounding out the group was Eric Gutterson, the American, assigned to them from the U.S. Army's Tenth Mountain Division. He was tall, blond, leanly built, from Vail, Colorado, with a boyish shyness and an easy smile. The smile was deceptive, however, as Gutterson could telemark down a ridge with the best of them and was also the most accomplished at climbing in the group. And he spoke the language a bit, as his father, a lift operator at a Vail resort, was of Norwegian descent. But it was generally the simplest phrases: *Kaldt I dag?* "Cold today, huh?" Or *For meg lutefisk.* "Pass the lutefisk." And with an accent that made him sound more Finnish than Norwegian. Certainly no one would want to rely on his language skills to get out of a jam.

The guys all ribbed him that he should stick to something familiar, like that game where you hit a ball with a bat, or tossed a ball in a basket, or whatever odd sports they played in the United States, not this type of work, which required an upbringing in the harshest conditions. Only a true Norwegian could handle what they would find on the vidda if they were sent in. But on every level of training the Yank proved to be a match for any of them. With his wiry blond hair and modest way, he immediately fit in. *Not a Northman, mind you*, they all were quick to point out.

But still *capable* . . .

"We'll be dropping a team of you back in on the vidda," Colonel Wilson explained to them, slowly pacing back and forth. "It's never been done before. But if an untrained engineer like Einar Skinnarland can pull it off, it ought to be berries and cream for experienced men like yourselves."

"You mean berries and *krumkak*," Jens joked, saying it in the northern dialect, producing a ripple of laughter from the group. "Remember, you're among Norwegians, Colonel."

"Yes, all right, *crumb cake*." The colonel smiled, pronouncing it in his deep Scottish accent. "The team will do recon for a larger operation set for a later time. For now, I won't say what that actual target is, or where. We're calling the operation Grouse. It's a bird that lives on mostly scrub and vegetation in the Arctic, so it's aptly named, if I may say so. What we have in mind will be demanding, but I promise it will also have the highest importance of any mission you will be a part of in this war."

He scanned the seated rows. Some smoked. Others just sat there with their legs crossed, holding back their excitement. The expression on every face said, without reservation, *We're up for it*.

"So when would we go, Colonel?" Claus Helberg asked.

"A couple of weeks. As soon as we can be assured of

darkness. From now on, you'll be separated from the rest of the ranks. Your training will become highly specialized. Oh, and just one thing more. You'll need a team leader. We'll pick one shortly. So that's it for now." He clapped his palms. "Unless there's something more?"

"I have a question," Nordstrum called from the back. "You say we'll be a team. A team of how many, if I might ask?"

"I assume you're speaking about the mission?" the colonel clarified. "How many of you will be going in?"

"Yes. If you can say."

"You'll be four," the colonel said, and, knowing that would raise some eyebrows, he seemed to make eye contact with everyone in the room.

Four. There were eight of them in the room. Each a top soldier. And each would do whatever it took to be a part of what was taking place.

"And this main squad . . ." Nordstrom pressed further. "The ones who will follow after . . . I assume they'll be from our ranks as well?"

Wilson gave a glance toward the planner, Henneker, who was standing to the side. "You mean are they to be Norwegian?" He stepped forward and took in a breath. "I'm afraid that's yet to be determined, Lieutenant. Anything more . . . ?"

12

Soon after, they learned what the ultimate objective was:

Vemork.

The tiny hamlet high above Rjukan where the Norsk Hydro chemical facility was located. With Einar gone, Nordstrum and Jens were the only ones who even had an inkling of the kind of work that was going on there.

No one was informed, even in the broadest way, about the mission's real purpose. Only that the four team members would be dropped on the vidda at night, they would camp out there in the strictest secrecy, confirm reconnaissance on the plant and its defenses, and then escort the larger party that would follow shortly after to carry out the raid. It was the end of September; nights were growing longer. In the long days of summer, nighttime visibility was always a threat—the slow-flying Halifaxes that would be used to drop in a team would be easy targets for German anti-aircraft batteries. With autumn came the cover of darkness, but with it the unpredictability of the weather as well.

And the storms.

Their training grew even more rigorous. The eight were sent back to the Highlands, where at the highest elevations there was snow, simulating as best they could the conditions they would find at home. In that clime they practised nighttime jumps, setting up a base camp in the most hostile conditions, skiing with eighty pounds of equipment strapped to their backs, quickly coding and decoding messages, and preparing a landing site for the main team. They also learned to use the brand-new homing machine called Eureka, which sent an electronic pulse to the crew in the Halifaxes when they came within range, identifying their location for the drop. They practised over and over what to do in case of capture; were put through grueling mock interrogations, some lasting as long as two hours. They went over what to do in case they ran into any civilians in the mountains. It was decided that they must be eliminated— countrymen or not. The mission was simply far too important to be jeopardized; too much was at stake. A stranger's loyalties could simply not be determined, Colonel Wilson drummed into the group, no matter how sympathetic they appeared. No one liked the idea of having to do this to their own countrymen.

"Anyone who is unable to carry this out," the colonel said to them, "perhaps it's best to call it a day now."

He waited. No one stood up.

"Good, then," Wilson said, pleased.

The mountainous terrain in Norway was not well suited to these kinds of air operations. Possible dropping grounds on the vidda were few and the weather could never be predicted. Sudden storms could flare quickly and alter the terrain of the landing site, even while the flight was in the air. The mountains in Norway were steep and closely situated. In the blink of an eye, valleys could throw up air pockets and shift atmospheric currents. As September turned into October the weather patterns grew particularly hostile. Driving storms and low cloud cover seemed to be daily reports. All they could do in the UK was wait. All the sitting around made the mood grow edgy. They already felt they were sitting out the war while the Nazis tightened their grip on their homeland. And now all they could do was delay and postpone and continue to train even more, each trying to make the case to be picked among the first four.

One day in the Highlands, they ran into a group of English paratroopers from the First Royal Engineers—hearty boys who skied serviceably and were skilled in physical fighting and marksmanship, but who seemed a bit out of their element in the snow.

"Englishmen on skis," Jens ribbed them. "Next you'll see Norwegians playing cricket."

They helped the Brits to adjust their boots and set their bindings to make the skiing easier, and talked about how to look for the firmer-packed snow, which was less taxing on the body.

"Keep in mind, this Scottish snow is nothing like the real thing," Nordstrum showed one of them, feathering the wet, heavy snow through his gloves. "And this weather, of course this is like summer to us."

"See our friend Gutterson here," Claus Helberg said, pushing forward the American. "He's actually a Yank, but we've made him half Norwegian. We could do the same for all of you if you stick close by."

"His top half maybe," Jens chuckled, with a knowing wink toward the Yank. "What's going on below, we're sorry to say, there's not much hope."

Everyone laughed. Even the British mates, who all seemed like good young men.

Another week went by. Then two. The final team was narrowed down. Poulsson, Haugland, and Helberg for sure. Each for their different skills. Poulsson was given the role of team leader. But Nordstrum and he had skied and hunted together in their youth and Nordstrum knew the Rjukan area, including the huts and cabins on the vidda, like the back of his hand. And he was also in as good shape as any in the group. When it came to the final spot on the team, everyone seemed to agree it would be him.

But as the rumors grew that it was only days now until they'd be leaving, the team was on a training exercise in the Highlands where the snow was exceedingly thin, practising shooting while on skis. Discharging his rifle, Nordstrum skied over a rock, and when he landed on one ski the gun went off again and he felt a stabbing pain in his left foot. He hobbled to a stop, knowing exactly what had happened.

He winced. There was a hole in his boot, blood oozing from it.

"Shit." Nordstrum looked at Poulsson ominously.

"Get the toboggan," the team leader said. "We'll help you down."

"I don't need a fucking toboggan," Nordstrom shot back angrily, and made it down the slope to the lodge on one ski, favoring the other.

"What's happened?" Colonel Wilson came over, having seen the commotion. In the lodge, Jens and the Yank, Gutterson, assisted Nordstrum into a chair.

"Kurt's so eager to shoot someone, he took it out on himself," Jens said.

"It's nothing," Nordstrum insisted. "The boot took the worst of it."

"Well, let's take a look, shall we?" The colonel peeled back the tongue.

They eased off Nordstrum's boot. Blood was all over his sock. Gerrie, one of the FANY nurses, came in and they carefully cut around it. It was nothing serious, thank God. The bullet had merely grazed his big toe, causing a lot of blood.

"It's barely a scratch." Nordstrum stood up, already putting pressure on it. "I'll be back on skis tomorrow."

"That may be." The colonel put a hand on his shoulder. "But you're out, Lieutenant. At least for now."

"Out?" Nordstrum protested in disappointment. "Give me a day or two, Colonel, and I'll be—"

"There's no appeal," Wilson said. "There'll be other missions. Sorry, I know how you feel, Lieutenant, but you'll be sitting this one out."

13

October 19, 1942

Three days later, as a crestfallen Nordstrum mended at Avainaire, Poulsson, Knut Haugland, Claus Helberg, and Arne Kjelstrup took off from the airfield near Wick in a specially designed Halifax and were dropped before midnight onto the ice and wild of the Hardanger plateau.

That evening, the BBC news opened its newscast with the greeting "This is the latest news from London," the slightest variation from the standard "This is the news from London," informing Einar Skinnarland, back in Rjukan now and the SOE's chief agent in the region, of his countrymen's imminent arrival.

It took over four hours for the bomber to reach the drop zone, avoiding the anti-aircraft batteries set up along Norway's western coast, a result of Hitler's fear that the invasion all knew was coming might be directed at the Scandinavian coast, with its endless irregular coastline.

This time the weather held.

Upon their return, Wing Commander Hockey and Flight Lieutenant Sutton reported they could make out winding fjords cutting into long, narrow valleys, snow-covered mountain peaks, even the lights of homes below, all lit by the bright full moon. The Hardanger was a mass of rock, ice, frozen rivers and lakes, too harsh for anyone to permanently inhabit, but it was about to become the first step in what was to be the most important secret mission of the war.

In his report, RAF dispatcher Hill reported that "the men jumped well and without hesitation," with no more than a "Good luck, lads" from him. As soon as they were gone, he tossed out two heavy containers after them, filled with their supplies.

What Airman Hill had no way of knowing was the difficult landing that awaited the four below. The area of the drop zone was nothing more than a barren ridge of rock, stones, and snow. Upon hitting the ground, Claus Helberg badly twisted his ankle. The rest quickly scrambled to gather up their chutes, knowing that the powerful winds and sudden gales that were common there could easily drag a man hundreds of yards, wounding him badly, separating him from his mates, and potentially hurling him over the edge of a ridge into who knew what.

Unable to locate their supplies, which were scattered all over the mountainside in the dark, the Grouse commandos spent that first night huddled in sleeping bags on the ridge, protecting themselves as best they could from the icy gales. For the first time Poulsson, the only one who'd been briefed, informed his mates of the true objective of their mission:

They were to be the advance party for a group of commandos to blow up the heavy water stockpiles at the Norsk Hydro factory in Vemork.

"Heavy water?" Knut Haugland said, huddling in his sleeping bag against the cold. "What the hell is that?"

None of the other three had ever heard the term before.

It took them two full days to collect their equipment, which had ended up scattered across hundreds of yards of rugged hillside.

Those first days, the weather held. The sky was blue and

the temperature manageable, and they were excited to be back in their homeland. But once they were able to get their bearings, the team was surprised to learn they had landed not in the marshy regions east of Uglflott, a short way from Vemork, but on a mountainside east of Songadalen, a good fifteen kilometers away.

Normally that was merely a half day's hike on skis for experienced hill men such as themselves. But they had to transport over seven hundred pounds of heavy equipment, comprising their rations for a month, a Primus stove, radio equipment, the Eureka landing signal, and their weapons. And making things even worse, their stove had been severely damaged in the drop. In the mountains, a stove wasn't just for cooking food; it was needed to dry out wet clothes, sodden from snow and sweat. What this meant was that they could no longer travel across the more direct route over the mountains, but had to traverse around them, cutting through the Songadalen Valley at a much lower elevation in order to find wood for fires, which would delay them another three days.

And as they set out, on the third day after they arrived, a snowstorm descended into the valley and the manageable weather that had characterized that autumn ended with a fury.

In the mountains, brutal storms can kill an inexperienced man in hours. Because it is a vast plateau, spotted with few high peaks, it is easy to forget that the Hardanger plateau is over three thousand feet above sea level, and its exposed, unencumbered terrain allows the winds to lash viciously across it on the path from the North Sea. To those familiar with the vidda, it is apparent why Scott and Amundsen chose this place to accustom their men to the brutal conditions they would face before their trek to the South Pole.

For the Grouse team, the temperature suddenly plunged well below zero; icy gales whipped up the snow, which blinded them. Lugging their cargo step by grueling step, the four Grouse members could barely see inches in front of them, heading into the blistering winds, fortified only by the inner belief that no one other than a hardened Norwegian hill man could withstand such a journey.

After a few hours, it was clear the storm wasn't letting up and they would have to find shelter.

Poulsson said he knew of a hut in the Haugedalen valley, where he'd hunted as a youth. In the sparsely populated wild, such dwellings not only provided needed shelter from a storm, but were frequently stocked with firewood and edible supplies for hunters and hikers to make use of and then replenish later. Ankle and all, Helberg said he would go with him to find the place.

Two hours in, with visibility nearly zero and the wind shrieking like a chorus of angry ghosts, Helberg turned to Poulsson. "When was the last time you saw this cabin?" he asked, shielding his eyes from the lashing ice balls.

"I don't know. When I was fifteen, maybe."

"That's thirteen years ago."

"Yes. I see you can count as well."

They trudged against the storm's fury to find it, only to come to the conclusion it had either been destroyed or moved. Now they had to trek the same two hours back against the frozen gales in darkness.

While they were away, Knut Haugland tried over and over to establish radio contact with SOE back in England, without success. In the narrow valleys, with steep hills on each side and high winds rushing through, it was next to impossible to find a signal. They were basically stranded; all they could do was hope that Poulsson and Helberg could make it back.

At Avainaire, Jack Wilson had no idea what fate had befallen their men. It was now three days, going on four, and still no radio contact. He feared that one or more of them had perished on the drop. Had their chutes been spotted, and now they were captured and presently sitting in an interrogation room of the local Gestapo? Had they already been taken out and executed as spies? The lack of news left the SOE planners in a state of near panic. The advance party was essential to getting the main team across the vidda to Vemork. Not to mention Nordstrum and Grouse's fellow countrymen, who every day pressed their British handlers for news.

As each day passed without word, panic turned to despair.

"What should we say?" Wilson asked his chief mission planner, Henneker. Final training was under way for the main raid that was scheduled to follow. Each day, German heavy water production was increasing. In London, Whitehall pressed them for answers.

Nordstrum and the rest of the team pushed the officers for any news of their friends. "There must be something. What have you heard?"

"Nothing," Corporal Finch, the radioman, told him. His answer contained a measure of worry. Everyone felt it. They could be dead. They had become close in the time here. One unit. With everyone's nerves frayed, the mission to destroy Germany's heavy water program simply waited.

It took six days, but at last the words everyone waited for came over the wireless.

"Sir . . ." The radioman rang Wilson, who was in bed. "Corporal Finch here. I know it's late, but I think there's something you should see."

Half dressed, Wilson rushed down to the radio room. The message from Grouse read: *Happy landing in spite of rocks everywhere. Sorry to keep you waiting for message. Snowstorm forced us to go down valleys. Four feet snow impossible with heavy equipment to cross mountains.*

He and Tronstad cheered. Their first reaction was elation. The mission was still on! But just as quickly, caution overcame them. Six days had been a long period without contact. What if the Germans had captured them and intercepted their code? What if they were being tortured and had divulged their mission? *Haugland might succumb to interrogation, and Helberg,* Wilson thought. *But Poulsson . . . never.* The man was made from a different mold. They'd have to kill him first.

The two had established a secret question and response for just such an eventuality. One that only they knew. Wilson wrote it out by hand and passed it to the radio operator. "Send this."

The wireless man looked at it curiously and raised his eyes.

"Send it, Corporal."

The radioman tapped out the cryptic message: *What did you see at the Strand on the morning of October 10th?*

They all waited. Everything depended on the reply. The mission. The heavy water production at Vemork. Likely the fates of their friends. Within seconds an answer came back. The radioman translated the code and handed the message to Wilson.

"Read it," the colonel instructed him.

"'Three pink elephants,'" the radioman said after a pause, and looked up with uncertainty.

"*It's them!*" Wilson shouted ebulliently, with a fist to the table. That was the answer they agreed on. Poulsson would never have betrayed it.

The opening act was set. The advance team was on the vidda.

Now it was on to the main show.

14

At the SOE headquarters, Jack Wilson and Leif Tronstad sat across the table from Major General Gubbins and Lord Brooks and Kelch from Whitehall, as chief planner Commander Henneker laid out the mission's plan.

Combined Operations had decided that thirty-four crack British paratroopers, all volunteers from the Royal Engineers, First British Airborne division, who'd undergone intensive training in the Highlands, would be flown in by two gliders towed by Halifax bombers and land on the marshy edge of Lake Mosvatn, approximately ten miles from the plant. The operation would be called Freshman. The gliders would be guided in and the landing site lit by the Grouse advance team, which was already on the ground. They had taken the decision out of Wilson's and Tronstad's hands.

"*Gliders*, you're saying . . . ?" Lord Brooks, Churchill's representative, raised a questioning eye. "On a frozen, mountainous lake?" The towing of gliders was always a hazardous undertaking, made even more so by the four-hour distance they would need to be towed and the unpredictable weather they might find at their destination, which could easily impact visibility.

"We've been over the various other options," Henneker conveyed. "But to parachute in, with so many men, they'd be strung out all over the vidda. It would take them at least a day or two to regroup, not to mention the possible shifts in the weather. To bring them in by sea . . ." The planner shook his head. "It's simply too far away in hostile territory to ensure the force would get there intact. The operation must be in and out. Speed and surprise are essential. We must get them as close to the actual target as we can."

Across the table, Wilson caught Tronstad's gaze with a cast of doubt in his eyes.

At first it was argued that the men go in by truck across the narrow suspension bridge at the front of the plant, dispatch the two sentries there, and then take care of the detachment in the guardhouse, estimated between twenty and thirty men. They'd been informed that after a visit by General Falkenhorst, commander of all Nazi armies in Norway, the plant's defenses had been bolstered. This included searchlights suspended from the factory's roof, a machine gun nest, and rows of mines and tripwires, predominantly around the large water conduits in the rear of the facility where it was thought any sabotage operation would have to originate. The west side of the plant, which faced the Rjukan gorge, was deemed to be unassailable.

Ultimately, they decided to traverse the vidda on foot, with the Grouse team leading them, and rappel down the cliffs.

"These men are up to this?" Lord Brooks enquired.

"They're the finest we have," Henneker assured him. "They've been training in the Highlands of Scotland for just such an action. Thanks to Major Tronstad here, and Jomar Brun, they know the layout of the plant inside and out. Once we neutralize the guards, we estimate the entire operation to destroy the high-concentration cells will last no more than fifteen to twenty minutes."

"It's not the inside of the plant I worry about," Leif

Tronstad finally cut in. "It's the vidda. The Scottish Highlands are one thing. But none of them have ever faced the fierceness of a Norwegian mountain storm, which can spring up without warning."

"Professor Tronstad has raised the possibility that the raiding party to carry out this mission should be comprised entirely of his own countrymen," Henneker declared. Like Wilson, he was an ex–Royal Highlander, and one who was certain the king's ranks contained the most capable fighting men in the world. "I have assured him these men are the finest caliber of troops there are."

"Still, just landing them on the vidda at night will be an accomplishment," Tronstad interjected. "The rest—"

"The rest will follow as planned," Henneker cut him off sharply. "Surprise and preparation will win out. There is no room in our preparation to fail."

Indeed, the men had gone through the most intensive mountain training procedure there was, equal to that of the Norwegians. They had even been dropped in remote Highland mountain settings in groups of two, with only maps and compasses to guide them, carrying the amount of weight on their backs they would have to bear on the mission, and similar rations to what they would have to consume.

"*Plus*, four of your men will already be there to assist." Henneker gave Tronstad a deferential nod. "Should the need be there."

"And what about *after* the raid?" Brant Kelch, Whitehall's scientific adviser, asked. "Assuming it's successful."

"It's been decided they will split into groups of two, each donning civilian garb," Henneker said, passing around the briefing sheet, "and make their way to Sweden. Each man will be provided with an escape pack filled with clothes, currency, and personal effects."

"We've even clipped their facial hair," Major General Gubbins chimed in. "So they will look like average Norwegians. And they each know a few words in the native dialect in the event they're stopped. Hopefully they'll blend in, like ordinary men."

"*Sweden* . . . ?" Brooks stood up and consulted the map. "I'm no logistical man, but it seems a way away."

"One hundred and fifty miles," said Tronstad. "With three hundred thousand Germans in the way. And if the men do reach the factory, every one of them will be on their tails. And if somehow the Germans don't manage to get them, you can be sure over that distance the weather on the vidda surely will."

"Some will no doubt be captured." Henneker nodded, clearing his throat. "Or be unable to complete the trip. But we believe the rate of success will be positive. And what's important is that we don't lose sight of the objective. If successful, this will set the Germans' heavy water experiments back three years."

"And if they're captured, they'll be shot as spies?" Brooks, who would have to manage the political implications, massaged his jaw. "These fine young boys, the finest caliber of fighting troops in the world, as you say."

"Each of them knows the mission's importance," Gubbins, the SOE chief, responded. "As well as the risk. Each and every one has volunteered."

"Still . . ." Lord Brooks's outward expression mirrored what was running through his mind. That this was indeed a one-way mission. That there was simply no plausible way for them to make it home. Nonetheless, the stiff-necked

Henneker was right on one thing . . . It damn well had to be done. Once achieved, any loss was acceptable.

And, yes, a few might well make it . . .

"All right, then." Brooks sat back down. He tapped his papers into a pile. "I'll brief the High Command." His eyes conveyed that in this war they had sent many men to their deaths. How many more would be lost if the Germans were allowed to develop their atomic research unimpeded? If they did nothing? And as the chief planner Henneker rightly said, these were stout men. The very best. Some would surely make it home. *The rest . . .* He packed up his briefcase, thinking, *Well, that's what medals are for.*

"So it's decided then . . ." Gubbins took a read of the faces at the table. "We're a go."

Kelch, Whitehall's scientific adviser, sighed. "The Germans have about one and a half tons of 'juice' already assembled. At five tons they'll be able to start production of a new form of explosive a thousand times more deadly than any in use today. So yes, I agree, it must be done. Whatever the cost."

He consulted Tronstad, across the table, who nodded, though with great reluctance. "I agree as well. The objective outweighs the risks." Trying something was better than nothing with the situation as it was. "As long as we all understand what they are."

He looked to Wilson, who nodded also. "Me, as well."

There was no objection. Lord Brooks ran his eyes around one more time and exhaled. "I'll get word to Mountbatten, then." He turned to Gubbins, fastening the clasp around his briefcase. "So when would they leave?"

"Soon," the SOE chief replied. "The next period of the moon. Moonlight is essential to the mission's success. November eighteenth to the twenty-sixth."

"A week, then." Brooks raised his eyes, taken by the suddenness of the date.

"The Grouse team, who've been on the vidda for a month now, have already been alerted," Wilson advised him.

"To our boys then," Brooks said.

"Yes, to our boys!" The cheer was seconded around the table. "And to the king."

Leif Tronstad cast a sobering glance at Wilson, then out the barred window. The skies had changed. The sun was no longer shining. Somber skies were not what he was hoping for. Not today.

But in truth, it reminded him of a typical Norwegian day.

15

Eight days later, at STS 41 in Wick, Wilson, Tronstad, and Henneker waited for word as the two Horsa gliders, each towed by a Halifax bomber, crossed the North Sea. No amount of smoked-down cigarettes or cups of coffee could mask their nerves.

They all knew the fate of the war might well rest on the outcome of the mission.

It was a four-hour flight, made in complete radio silence over the dark and frigid waters. Wilson knew that inside their gliders the men would be knee-to-knee, their stomachs tight with nerves. They may well be the best-trained fighters in the world, able to stand up to a test as well as anyone, but bouncing around in a cramped space at the mercy of a sixty-foot metal tow line, the craft shaking like a baby's rattle from pockets of rough air, or now, as he checked the time, likely from German anti-aircraft flak as they crossed the coastline, not knowing what outcome awaited them on landing, would test the mettle of even the toughest of men.

"They're likely passing over the coast about now," Henneker said at 10 P.M. "Here's to them."

"And to Grouse," Tronstad added.

"And to that damn Eureka machine," Wilson chipped in as well, knowing how crucial it was that they land at the designated spot, not ten miles from the target.

By now the Grouse team had made its way to the outskirts of the frozen Lake Mosvatn to await the team's arrival. They had radioed in earlier that they had set landing lights on the lake and that the signal from the radio beam was solid.

For about the hundredth time Wilson checked his watch. 10:30 P.M.

It shouldn't be long now.

Another dreadful hour passed without news. Even upon landing, the strictest radio silence would be observed, so as not to alert the German W/T operators on the ground as to their location, even if they had been seen coming in. The lake was a solid two hours' trek from the target.

After another hour, Tronstad muttered, "They're either engaging the enemy now, or . . ."

"Or, what?" Wilson questioned.

He tapped out his pipe. "Or every German in Norway knows they're there."

By midnight they could only surmise that their boys were in action now.

Wilson knew that in these things the waiting without knowing was by far the toughest part. If he was a younger man he would gladly have been aboard one of those gliders himself. Twice already, Gubbins with Combined Operations had checked in from London. "Nothing to report," was all Wilson replied to his boss.

"Is that bad?"

"Not bad at all. We don't want to alert the Gerries to them. Let's just wait."

By 1 A.M., Wilson wasn't so sure at all what was good and what wasn't anymore. His insides were gnashing. Ashtrays of cigarette butts and pipe bowl droppings marked the time. The tension of what was at stake was clear in the faces of Tronstad and Henneker, both seasoned operators.

"Won't be long now."

Then the first word came in from one of the Halifax pilots on his way back to England. Henneker, who intercepted the transmission, read it aloud. "It's from Taxi Two." The tow plane for the second Freshman team. His face became wan. "They're saying they were unable to locate the landing zone. They decided to turn back for home, but it seems the tow line froze." He looked up. "And then disengaged."

"Disengaged?" Wilson looked at him in horror.

"Apparently it crashed." Henneker put the message down. "It reads, 'Glider released into the sea.' "

"*The sea?*" Wilson drew in a breath and turned to Tronstad. There was no hope of rescue there. "My God."

Seventeen men. Good ones. *Still* . . . That left only Freshman One. Such a loss of men would be inconsolable, a huge blow, but the mission could still be accomplished.

"Do we tell London?" Henneker asked.

Wilson said, "Not yet. Till we know that the mission is completed. There's still hope."

At 3:30, with the men on the verge of losing their wits, Corporal Finch, the radioman, ran into the briefing room with a message. "It's from Grouse, sir."

Wilson saw what it contained from the pallor on the radioman's face. He stood and beckoned the corporal over. "It's from Haugland." Wilson took the message and read. "He says they heard noises in the air over a wide circle, but no contact. Nothing landed." A pain knifed through his gut. "There was an explosion, however. On the far side of the lake. A fireball." He swallowed and sat back down. "They saw evidence of nearby German activity in the area."

There was no word at all from Freshman themselves.

At 4 A.M., Wilson called Gubbins at Combined Operation

HQ. "It does not look good, sir," Wilson said. "The men have failed to land."

There was a long pause on the other end. "I assume they're on their way home, then . . . ?"

"No, sir." Wilson cleared his throat. "It appears they've crashed."

"Crashed? Freshman One or Two?" the head of SOE enquired.

"Both, sir, I'm afraid. I fear both teams are gone."

16

The morning of November 22, German radio broadcast the following news item, which was picked up, without further commentary, in newspapers across the British Isles:

> On the night of November 19–20, two British bombers, each towing one glider, flew into southern Norway. One bomber and both gliders were forced to land. The sabotage troops they were carrying were put to battle and wiped out to the last man.

17

The mood was heavy in the SOE planning room on Baker Street that morning, thick as a fog in Wales.

Thirty-four crack soldiers and six brave airmen were dead. Months of planning and preparation down the drain. The stock and credibility of SOE shattered.

Wilson's team had helped train the soldiers, and their loss weighed heavily on them all.

On the strategic front, the toll was even higher. The Germans had now been alerted as to the ultimate target of the raid—the heavy water facility at Norsk Hydro. No doubt the plant's defenses would be strengthened even further. All knew it would take months to even think of another raid. And every day the German heavy water production was allowed to continue was another day they got closer to a weapon that could win them the war.

A further cost, Wilson and Tronstad knew, was that it was now likely the Germans would sweep the Rjukan area and pick up anyone on the ground even suspected of aiding the raid. Which put the Grouse team, still hiding on the vidda, in even greater danger. In order to remain hidden they'd have to head for the most remote and inhospitable regions. The rations they'd brought with them were intended to last for weeks, not months. The morning after the raid, Wilson's first communication to them urged that it "is vitally necessary that you should preserve your safety at all costs." The second

99

was that at the same time, they required updated information on the status of new German defenses around the plant. *Keep up your hearts*, he urged them. *We will do the job yet.*

But in fact, they had to start over completely. The Home Office had the grim task of explaining the loss of forty elite men to the country. For reasons of secrecy, any mentions of the raid were completely expunged from the official records, lest people on the home front, specifically the press, ask questions as to what it was these men had given their lives for. Everyone knew recommending a new plan of attack would be no easy task now. Who would dare even authorize such a mission? Not to mention that the chance for favorable weather over Norway was narrowing by the day. The feeling at SOE was that if the disastrous mission had proved one thing it was that just landing a sizable party on the vidda was next to impossible, much less getting that team across it. So what would a new plan of attack be? Who would carry it out?

"Do we go for it again?" Henneker, whose stock had precipitously fallen, asked around the planning table.

"Getting any kind of approval from the Home Office will be next to impossible now," Lord Brooks replied. What had now become clear, if it ever was in doubt, was that the likelihood of any of their men actually making it out, even if the raid had proven successful, was more than remote, if not impossible.

"Anyway, the window of weather to even contemplate such an undertaking is narrowing," Henneker said. "And to drop a party of that size into the area, with enough firepower and supplies to get the job done . . ." To throw good lives after lost ones, he was saying. It would be the toughest decision they would ever have to recommend in their lives. Not only in terms of their consciences and careers, but in achieving the objective, which was to set back the German efforts to obtain the decisive weapon of the war.

"I'm open to all suggestions." Gubbins looked around the room.

No one raised a hand.

Finally Leif Tronstad spoke up. "To my mind, the stakes haven't changed, have they?"

"If anything, they're only higher," Brant Kelch, Whitehall's scientific adviser, confirmed. "The Germans are said to be closing in on a critical mass, and from what I'm told, the combined American and British teams are still at least a year away."

"So then our only choice is to bomb the damn thing into oblivion," Henneker finally said. What the others were likely thinking. "Our new Sterlings can make the trip there and back. The Americans have their B-17s. Once past the coast, I'm advised the German air defenses aren't anything to worry about. A day of heavy bombardment, we'll level the place."

"No. You won't." This time, Tronstad looked him squarely in the eye. "The gorge is far too narrow and the plant too protected by the overhang of the cliffs. The planes will have to fly in low, so who knows how many you'll lose. In addition, the town of Rjukan is only a short way away. All that will happen is that your bombing will end up not achieving its ends and hundreds of innocent lives will be lost."

"You were willing to risk British lives when they were on the table," Henneker said with an edge of a challenge.

"I told you from the start your raid wouldn't work. And we won't slaughter innocent citizens." The Norwegian scientist turned intelligence officer put down his pipe. "Especially when the prospects of success are so low. *And* when there is still another way."

"And what way is that?" Gubbins asked, seemingly taken by surprise.

"One last raid."

"*Another raid . . . ?*" The SOE chief took off his glasses. "I just informed you what the climate for that kind of action is right now. How would this one be any different?"

"Because this time we'll do it with men who have a fighting chance of carrying it out. My boys," Tronstad declared.

"*Your* boys?" Lord Brooks looked at him.

"Norwegians?" Gubbins said. "You're talking exclusively?"

"And why not? We have four already in place. A team of say, five or six more, equally trained. Who are as brave as any Brit and just as willing to put their lives on the line. Who speak the language and know the region like the back of their hands. Who better?"

"Members of the Linge Company have never been sent into battle," Gubbins said. "This may well be our last chance at the target."

"They were in battle before they came here. And if Grouse has shown you anything, it's that they're as resilient and committed as any of yours."

"*Ten men . . . ?*" Henneker sniffed skeptically. "Even if they do make it there, there are now thirty to forty German guards they'd have to get past before they even reached the objective. Forgetting the terrain."

"Aye, and ask anyone," Tronstad said, "the odds won't bother them. And the terrain is their friend. They know the region and how to survive there. And they're as good fighters, and as prepared, as any in the corps. Am I wrong, Jack?" He turned to Wilson. "We should have done this the first time. Is that not so?"

The head of the Norwegian section looked around the table. Gubbins had given him his job and he had known the man many years. But now it was time to do what had to be done, and do it right. "He's right, sir." He gave the SOE chief a nod. "They're as capable as any men we have. And they're eager to go and fight. So I agree, let's send them in. I'll stake my rank on it. They'll show you results."

"A team of ten Norwegians to save the war for England and the rest of Europe?" Henneker laughed, searching the table for agreement.

"You're right." Tronstad thought about it a second and then conceded. "It may take eleven."

There were a few restrained chuckles, but when they died out, no one seemed to challenge the idea. Bombing was always a risky proposition. Better a few Norwegians dead, after Freshman, some were likely thinking, than a wing of new Sterlings down and nothing to show for it.

A few Norwegians wouldn't even make the evening news.

"All right then." Gubbins nodded, receiving a confirming nod from Brooks. "Take your boys, as you call them, Colonel, and do the job. This may be our final chance at it. Keep your damn rank. Just get the blasted thing done."

18

Nordstrum was exercising at Avainaire when the official car drove up to the lodge. Wilson and Leif Tronstad stepped out.

"Colonel." Nordstrum saluted, happy to see them back. Everyone knew they'd been attending an important meeting in London. Something in their faces said that something big had been decided.

Wilson came up to him. "How's the foot, Lieutenant? Good to go?"

"Completely healed, sir." Nordstrum bounced on his toes to demonstrate he was ready. "What's the news?"

"You all know about Freshman, I assume?"

Even tucked away in the Highlands, word had reached them of the catastrophe that had taken place in Norway. The Linge Company had trained with those boys, so the loss of so many hit hard. No one knew precisely what had taken place—only that the job, whatever it was, important enough that they had risked forty British lives, hadn't been accomplished. And there was also the fate of the Grouse team, their close friends, who hadn't been heard from in a while, and who would now have to go deeper onto the vidda just as the weather was worsening. "We're all sorry about your boys. But ours are stuck there. We'd all do whatever we can to help them."

"Then gather the group, Lieutenant," the colonel said. "We have a job for them. And I'm asking that American lad in too, what's his name?"

"Gutterson, Colonel."

"Gutterson, yes. He's good in a pinch as well."

Nordstrum looked at them expectantly.

"The news, Kurt"—Tronstad put his hand on Nordstrum's shoulder—"is we're sending you in. A small team to meet up with Grouse, and finish the job that Freshman was sent to do."

The job, as everyone now knew, was the destruction of the heavy water facility at the Norsk Hydro plant in Vemork.

"You're talking about sending in Norwegians?" Nordstrum said, elation building inside. "Into Norway."

"Aye. Plus the Yank. You'll need the best climber you can find. And he's earned his spot."

"Don't you worry, we'll keep an eye out for him." Nordstrum grinned. "I know the boys'll be pleased, sir. How soon, if I may ask?"

"Half an hour. In the great room. Before lunch." Wilson glanced at his watch.

"I meant how soon until we go in." Nordstrum smiled.

"Yes, of course," the colonel said. "We'll need one more round of training. Industrial sabotage, specific to the target itself. But soon, Lieutenant. Whenever the weather permits. Grouse can only hold out so long."

19

In Rjukan, Dieter Lund gathered his men together as well.

News of the failed glider mission had reached them the day after it occurred. Two planes down in fiery crashes, dozens of British airmen dead, not thirty kilometers away. The Norsk Hydro plant in Vemork had been the target. Not a month ago, the local Gestapo had issued a new order on saboteurs that had come direct from the Fuhrer himself:

> From now on, all opponents brought to battle by German troops in so-called Commando operations in Europe or Africa, even when it is outwardly a matter of soldiers in uniform or demolition parties with or without weapons, are to be exterminated to the last man in battle or while in flight . . . Even if these individuals on being discovered, make as if to surrender . . .
>
> Should it prove advisable to spare one or two for reasons of interrogation, they are to be shot immediately after interrogation.

It was a futile mission, Lund knew. Even if they had somehow reached their objective, these men never stood a chance.

Things were now in a high state of activity in the area. Fresh troops were being brought in and stationed at the plant. New rows of mines were being laid, plus additional rings of barbed-wire fencing added. Even in Rjukan, you could see the beams from the searchlights crisscrossing the ravine from the suspension bridge at night.

Muggenthaler, the local Gestapo chief, had issued strict

commands to find all illegal radio activity in the region. "These commandos had to have assistance on the ground," he said to Lund. "Sniff them out. These are your people, Captain. I urge you to find them."

"Yes, Herr Obersfuhrer." Lund saluted with a snap of his heels.

In the mountains, German mobile W/T vehicles searched hut to hut for signs of radio transmissions. These signals were generally hard to detect, and had to be listened for with painstaking dedication, as only an active transmission could be traced, and in the mountains, with vast distances, it was difficult to get there in time. When caught, violators were generally shot on the spot. In town, Lund's own men went street by street. Any suspicious electronic equipment was confiscated without explanation. Those even suspected of having ties to the resistance were brought in. Cause was of no concern. Twenty had been rounded up in the past twenty-four hours alone. What ultimately happened to them, Lund himself couldn't even be sure. They were probably beaten senseless in the basement of Gestapo headquarters and, whether they admitted anything or not, sent off in the middle of the night to the concentration camp at Grini where all the Jews and suspected troublemakers were sent. Their wives and mothers would beat down the door at police headquarters. "What's happened to my son? I know he was brought in. Where have you taken him?"

"I cannot say, madame." Lund would simply shrug or throw his hands up to suggest the matter was on a higher level than him. "It's out of my hands," he would say, though he suspected what their fates were. "He shouldn't have been engaged in any illegal activity."

"*Illegal activity?* He was just a fisherman," their loved

ones would protest. "You serve these animals, Lund." They pointed, accusation in their eyes. "*Why?* His blood is on your hands."

Why . . . ? That he would never answer. Because it was his only way of coming out of this war with his hide, and, hopefully, a few kroner thrown in. And, he had to admit, maybe because he enjoyed seeing these same people humbled and in anguish. All the ones who once thought him no more than just an ox in the back of the classroom who would never amount to a thing. They didn't snicker at him any longer. Now he had the power of life and death over them. And just whose blood, when he looked at his palms, did they think he actually had on him?

Now, in the courtyard of the station, Lund blew his whistle and his troops came into formation. Twenty-two of them. Not exactly God's gift to the Master Race, true, but those, like him, who had made the wise, if not popular choice to side with those they thought would be the winners in this war. Yes, some could be called crooks and thieves, facing prison sentences if they did not commit. Some were a little slow, perhaps, in the noggin. Others were just not brave enough to have joined the fight against the Nazis.

And a few simple opportunists like himself who had made the same bet.

But the Gestapo chief was right on one thing: these British commandos had to have had locals in the population to assist them. There was simply no way they could ever have hoped to make it to the target, over such unforgiving country, without such help. Someone here had to be providing them intelligence on the site.

Which meant these people were still out there. In town.

Or up on the vidda. Rooting them out would be no easy task. The vidda supplied an almost inexhaustible network of huts and cabins. Safe havens. It would take an army to cover the entire map.

But one way or another, he would find them. In his kind of work, there were always other ways.

"Take your men and split into two groups," Lund instructed his lieutenant, a willing but rather sluggish farm boy named Voss. "The first will follow the W/T vehicle as it searches for radio signals. Bring in anyone they find."

"Yes, sir." Voss clicked his heels and gave him a heil.

"Group Two, Sergeant Karlson, canvas the streets in town. Pick up any new face you see on the streets and bring them in. We'll sort out later who they are."

"Sir." Karlson snapped a nod and stuck out his arm.

"And Sergeant . . ." Karlson turned back. "On your rounds, take two of your men, and go down the road to Vigne. Number seventy-seven."

"Seventy-seven, sir . . ." The officer stared back at him, not quite comprehending.

"I want you to keep a particular eye on the man who lives there. All comings and goings. Anyone in or out. He's an old one. You shouldn't have much trouble. But he's canny. And watch he doesn't surprise you with his shotgun."

"I'll handle it myself, Captain. What is this trouble-maker's name?"

"Nordstrum," Lund informed him.

"Nordstrum? Kurt Nordstrum's father?" the sergeant said, widening an eye.

"Just see that the old man is under our watch. Report all comings and goings to me directly." If his son was here, someone may well be feeding the old man information.

An eel could be caught, no matter how deep or cold the water.

This would be one way to fish him out.

20

"This is what you'll all be gunning for, men." Colonel Wilson tapped the screen in the great room turned briefing room at Avainaire.

The seven commandos, Ronneberg and the Yank, Gutterson, included, sat in front of the large screen on which an aerial photograph of the Norsk Hydro plant supplied by the RAF was projected.

"Some of you may already know it. The Norsk Hydro hydroelectric plant at Vemork. You may also know that it once was principally used to make ammonium nitrate for fertilizer. But since the Nazis took it over, that's no longer the business that concerns us. The equipment we're looking to eliminate is located in the plant's basement. As you can see"—he tapped his pointer to the screen— "getting to it, without detection, will be no easy feat."

A few of them murmured that indeed they knew the place and the colonel was right.

"The facility is built on a rock ledge blasted out of an almost vertical mountainside," Wilson continued. "So sheer is the drop from that height that a stone thrown from the edge will not land until it hits the valley floor six hundred feet below, where the icy flow of the Mann River winds its way through the gorge.

"Above it"—Wilson elevated his pointer— "the mountainside rises nearly as steeply, to over three thousand feet, where lakes, dams, and mountain rivers feed water to the twelve huge penstocks you see here, which carry it down to the plant's turbines. There are only three ways to reach this ledge on which the plant lies: the first, the suspension bridge you see here leading to the opposite side of the gorge and on to the town of Rjukan, two kilometers below. The second, a series of steps leading down from the penstocks, which, we're told, are mined. The third, a single-track railway used for bringing in heavy equipment that was hewn out of the mountainside and leads all the way down the valley. I think it's safe to say if Thor himself had chosen to build a lair on earth that could not be taken by human assault, he could have done no better than what you are seeing."

"I know the place." Nordstrum nodded.

"Me too," said Jens. "As I recall, there's a dirt road on the other side of the gorge leading down from the top shelf of the vidda near a tram. It's called the Ryes Road."

"There was a cable car leading above it," Nordstrum added. "It was built so that the townspeople of Rjukan could have a chance to go up and see sunlight in the winter."

"The Nazis have closed it," Tronstad said. "It's also possible the road's been mined."

"Since the penstocks and the plant are here on the south side of the gorge," Colonel Wilson went on, "the Germans assume that any attack against it would naturally come from there, and they've defended the place accordingly. This area here"—he pointed to the bottom of the cliffs— "is heavily mined. They've also placed machine gun batteries at the valve house, here, and at the upper end of the penstocks, and all sorts of trip wires and booby traps along the steps down the mountainside. Everywhere else," he said, "as is evident, is nothing but a sheer drop into the gorge below."

"In our view, this pretty much rules out any approach to the plant from the southern side." Tronstad took over from Wilson with a drag off his pipe. "We believe you must proceed from here, the northern side, which means you'll have to cross the gorge and the river at night, get yourselves back up to the level of the factory—six hundred feet, and not an easy climb, especially in darkness and with weapons and explosives strapped to your backs. Assuming that it can be done . . ." He caught himself and smiled. "I should say *when* it's done—the facility is guarded by some twenty to thirty German troops, most situated in a guardhouse." He indicated a small house next to one of the valve buildings. "As well as the two who are rotated hourly on the suspension bridge over the gorge."

"Why don't we just storm the bridge and cross from there?" Joachim Ronneberg proposed. "Silencing a couple of guards shouldn't present much of a problem."

"All true," Wilson agreed. "But then there's the possibility the guardhouse would be alerted, and then it's an all-out fight."

"So? Twenty or thirty shouldn't be much of a problem either," Jens laughed, producing a murmur of agreement.

"I'm sure you're right on that, Sergeant." Wilson nodded. "But I neglected to mention the two to three hundred who are stationed in the towns of Rjukan or Mosvatn, only a mile or so away, should the alarm be raised."

"As you were saying then, Colonel. . . ." Jens cleared his throat to a few amused laughs.

"So let's look a little closer at the target itself, shall we?" Wilson signaled to the aide operating the projector. The next photograph was a close-up of the main building, taken by Einar Skinnarland from across the gorge. The structure was seven stories, built of white brick and concrete. "As I said, our target is located in the basement. Thanks to Professor Tronstad, we're familiar with the layout. There are only three ways for anyone to get inside. The first, the steel outer door leading to the basement, here," Wilson pointed, "which may or may not be locked, as there are regular guard patrols that go inside every hour. Another, a door on the south side of the building, which leads to the first floor. Which means, once inside, you'd have to get yourselves around, and who knows what you'll encounter. The third option"—Wilson tapped his pointer at a spot on the northern side of the building three times— "and not a happy one, is a tiny crawl duct that only a few people who work in the plant even know about. This leads directly to the basement, but unfortunately is only large enough for one person at a time—and time *is* of the essence here. If all else fails, there's always blowing the outside basement door, of course, but doing that, the cat's out of the bag, and will undoubtedly alert those stationed in the guardhouse."

"In the basement," Tronstad went up to the screen, "are eighteen high-concentration electrolytic processors. Which look like these . . ." A new photograph came on of a series of five-foot cylindrical tanks with a maze of tubes, hoses, and dials emanating from them.

"As long as we don't have to explain what they are, I'm sure we'll have no trouble destroying them," Olf Pedersen called out.

"In that case, be my guest and just call them high-concentration cells." Tronstad laughed. "In the next few weeks I daresay you'll get to know these things as intimately as you would your own mother's face. As well as how to neutralize them. In addition, the storage canisters of finished product are kept here as well. At all cost, these canisters must be destroyed, as much as the equipment. As critical as this mission is, let's just say it pales in comparison to the damage that would be caused should these canisters ever be allowed to reach Germany."

The saboteurs nodded soberly that they understood.

"So that's it for now," Wilson said. "Over the next weeks we will tailor your training to fit precisely what we are asking you to do. Any questions?"

No one spoke at first. Then Nordstrum raised his hand. "Only one. Just what is it that's in these canisters, or these 'high-concentration cells,' that makes them so damn dangerous? That you've already lost so many lives for?"

Wilson looked to Tronstad. The scientist turned intelligence agent nodded and inhaled a breath. "Something you likely have never heard of. It's called deuterium oxide."

"You're right on that one!" Jens looked around to a ripple of laughter.

"Heavy water, it's also known as," Tronstad said.

"*Heavy water?*" Pedersen let out a laugh. "You're talking beer, I assume?"

Now the entire group joined in the laughter as well.

Even Tronstad, who bit on his pipe with an amused grin. "No, not like beer at all, I'm afraid." His smile melted away. One could see in his hooded eyes this was of the highest seriousness.

"Okay, heavy water, Professor," Olf Pedersen pressed. "If it's not like beer and it's so fucking dangerous, what exactly does it do?"

They waited for Tronstad to answer. He just gave a glance to Wilson and bit on his pipe. The silence seemed to carry a weight. He restrained from saying any more. Then the colonel rubbed his hands together. "I'm afraid that's all we're prepared to discuss right now. You'll be shipped south in a week or so. Training begins for real then. If that's all, we'll just say good luck."

21

They named the operation Gunnerside, after the small town in Wales where Major General Gubbins went in the autumn to shoot grouse. There was Nordstrum and Jens; Joachim Ronneberg, who was named the leader; Olf Pedersen; Hans Storhaug; Birger Stromsheim, who knew more about explosives than any of them; and Eric Gutterson, the American from the Tenth Mountain Division.

They trained intensively for another month. Two weeks in Scotland at Special Training School 17, focusing on industrial sabotage, going over how to quickly assemble and ignite explosives until they had it down as routinely as turning on a light switch in their own home. Then they were moved south to STS 61, near Cambridge, a stopping-off station for agents being sent back into Europe. There, they went over the most recent layout of the plant and its grounds as determined by aerial photography taken from reconnaissance runs and from Jomar Brun, the ex-chief engineer of Norsk Hydro, who had recently defected.

They were told of the risks they would face, as both Tronstad and Wilson were finally clear about the full fate of the Freshman party, and that, if caught, they would in all likelihood face a similar outcome. They also practised the demolitions on exact-size models of the processors at Vemork, which had been constructed, until they had the entire operation of setting the charges to destroy the equipment down pat. Soon they knew every inch of the inside of the factory—

not only its layout and defenses, but every stairwell, every broom closet.

All that held them back now was the weather. The storms were relentless over Norway that winter, and equally hard to predict. And the longer they were forced to wait, not only did the Nazis continue their production, but the Grouse party had to hang on on the vidda, staying ahead of the Germans by going hut to hut in the frozen wilderness, scavenging whatever they could find to live on.

The drills grew even more intensive. Nighttime jumps in the mountains, traversing with eighty pounds of equipment strapped to their backs, climbing and rappelling down cliffs in the dark. Infiltrating the target; setting the explosives. Speed was essential. Everything had to be done at a quicker pace. Fifteen minutes in and out. Their route was mapped out to the smallest detail: They would land in the mountains, and after hooking up with Grouse at Lake Maure, they would proceed to the target, rappel down the cliff side near the hamlet of Vaer, cross the Mann, which was low now and blocked with ice, making it fordable, and then follow the railway lines up the slope to the Norsk Hydro factory, where they assumed there would be fifteen to twenty soldiers on guard. Once the mission was completed, if possible they were to leave by the same route, back up to the vidda, and ski their way to Sweden.

Nordstrum was named to head the four-man explosive team that would enter the building. The rest, under Poulsson, would act as cover outside and engage the enemy if it became necessary. What mattered most, it was beaten into them over and over, was that the stocks of this mystery liquid stored in metal canisters, "juice," as they called it, be destroyed.

*

Near the end of their training Nordstrum found Tronstad at his desk in the room at STS 17 that the planners used as a makeshift office. It was the thirteenth of January; there were only two days remaining before they were set to go. "This heavy water . . ." He came in and sat opposite the scientist's desk. "It's already cost a lot of lives. Just what is it, Professor?"

The scientist turned intelligence leader pushed back his chair. He rubbed his mustache, deliberating how to respond. This time, his fellow Norwegian seemed to trust him. "Have you ever heard of splitting the atom, Kurt?"

"Somewhere. Is that what this is all about? The atom?"

"It's a lot of science." From a briefcase under his desk Tronstad removed a black folder marked STRICTLY SECRET. FOR THE PRIVATE ATTENTION OF THE ALLIED MILITARY COMMAND. He pushed it across to Nordstrum. "I promise you won't understand a whole lot. Even as an engineer. It's just a lot of complex equations. But let's just say, if the Germans get there first, it will lead to some of the nastiest business that can ever be imagined. Not to mention it'll win them the war."

"And are we up to the same?" Nordstrum leafed through the report. Pages and pages of formulas, opinions. U-235. U-238. He looked up. "Trying to split the atom?"

Tronstad tapped out his pipe. Likely something he shouldn't be answering, Nordstrum could see, but the scientist slowly nodded. "Of course."

"And if we get there first . . . ?"

"Then we'll win the war." Tronstad shrugged with a smile.

"I see." Nordstrum got up. "Seems a lot of trouble everyone's going to," he sniffed, "for something so small."

119

"Λyc." Tronstad put the black folder back in his case and locked the clasp. "That it does."

Now they had only to wait for the weather to clear.

The skies along the North Sea remained perpetually leaden that winter. The January 15 date came and went. February came. All the while, the heavy water production in Vemork continued and the Grouse team, so essential to the execution of Gunnerside's mission, stayed huddled in the barren, frozen wilderness without supplies.

One day the mission team were all brought into a briefing room.

"We're at the very last part of your training," Colonel Wilson said. He leaned on the edge of the table. "By this time you all know what you have to do. But we'd better be honest here. The Germans have a strict policy when it comes to saboteurs, in or out of uniform. And it's not pretty. So you'll all be handed one of these."

One of his lieutenants passed around two blue pills in a small, clear container. Everyone stared at them, knowing without directly hearing it precisely what they were. To Nordstrum the capsules looked as harmless as what you would take to cure a headache from too much alcohol. The sight of them only reinforced just how much was riding on what they were set to do.

"You have to assume, if you're caught, you'll be executed," Tronstad said, going eye to eye as they passed the little vial around. "But not before they try and get you to give up what you know. Which I promise won't be fun at all. I'm told these are painless. But don't hold me to that. I haven't had the pleasure."

A few chuckled lightly, staring at the capsules.

"And quick. Like a light switch going off." Wilson snapped his fingers.

"Quick as a German peeing in a Norwegian snowstorm," Jens called out. A trickle of laughter filtered through the room.

"Yes," Wilson said with a restrained smile, "that quick. Anyway, the last thing any of you would want to do, I know you'd all agree, is give up your own mates under interrogation."

"You don't have to worry about that," Ronneberg spoke up. "Except maybe Jens there." He turned around. "Can't get *him* to shut his mouth even when he's taking a shit."

"Yes, it will be a relief to put a gag on him at last," Nordstrum said. "I've had him with me for two years."

"All right, all right, maybe I can go on a bit," Jens said. "But giving up my friends . . . I'd rather die first." He looked around the room, and everyone backed him up with an "Aye!"

"Anyway, pass them back, if you don't mind," the colonel said. "Don't want anyone confusing them for aspirin before you go, if you've had a bit too much to drink."

There were a few more good-natured laughs, then everyone settled down as the pills were handed back.

"We'll be at it soon then," the colonel said. "I'm told the weather is in for a change. There's a lot riding on you boys, but I know you're up to it. All we need now is a break in the clouds."

22

February 15
Communiqué from Combined Operations,
Weather Services, in Sussex.
To SOE. Mission Planners. STS 61:

Latest weather forecasts for the eastern North Sea and southern Norway for the nights of February 16–17:

Expected break in cloud cover. Three-quarters moon. High visibility anticipated for this narrow window only. Low winds. The following days have a higher level of unpredictability. Front forming in the northern Atlantic.

"So, there you have it," Wilson said to his adjunct, Commander Welsh. "We have our date. The sixteenth."

"Tomorrow night, then." Welsh nodded back. "I'll tell Ronneberg to get them prepared."

"No, let them blow off a little steam tonight. We'll brief them tomorrow. But alert Colonel Maxwell, if you would." The RAF commander at the base. "Tell him to get his crew prepared."

"Yes, sir." Welsh went to leave.

"And Commander . . ."

He looked back.

"Get word to Grouse on the ground to get that Eureka machine warmed up. They've got company on the way."

23

On the morning they were to leave, Nordstrum awoke to a high pitch of activity on the base. He went to the window and looked outside. An RAF Halifax was on the tarmac, its propellers revving. Maintenance crews were getting it prepared. In one of the hangars, metal containers were being assembled and bolted shut.

"Something's going on," Nordstrum said.

Birger Stromsheim ran over and looked out with a gleam of anticipation. "Jesus, Kurt, I think we're on."

Before breakfast, Ronneberg went around to the bunks and assembled the team. "Boys, the colonel just informed me. We're going tonight."

"Tonight we'll be sleeping in Norway," Hans Storhaug said, hopping out of bed.

"Tonight! How's that, Yank." Nordstrum slapped Gutterson on the shoulder. "You'll finally be able to use some of that Norwegian you've been practising."

"*Jeg ur klar*," the American said, grinning. *I'm ready*.

"*Jeg er klar*," Nordstrum corrected him. "But who's counting?"

There was plenty for them to do that day to keep their nerves under wraps and their thoughts occupied.

They fitted their ski equipment, distributed the weight evenly in their packs. Each was filled with food, extra socks and gloves, burners, explosives, Thompson machine guns, and hand grenades. And two suicide pills. Each pack weighed over seventy pounds. They were set to leave at 2100 hours, the word was, which would put them over the mainland in early morning. They were supposed to be landing at Bjornes- fjord, a lake near Lake Maure, where they would rally up with the Grouse team, who was nearby, and who'd been alerted to their arrival. They'd finally get to see their country- men.

After lunch, Ronneberg came in and said Wilson and Tronstad wanted to see them all.

In the briefing room where RAF bombers received their final instructions before their flights, Tronstad, dressed in a heavy wool sweater and with his ubiquitous pipe, put his foot up on a stool and said to them, "Boys, you know by now that the Germans will never take you as prisoners. For the sake of those who have gone before you and are now dead, I urge you to make this operation a success. You have no idea how important this mission is, only that what you will do will live in Norway's history for years to come."

He went up and individually shook each man's hand. Each felt in return they were doing the highest service to their country. As they filed out, everything set to go, Tronstad went up to Nordstrum and took him by the arm. "Kurt, can you stay behind a minute?"

Having been pulled at the end once before, Nordstrum felt a jab of apprehension shoot through him. But he merely nodded back. "Of course."

After the rest filed out, Tronstad and Wilson stayed behind in the briefing room. There was an empty chair at the desk. Tronstad motioned to Nordstrum to take a seat.

"If it's all the same . . ." Nordstrum said. He remained standing.

"Of course." The colonel rubbed his hands and started in. "We just wanted to be sure, Lieutenant, as leader of the explosives team, you fully understood the mission's main target is the stocks of fluid stored in the plant's basement. These must be destroyed at all costs. Regardless of the remaining cells, and even if your position is surrounded and it involves a heavy loss of life."

"We all understand that, sir." Nordstrum looked back at him. It had been drummed into their heads a hundred times. "And that's what we'll do."

"Good." The major smiled a bit contritely, as if caught in a ruse. "Seems a bit late in the game on that, I suppose. . . ."

Clearly something else was on their minds.

"There *is* one more thing . . ." Tronstad came over and sat across from Nordstrum, against the table. "We all know how much you're itching to get back there, Kurt."

"Yes, Major." Nordstrum nodded. "We all are."

"You're likely as at home in the mountains around Rjukan as any on this mission. You know how to keep low and how to survive in a pinch, should things come up."

"*Things*, sir . . . ?"

"Yes, Lieutenant." The colonel stood up as well. "We'd like to ask something of you—entirely your choice whether to accept it or not, of course. We can always go to someone else."

"And what is it?" Nordstrum looked at them plainly.

"We have some matters that will need to get done there, if everything goes according to plan. After the operation. The only thing . . ." The ruddy-complexioned colonel cleared his throat and looked Nordstrum squarely in the eyes. ". . . is that to carry them out, it may well put you in a bit of danger. . . ."

Nordstrum glanced at the empty chair. The colonel waited.

This time, Nordstrum took a seat. "Tell me what it is you need."

24

For a mission that required a clear, bright moon to ensure a successful landing in Norway, it was raining cats and dogs in Scotland the night their Halifax left the ground.

The seven men of Gunnerside squeezed into the fuselage in white camouflage suits, their chutes strapped on tightly. With them were twelve sealed containers of supplies.

As the bomber took off, the men didn't show a lot of nerves or worry. They'd been over what they had to do so many times, it was in their blood now. They knew every aspect they could control. Plus, they were headed home.

From the tarmac, Wilson and his adjunct, Welsh, watched the plane lift off and disappear into the low ceiling of clouds. The two exchanged a hopeful glance.

"It's a wet one," the commander said.

"Damn well is." Wilson nodded. "But hopefully not there."

Leif Tronstad was in the midst of a letter to his wife and children back in Trondheim. Hearing the bomber take off and climb, he put down his pen. "For the king," he whispered, momentarily shutting his eyes. "And for mankind."

He picked up his pen again, but found it difficult to go on.

For the men of Gunnerside, the ride was long and bumpy over the North Sea. For over four hours, the seven crammed into a narrow space on makeshift seats. With every bit of turbulence or sudden dip in altitude, they exchanged expectant smiles. Luckily, the winds died down and it was calm as they crossed the Norwegian coast, and, even more encouraging, the German defenses were quiet.

"Boys, look!" Jens pointed with a hopeful smile through the one small round window in the fuselage—the moon. It was bright and full. Exactly what they'd hoped for. From a teeming night in northern England, they'd come home to a clear, moonlit sky.

The copilot turned back to them and called back, "We're over Norway now, boys. Welcome home. Stations all."

Ten minutes to the drop.

The jump dispatcher got out of his straps. "Time to get ready, gents."

He bent down and pulled open the specially designed hatch. It opened to moonlit-frosted peaks of mountains and valleys of endless snow, the sight of which made each of them smile. One by one they got out of their seats and attached their jump cords.

"Leveling at eight hundred feet," the pilot announced.

Ronneberg was up first and edged himself over the hatch. All that had to be done to jump was to go through the open chute. A sixteen-foot cord and the force of the wind taking hold of you did all the rest as soon as you cleared the plane. It took only two to three seconds for the chute to deploy—at eight hundred feet, a jumper didn't want to be held in suspense too much longer.

"See you all on the ground." Ronneberg took a last look at them and winked. Then, with a tug on his cord, he wiggled into the jump chute.

The green light went on.

The jump dispatcher tapped him on the shoulder. "*Now!*"

Shouting "To Norway!" Ronneberg lowered through the hole and disappeared into the darkness.

"Next up. Quick." The dispatcher pulled the next in line. Stromsheim.

At sixty meters per second, even a moment's hesitation could mean hundreds of yards of separation on the ground. Not to mention possible peril in the vidda's unpredictable terrain.

With a whoop, Stromsheim followed Ronneberg. Then Storhaug. Olf Pedersen was up next. Both waved and proceeded quickly out of the plane. The line moved forward. Then it was the Yank. "Not sure how I ever got into this bloody outfit," he said with a grin. Then he pulled his woolen mask over his face and disappeared.

Jens was next. Nordstrum knew jumping was his least favorite part of training. As he stood over the edge for a couple of seconds, his stomach always seemed to turn a bit.

"I think I forgot to turn out the light in the barracks," he said, turning to Nordstrum.

"They'll forgive you. See you on the ground."

"Quick, out you go!" The dispatcher gave Jens a push, and with a yelp, he disappeared.

"You're the last," the dispatcher said to Nordstrum. "God's speed to you, whatever it is you're doing."

"Thanks," Nordstrum said. "Don't forget the packs."

"They'll be along." The dispatcher pushed him over the hatch.

He pulled up his mask and jumped.

Suddenly the air gusted cold and he was flung sideways, free of the plane. The chute cord extending jerked him upright. Above him, the chute deployed with a loud whoosh. He tugged on the straps. Below, he saw six other white chutes illuminated by the moon; all seemed to be descending in slow motion. Above him, one by one, their supply containers

128

started to come out, until there were twelve, their chutes automatically deploying in the same way. It was quite a sight, Nordstrum couldn't help but reflect. Nineteen white chutes lit up by the full moon and reflected against the sheen of the snow on the ground.

Norwegian snow!

Slowly they all drifted down and hit the ground. Nordstrum came in last and the wind blew him hard against the snow. One by one, the supply containers landed all around with loud thuds, wind gusts picking their chutes and dragging them on impact. Any one of them could have knocked a man unconscious if he'd been struck. For a moment, Nordstrum just sat in the soft, cold snow, letting his hands run through it. It felt good to be home. But it was important for them to extricate themselves from their chutes as quickly as possible. A strong gust could take a man off his feet and drag him, without him being able to do a damn thing about it, right off a ridge. He stood and unhooked the chute's lines.

The good news was that the weather had held.

He heard a yelp. It was Jens, who'd landed just before him. His friend was struggling on his feet with his chute, being lifted up and dragged like a marionette across the snow. If a strong gust took him the wrong direction, there was no telling where he'd end up. There could be large rocks or even crevices; he could end up a mess of broken bones. Or worse.

"Jens!" Nordstrum hurried across the snow and cut into his friend's path. "Give me your hand."

Jens was frantically trying to free himself from his straps, digging in his boots as the gales dragged him about. "I can't."

"Just give me your hand!" Nordstrum reached out for him again. "I'll hold you." But the ski suits were slick and he kept tumbling. If Nordstrum missed him, it could be disastrous.

"Jens, grab on!"

Finally Jens clasped onto Nordstrum's forearm. He dug his boots into the ice and skidded to a stop. At last he was able to free himself from the chute, which was picked up by another gust of wind and carried off like a weightless piece of paper.

"Jesus . . ." Jens blew out his cheeks. "Thanks . . ." He looked to see where the parachute had ended up—over a ridge, a drop of about fifty feet down to snow-covered rocks and boulders. "Wasn't exactly by the book, was it?" He looked at Nordstrum and shook his head.

"Not my book," Nordstrum replied. He had only the smallest smile in his eyes, all that was visible above their woolen masks.

One by one, the team came together on the ridge where they'd landed.

"Any problems?" Ronneberg asked, as Jens and Nordstrum came up.

"None here," said Nordstrum.

Jens kicked the snow from his boots. "Me neither."

"Any idea where we are?" Ronneberg asked.

Nordstrum looked around. He didn't know the place. It was the dead of night and heavy accumulations of snow could change the look of it from storm to storm. "Near Bjornesfjord, I'm hoping." Ten kilometers from Lake Maure and Grouse. "But it doesn't look familiar."

"Bjornesfjord would be good. All right, everyone." Ronneberg clapped his mitts together. "Let's gather the gear together and find our mates."

They each went across the ridge, locating as many of the

twelve containers as they could. Most were scattered about in the snow. They lugged them all together, tiring work without skis, as some of them were a good distance away.

Ronneberg did a count. "Shit, there's only eleven."

To their dismay, they discovered one had been dragged even farther by the gusting gales and had tumbled into a deep crack in the ice where it was wedged some ten to twelve feet down.

"That's going to be a problem," Ronneberg sighed, peering over the edge. The containers weighed up to eighty pounds, a prodigious weight to haul back up without a place to plant your footing. "What's in it?"

The markings on it couldn't be seen. There was no telling what was inside.

They couldn't take the chance to leave it.

"One of us has to go in." Ronneberg knelt over the edge, his face acknowledging the danger. Any man knowledgeable in the mountains knew these cracks could shift or cave in if one stepped on the wrong spot.

"I'll go," Nordstrum volunteered. He was likely the strongest of the group. "We'll find some rope and I'll climb down and hoist it back up."

"No, it should be me." Gutterson, the American, raised a hand. "I'm the stronger climber. I can winnow myself down and wedge it free. With any luck, we can pull it up by its cords." The cords had held the weight in its descent, after all.

Nordstrum gave Ronneberg a shrug, nodding. "Worth a try."

"All right, Yank, you're up." The lieutenant got back up. "Olf and Jens, start unpacking the packs and locate our skis. "Hans . . ." He pointed Storhaug toward a nearby rise.

". . . Maybe you can go up that ridge over there and see if you can get our bearings."

"Aye," everyone said, shifting into motion.

Nordstrum, Ronneberg, and the American knelt and peered into the crack in the ice. Fortunately, the walls seemed stable, around five feet apart at the top, then narrowing. The crate was lodged on its side. There were small ledges of rock and ice to support Gutterson's feet.

"See you down there." He bent down and started to wedge himself inside, supporting his weight with a hand on each side, deftly lowering himself down a foot at a time, his boots searching out and testing the firmness of any ridges he found. He was an experienced climber, and within a minute had maneuvered his way to the crate.

"I'm down." He looked back up.

"Well done," Ronneberg called.

Then, supporting his weight on the ice and pressing his back against the frozen wall, with a grunt Gutterson yanked the crate out from where it had lodged. "I think it's free!"

To do this took a good amount of strength. The Yank leaned his shoulder into the crate and with a grunt began to raise it onto his back, all the while making sure his toe support would hold. Nordstrum shimmied down a few feet and took hold of the parachute straps, which were still attached to the crate. Then he and Ronneberg hoisted it the rest of the way, praying the bindings held, as Gutterson remained directly below it. All they needed was for the damn thing to break free and go tumbling down on him.

As it neared the surface, Ronneberg knelt and he and Nordstrum rolled the crate back over the edge onto the snow.

"Good work, boys!" Ronneberg extended a hand and helped Nordstrum climb back out.

"How is it down there, Yank?" Nordstrum called to Gutterson. "We can always leave you and come get you after the mission."

"Thanks, but I think I'll stick with you, if it's all the same," he said, then made his way back up with an equal display of agility. Nordstrum pulled him up the last of the way.

They sat there, spent, blowing air out of their cheeks, regaining their breath. "'EXPLOSIVES'." Ronneberg read what was stamped on the crate's side. "That wouldn't have worked at all if we left it there."

"Now, all we have to do is lug it back," Nordstrum said, getting up and taking hold of one of the straps. Ronneberg grabbed the other. It was a couple of hundred meters, which would have been a whole lot easier with skis on.

"So, they have snow like this back home in Colorado?" Nordstrum said to Gutterson as they hauled the crate over deep drifts. Everything around them was a blanket of white.

"No." The American picked up one of the lines from the rear. "Deeper."

"*Deeper* . . . ?" Nordstrum and Ronneberg looked at each other with a hearty smile and laughed.

Nordstrum looked back at him with a crooked grin. "Just wait."

25

They broke out their packs and skis and hurried to bury what they didn't immediately need in the snow, marking the spots with stakes so they could locate them again, in a race against daylight lest German reconnaissance planes flying over spot them.

Then, taking their best guess as to where they were—near the Bjornesfjord, as Nordstrum had said—they decided to head west. Toward Lake Maure, ten kilometers away. Grouse's last radio transmission had given the lake as the location of their cabin.

The snow was packed and icy and they made excellent time, skiing at five-meter intervals and whooping with excitement to be back on Norwegian snow, not in the Scottish Highlands. Above them, the sun came up in the sky and daylight brought a good sign: The sky was blue.

"So where's all this dreaded weather of yours I've heard so much about?" the Yank called out cockily.

"Just count to ten," Jens warned. "It'll change."

"One, two, three . . ." the American said, skiing ahead of them.

"Don't tempt the gods, Yank," Storhaug cautioned. "You'll regret it."

They skied about two hours, hard work with the seventy-pound packs strapped on their backs. But soon they began to suspect that their bearings had been wrong. They were nowhere near the Bjornesfjord, Nordstrum came to sense.

The lake should have been in sight by now. They stood around and chewed a jerky strip and tried to get a fix.

"If we're not in Bjornesfjord, then where?" Ronneberg asked. "Skrykken?"

"Skrykken? Let's hope not. That's almost thirty kilometers off," Nordstrum said with dejection. "And look . . ." He pointed east.

The mountains that were in sunlight only a moment ago were suddenly covered in clouds. With the swiftness of a squall at sea rising up out of nowhere, the skies darkened and the winds kicked up.

"Well, seems you're about to get your wish, Yank," Ronneberg muttered. "Button up."

The wind seemed to sweep in the clouds, and in an instant, they could feel the temperature plunge. There was no doubt. A storm was coming in. They were miles from any shelter they knew of. These could last an hour or a couple of days. You never knew how long or how strong it would be.

"Which way?" Ronneberg deferred to Nordstrum. One thing they all knew, they couldn't stay there. There, they'd be at the mercy of Nature.

He checked the winds. "Your guess is as good as mine. I say continue east."

"Into the teeth of it?" Pedersen questioned. The winds had now started to howl, even knocking Gutterson's hood off, and snow was starting to swirl.

"We'll never outrun it," Nordstrum said, tightening the toggles on his hood. "Button up, Yank," he turned to Gutterson, "we're about to see firsthand if you were born to be a hill man."

Within minutes, whatever hope they had that this was just a passing squall was dashed. The winds sharpened into icy gales, howling like sirens; frozen snow, hurled around like sand in the desert, bit at their eyes. Large drifts piled up around their skis, making every step a task, the weight of the packs on their backs bringing them to a virtual halt.

Visibility became zero.

"Pull up your mask," Nordstrum yelled to Gutterson above the howl of the wind. Inside their hoods they had only the narrowest exposed slit for sight, but they could see only an endless sea of white anyway. As the temperature dropped, the wind drove arrows of frozen snow into their eyes, clamping them shut. Virtually blinding them.

The only benefit of such a storm, though a small one, was that the blanket of blown snow would cover their tracks and eliminate any trace of them if the wrong people happened to pick up their presence.

They leaned into it, pushing against the gales, a step at a time.

In minutes, each became covered in white.

An hour of slow going passed. Nothing familiar appeared. Then two hours. They were only able to go about a kilometer. It was becoming nearly impossible to carry on. And Nordstrum knew they were now completely lost. Worse, without shelter, he knew they'd have to dig in somewhere on the side of a slope with Nature's fury raging all around. This was a bad one, it was becoming clear, and in this kind of storm, even the most experienced of men could only hold out so long. But just finding such a sheltered spot was next to impossible with the snow-swept gales battering them and snow so thick you could barely see your hand in front of your face.

"Come on, all of you, we have to go on." Ronneberg pushed them on. But his eyes connected with Nordstrum's and betrayed an expression of concern, which Nordstrum rightly read as, *We're in for a tough fight here.*

They trudged about another kilometer, almost to the point of giving up, when suddenly Pedersen, who had assumed the lead at that stage, pointed ahead with joy. "Look!" You could barely hear his shout above the shrieking gales.

It was a hut. A hunting cabin. Almost entirely encased in a blanket of fresh snow. The winds blew so fiercely and visibility was so limited, they didn't come upon it as much as bump directly into it.

"Thank the trolls!" Jens thrust his poles in the air triumphantly.

"Fuck the trolls, thank whatever beautiful sonovabitch who happens to own this place," Hans Storhaug said. He loosened the icy doorframe with an axe, pushed it open with his shoulder, and the seven of them tumbled inside.

At first they just collapsed on the floor, their packs still on. Elated, exhausted, breathing in heaves and gasps. There was no way they would have survived more than another couple of hours in a storm of such ferocity.

"Look. Over there by the stove," Jens said, peeling himself off the floor. "Is it a mirage or am I dreaming?" As luck would have it, there was even a bundle of birchwood for a fire.

"You're not dreaming," Pedersen exclaimed, extricating himself from his pack, going over and checking for kindling.

The most important thing now, other than getting a fire going and drying out, was to figure out where they were and chart a course to Lake Maure, where they were supposed to meet up with Grouse.

But there was little more they could do once the fire was

going than open some food and get ready for sleep. They'd been up for almost twenty-four hours.

"Yank," Ronneberg said.

"Yes, Lieutenant."

"Take the owner's bed. You've earned it tonight."

"Me?" Gutterson questioned.

"And remember, we only give the owner's bed to true hill men," Pedersen explained.

"Aye," the others chimed in.

"Thank you." The soldier looked around, unsure but pleased.

"Just don't get too comfy. You're up in an hour, lad, and then the bed's mine," Ronneberg said. "I'll take the first watch." He settled into a chair, holding back his smile.

"Yes, enjoy your beauty sleep, Yank," Birger Stromsheim chuckled.

They rolled out their sleeping bags and bedded in.

"Feels good to be home, right, boys?" Ronneberg said.

"Aye," one or two muttered. "It does."

And then it was quiet.

Outside, the winds grew to a howling high pitch and the snow fell in waves. The shaking wooden walls made it feel like the hut was about to be lifted right off the ground and blown away. In his sleeping bag, closing his eyes for a few hours before it was his turn to watch, Nordstrum prayed that when they awoke this hellish nightmare would have moved on.

26

But the storm didn't move on.

Instead, it grew even stronger. They woke in early afternoon to winds even more formidable and howling than the night before.

At least three feet of snow had fallen. The drifts against the house piled up closer to five. Every hour, more continued to fall. They had a mission to fulfill and their countrymen to rescue, who were in dire conditions themselves. Ronneberg and Nordstrum tried venturing out to see if continuing was possible, but they could barely get ten feet before the gales pushed them back.

"What do you think, Kurt?" Ronneberg put his face close to Nordstrum's and shouted above the wind.

Nordstrum replied, "I think this storm will kill us before the Germans ever get off a shot."

"I've never seen one as strong as this," Ronneberg said, struggling even to stand upright.

There was no choice but to go back inside. Their only prospect was to wait out the storm and hope it would blow itself out.

Wherever they were, the Grouse team was enduring the same conditions.

The first order of business was to determine precisely where they were. They went about examining the hut for any clues. In the back of a drawer Gutterson found a map, and on it, there were a couple of hand-drawn circles and a greased thumbprint, unfortunately not in the area of

Bjornesfjord, where they assumed they'd been dropped, but near Skrykken, some thirty kilometers away.

Thirty kilometers back the way they'd come yesterday.

"That would be bad," Nordstrum said, poring over the map. "You can see there's no easy route to Lake Maure from Skrykken, if in fact that's where we are. Or any shelters I know of. And, unless we want to turn two lost days into four, the mountains we'll have to cross to get there are some of the highest elevations on the vidda. Over a thousand meters. It'll eat into the rest of our provisions."

"Then we'd better damn well be certain," Ronneberg said. "There has to be something here. Turn the place upside down if you have to."

Pedersen and Storhaug went through the kitchen. Only old cookware and a few tools. Stromsheim and Gutterson searched the living area. The only books were folk tales and hunting catalogues. Nordstrum and Jens went through the owner's bedroom. They found nothing, not even in the bed-side table drawers. Only a Bible and a book on local animals of the wild.

There was always a respect for the owner's privacy when you used their lodging, especially in a place that had saved their lives, but Jens said, "The hell with it," and jimmied open the locked closet. Again, they found nothing at first, but in the pocket of one of the owner's oilskin jackets, he came on something. It was a notebook titled "Fishing Log Book for Skrykkenvann."

Ronneberg let out a deflated sigh as Nordstrum dropped it on the kitchen table for all to see.

Skrykken, it was.

They realized what a mess that was. Whenever the storm finally broke, not only did they have to retrace the hours they

140

had trekked yesterday, but they had a good thirty kilometers more to get to the hut where they hoped the Grouse team would be waiting for them.

This would have seemed a good time to use the radio equipment their SOE planners had elected not to send along with them—as they thought it was heavy and would slow them down, and they'd be meeting up with Grouse upon arrival anyway. Though in this mess there was no way they would have been able to find a signal.

Outside, it sounded like the roof was being ripped off the hut.

Dejectedly, Ronneberg said, "Tomorrow we'll try again. Let's make a fire. This has to blow over."

But the next day the storm continued with the same fury. And the day after as well. By day four, their food supply was dwindling. They'd only brought enough with them to get to Grouse and complete their mission, which they'd thought would be a matter of days. The rest, for their journey to Sweden, was buried back at the drop site.

With no other choice, they decided that a party had to go back to replenish their supplies. Nordstrum and Jens volunteered to make the trek. For Nordstrum, sitting around and doing nothing was making him stir crazy anyway. They set out at 9 A.M. The snow was coming down so heavy it was barely possible to even see your hand in front of your face. By 1 P.M., exhausted and famished, they finally made it back to where they thought they'd landed. At least that's what their compasses read. But four feet of snow had made everything appear different.

"What do you think, Kurt?" Jens asked, shouting above the gales.

Nordstrum shielded his face from the wind and checked the compass reading. "They have to be here."

They searched all around. But after three grueling hours, they had no choice but to give up. The marking stakes they'd left were completely buried. They dug futilely, but never found a thing. They had no other option but to turn back for the hut. Back into the teeth of the very storm they had just braved, with nothing to show for it.

Empty-handed and exhausted, the two made it back to the Skrykken cabin after dark.

The thought occurred to all: What if Grouse, knowing Gunnerside had landed, had sent out a search party to find them? In this weather, they would surely be dead by now. Or what if they had lost hope and managed to get word back to SOE that they, Gunnerside, had likely perished? There was no choice but to wait it out, the mission still in the balance. Not to mention their friends' lives. It seemed to them all that Nature herself had taken sides in the conflict.

By the fourth day, their own provisions had now grown perilously thin. The kind of trekking they had to do required nourishment. And they were at least a full day's journey from where they had to be. Pedersen and Gutterson had come down with colds and swollen glands. Somewhere nearby, the members of the Grouse party were starving with no news of them.

"What are you thinking now, Yank?" Storhaug chided Gutterson, who stared out the window, which was half covered by mounting drifts.

"I'm thinking, you win," the Yank said. It was the only laugh they had the whole day.

The fate of the war was being decided by a ferocious storm that seemed like it would never end.

27

In the tiny cabin at Lake Maure, the situation for the Grouse party was growing just as dire.

They'd had word from England that Gunnerside had landed successfully and were likely on their way to them. But they were both riding out the same storm. Poulsson and his men feared there was no way, unless the Gunnerside crew were lucky enough to have somehow located a hut, they could survive in such hostile conditions.

More than likely, they were dead.

Poulsson and his men had been holed up on the vidda for four months now. Their food stocks were long gone. They were living on whatever they were lucky enough to catch, as well as using survival tricks Poulsson taught them, like sucking out moss from rocks, a high form of protein and nutrition, which he said the reindeer nourished themselves on when there was nothing else to eat, and which they heated into a repugnant-tasting paste. Each had lost a good 15 percent of their body weight. Their hair had grown straggly, their beards long and tangled. In this storm there was no way anything could be hunted, nor could they get a visit from Einar Skinnarland, who occasionally skied up from Vigne with food. Worse, they were running perilously low on firewood.

When it came to Gunnerside, the four were not of one mind about what to do. Claus Helberg wanted to send out an expedition to Bjornesfjord and look for them. Poulsson said no; it was far too dangerous. And anyway, if the bomber pilot had been unable to find the drop zone, which was well lit with their Eureka beacon signaling, they could be anywhere, miles and miles away, in the worst storm many of them had ever lived through.

They started to think that their friends, not to mention the mission, had met with a tragic end.

Still, Poulsson argued, if anyone could survive such an unsurvivable ordeal, if there was one man, two, maybe, who could withstand whatever Nature threw at them and steer their team through, it was Kurt Nordstrum and Joachim Ronneberg.

Anyone else, and the Nazi heavy water production would have claimed seven more lives.

28

On the fifth morning, the men of Gunnerside awoke to a long-awaited sign.

The winds that had battered them for four days had calmed. Sunlight angled into the cabin, where in the teeth of the storm the steady blanketing of snow only made it appear to be night.

Nordstrum got up before the others and crawled out of his sleeping bag to the window. It was covered nearly to half its height with drifts of wind-blown snow.

Birger Stromsheim, who had taken the last watch during the night, was looking out. "It's finally over," he said.

The sky was a brilliant blue.

One by one everyone rose, buoyed by the change in fortune. They dressed, made some food, packed up what was left of their provisions. The first order of business was to retrace their steps back to the drop site, where they had buried the balance of their supplies. Ronneberg ordered their packs reduced to fifty-five pounds and Storhaug and Pedersen fashioned whatever wood they could find into a makeshift toboggan to cart the balance. With relief, they finally bid good-bye to the Skrykken cabin. It had held together in the worst storm any had remembered having to endure. The little hut had surely saved their lives.

Outside, where slopes of rock and even valleys and lakes could be seen five days before, now there was only an endless vastness of white. Climbing proved to be tougher; they were weighed down by even the reduced packs on their backs and lugging the heavy sled. Even gliding, where on the downslopes they could normally catch their breath and rest their muscles for a bit, was a taxing effort in all the snow. Still, it was exhilarating to see their short herringbone patterns in the snow as they climbed the ridges, and they whooped like boys on a day's outing, hopeful now that they were only hours from finally meeting up with their stranded countrymen.

It was an exhausting, four-hour effort to even get back to the ridge they had parachuted onto five days before. But when they did, or at least the compass readings assured them it was so, everything had changed. They were no longer in a valley on a rocky face, but in a large basin covered by a blanket of white. Famished and exhausted, the seven searched around for any sign of the stakes they had planted as markers, which were now completely buried in snow.

Nordstrum finally came upon the handle of one protruding through the snowdrifts. "Over here!" He got on his knees and pawed at the thick, wet snow until he finally unearthed the buried container four feet below.

They all began digging in the same area, until, one by one, an hour later, all twelve supply crates were recovered. They brushed them off, reloaded their packs with needed food, then sat around chewing biscuits and cured venison until they regained the strength to continue.

It was still a thirty-kilometer trek to Lake Maure, a trip even most trained mountain men would find unmanageable.

"Kurt, you know the way?" Ronneberg asked when everyone was ready.

"I do now." He nodded. He started out, east, pushing off and climbing the first ridge.

Reenergized, they all followed in line with yelps of excitement, Pedersen and Gutterson dragging the sled behind, the herringbone pattern of their skis up the first climb a beautiful mosaic in the sunlit snow.

But it was exhausting work. Each ridge left them gasping for air, their thighs burning from exertion. In normal snow, a trek like this would take a good half day, but now they were loaded down with packs and with more snow to push through than any of them had ever seen. They kept their eyes peeled for strangers along the route—but for the first few hours they didn't even see a deer or fox, much less a human. And their gazes were trained toward the sky as well, for German planes—though in their camouflage suits, their packs and weapons painted white as well, they would be difficult to make out from up there.

"So, tell us, what's it like back in Colorado?" Pedersen asked Gutterson, as he skied up from behind.

"The mountains are rockier and taller," said the Yank, "and the valleys wide. But it's all green in the summer. Greener than anything you've ever seen."

"I didn't ask for a postcard," the Norwegian said. "How are the girls? Are they pretty?"

"They are," the American said.

"As pretty as here?"

"So far the only Norwegians I've seen here are all of you. So yes, far prettier, in my view. But when I do see a girl or two I'll let you know."

"Not to worry," Nordstrum said from behind him, "if you meet one they won't understand you anyway, with that accent." He skied on ahead.

About two hours in, Jens, who had taken the lead at that stage, stopped suddenly and pointed ahead. "Hold up! Look!"

In the distance, something was moving through the sea of

white. A black speck, below them in the valley. Not yet in binocular range. Whoever it was was heading directly toward them. In their white suits, there was no way he could have noticed them yet, so far away.

They decided to take cover on the slope, hoping the traveler would veer off and avoid them, but he didn't change his route. Nordstrum skied down a bit closer and focused his binoculars. "It's one man. Heading directly toward us, I'm afraid."

They stopped on the slope of a hill nestled between two peaks. There were large ice boulders, but truly nowhere to completely hide. Anyway, when the man got to them he would surely come upon their tracks. He appeared to be dragging a sled behind him.

Ronneberg took the glasses. "You think he's from Grouse?"

Nordstrum shrugged. "A hunter, more likely. We're still too far away. And he's alone."

They watched him come closer and closer, headed straight for them, until it became clear there was no avoiding the man.

"All right, Jens, Olf, go down and bring him here," Ronneberg finally decided.

Colonel Wilson and Tronstad had been clear: They were under the strictest orders to liquidate anyone they might run into, friend or foe. The stakes were simply too high. In England, each swore to a man that he was capable of carrying it out. But as the traveler came into view, in a deerskin coat, climbing at a good pace, a rifle slung over his shoulder— clearly a man used to the mountains, like themselves—they had to ask themselves again if they could.

Lugging a toboggan, the man stopped in his tracks when Olf and Jens skied down into his path, their weapons drawn.

"I've got a little money in my jacket," the man said. He put up his hands. "You're welcome to it. As you can see, I've caught no prey." He pointed toward his sled.

"What's your name?" Ronneberg said, coming down from his cover. "And what are you doing up here?"

"My name's Kristian Kristiansen." The man removed his hat. "And I do a little hunting." He was large, balding, and broad shouldered with a thick reddish beard, and his eyes went curiously but methodically from man to man, trying to figure out just who he had stumbled upon in the wild, watchfully taking note of their drawn machine guns.

"Anyway I've just set out. From Uvdal. It's a town on the edge of the vidda. About thirty kilometers from here. I spent the night in my brother-in-law's cabin a few kilometers down—"

"We know where Uvdal is," Nordstrum said.

"You do? Then you also know food there is pretty slim these days. Which should answer the question of why I'm out here."

"Weapons are strictly forbidden by the German authorities, are they not?" Ronneberg went up and indicated for him to remove his rifle. Like radios, being caught with them was punishable by death.

"They are." The hunter nodded, still unsure whether he was talking to friend or foe. He likely assumed only Germans or Quislings could possibly be up here with weapons of their own. "I beg you, it's only for shooting deer. I have no politics."

"Black market?" Nordstrum questioned. The trade for deer meat above what their ration cards allowed would make such a trip with two or three trophies worthwhile.

"War or no war, people still have to eat," the hunter said. "So who are all of you?" He looked around warily.

"No matter to that. Are you NS . . . ?" Ronneberg grilled him. The Nasjonal Samling party. Quisling.

The hunter eyed them with circumspection, factoring in the sight of their camouflaged weapons and military uniforms peeking out from under their snowsuits. The idea that they could be free Norwegians in military uniforms carrying heavy weaponry surely never occurred to him. "Sure. NS. I've been known to be in favor of them." The man nodded with a bit of an obsequious grin.

"And if we asked around down in Uvdal," Ronneberg said, "would people there bear that out?"

"Back there . . . ? I have so many enemies in town, they'd probably say I hate the Nazis just to cause me some trouble." The hunter laughed and looked at each of them. "But I don't."

"And why so many enemies?" Nordstrum pressed him.

"Because in times like these you do what you have to do; I'm sure men like you understand. The deer, they don't just come up and bite you on the ass. You don't expect me to just *give* them away."

"A profiteer, then?" Nordstrum said. He probably sold what he caught for five times what it was worth.

"And what of the king?" Ronneberg continued to question him.

He pulled open his ski suit and divulged his British uniform underneath, not German or NS. "No sympathies for him then?"

"King Haikon!" The man's eyes doubled in size. "Good God, you're all true Norwegians then?" he said with a laugh. "How the hell was I to know?" A grin cracked through his heavy beard. "Norwegians bearing arms, on the vidda, blessed God! Yes, I'm a devoted supporter of the king. Ask anyone there, they'll tell you where my sympathies lie. I had no idea who you were."

"You seem to be supporting anyone. Let's see what's in your pockets then," Ronneberg said.

They searched him. They found an identity card verifying his name, about three thousand kroner in cash, and a black notebook with a lot of scribbled names. "You keep lists on people?"

"My customers," the hunter said. "You can check them. Everyone knows me. Kristian Kristiansen. Ask anyone, they'll tell you I'm a man of my word."

"Other than your enemies," Hans Storhaug said with a snort.

"Well, maybe I overstated that just a little . . ." The man grinned a bit guiltily.

NS or patriot, he was a profiteer, and didn't know quite how to answer. Or if he was in any trouble, trying to judge the reaction of the group, trying to laugh it off, but still, with worried, flitting eyes.

"Watch him, Eric," Ronneberg said to Gutterson. "If he makes a wrong move, you know what to do."

"Aye, Lieutenant," the Yank said, motioning with his gun. "Come on, pull out some water. You can sit over here."

The rest huddled a few yards out of earshot. Each knew what they'd been ordered to do. Ronneberg looked around for the feel of the group. "So . . . ?"

"I don't like it," Storhaug said. "There are Germans in Uvdal. If we let him go and he opens his mouth back there, we'll have two divisions up here after us."

"That may be, but Norwegians don't kill Norwegians,"

Nordstrum said. "Unless they've betrayed their homeland. And there's no proof he has."

"He said he was NS," Jens said.

Olf Pedersen nodded. "Yes, he did."

"He would have said anything to save his skin," Nordstrum argued. "He had no idea who we were. What would you have said?" He looked at Storhaug. "He likely thought we were Quisling."

"It's not just about the politics." Storhaug took a swig of water and spat it out. "If we let him go and he runs his mouth off over a beer at the local pub, who guarantees who that person will tell? Or if the Germans offer him a wad of money for something he claims to know? He's already admitted he's a profiteer. You think he'd turn down a payday out of any allegiance to the king?"

"How about if I keep an eye on him?" Nordstrum said to Ronneberg. "We can take him along to Grouse and then tie him up there in the cabin. When we get back we can set him free."

"There's no guarantee we *will* get back." Storhaug kept at it. "All that you'll do for him then is drag him along a long way to make him freeze to death or starve."

Nordstrum nodded, though his instincts insisted the man was who he said he was. But there was a case for disposing of him as well. And no doubt Wilson and Tronstad would have argued for it without hesitation.

He looked toward Jens.

"I'm afraid I'm with Hans on this one, Kurt." His friend shrugged guiltily. "It's simply too much of a risk."

"Me as well," Olf Pedersen said. "You may be right, Kurt, he's just an average guy trying to make the best of it in a war. But if you're wrong and he does like Hans says . . . ? What if we're facing German half-tracks up here in a day? How would you feel then about letting him go?"

Stromsheim looked at Nordstrum and nodded. "Me too, I'm afraid."

Nordstrum saw it was a losing cause. And maybe they were right. They looked back down the hill. The hunter just stood there, chatting with Gutterson, puffing on a cigarette, but at the same time, intermittently glancing up at them with unease.

"So, it's decided then," Ronneberg said, capping his canteen.

"I'll make it easy on you." Storhaug exhaled. "Since I was the one who argued for it." He pulled his tommy off his back.

"At least make it quick," Ronneberg said, shaking his head.

With a nod, Storhaug headed back down the rise. "I see the two of you seem to have become fast friends . . ." he said amiably.

"Our families are from the same region," Gutterson said. "The Sognefjord."

"Is that right? Come, we need to check out what's in your packs," Storhaug said, a hand on the man's back. "So you say you're a supporter of the king, are you . . . ?"

"Absolutely," the hunter said and went with him, looking back at them once, not sure if he should be worried or relieved.

"Then that's too bad then." Storhaug stopped and pulled back the bolt on his Thompson. "I'm sorry, friend."

"Listen—" The hunter put up his palms. "Just hear me out—" Storhaug let off a short burst, sending the man backward into a drift, his arms spread wide.

Then he went up and stepped over him. The man's eyes

were wide, his deerskin coat pelted with black, wet dots. He put one more burst in his chest, just to be sure.

Gutterson stared at him, his eyes lit with anger. "He was just a trapper. He was no more a threat than me."

"Had to be done," Storhaug said. "Sorry, lad." He slung his tommy back over his shoulder. He went up and put a hand on Nordstrum's shoulder. "Sometimes you're a bit too honorable for your own good, Kurt. That'll come back to bite you in the end."

"We should bury him," Ronneberg said.

"Of course." Nordstrum nodded. "Who'll help?"

"I will," Gutterson offered.

"I guess I should too." Storhaug shrugged. "Considering."

"And if any of you know anything, it might be right to say a few words," Ronneberg called after them. "I'm afraid I'm not very good at that kind of thing."

"I know a few words," Gutterson said. "I'm Lutheran."

They dragged the hunter's body over to a tall drift and swept fresh snow over him. Come spring, when it melted, someone would find him. Hopefully before he became a target for wolves. But for now, as time was short, it was all they could do. It took a while to fully cover his boots. In a couple of minutes the large man had completely disappeared. They decided against putting his rifle in the snow as a marker and buried it with him.

The group settled over him and they all pushed back their hoods.

"Heavenly Father," Gutterson started in English, "receive this soul and forgive him for his sins . . ."

Jens said, "That's all?"

"I guess I didn't go so often." Gutterson shrugged.

In war, Nordstrum said to himself, sometimes things you

wouldn't do in life were unavoidable. Things that one day you might look back upon with regret. In the end, it was all best left unsaid. What did it really matter for Kristian Kristiansen? NS or patriot, all he'd been was an unlucky man who had skied the wrong path.

It was God's job to do the judging.

"At least one good thing," Nordstrum said. "We can make good use of the sled."

They loaded several packs of their supplies on the hunter's sled and then headed back to rejoin the men.

"We ought to move out now." Ronneberg pointed toward the sun. "We've lost a lot of time."

They strapped their packs back on and each skied by, Gutterson and Storhaug dragging the hunter's sled. There was no sign of blood. No sign he'd even been there, Kristian Kristiansen, other than the lonely herringbone pattern of his tracks in the snow, which the seven skied quickly over.

29

It was still a couple of hours' trek over the Songvaln to Lake Maure. The sun had started to wane. Tired and winded, they came upon the flat-roofed cabin Kristiansen had mentioned that he'd stayed in the night before.

Early the next morning, they were off again at first light. Nordstrum thought the lake was still a two-hour trek, but much of it downhill. And the morning was clear.

They skied in a line, each gliding in each other's tracks at five-yard intervals when a buzzing was heard overhead. "Everyone get down!" Ronneberg yelled. "The sleds."

Pedersen and Jens scrambled to drape a white tarp over all the cargo, then they dove headfirst into the snow.

Coming into view from over a peak was a Storch Fokker, a German reconnaissance plane. It came in and circled the valley, its twin propellers buzzing. Only three or four hundred feet above them, they could clearly see the black cross on the fuselage and the machine guns on its wings. They pressed themselves into the snow. If they were spotted, the Germans could tear them to shreds with those guns, or at a minimum, alert the enemy to their presence. After a quick circle, finding nothing of interest, the plane seemed to move on. They all stood up and watched it disappear.

"There's always the chance they saw our tracks," Nordstrum said. The good news was that they'd all been careful to ski in the leader's tracks, so even if they were spotted, it would only appear to be a single skier, not a party of them.

They took turns dragging the sleds, which now weighed a couple of hundred pounds each, with the additional supplies. Nordstrum didn't know the exact location of the cabin where the Grouse party was holed up, only the general region. They didn't even know for certain that their friends would even be there, or how they had managed in the storm. Only that that had been the site of SOE's last communication with them. Things had a way of changing rapidly out here. The day became bright and crisp, and progress was good. Along the way, they spotted animal tracks and droppings, signs that reindeer were in the area.

Kristian Kristiansen had followed his nose in the wrong direction and it had cost him his life.

Nordstrum now had a feel for where he was and took the lead. Who knew what condition they would find their countrymen in? Or what sort of food they'd been able to find? The sight of reindeer near was a positive sign, but four months . . . Four months was a long time, even for the hardiest of men. You never knew what sort of—

Suddenly he spotted something far out in the snow. Ronneberg skied up. "What is it, Kurt?"

Nordstrum pointed out toward the valley. "We have more company."

Several hundred yards ahead a figure on skis was coming up a frozen lake. Twenty yards behind was another skier. From this distance, even with their binoculars, they were no more than moving specks.

"You think there's a chance it's a German patrol?" Ronneberg asked.

"There's always a chance. What if that plane spotted our tracks?"

"Better not take a chance. Everyone, take cover!"

157

Ronneberg waved to the men. They all crouched down and scanned over the valley from behind some boulders.

"They might also be our guys," Nordstrum said. "We can't be that far away."

"You know them best, Kurt. I don't want them to see the rest of us. Why don't you go ahead and check. And take a gun. Eric, you and Storhaug take a position near those rocks down there. If you're in any trouble, Kurt, remove your hood as a sign. You won't have to worry about them after that."

Nordstrum slid out of his pack and grabbed a Colt pistol, which he put inside his suit.

"Remember, lose the hood and we'll open fire on them," Ronneberg said. "And don't take any risks."

"Don't worry," Nordstrum said.

He skied down a way and focused in on the two men through his binoculars. They were still about three hundred yards away—with no idea anyone had spotted them. They were not even skiing toward him but actually away from him across the lake.

As they came in range, Nordstrum focused on the figure in front. He had a long beard and wore a flat cap on his head. But he wore no uniform Nordstrum could see. Hunters, most likely. Like Kristiansen. The proximity of deer would bring more hunters out, which wasn't good for maintaining their secrecy. *Or . . .* He peered in more closely. *Could it be Arne Kjelstrup? Or Claus Helberg?* It didn't look like it to him. But there was simply no way to tell.

Nordstrum thought it best to take no chances and come up on them from behind. Who knew how someone confronted might react? He maneuvered himself to a spot where the sun was behind him as they trekked across the lake. By now, the second man had caught up with his partner. But they looked so haggard and unkempt, with their long, straggly hair coming out of their hats and beards, they appeared more like beggars than anyone he knew.

Yet he saw they carried rifles.

Finally Nordstrum maneuvered himself into position. If they wanted to take a shot at him, they'd have to do so directly into the sun. He took a final glance up the slope, at Gutterson and Storhaug. Then he silently began to ski up to the two, who still had no idea he was there. He got within thirty yards and put his hand around the Colt in his suit. He knew that Storhaug and the Yank had their rifles trained on them in case there was the slightest trouble, awaiting his signal.

"*Arne? Claus . . . ?*" Nordstrum called.

The two turned around, their hands instinctively reaching for their guns as well.

Nordstrum was about to go to his knees and pull out his. Then he couldn't believe what he saw. Underneath the straggly beard and the gaunt, sunken cheekbones was a face he had known for ten years. "Jesus, *Claus?* It's Kurt."

He threw his arms in the air and waved to his men up on the hill. "Don't shoot! Don't shoot! It's Kurt!" he yelled again to his two countrymen.

"*Nordstrum?*" Helberg finally lowered his rifle and uttered in disbelief, "My God, Kurt, you're alive!" They each took off and skied toward each other, jubilantly, and hurled their arms around each other.

"Jesus," Arne Kjelstrup looked at him, "where the hell have you been? We were sure you hadn't survived the storm."

"*Storm . . . ?*" Nordstrum said deadpan. "What storm? Did you have weather here?" Then he broke into a wide grin. "That was the mother of all storms, wasn't it? We were lucky to have found a hut. But look at you both! God, it's good to see you."

The rest of the Gunnerside contingent left their packs and skied down to the lake, whooping with joy.

"You folks didn't happen to bring along any food, did you?" Kjelstrup asked. It looked like he hadn't had a good meal in weeks.

"Food?" Nordstrum shrugged. "Hmm, no, no one mentioned. Are you short?" Then he laughed. "Of course we have food. A sled full of it! Jesus, what the hell have you been surviving on?"

"We'll tell you, but you won't believe it," Claus Helberg said. "We're just happy you're here."

The rest of the team arrived. Everyone hugged and cheered, slapping each other on the back. They'd found them. Amid the Germans and the worst storm any had ever seen, they'd found their friends. Alive.

Now it was time to get on with why they were all here.

30

Dieter Lund motioned the old man into a chair across from his desk at the Nasjonal Samling party office in Rjukan. "Pere Nordstrum . . . Please, sit down. Over here will be fine. You can wait outside," he said to the Hirden sergeant who had brought him in.

His police office was on the second floor of the old Hanseatic trade building on King Gustav Street, the basement once a place where grain and cattle were stored, now converted to jail cells, which were amply filled. Lund had put his best uniform on, starched and pressed, with shiny metal buttons polished and fastened to the top.

He stood up. "I am very sorry for the manner in which we had you come in."

Nordstrum's father was a thin, weathered man, in his late fifties only, but a lifetime of heavy work and bitter winters had stooped his back and made him appear much older. He was bald on top with bushy, gray hair on the sides, thin, rough lips, and calloused fingers. Narrow, suspicious eyes. Still, Lund observed, he had the look of a man who could still handle himself in a tussle or in the outdoors if necessary.

"Go ahead, I assure you it's all right." Lund gestured to the chair. "I just wanted to have a little chat. May I offer you some coffee?"

"For yourself, maybe. None for me." The elder Nordstrum followed Lund as he got up and stood over a tray on the right side of his desk and poured himself a cup.

"Please, don't stand on politics. It's so rare these days to find the real thing. So much of it is watered down. I'd be honored if I could share a cup."

"I said not for me." Nordstrum's father waved it off again. "Just tell me, why am I here?"

"Why you are here . . . ? Of course, we shall talk about this. But first—" Lund took a long sip of the coffee, savoring the smell. "To the new Norway . . ."

"I don't have time for the new Norway. I have a farm to manage. I must insist, Captain, on what grounds have you brought me here?"

"You are here, of course," Lund sat back down, "it's sad to say, like so many others, through no fault or action of your own. But only because keeping the order requires different measures now, as outside agitators are in this country and bent on doing their new state harm."

"Doing harm? I'm a farmer." The old man glared. "I've always shunned politics, war or no war. What do any outside agitators have to do with me?"

"Not with you exactly, perhaps. I perfectly understand the confusion." Lund pushed back his chair and crossed his legs. "But, perhaps, with your son."

"*My son* . . . ?" The old man's dull gray eyes suddenly came alive. "My son is dead, I'm told."

"Dead?" Lund laughed dismissively. "Then I have wonderful news for you, Pere Nordstrum. Your son has made a remarkable recovery. Almost Christlike, I would say. In fact, I am sure your son is quite alive. Possibly in England, training with those who would disrupt our national unity party. But more likely—and forgive me for thinking this might not be news to you—perhaps even back at home. In Norway. As we speak. Though whatever business he is on, he will no doubt not be showing his face much around here, as he is wanted by the state."

"Wanted? My son fought for the king like many boys did. He was a soldier. Not a criminal. That's no offense. What do you say he's done?"

"He is wanted for crimes committed against the Nasjonal Samling party. Murder, in fact."

"*Murder?* You must be mad."

"I'm afraid I'm not. Against a member of the Hirden guard, to be clear. As well as the illegal appropriation of state property, specifically a coastal steamer, used in his escape. To England."

"My son was a soldier." The old man sniffed back. "One of his regiment came to me a year ago and told me he was killed in the Gunbraval Valley. I told him from the start not to get involved. That whoever wins, it would only end up with him dead and everyone else still fighting it out. And so it is. I haven't heard from my son for two years. Yet you say he is wanted for crimes against the state? You will have to tell me, Captain, with all the murder, bribery, family inform- ing on family, and the disappearances in the dead of night that go on here in the name of keeping order, how can you call anything that defends against it a crime?"

Lund put down his cup and leaned back with amusement. "You say you are a farmer, Pere Nordstrum? You should argue in a court of law. You are almost convincing. I brought you here for a chance to make your own situation easier, not for us to devolve into a dispute over this side versus that. Or, who holds the cards in this matter, and who does not . . ."

"Cards . . . ? What cards do you hold?" The old man looked back.

"Enough playing around. Your son, Herr Nordstrum. I want to know if he has been in touch with you."

"You drag me in here to, what . . . ?" The elder Nordstrum forced a smile in the eyes of the man with the light hair slicked to the side, a smooth face with sideburns that had barely filled in, eyes the color of rain. "Inform against my son? Turn him in? You have your thugs remove me from my home, without a thimbleful of cause, and you expect me, even if I knew, to divulge his whereabouts? I'd rather you take out my own eyes, Herr Lund. Or my heart. Kurt is a resourceful boy. I say he's dead and you say not, we'll see. . . . But if he is not . . . If he is somehow back here as you suggest he is, it will likely be all the same in the end because I promise you will never find him until he has done whatever he has come to do."

"Listen, old man." Eyes narrowed, Lund leaned forward. "Let me be clear. When I spoke of holding cards, it was not some metaphor. I believe your daughter, Kristin, and her two children live in Trondheim with her husband. Trondheim is a long way away, but not so long when it comes to the reach of the law. I could have them here in days. I could put them, and I'm just speaking as a possibility, in the very cell underneath where we are now sitting. That would be a cruel and almost unjust irony, would it not? Perhaps she could persuade you of the wisdom in cooperating on this matter. I'm sure you have also heard of the detention camp outside Oslo at Grini. They are always accepting new residents, I am told. Women and children too. I assure you, they don't ask too many questions there. So in this matter I simply want you to understand your choices. If I choose to leave her be, you will be under watch, and we would expect to know if he is in the region the moment he makes contact with you. And

164

if not . . ." Lund pushed the saucer and dish away. ". . . then it is not as if I did not offer to help."

The elder Nordstrum's hands balled into fists and he gazed with simmering anger at the policeman. Yes, he was a weakened man these days, but still capable of lunging across this desk, putting his hands around the man's skinny neck, and doing what the whole town would regard as a blessing. "Herr *Lund* . . ." He paused on the policeman's family name. "Your father was the tax collector in Vigne for many years, I believe?"

"I am honored that you remember him. Sadly, he died three years ago."

"From drink, the world knows. Or greed. His reputation, if I may say, was 'two coins for the town, one for the pocket,' if you know what I mean. Not only a drunk and a wife beater, but a gambler, and with other people's money. I used to see him holding his cards and sweating like a fish in the Oar and Bow. Was that the man, Herr Lund . . . ?"

"*Captain* Lund," the policeman said, his jaw tightening and his smile disappearing. "A rank you ought to pay a bit more heed of."

"*Captain* Lund . . ." the elder Nordstrum said as if with a vile taste on his tongue. "Even as such, it would seem when it came to character he had far more than he passed on to you. For even a thief like your father would never have traded in his country for some well-pressed uniform and phony ribbons on his chest. So must ask you again, under what law do you restrain me here? I have committed no crime. I ask you to cither show me that I have, or let me go."

"You are not restrained, old man. Pick up your filthy mule outside and go. But just know, I need no law to do what I said regarding your daughter. I am the law here now. So do your family a favor and give heed to what I said . . ." He stood up, and with a wave, indicated his patience had ended.

The old man got to his feet as well and tugged at his trousers. "I'm just an old mechanic, Captain Lund, turned farmer. Not trained when it comes to expressing myself. So I hope the right words come, to convey what is in my heart. That thugs like you will never, not for a single day, be thought of as the *new* Norway. The true Norway will lie buried a thousand years before the people turn to cowards and traitors like yourself. And if my daughter or her children are harmed, one day, whether I'm around to drop the noose or not, you will surely be hanged for it. That is, if that ghost of a son of mine doesn't come back and do the job himself. So take me away, put a bullet in me, if you must. Like so many others. But no . . . I suspect if what you say is true about Kurt, I'm far too valuable to you alive. But for now, I'm just a man who has lived too long and seen too much of this new Norway."

"*Shoot* you . . . ?" The Hirden laughed. "Where did you ever get such a notion? Not a chance. But you are right," he fixed on him, "I'm going to enjoy having you around. I want you to be the one to confirm it when I bring his body and throw it like a dead fish on your doorstep. Now back to your fields, old man. You've wasted too much of my time. Sergeant, escort this old farmer back to his mule."

31

It took a few days to nourish the Grouse team back to full strength, with the provisions the Gunnerside team had brought from England and a reindeer they managed to kill on their way back to the cabin.

They spent the time sharing how each team had remained alive during the storm, and then going over the best route for them to make their way across the vidda to the target. Claus Helberg knew of an abandoned hut just a few kilometers from the edge of the plateau above Vemork that would suit their purposes.

By latest accounts, there appeared to be around fifteen Germans in the guard hut at any time of night, plus two more on the suspension bridge spanning the gorge. Another patrolled the giant penstocks that supplied the Norsk Hydro plant's massive turbines their water for power. The guards worked two-hour shifts and changed like clockwork due to the extreme cold.

Additionally, there was also the possibility two more guards might be on rounds at any time inside the factory. As well as a Norwegian watchman or two stationed inside the electrolysis room itself, who might have to be subdued. It was clear that if they had to engage the main detachment stationed in the hut or on the bridge, the alarm would quickly bring reinforcements from Rjukan or Mosvatn, only a few kilometers away, where hundreds of troops were stationed. Then even if they did manage to take out the targets in the plant's basement, it would basically be a suicide mission. There would be no way back.

So secrecy, not a direct assault over the bridge, was deemed to be the best plan. But that meant taking on the most challenging terrain in all of Norway to best approach the target.

The cliffs above, which rose to three thousand feet, were considered far too steep to rappel down at night, even for experienced climbers. The area around the giant conduits, which brought in the water from rivers, lakes, and mountain streams on the vidda to run the giant turbines, had been heavily mined.

On the other side of the river, the slope was more forgiving, but it also came with the risk of crossing the river at night with searchlights fanning the valley, and then making their way back up the rocky heights at the rear of the plant, a difficult climb in daytime, not to mention in darkness with heavy packs of explosives on their backs and weapons strapped on. If they made it up there, Claus Helberg said, the railway tracks leading to the plant had not been mined, but getting to them would be no easy feat. The plant's defenders, however, did not think it possible any threat could come from that direction. The Germans considered the only real threat to storming the facility was from a direct assault over the suspension bridge that led to the front.

Once on top of the ledge, the saboteurs could break into the plant by one of the three ways Tronstad had mapped out in England: It was possible the steel side door would be left open, since guards routinely patrolled inside. If it wasn't, there was the side door around the north side of the building on the first floor, but who knew what was inside? Lastly there was the narrow valve duct Jomar Brun told them about that led from the outside literally to the basement where the heavy water stocks were located, an access even many who worked in the plant didn't know of. However, as Tronstad had explained, this entry could only accommodate one person at a time, crawling on hands and knees, and once inside, any second they delayed setting the charges could be critical.

"If everything is locked, and the valve duct unavailable, we blow the basement door," Ronneberg declared. "That will, of course, alert the Nazis." He looked at Poulsson, Gutterson, and Kjelstrup. "Covering team, you will have to take care of them then."

"That's no problem." Poulsson shrugged. The flimsy exterior of the hut wouldn't provide much protection against a hail of bullets, and with three submachine guns trained on them, anyone who managed to make it out wouldn't get far.

Once inside, Nordstrum and Stromsheim calculated, it would take around fifteen minutes to get to the target and set the charges. It would be early Sunday morning and Tronstad and Brun estimated the crew inside would be light, maybe only a single guard. That left only two minutes to make their way back out of the building since the fuses couldn't be any longer; the last thing they could accept was to allow a German or watchman to stumble on the charges after they'd been set and disengage the wires. They reasoned that the explosion from the blast would be loud; Stromsheim, who among them knew most about explosives, thought it was possible that the entire building would go up. Who knew what chemicals were stored inside? Which left no doubt in anyone's mind that the soldiers in the guard hut would be alerted right away. At best then, they'd have to fight their way out and back down the mountain. And at worst, in minutes every German in the valley would be on them.

Which made the choice of their escape route all the more crucial. Otherwise, it would just be a one-way mission. Poulsson and Ronneberg, the two senior men, made the case for fighting it out back across the bridge.

"Getting past the guards won't be the problem," Poulsson argued, "but climbing back down the cliff to the river will be slow. And we'd be sitting ducks for the searchlights over the river and the valley. We'll never be able to retrace our steps to here. Therefore, it makes sense to go back up via the cliffs."

"So then we don't come back here," Nordstrum said. "But climbing three thousand feet in the dark, with heavy packs on our backs and weapons, is no easy feat. We'll get separated and we'll be easy to pick off. I think it's far better to have the darkness and the rugged terrain in the gorge working for us and go back up the way we came. Do you know if the Ryes Road is mined?" he asked Helberg.

"I'm told it's not," he said. "So yes, we can cross and go back up the cliffs that way, underneath the tram. It's steep. One advantage, of course, is they'll never think it possible we went that way. Once on top, we could make our way back to the cabin. What do you all say?"

So they voted: straight up the cliffs or back across the river and up the Ryes Road?

Most sided for the Ryes Road.

One who sounded a differing voice was Olf Pedersen. He was the weakest climber in the group, and had always been unsure of the trek up and down the mountain. "To be honest, I never expected to see Sweden anyway," he said. "I knew that when I volunteered. So I'm for whatever is agreed to."

"If we make it out of that plant, I'll make sure you make it back to your skis," Nordstrum said to him. "That's a promise."

"And I'll be there as well," Gutterson said. "We're one in this all the way."

"Thanks, boys."

"Okay, then it's settled. We'll go back down the way we came." Ronneberg spoke for the group. "And pray the Germans don't shine their lights on us."

Also on their minds was the risk of reprisal in case any of them were captured and were found out to be Norwegian. That's why they would all wear British uniforms and had their suicide pills. Helberg, Poulsson, Jens, and Nordstrum all came from the area and still had family there, who would certainly be among the first lined up against a wall if their identities were discovered.

On that subject, each knew that not everyone would make it back out alive. It was likely a few might be trapped inside the plant, or shot on their way out, or surrounded on their escape back across the valley. They had a frank and lengthy conversation, including a bet on just how many would make it out.

No one seemed particularly optimistic.

It might not be a suicide mission, each man knew, but it surely was the next closest thing.

32

The morning of the raid Ronneberg asked Claus Helberg, who still had contacts in town, to go into Vemork on a final reconnaissance trip to scout out the best route into the gorge and up the rock face on the other side.

Dressed in everyday clothes, he skied off bravely with a wave, leaving a trail of powdery snow as he took off down the mountain.

It took only about an hour for him to get there. Setting eyes at last on the giant Norsk Hydro factory they'd talked so much about was both exhilarating and terrifying. Not to mention the sight of Germans all over his home village. That he hadn't seen before, and it made his chest tighten with resentment and anger.

Posing as a factory worker, he walked in plain view down the main road that wound from the suspension bridge down to Rjukan, past traffic headed up to the factory and German troop trucks rumbling down the hill. From a side construction road on the less steep side of the gorge, he found what he thought was a manageable route down into the valley.

Looking further, he hid his skis in the snow and followed the steep terrain all the way down to the river, sliding on some icy spots, grabbing on to bushes to break his fall, sometimes stepping all the way up to his waist in softer, sunlit snow. On the valley floor he found the Mann to be little more than a trickling, frozen stream—which answered one of their big concerns, whether they'd be able to cross it. He then kept on going all the way over to the other side, to the rock face at the back of the factory, which loomed above him like an impregnable fortress six hundred feet up. He searched around for some way to navigate up the slope, and in spite of its steepness, he spotted something that made his heart rise happily.

To mark the spot he pulled out a handful of berries.

Six hours later he returned to the hut with a grin on his face.

"The good news is there is a way down," he said. "By the wide bend on the Rjukan road. It will be dark and slippery, but it's definitely doable. Even at night. I made the trip myself. And the light from the searchlights on the bridge won't reach there, but should illuminate the way."

"And the river?" Ronneberg asked. "Can it easily be crossed near Vaer?"

"Even better," Helberg said. "Closer to town, the river is completely iced over. It won't be a problem at all. Unless it warms, its flows are no more than a trickle. On the other side, it's steep back up the cliffs, I admit, underneath the factory. But there's a route up that I found. Leading straight up to the railway tracks."

"You're certain it can be climbed?" Nordstrum pressed. He had grown up in the region, but he had never been in the gorge that deep. None had. "Even with heavy packs on our backs, and weapons?"

"Look." Helberg dug into his pocket. He held out his hand. "What do you see?"

Nordstrum looked with interest. "Juniper berries."

"Where juniper bushes can go, so can man," Helberg said with a sage grin. "I even went a third of the way up to be sure of it myself."

*

While Helberg was away, Nordstrum's old friend Einar Skinnarland had skied up from Vigne and met them at the hut where they were located.

He, Nordstrum, and Jens all exchanged hugs and warmly patted each other on the back, as they hadn't seen each other since their first days in Britain, after commandeering the coastal steamer.

After explaining how the past months had been for him back here and providing some recon himself about the inside of the factory, Einar said to Nordstrum, "Kurt, I've something to talk to you about. Can we step outside?"

"Of course."

The two went out and stood on the snowy ridge on the edge of the iced-in lake. "Look." He pointed to a stubborn rodent digging out of the snow. "Even in this frozen wilderness, there's life."

"He's lucky he didn't show his face until we got here with food," Nordstrum laughed, "or I'm certain the Grouse team would have made him dinner."

"A little salt and margarine," Einar shrugged, "yes, not so bad. . . . Look, Kurt, I've got some things to tell you about. On your father . . ."

A stab of worry shot through Nordstrum. "Is he dead?"

"No. He's not well, of course, but he's still around. But he's been brought in by the police. Luckily, he wasn't arrested. I'm afraid many in town have been by now."

"*The police?* For what? He's never been political in his life." Nordstrum chuffed out a disgusted breath. At the same time, he felt a weight in his chest, because in his heart he knew the answer. "Because of me, naturally."

"Look, no one needs a reason anymore. The NS and the Gestapo have their grips on the whole area. Because you're

174

his son, that's all the reason they need. The local militia chief here, Lund . . . you may remember him from school?"

"*Dieter* Lund . . . ? That eel. His father was tax collector in Vigne, if I recall?"

"He is an eel, but he's the eel of the local Gestapo chief, Muggenthaler, now. You remember how he always sat in the back of the class, never saying a word. A real ass-sniffer, who always thought he was smarter than everyone else. Well, a uniform has only made him more so, only far more dangerous. And from what I hear, he seems to have a real wart on his ass for you."

"Me?"

"About that mess on the ferry last year when you came back to Rjukan. Someone must have talked."

"The Hird . . ." Nordstrum recalled. An impulsive act, he always knew. One that one day might come back to haunt him. And now it had.

His father wouldn't survive a week in jail.

"Look, even rats come to the defense of their own," Einar said, "and this one is one of the worst. Anyway, the good news is your father's still on the farm, not in the basement of the police station in town. Or shipped out to Grini yet, where he would stand no chance. But who knows how long he has? We looked in on him from time to time, brought him some food. But he was under constant watch. After a while it simply became too dangerous."

Nordstrum put a hand on his friend's shoulder. "I appreciate that, Einar. You've been a good friend. And you've nothing to apologize for."

"My wife." Einar pushed back his wavy, dark hair. "She brings out all my best qualities. You should find one yourself one day. When all this subsides. I mean—" He stopped, looked at Nordstrum with a sniff of apology. "I'm sorry, Kurt. I didn't mean to bring all that up."

"No apologies necessary. And be certain I'll look into it," Nordstrum said with a half smile, "if after this is over I'm still around."

"If we're *all* still around." Einar nodded in agreement. "Our transmissions are becoming harder to conceal. The Germans have their W/T trucks sniffing everywhere. Especially in town. And this raid will be no sail on the lake, you know that? Anyway, I'm sorry to have to tell you this news."

"Thanks." Nordstrum patted his friend on the shoulder. "I wonder if there's a way to get him out?"

"He's under constant watch and in poor health. Where would you take him? And it's not as if you don't have enough going on here."

"Of course." Nordstrum kicked the snow off his boot. "I meant after."

"*After . . . ?*" Einar stared, probing for his meaning. Afterward, he'd be on the run. To Sweden. "What do you mean?"

"There's something I need to tell you too. Something Tronstad asked of me. When this is all finished. But look, there's Claus returning from town." With a wave, Helberg had pulled himself up the last ridge to the cabin. "Let's hear if he's found a way to get us near the plant, or if tomorrow, we'll all be dead on that bridge."

33

Before they left that night, they went over the plans one last time.

Ronneberg said to Nordstrum, "Once we get into the high-concentration room with the explosives, Kurt, you're in charge. We've estimated it should take *what* to do the job . . . ?"

"Seven minutes," Nordstrum confirmed. They had done the drill at least a hundred times in England on exact replicas of the factory and compressors. "Depending, of course, on what else we encounter in there."

"Of course. The only sure sign that the charges have gone off will be the sound of the explosion. By then, if all goes well, we should all be out of the building. The password for withdrawal, as you all know, is . . ."

"Piccadilly," Hans Storhaug said.

"And the reply?"

"The reply is Leicester Square."

"Good. Should anything happen to me or upset the plan, everyone must act on his own, with the one goal in mind to complete the mission. If we're detected, or if the alarm is sounded in any way, the covering party will attack the German guards immediately."

Poulsson, Gutterson, and Storhaug nodded.

"The demolition party will concentrate on getting inside the plant no matter what it encounters, but if they're killed or disabled before the plant is reached, the covering party will take over the placing of the explosives. All that matters is someone must arrive at the objective to do the job."

It was basically an admission that they would all die trying to complete the operation.

Poulsson nodded again. "We'll be there."

"And finally, just to repeat what we were all told in Britain, Hitler has ordered every commando or saboteur, whether in uniform or not, to be interrogated and shot. So if any man is wounded or about to be taken prisoner, you have your pills. I know it's a bitter thought, but in the end, it's pretty much the same outcome."

It was one thing to talk about suicide in the highlands of Avainaire when it was just a concept that might never come to fact, another thing entirely when you knew that many in the room might not make it through the night. But the truth remained: If you were injured, there was virtually no chance of making it back up to the vidda, much less all the way to Sweden.

"Count me in," said Poulsson, with a drag from his pipe, standing up and turning toward the window.

"Me as well," said Nordstrum. In effect, it was the same result. Might as well spare yourself the pain.

"And me," said Jens.

One by one, they all agreed. All that was left for Ronneberg was to add, "We leave here at twenty hundred hours, to give ourselves enough time. Claus, you'll lead the way from here to the power line road. After we leave our skis, he'll also take us down the gorge and up to the railway tracks. There's a change of guard on the suspension bridge every two hours, on the hour. At half past midnight, we start our attack."

34

Before the war, when Nordstrum was in engineering school in Oslo, no one knew, in spite of the troublesome events taking place on the mainland of Europe, if Norway would be dragged into the widening war.

The country had managed to stay neutral in the last war, and Sweden and the king tried to hold firm to that again, despite both the British and the Nazis escalating tensions by clashing in their sovereign waters.

Waiting those last hours before leaving the hut, Nordstrum remembered those days.

The liberals rallied around France and Britain. Others railed at the Brits for threatening to mine the harbors of Bergen and Narvik. They saw the Germans as the saviors of Europe. Both factions turned their eyes to the country's north, with its ice-free ports and overland transport routes for the valuable iron ore from Sweden.

The night of April 8, 1940, made everyone take sides. Germany surprise-attacked by sea and air. In days, Bergen, Trondheim, and Narvik were overrun by advance troops from German destroyers. An enemy detachment headed down the Oslofjord toward the capital.

In a day, the city was in turmoil. Everyone knew Norway's army had no chance against the Nazi blitzkrieg. But to a true Norwegian, their homeland was their mother. Overnight, arguments over beers in the pubs in Oslo escalated into impassioned recruitment rallies. They cheered when the artillery and torpedoes sank the German flagship *Blucher* in the Oslofjord, allowing the king and his family to flee the city and set up a government in Elverum.

Pandemonium reigned. Students were signing up in the king's army; others fled to the supposed safety of the north, or to the east and to Sweden. Nordstrum, a person whom his peers always seemed to look up to, felt pressure both ways. His father had begged him not to do something rash. The king's army was no match for the Germans. In the end, they would all be killed or put in prisons. In his heart, Nordstrum knew what he had to do. What all true patriots were doing.

But he also had to think of Anna-Lisette.

They had known each other two years—she was in her final year in economics—and they had talked of getting married after her graduation.

"We've got to make sure you're safe," he said in the apartment he shared with two other students near the university. Oslo had become a maelstrom of fear, false information, people fleeing ahead of the German advance amid overtures of welcome by Vidkun Quisling and his Nasjonal Samling party, who had seized control of the public radio station in an ill-timed coup.

"I have an uncle in Malmo," Anna-Lisette said. "The trains are still running. If we leave now, we will be safe. They'd never dare invade Sweden."

They threw their belongings into suitcases. The city was rapidly becoming a ghost town. The Nazis could be there any day.

"I have a friend," Nordstrum said. "A Jew. His family is leaving for Stockholm tomorrow. You could go with them."

"You could go as well, Kurt. When I spoke of Sweden, I was speaking of both of us, not just me."

It only took one look at him for her to see he had already made up his mind. "You won't be coming, will you?"

He let out a helpless breath. "Anna-Lisette . . ."

She sat next to him and put down the sweater she was folding. Her eyes seemed to reflect the same worry raging in his own heart. "You'll only get yourself killed, you know. You all will. But if you won't go, neither will I. I speak some German. They'll need someone here to help with getting information through the lines."

"The fighting won't *be* here," Nordstrum said. "It'll be up north. I've talked to Gries and Karlsson. They're sending people up to hold the lines at Narvik."

"So that's where you'll be heading?"

"Yes." Slowly he allowed himself to nod. "Tomorrow."

"You knew all this, Kurt, and yet you didn't say?"

He put his hand to her face. "I can take you part of the way by train. As far as Lillehammer. Your folks are there. You should be safe. I can't imagine what the Germans want with a bunch of cows and ski trails. If we can't stop them at Narvik, I'll make it back there and we'll cross over the mountains to Sweden together. I give you my word."

She looked at him and smiled, wanly but bravely, filled with both affection and inevitability. "I know you, Kurt. You'll never join me. You'll keep fighting. Until someone wins."

He put his arms around her and pulled her close. "You're wrong. I will."

She buried her face into his sweater. He felt tears there. He sensed there was something she was holding back from him. Like she knew then. Knew better. "No, you won't."

They took the train the next day, and he went on to the north to fight.

And she was right. After Narvik it was Honefoss. And then after Honefoss it was Tonneson, Haugsbygda, and the Gudbrandsdalen valley.

What she held back from telling him in Oslo never reached him.

Who knows, maybe she didn't even know right then. *It's not just me, Kurt.* And would it have made a difference? The fight needed him. Needed anyone who could shoot and had the nerve to hold a line.

It was almost a year, months after she'd been killed, that the letter finally reached him, passed along by friends, soldiers in other regiments.

From her mother, Regina, who Nordstrum had always liked, who wrote to him that Anna-Lisette had been carrying their child.

They sat around waiting for 8 P.M. They checked their guns and waxed their skis one last time, filled their rucksacks with tins of food, compasses, flashlights, bandages, chocolate bars, waterproof maps made of Chinese silk, extra bootlaces, and gloves. Nordstrum and his demolition group packed up their explosives, fuses, detonators, spools of wire, lighters, and small-nose pliers. Those in the covering detail took extra ammunition, hand grenades, even knives. Storhaug had a large wire clipper that he had brought with him from England. "You watch," he made sure everyone saw it, "you'll thank me for lugging this damn thing around."

Everything of foreign origin that might betray where they'd come from was destroyed. Empty food tins, fruit and chocolate wrappings, cigarette packs. To fill the time, a few of them cleaned their weapons. Others smoked and talked about family and heading home one day, so close were they to those they loved that it was painful not to be able to visit them, even for an hour, or get word to them that they were here.

Storhaug even closed his eyes and caught a nap.

Nordstrum's thoughts drifted to his father. As a boy, after his mother's death, he'd had to bring him home from the pub many times when the old man had had too much to drink, driving at fifteen—everyone knew and looked the other way—dragging him up the stairs against his stubborn grunts and groans, and tucking him in bed. He'd been forced to be a man before he could shave.

He'd been so close his last visit, his father in the window, knowing Nordstrum was there, waving him on. He might never see him again. He thought of him coughing and hacking in a frigid basement jail.

And then his thoughts turned to how they had to succeed, no matter how long the odds. They had to. Not just because everyone was counting on them in England. Or because of the stakes. *It's important to the world.* But because something had to matter in this war. Something had to make his choice mean something.

His choice not to come back for her.

Because he'd kept on fighting, as she had always said he would. He'd never taken her to Sweden. And she had stayed and died, carrying his child.

And because knowing that now, it was too late to undo it and bring it all back. He reached in his pocket and took out the baptism cross she had given him on the train. He pressed it to his heart. That's why they had to succeed tonight. Some good had to come of it all. His choice to stay and fight.

Because in the tremors of his heart, as he waited for the call to go, nothing else did matter.

35

At 8 P.M., skis on, packs strapped to their backs, weapons over their shoulders, Ronneberg looked at the nine men who had taken the fate of the Allied war machine onto their backs. "All right, boys, let's go."

They took off down the mountain, single file, no celebratory yelps this time. In silence. Claus Helberg led the way, having made the trip down just that morning. The rest followed in his tracks.

At first the slope was steep and straight, and they maintained a steady pace. An icy wind had kicked up, and the moon was bright; too bright for Nordstrum. As they made it down the mountain and approached Vemork, the hum of the factory's giant turbines could be heard in the distance, a steady, deep, bellowing *whoosh*. On the valley floor, a thousand feet below, the lights of Rjukan came into view.

They swept down over the edge of the vidda on the western side of the gorge. The woods grew so dense that they had to remove their skis. The snow was alternately deep and soft, then hard and icy, depending on its exposure to the sun. At one point, they sank in all the way up to their waists and were barely able to take a step at a time, struggling with their packs. Other times, they slid on their backs on the hardpack, grabbing for shrubs and tree limbs to stop their descent. Using the telephone poles that ran from the valley to the top of the mountain as a guide, they slid from pole to pole, latching onto whatever they could, the wires above them sagging from the weight of the snow. It wasn't cold. In fact, the wind down here was warm, and silently Nordstrum feared a *foehn,* which could melt the ice on the river and make their escape back up the side of the mountain even slower and more treacherous.

Finally they came out at the upper end of the main road, which Helberg had traveled earlier that afternoon, and slipped their skis back on.

They continued along the edge of the darkened road. The ice made it as hard and slippery as a skating rink, their skis clattering. Maybe the blowing snow and difficult conditions were, in the end, a good thing, Nordstrum thought to himself, for there was no sign of anyone out and around. It would be easy to spot a vehicle coming in either direction. The headlights, plus noise from its engines, would easily give them time to prepare.

Then all at once, as they came around a bend, each of them stopped.

Across the gorge, lit up by the moon, they saw their target for the first time. It was perched on its seemingly impregnable shelf of rock. The mammoth seven-story hydroelectric building towered over the valley and the Mann River that cut through it far below. Above the plant, huge conduits with diameters five and a half feet wide funneled endless supplies of water from above, some 1,750 cubic feet per second, powering its massive turbines. Only the narrow-track railway that led from its back gate down the gorge, and the slender suspension bridge that crossed the valley, connected it to the world below.

Though they knew every inch of it and had seen the photos a hundred times, each man felt his heart stop for a second, staring at it, consumed with the sheer impossibility of what they were here to do.

185

They arrived at the large U-bend in the road near the tiny hamlet of Vaer, where Tronstad had initially thought it most practical to ford the river. No one was around. From here, they would continue down the slope to the dirt power line road on the bend below, to circumvent the small town. The slope was sheer though filled with scrub, dead trees, and bushes to latch onto. The main road wound back from a wide U-curve directly below them.

At a rock, Helberg stopped, seeming to recognize a clearing. "This is where we head down."

They removed their skis and, because of the steepness of the grade, let gravity take them, clutching onto brush and tree limbs with one hand, their skis with the other, the moon peeking through clouds and trees. It took fifteen minutes to get most of the way down, digging their heels into the snow to keep from sliding out of control. As they got close to the main road again, on a bend, Nordstrum, who was near the lead, suddenly became aware of a rumble ahead of them, which grew increasingly louder. Then ahead of them lights flashed, moving toward them at a fast pace.

Headlights.

"Hold up!" he yelled, latching onto a shrub to bring himself to a stop. He put up his hand to make sure the rest understood.

They were all still covered by the brush, but the slope they clung to was steep enough that any of them could have slipped and fallen out into the road and into plain sight at any time.

The rumble grew louder. Then headlights came around the bend.

A bus.

Not one bus, two.

Heading up from Rjukan, and likely carrying the night shift up to the plant. All of them remained perfectly still, holding their breath as the two vehicles rumbled past them, praying their camouflage ski suits would blend into the snow and that the headlights that had just cast their light over them hadn't exposed their presence.

But the buses moved by, Helberg and Ronneberg hanging on to a tree limb so that they literally would not fall on their roofs as they passed by underneath them. Then it grew quiet again. The vehicles made their way around the wide U-bend and headed farther up the mountain.

They'd been lucky. A minute later, and they all would have been scrambling to dive off the road out of their path.

With Helberg taking the lead again, the ten hurried along the main road until they came upon the power line road he had found that afternoon. There, they would change out of their ski suits and hide their equipment and rucksacks until they came back to pick them up on their escape. From that point on, they'd be wearing the uniforms of the British Army, so as to avoid any reprisals against the local population if they were captured or killed.

The heavy drone of the factory was even louder now in the lower part of the valley: the whoosh and whir of its giant turbines; the steady thunder of rushing water plunging through its massive penstocks.

They stripped out of their suits, taking with them their tommys and Colt .45 pistols, and as much ammunition and grenades as they could carry. Nordstrum and Ronneberg transferred their explosives and charges into smaller sacks especially designed for the climb. Arne Kjelstrup came out with his armorer's shears and some rope over his shoulders. He tucked the shears into his belt,

Ronneberg warning him, "Those better not clatter against the rocks or we're dead."

"Don't worry, they won't. You'll be happy to have them."

Then they scattered their belongings in a nest of spruce leaves and balsam needles to collect later, when they made their way back. The time was ten o'clock. They still had to ford the river and make the six-hundred-foot climb to the factory ledge.

"All right, let's go." Ronneberg waved them forward. In a whisper, "Claus, you're still leading the way."

Not another word was said as they continued, sliding down channels in the rocks to the bottom of the gorge another hundred feet below.

They were there.

No one knew how many of them would make it back.

36

As Claus Helberg had assured them, the Mann River, which in spring cut through the gorge with a current fed by the mountain's runoff, was no more than an icy trickle now, barely three inches of water on its surface. He had done his job well and had found a narrow route to cut across it, the ice crackling underneath their boots.

From there they ran fifty yards and huddled up in the shadow of the steep rock face underneath the factory that rose from the valley floor.

Above them, massive searchlights fanned the valley from the narrow suspension bridge. If any one beam centered on them, it was over. But none went deep enough in the valley to reach where they were. Or near the rock face they were about to ascend.

They looked up. Six hundred feet, the bottom third harrowingly steep. While Helberg was right—that much of the way seemed to have spruce shrubs or at least little ledges to grasp onto in the dark, with their weapons slung over their shoulders and the equipment weighing them down, even an expert climber would find the climb a challenge. Any fall could mean instant death, or worse, maybe, to be left there, at the bottom, with badly shattered bones.

"I'll go first," Helberg said. Only because he had plotted out a pathway up that afternoon.

"Then me," volunteered Gutterson, granted the most agile climber of the group. He noticed Olf Pedersen's hesitation, staring up at what they had to get up. "Get behind me, Olf. It'll be a cinch. Just follow my path."

"And I'll be right behind," Nordstrum said. "Between us you're in solid hands. Just think of it as a waltz, Olf, not a jitterbug," he said with a grin.

"Thanks." Pedersen blew out his cheeks. "I wish that made it easy."

"Well, whatever you do, if you fall," Arne Kjelstrup elbowed him with a wink, "just don't scream. You'll give the rest of us away."

"Yes, of course," Olf said with a brave smile.

"Hand me your gun," Nordstrum said to him. "I'll carry them both."

"No, I can make it," Olf insisted.

"Just give it to me," Nordstrum said, taking it out of his hands. "You might well need it up there."

"So . . ." Ronneberg looked around and nodded. "Ready? Let's go."

Helberg started first, trying to re-create the route he had mapped out during the day. Gutterson went next. Then Olf, hesitantly, one step at a time. He hoisted himself up, following the exact path the Yank took ahead of him, tentatively grabbing rocks and shrubs, testing which were firm and secure, and which seemed loose and would give way. Helberg got to about thirty feet up, turned back, and waved for the rest to follow. "It's easy to here."

"This one's a little loose." Gutterson shifted around and warned Olf, pointing out a ledge to avoid.

"Thanks."

Grabbing on to branches and testing for stability, Gutterson caught up to Helberg and took the lead. An able climber, his technique was to reach with his hand and make sure his toe was stable, then rest a moment, putting pressure on his toehold, before continuing on. "How are we doing?" he yelled down to Olf.

"Fine so far," Pedersen called, eight feet below him, cautiously trying to wedge his boot into a small crevice.

Nordstrum was four feet below him, and then the others followed in a line, Poulsson picking up the rear. The slope was steep, but manageable if you kept your eyes straight ahead and not down. Though sometimes someone would kick away a piece of loose rock and it would dislodge, narrowly missing the climber underneath. On one occasion Gutterson had to manage with a single handhold and held on for his life, stabilizing his two feet before reaching up for a higher hold.

"Here." He pointed out a foothold that was secure. Sometimes someone's leg simply gave way from fatigue and he had to rest there, perilously clinging to a ledge, while he shook it out and recovered his strength.

Around 150 feet up, Pedersen seemed to find himself trapped in a spot he did not trust and let out a long breath of concern. One of his legs swung out from the rock and suddenly he just hung there, dangling over the sheer face, supported by only one hand, one leg hanging free. Everyone held their breath.

"Olf," Nordstrum said calmly, spotting his friend's dilemma.

Pedersen's face was as ashen as the moon and drenched in sweat. "I'm okay," he said, but every time he tried to dig his foot into a new toehold his boot gave way and his predicament became even more dire.

No one knew how much longer he could hold on.

"Just stay where you are, Olf," Nordstrum exhorted him. "I'm coming up to you. Hang on."

Testing the stability of the branches, grabbing on to a spruce in the narrow cracks, Nordstrum swung himself over to Pedersen's right, and steadily climbed up, until he stood parallel to him, just a few feet away.

"You see this rock?" Nordstrum reached out and tapped a support that was within Olf's reach. Olf was rigid, like a skier on a steep slope beyond his abilities who was paralyzed as to what to do next. He nodded.

"Just swing yourself around," Nordstrum instructed. "Put your right foot on that ledge—yes, that one. . . . Then all you have to do is reach up and grab on to here."

His fingers straining, Pedersen sucked in a breath and nodded. "Okay." It was not that he was afraid of heights—he had jumped out of a plane many times and he could ski the steepest slopes tirelessly. And he was also a man of enormous bravery. To have come all this way, braved the elements, to be within an arm's reach of their goal, and then to falter, to let down his mates—it all seemed to give him renewed determination. "I'm coming."

Feeling along the rock with one hand, he desperately tried to locate some sparse growth to wrap his fingers around. He got his foot to the stable nook Nordstrum had pointed out.

"That's good, Olf. You're almost there."

At first it slipped off, and everyone expected the worst. A wrong move and he would plummet to the bottom of the rocks.

"Olf, come on," Nordstrum said, meeting his eyes firmly.

Pedersen took in a breath, locked on Nordstrum. "All right."

At last finding the courage to take a step with his full weight, he transferred himself over, beads of sweat pouring down his face. He hoisted himself up, fingers straining for the sparse clump of pine needles Nordstrum had pointed out, and pushed on his feet and grabbed on.

The clump held.

"Ha." Pedersen gave out a kind of fatalistic laugh, blowing out his cheeks. "Got it now. Thanks, Kurt."

"You're in luck, the slope levels out up here," Gutterson called from a few feet above them. "It's much easier."

"And just when you were getting the hang of it, huh, Olf?" Nordstrum gave Pedersen a smile.

One by one they crawled up to where Gutterson was resting, Nordstrum remaining behind if anyone needed help. Remembering their training, they kept their sights straight ahead of them and upward to their only goal—the shelf of rock perched above them where the railway tracks led—not backward, to the gorge, where the icy river was now merely a thin ribbon of white cutting through the canyon's walls. And as, step by step, they began to climb the rest of the way, the wind suddenly picked up. The thought passed through everyone's mind just how lucky they had been. A few minutes earlier, on the sheerest face, a gust like that would have surely swept them off the ledge to certain deaths.

It took an hour. Inch by hard-fought inch. The last hundred feet, Nordstrum's fingers were bloody and his arms felt as heavy as rocks just to thrust one forward. He had to will himself to continue to push each boot up one more step, his gaze fastened up ahead, so tempting was it to stop, let out an exhausted breath, and look down.

One by one they finally all crawled up to the top of the ledge, the ones before helping the next in line. Even Olf, who rolled over it with an exhausted sigh, gasping, laughing, seemingly amazed he was alive. For a few minutes, they sat there in the snow, spent, almost numb, letting their lungs recover and contemplating, for the first time, as they finally looked down at the tiny river below them, what they had accomplished.

"Here," Nordstrum said, handing Pedersen back his tommy. "You'll be needing this."

"Thanks, Kurt." He gave Nordstrum a grateful nod.

For a while they all just sucked in air, ate a few bites of chocolate and dried fruit, recovering their strength. It was a few minutes after eleven. The steady churning of the massive turbines was louder now, as if it literally shook the rock shelf they were on.

And the danger now was no longer the climb or the elements, but, for the first time since they came back to Norway, the Germans.

37

The night had turned cold and blustery. Around them, tracks in the snow were visible where German patrols had trekked recently. Though not even the most thorough defender could have imagined a threat coming from the incline over the gorge.

"Let's get closer." Ronneberg rallied them together as soon as they'd regained their strength. "Covering team, you take the lead. If we encounter mines, whoever is left has to shoot their way into the plant and carry out the mission. Are we all agreed?"

This time, it wasn't so much a collective yes as it was just everyone standing up and strapping on their weapons and packs with a nod.

"All right, let's go then."

Joaquim Poulsson, who was in charge of the covering team, headed out along the tracks, followed closely behind by Helberg, Gutterson, Storhaug, Pedersen and Arne Kjelstrup.

Ronneberg waved Nordstrum forward. "Demolition team . . ."

Slinging the explosives over his shoulder, Nordstrum and the rest fell in line.

They scampered along the rail tracks toward the noise. The constant whooshing and shuddering of the plant's dynamos again gave the sense that the entire ledge they were on was shaking, and drowned out any noise they made. They were only a few hundred yards from the target, with a detachment of enemy soldiers waiting for a mine or a tripwire to engage them, yet Nordstrum detected not a scintilla of hesitation or fear in any of the group.

The only German guards visible were the two sentries patrolling the suspension bridge far below, searchlights fanning the valley.

In fact, they were the first actual Germans any of them had seen on the mission. Nordstrum couldn't help but think that not far away, the people of Rjukan, family to some here, were in their beds asleep, with no idea that only a mile or so away their sons and brothers were back, lugging enough firepower to blow up half the mountain, about to put their lives at risk for a threat no one here knew existed.

It was enough to make him shake his head and laugh.

"What?" Ronneberg asked from behind him.

Nordstrum just smiled. "Nothing."

The night had become dark, with no moon. A strong southwest wind beat into their faces, but it also pushed back any noise they made. In a crouch, they followed the railway tracks up the hill. Poulsson, a few yards out in front, came upon a path alongside the tracks, which they assumed was for authorized personnel and therefore wouldn't be mined. Ahead, the plant's massive two buildings grew closer. At half an hour before midnight, they came upon a shack. A transformer station, maybe five hundred yards away from the back gate. Empty.

Ronneberg put up his hand. "Let's wait here for the change of sentries."

With Helberg and Stromsheim keeping watch, the rest took cover, taking off their packs, unwrapping a sliver of chocolate. They knew that a short distance away, fifteen to twenty German soldiers were playing cards or huddling by the stove to keep warm, ready to engage them at any false move or the sound of an alarm.

Yet the mood remained surprisingly relaxed. Helberg directed Gutterson's attention to a series of lights on the far side of the valley. "My cousin's house is right over there. In Vaer." He pointed. "You see the two lights?"

"Underneath that ridge?" He used the Norwegian word, *mone*.

"It's pronounced *menn*, Eric. But, yes, where those two roads intersect. He moved from Oslo when I was in school here. He was a horse trainer."

"My mother's family were horse trainers too!" Gutterson said, surprised. "Quarter horses. In Colorado."

"Quarter horses?"

"They're race horses. Bred to be very fast."

"You mean like in the Kentucky Derby?"

"Derby horses run a mile and a quarter. These are bred for a quarter mile. Like a sprint in the Olympics." He snapped his fingers. "Like lightning."

Joaquim Poulsson knelt next to Nordstrum and pointed across the valley too. "You see the tram?" Underneath it was the Ryes Road, zigzagging its way up the mountain, their planned route of escape.

"Of course." Nordstrum had ridden it to the top many times.

"When we were kids, my friend Kjell and I snuck past the watchman and slept in one of the cable cars at night."

"No kidding?"

"It was a dare. From Agnes Hovland. You remember her?"

"I knew Agnes. Or I knew her younger brother, Karl," Nordstrum said. "We used to snowshoe together. She was a beauty. I probably would have done anything she dared me, too."

"Kjell said she let him have a feel. But all I got was a dance at the Telemark Fair."

"A dance with Agnes Hovland wasn't the worst of things." Nordstrum shrugged. "Anyway, you got to spend the night in a cable car."

Poulsson spat. "Actually we got caught by the night watchman and I wasn't allowed to go out at night for a solid month. Pretty stupid, huh . . . ?"

At precisely three minutes to midnight, two guards stepped out of the guardhouse and headed toward the sentries on the suspension bridge.

Nordstrum drew Ronneberg's attention to them. "Look!"

They were way too far away to overhear, but he imagined the conversation going something like, "What the fuck took you so long? We're freezing our asses off out here."

The two relieved sentries clapped their hands to get the blood going and picked up their pace back to the hut. Maybe one of them had been holding back a pee. The two on the bridge then looked out into the valley; one spat over the edge as if cursing his luck to be out there, then they started to cross the bridge at a deliberate pace, to the Rjukan side of the gorge, rifles on their shoulders.

"Another half hour," Ronneberg said. "To give the men relieving them some time to relax."

As these final minutes passed, everyone's nerves finally did come to the surface, and the men were quiet. All there was to do was wait. Everyone's thoughts seemed to take them somewhere. Oddly, Nordstrum's roamed to his mother. When her leukemia got worse she was taken from Rjukan to a private clinic in Oslo. Once, when he went to visit her near the end, she took his hand in hers, bony and withered, her face deathly pale. "You'll have to be the man now, Kurt," she said, her voice no more than a whisper, but yet firm. "You'll see. He's no angel. He will need you."

"Don't be silly," Nordstrum had said. "It's still your job, Mom. We'll keep it open for you. You'll be home soon."

She'd tightened her grip on him. "Promise me, Kurt. He plays so tough and thick-skinned. But this will kill him, you can be sure. It will kill him."

"I will, Mother," he had to promise before she let go.

A week later she was gone.

As he stood there, he wasn't really sure if he had done his job well.

They heard a rumble. From across the gorge, a truck came over the bridge. It looked like more workers coming up from Rjukan. It stopped at the gate. The guards came up to it. There was no way to hear what was said, but one of them opened the gate as the other waved the truck through. It drove in and wound around to Building Number Two.

Twenty past twelve.

Jens came up, looking out at the bridge. "Remind me again why I'm about to get my ass shot off for a few liters of fucking water that costs more than champagne?"

Nordstrum shrugged. "Maybe because you like playing the hero?" He kept an eye on the two German sentries pacing back and forth on the bridge.

"If I just wanted that, I should have stuck with football." In school he'd been a promising player. A coach even came to look at him to train for the national team.

"You really weren't so good at that either," Nordstrum said with a straight face. "Who knows, maybe it's just because you're a Northman. And because no one else would."

"A Northman . . . ?" Jens gave him a snort. "I guess that explains it."

"You know, I've been thinking . . ." Nordstrum rested his tommy on the shed. "If I die here, there's not a single person in the world who would really miss me. My mother's dead. My father's in failing health and might end up in jail; he can't last long. Anna-Lisette . . . The truth is, I don't have a single lasting attachment in the world."

"Yes, you did, Kurt. The war took it."

"I'm not so certain the war is an excuse."

"Well, I'd miss you, Kurt," Jens said. "Look around, we're all in the same boat."

"You would, huh?"

"Sure." Jens grinned. "And sorry to tell you this, but I don't intend on dying."

The American came up to stand beside them and looked down at the bridge. "I'm actually a little scared, if I can say. You men have all seen some action. This is my first."

"You'll be fine," Nordstrum said. "Just do what you're trained to do. The mind follows. Look around, we're all a little scared."

Ronneberg put his gun over his shoulder and announced, "Twelve twenty-seven. It's time. Remember, if the explosive team goes down, the covering team takes up their place. At all costs."

Quietly now, everyone gathered up their equipment. Poulsson stamped out his cigarette. Nordstrum strapped his pack of explosives on his back.

Ronneberg went in front. "All I can say is, if there was any team I could have chosen to be with on this job, you'd all be on it. Even you." He grinned at Gutterson. "Despite the accent."

Snow had begun to fall. Nordstrum put out his hand. Large, soft flakes fell into his palm. Snow was always a good sign. Like most of the men who'd grown up here, he'd been on skis before he'd learned to ride a bike.

"See, the trolls are smiling on us." He elbowed Jens.

"I can't say I believe in the trolls," Jens sniffed back.

"You don't?"

"All right, on my signal . . ." Ronneberg whispered down the line. "Covering team, take the lead."

As the guard on the bridge headed back toward the far gate, the lieutenant lowered his arm.

One by one they stole away from the shed, Poulsson in the lead, then Helberg, Storhaug, Kjelstrup, Gutterson, and Pedersen. Watching them go, Jens turned back to Nordstrum. "And I've known you a long time, Kurt. And neither do you."

38

At STS 61, near Cambridge, Colonel Jack Wilson was about to pack it in for the night.

Gunnerside had been back in Norway for nine days. For the first six, until the team met up with Grouse, they hadn't had word from them. Whether they were alive or dead. Finally, Knut Haugland, the Grouse radioman, in his understated way, messaged in: "All partics together. Good to see the mates and building ourselves back up. Will advise on future preparations."

Since then, it had been quiet again.

The last thing Wilson wanted to do was flood them with questions. German wireless antennas were desperately trying to narrow in on anyone transmitting in the area. It was best to keep traffic low. Still, they were aching for some news. Major General Gubbins checked in every day, with entreaties from Lord Mountbatten. "Winnie wants to stay informed." Which only went to show the importance behind this mission. Wilson would be on that vidda himself, he knew inside, if only he was twenty years younger and could ski.

Still, the silence was like a prod that kept him awake most nights. On his way out that night, out of sheer frustration, he stopped in on Tronstad, who was in the midst of drafting a letter to his family, sipping a whisky, his ubiquitous pipe in a bowl on his desk.

"Colonel." The scientist looked up. "Drink . . . ?"

"I wouldn't turn one away." Wilson pulled up a chair.

Tronstad opened a drawer and took out a half-finished

bottle of eighteen-year Aberlour. "Picked this up in Scotland," he said. "Made all that damn waiting a bit more worthwhile." He poured one out for Wilson.

"How do you keep it together?" Wilson asked, tilting his glass in salute.

"I'm Norwegian. Give us a little wind and rain, we don't worry about much else."

"You don't?" Wilson took a long sip and nodded. "To our success."

The scientist smiled. "At least, on the outside. On the inside we're just as riled as—"

There was a knock and the door sprang open. It was Corporal Finch, out of breath, who had come after Wilson from down the hall. It was his job to field the wireless traffic from Norway. "I'm glad I caught you, sir."

Wilson put down his drink and stood up. "What is it, Corporal?"

"This just came in. From Grouse." He handed the message to Wilson.

Tronstad stood up too.

It was from Haugland. He and Einar Skinnarland had broken away from the main group, as it was vital that information be sent back to England, and God forbid the only person capable of transmitting it was killed in the raid.

"What's it say, Jack?" Tronstad stood waiting.

"It says, 'Everything ready. Festivities set for tonight. Will advise upon completion.' "

Wilson looked up. "So it's tonight, then." His ruddy face grew bright with excitement. "Corporal, see my car is canceled. Looks like I'll be spending the night."

It was going to be a long one, Wilson knew. Ten brave men were about to put their lives on the line. The funny thing

203

about bravery, sometimes it was no more than people being afraid to shrink from doing the right thing. When the story of this war was written, he reflected, the outcome might well rest on a team of ordinary Norwegians pulling off what the best-trained troops of the British army were unable to do.

"To my boys, then," Tronstad said, tipping his glass toward Wilson.

"Yes, to your boys." Wilson clinked glasses, and they both threw back a gulp. "And I'm sure Winnie will want to know as well."

An ocean away, an aide slipped into the Blue Room next to the Oval Office, which Franklin Delano Roosevelt used as a greeting room, interrupting a reception between the president and a group of female volunteers from Indiana who had won a contest for outstanding results under the War Bonds program.

"I have to excuse myself for just a moment," Roosevelt informed the group's headmistress, a Mrs. Lois Ingram. "Please be assured I will return as soon as I can."

In the adjoining office, Henry Stimson, his secretary of war, was waiting for him. "We just received a cable from Whitehall, Mr. President. The prime minister thought we'd like to know that that effort to derail the Nazi heavy water facility in Norway we all spoke of back in June last year—"

"Yes, up in New Hyde Park." The president nodded. "I recall."

"That's correct. Anyway, they want us to know, it's scheduled for tonight," said the secretary of war.

"Tonight?" The president wheeled himself to his desk. "After that last fiasco, they actually threw more Brits on it? I'll be damned."

"Not Brits." Stimson handed him the transmission. "A bunch of Norwegians, it seems."

"Norwegians . . . ?" Roosevelt read over the cable. "I'll be damned."

Ever since Albert Einstein had first alerted him to the prospect that a nuclear chain reaction might be used to create bombs of unimaginable destruction, it had become a race that would decide the war. The ultimate race, he knew. An outcome determined by a clear, harmless liquid fit for even a child to drink, where the world's total supply lay in ten small drums held at the most-guarded scientific facility in the world.

"Inform General Groves," the president said. The military head of the Manhattan Project. "And let me have a few minutes, if you would, Henry."

"Of course, Mr. President." Stimson went to leave the room.

Roosevelt sat back and closed his eyes. He remembered Churchill's worry on this matter, and anything that could make *that* man worry must be quite a scare. Hell, he recalled Albert Einstein's worry, and that's what really troubled him.

He laughed.

"Sir?" Stimson turned at the door. "Something struck you as funny."

"Nothing, Henry." He shook his head. Other than the fate of the world now resting in the hands of ten bloody Norwegians, there was nothing funny about it at all.

In fact, it was the most serious damn thing Roosevelt had had to ponder as president since the attack on their navy at Pearl Harbor had brought his country into the war.

39

The ten crept silently along the tracks and came upon another shed, this one a tool shed, no more than a hundred yards from the wire gate. It was all that barred the way to one of the most important military sites in Europe. It was dark, and other than the whir of the giant turbines the place was deathly quiet.

Nordstrum checked along the perimeter of the wire. There was no sign of anyone around.

"Arne." Ronneberg called Kjelstrup forward. "I think this is your moment."

"Aye, Lieutenant." Kjelstrup grinned. He reached into his rucksack and took out the wire shears he'd lugged all the way from England. "I told you these would come in handy."

Ronneberg motioned him forward to the gate. "Be careful. And watch out for any guards. Good luck."

In a crouch, Arne followed the railway tracks directly up to the rear gate. The moonless night hid his approach. With the precision of an expert plumber, which was what he was before the war, he examined the wire mesh for a weak spot and found the perfect point, where he executed a single, well-placed snip. He pulled the wire back and stretched it wide, making a gap. Then he turned back and waved everyone forward.

One by one, the covering team headed off in the darkness to meet him, their footsteps muffled by the constant whoosh from the factory's dynamos and the steady westerly wind. Nordstrum and the demolition team followed closely behind.

At the gate, there was barely a moment's hesitation. Ronneberg held it wide for the rest and one by one they scurried through. Poulsson and Gutterson continued straight to the front of the building where the high-concentration tanks were located, taking cover behind a group of storage drums, not twenty yards from the guard hut. With its flimsy wooden walls, the structure would offer only scant protection against the hail of automatic weapons should they have to open fire. Kjelstrup continued farther down to a thatch of bushes to keep watch over the two guards on the bridge. Storhaug and Pedersen slipped around to the north side of the building to keep an eye out for the sentry patrolling the penstocks. Helberg remained at the gate, covering the escape route for when they all had to beat a hasty retreat.

It appeared that not a single guard, German or Norwegian, patrolled the upper grounds.

The Norsk Hydro factory, which looked like a brightly lit, impregnable fortress at every point of their approach, now loomed even larger directly in front of them. Its massive, humming turbines, swallowing an endless flow of water from the vidda, gave off a sensation of awe and dread for what they were tasked with pulling off.

"Jens, Kurt." Ronneberg waved his fellow team members forward. "This way."

The four-man demolition team split into two pairs—Nordstrum and Stromsheim, and Ronneberg and Jens—each team with enough explosives to accomplish the job in the case that the other unit didn't make it in.

They both scrambled silently across the grounds to the steel door that led to the basement, the fastest and most direct point of access.

So far, it was all working like clockwork.

At the door, Ronneberg tried the handle, pushing his shoulder against it.

It didn't budge.

"Shit," he whispered, and tried again.

It was locked.

That left the other door on the north side of the building that led to the first floor. Much faster than the duct Tronstad had spoken of, with an opening only wide enough for a single person at a time.

"Kurt, Jens and I will go around the side and check out the other door," Ronneberg whispered, pointing to the other side of the building. "You and Birger search for that pipe duct."

Three minutes had gone by. Now it was all about the time.

Hugging the exterior, Ronneberg and Jens disappeared around the side into the darkness.

"Let's go." Nordstrum waved to Stromsheim. They ran off the other way, the giant factory whooshing and belching so loudly the building seemed to vibrate.

Next to a closed, corrugated metal service door, Nordstrum spotted a small wooden ladder, only three rungs tall. It was perched in the snow under some kind of opening covered over by a wooden door fastened with a cheap lock.

"This has to be it." Nordstrum pried the door open, busting the flimsy latch, the sound covered by the building's noises.

It led to a long, dark chasm, narrow as a cave. "This is it!" The passage was narrow and unlit, and seemed to have various things blocking the way: hoses, cables, pipes.

"Should we wait for Joachim and Jens?" Stromsheim asked. He removed the pack from his back.

"You heard him." Nordstrum shook his head. "We're each on our own. There's no time to find them now. We go right in." He handed Stromsheim his gun, then hoisted himself up into the narrow opening and wedged himself inside. It was barely wide enough for him to fit. Ronneberg, who was even taller, would have even greater difficulty, if he had to enter this way.

"C'mon, let's go."

Nordstrum went forward on his hands and knees. He had to remove his explosives pack, as the passage wasn't large enough for it to fit through on his back, so he put it in front of him and nudged it forward with his knees. Stromsheim climbed in after him.

The passage was dark and they had to push hoses and heating cables out of their way as they crept along. The only light in there was a small flashlight that Nordstrum trained ahead of him, while feeling for metal pipes, ducking, pushing along their equipment and weapons. The duct gave off of a musty, metallic smell. Like the blind leading the blind, they crawled slowly along, doing their best not to make any noise.

According to Tronstad, the duct took a direct route over the basement to the heavy water processing room, the very place they were trying to reach. He had told them it was about fifty yards long, but in the dark, inches at a time, the distance was hard to gauge. It took a lot of time, and they had no idea where Ronneberg and Jens were; there was no sign of them behind them. Nordstrum kept his ear pitched for the sound of gunfire, knowing, if he heard it, he would likely never leave the building alive.

"Look." He pointed up ahead. He saw a light. There was a small opening, no more than six inches wide, where some pipes passed through into the basement. As he reached it, he stopped, his heart picking up with nerves for the first time, and put his face through the small opening to take a look.

They were over a corridor. Ahead, he spotted a locked door with the sign NO ADMITTANCE EXCEPT ON BUSINESS. That had to be it.

The high-concentration room.

"We're in luck. It's just ahead." Nordstrum pointed forward. "Just a few meters more. Watch out for all these pipes." He went on, having to duck and twist himself around to get past them.

They were only a few yards away.

Suddenly he heard a loud, metallic clang on the floor.

Behind him, Stromsheim dropped his head and groaned. "Shit."

In trying to avoid the pipes, his knee had sent his Colt through the opening in the duct. It was now sitting in the open for anyone to see. The sound of it landing seemed to reverberate down the entire floor. Nordstrum and Stromsheim had no choice but to remain precisely where they were, not daring to move a muscle, fearing that the door below them would open any second and a guard would peek outside, spot the gun there on the floor, and look upward.

Remaining perfectly still, Nordstrum reached for his tommy and quietly drew back the bolt.

After a minute or so, no one had come out. Thank God. The building seemed to have a lot of clanking, grating sounds—compressors, water pipes, currents rushing through turbines. The sound of the gun hitting the floor was only one more. Still, at some point a night watchman would come by.

Holding still until they were sure it was safe to continue on, they finally pushed ahead. After another twenty feet, Nordstrum came upon a wider opening in the duct. This one had to be inside the high-concentration room for sure. Putting a hand to his lips for his partner to remain silent, he stuck his head through the hole and peered inside.

What he saw was a large room. To his right was a man, sitting behind a table, making notes in some kind of notebook. He was older, with white hair under a flat wool cap, dressed in civilian clothes. Not a guard; likely Norwegian. Maybe a watchman in the room to take a reading.

And beyond him, to Nordstrum's elation, identical to the models they had practised on in Britain, were the eighteen high-concentration compressors, hissing steam and emitting the slow, steady drip of heavy water into the very same cylindrical steel canisters they had come to destroy. He looked back at Stromsheim with a triumphant nod.

They were here.

40

Hugging the shadows, Ronneberg and Jens hurried around to the north side of the building. They found the closed steel door that led to the first floor.

No one was around.

Ronneberg twisted the handle and tried to push the door in with his shoulder.

It was locked as well.

That left only the duct as their last possibility. And Nordstrum and Stromsheim were somewhere on the other side of the building.

"Quick, let's head back around and find them," Jens said, checking his watch. Seven minutes had elapsed since they'd first come through the gate—an eternity to those who were keeping watch on the Germans and didn't know their progress—and they were no farther along than when they arrived.

"All right." Ronneberg nodded and started to head back. Then suddenly he grabbed Jens's arm. "Hold it!"

There were windows at their feet, all blackened out with dark paint of some kind. The electrolysis compressors were in the basement. These windows had to lead somewhere.

Ronneberg said, "I'm going to take a look." He got down on a knee, making his way along the base of the building, trying to locate some section of a window he could get a view through. Finally he came upon a corner where a narrow ray of light shone through. He reached into his pocket for a small knife and scratched at it. A residue of black paint chipped off into his hand. He leaned in closer and put his eye to the tiny opening.

As if in a dream, the eighteen electrolysis chambers were visible at the far end of a large room. Nearer to him, he saw the back of a man jotting in a notebook at a table. The man was older, with white hair under a flat wool cap.

Not a German in sight.

"Anything in there?" Jens leaned over and asked under his breath.

"Yes." Ronneberg turned around with a broad smile. "Our target."

41

Taking his weapon, Nordstrum slipped silently through the hole in the duct and down into the large room. The compressors were hissing, clanking, synthesizing their precious by-product, drip by dreaded drip.

Stromsheim followed close behind with the rucksack of explosives.

The watchman made notations in his notebook, seemingly humming a few bars of a tune while he jotted, completely oblivious to them.

Nordstrum pulled back the bolt of his gun.

With a jolt, the watchman looked up, blinking twice at the sight of a man in a non-German military uniform holding a gun on him, and another right behind.

He took off his glasses and rubbed his eyes.

"I assure you we're quite real." Nordstrum advanced toward him. "And if you want to continue to live through the next few minutes, you'll do precisely what we say. Now put your hands up."

"Don't shoot," the man said, doing as Nordstrum instructed. "Who the hell are you? And how did you possibly get in here? The door's locked."

"Never mind that," Nordstrum said. "Haven't you ever seen a British soldier before? Now get up and away from there, and keep your hands in the air."

"Brits? This is truly amazing." The watchman stood up and followed Nordstrum's instructions. "What do you want in here?"

"First, where's the key to the door to the outer yard?" Getting out that door was their only means of a quick escape.

His palms still wide, the watchman slowly reached to his vest pocket and came out with a ring of keys. "May I?"

"Put it on the table." Nordstrum directed him with the gun.

The man wound clumsily through the keys until he found the one he was looking for. He put the entire ring, with one key sticking out, next to his notebook. "You know if the Germans find you in here, we'll all be shot."

"Then you better do your best to keep that from happening." He turned to Stromsheim. "Go check outside the door and retrieve your gun," Nordstrum said in English.

Stromsheim headed to the basement door, opened it slowly, and stuck out his head.

"Tell me your name?" Nordstrum said to the watchman.

"It's Gustav. Fredrickson."

"So, Gustav Fredrickson, do what we say and you've nothing to worry about. Don't, and all bets are off. How often do the guards come around?"

The watchman glanced at the clock on the wall. "Once an hour, usually at ten minutes past. Punctual to a T." It was 12:48 now. That gave them twenty minutes. "They check the water levels, make a lot of notes. The bastards can't afford to lose a precious drop. But there's others in the building . . . My foreman. He comes around. I'm not sure you can count on him."

"And we can count on *you* . . . ?" Nordstrum questioned.

"Me, yes. British commandos? With a grasp of Norwegian. Look, I know what you're here to do."

"You do, do you?" Nordstrum opened the rucksack of

explosives and placed it on the table. "Then we best get started, don't you think?"

Near the German guard hut, Poulsson and Gutterson hid behind the storage drums, barely ten meters from it. It had been almost twenty minutes since Ronneberg and the demolition team had gone inside. Amazingly, not a single guard or watchman had wandered by.

They waved to Arne Kjelstrup, who was crouched in a clump of bushes, watching over the sentries on the bridge. From inside the hut, they could hear the chatter of voices, some laughter at intervals. Who knew how they were passing the time in there? Drinking coffee. Playing cards. Sharing photos of some Nazi film star. It took all the restraint Gutterson and Poulsson had not to just riddle the hut with bullets and put an end to them.

12:46.

Separately, each of their minds drummed with worry. *What could be taking so long?* Had any of the teams reached the target? Did they encounter any opposition? Were the two of them crouched here, the minutes ticking achingly slowly, and their countrymen were trapped inside?

No, the alarm hadn't sounded. Or gunfire. If they'd been caught, they would surely know by now. They just had to be patient and maintain the watch. But every minute that passed stretched on as if it were an hour. Poulsson, who spoke a little German, strained to listen to what was being said inside the guard hut.

They heard a sound from within. Suddenly the door flung open.

Gutterson's heart stood still.

A German came outside, stretching his arms. He wore no

216

jacket or helmet. His uniform shirt was open. The stripes on his arm indicated he was a corporal. "It smells like a barnyard in there tonight. I'm going to take a piss," he called back over his shoulder.

The guard took a look around, basically staring directly at Jens and Poulsson, crouched behind the drums, as if he knew they were there.

Gutterson wrapped his finger around the trigger.

Then, slapping his sides for warmth, the guard stomped around the back of the hut, and shortly they could hear the tinkle of urine as he relieved himself in the snow with an audible sigh.

"Every time he pees, Helmut sounds like he's having sex," someone said inside, loud enough for all to hear, followed by a cackle of laughter.

"Yes, well, at least I know the difference," the peeing guard shouted back. "Which is more than I can say for any of you."

When he finished, the guard hustled around again, with a "*Brrrr* . . ." and opened the door and ducked back inside.

Poulsson and Gutterson took their fingers off their triggers. Another situation like that, both seemed to know, and it would be hard to hold back.

Where were Nordstrum and Ronneberg? They had to be out soon.

It was now 12:51.

42

Stromsheim hurried back into the high-concentration room, now holding his Colt. Nordstrum tossed him the open rucksack of explosives. Immediately, the sapper expert began setting them out.

The watchman's eyes went wide.

Eighteen adhesive, sausage-shaped charges, each about a foot long, made of nitro-cellulose, with a detonator fuse 120 centimeters long. Since it took one second for each centimeter to burn, two minutes were all they had to get safely out of the building.

As he saw what was happening, the watchman stood up. "That's enough to take the whole building down. You'll never get out of here."

"Then at least we'll die knowing we did the job, don't you agree?" Nordstrum said. "Now sit back down."

Where the hell were Ronneberg and Jens? One way or another, they should have been in here by now. Time was running short. If no one showed, he'd have to put down his gun and help Stromsheim with the charges or they'd never get it done in time.

12:53.

"Don't make a move, Gustav," Nordstrum said, heading to help his friend at the concentration cells. "Otherwise, I'll be forced to—"

Suddenly there was a crash, the sound of glass shattering. Nordstrum spun and aimed his tommy at the blackened windows behind the desk. Shards of glass fell onto the floor, a rifle butt coming through.

"Just keep at it!" he yelled to Stromsheim. "If they're Germans, set the fuses to go." If it was indeed someone unwelcome, he'd give his friend as much time and cover as he could. He leveled his gun at the person climbing through, prepared to pull the trigger at the first face he saw.

To his delight, it was Ronneberg's.

"Jesus, another second and I would have pulled the trigger," Nordstrum said, scurrying over. "Where the hell have you been?"

"What did you expect us to do—knock? This was the only way we could find to get ourselves in," Ronneberg said, maneuvering an arm through, kicking out a last piece of glass, and pulling himself through. "I'm glad to see you here though."

He jumped onto the floor.

Jens was next, tossing the lieutenant his backpack of explosives. "Lieutenant." He nodded, pleased to see him there.

"Say hello to Gustav." He introduced the watchman in English.

"Lord in Heaven, just how the hell many are you?" The watchman stretched his eyes wide.

"Gustav says the Germans come by every hour to check the water levels. At around ten after," Nordstrum said.

"Not around, *exactly,*" the watchman declared. "There's usually two of them. They leave their guard hut on the hour, but that's what it takes to get here and maybe have a smoke on the way."

"That gives us about five minutes before they leave the hut, and we'd better be out of here." Ronneberg looked at the clock. "Kurt, how long did you say it would take?"

"Seven minutes. Depending on what we found in here."

"Seven minutes . . ." Ronneberg checked his watch concernedly. "We'd better get cracking."

Donning rubber gloves, each of them knelt and worked their tasks with the precision of a craftsman who could do a specific job over and over in his sleep, molding the charges to the belly of each steel compressor tank and connecting the wiring.

Each tank was four feet, two inches tall, jacketed in stainless steel with lead pipes, condenser tubes, water seals, rubber tubing, anodes, cathodes, water jackets, flanges, and dials coming out of them. Things Nordstrum knew nothing about or how to read, only that the microscopic extract of the concentrated solution that fell drop by drop into the cylindrical metal tanks was more important than the largest rocket in the Nazi war machine.

It had been four minutes now since Jens and Ronneberg had come in.

"Be careful. There's a lye discharge that comes off them," the watchman warned. "It's very caustic, so avoid getting it on your skin or clothing."

"Thanks," Nordstrum replied. The last thing he wanted was to have to kill a fellow Norwegian, and for what it appeared, Gustav was doing his best to cooperate with them.

They had wired twelve of the eighteen compressors.

Five minutes now.

There were eighteen fuses altogether, but Ronneberg went from processor to processor, coupling the finished ones, so there would only be nine to light at the end. Then he attached a second thirty-second fuse to one, which would presumably ignite them all, the longer ones acting as a form of insurance in case the shorter fuse failed. They could not take the chance

220

that, once they left, someone would stumble on them before the charges exploded and defuse them.

When Stromsheim and Nordstrum had finally molded the last of the charges to the cells, Ronneberg set another around the group of steel storage canisters in the corner, next to a water drain.

The entire inventory of finished heavy water product in the world.

When he was done, everyone stood silently for a second. All they could hear was the steady *drip, drip, drip* of the deuterium oxide into the collection bins.

"Okay." Ronneberg let out a breath of anticipation. Everything was set. Seven minutes had elapsed, exactly as planned. That left them ten to get out before the watch arrived and back to the gate before the whole building became a giant fireball.

Nordstrom and Stromsheim went from cell to cell, doing a final check on the charges and detonators. "They're all good." Birger gave a thumbs-up to Ronneberg and removed his gloves.

All that was left was to set the fuses and leave.

Nordstrum turned to the watchman. "All right, you and I are going to get that outside door unlocked now, Gustav." He led him out by the arm and into the corridor. It was only a dozen or so more steps to the steel door that led outside. Nervously, Gustav fumbled while finding the key. "C'mon, old man. No foolish moves. The last person I'd ever want to hurt is a Norwegian."

"You don't have to worry about me. I promise, I'm on your side in this."

Finally the watchman inserted the key and turned the latch. Nordstrom cracked open the door. Cold air rushed inside. Everything seemed quiet outside. No sign of anything troubling in the yard.

"It'll lock on closing?" Nordstrum made sure.

"It should. That's how it's set up," the watchman said.

"Then we'll leave it ajar. Okay, back to the cells."

In the high-concentration room, everything was ready to go. Ronneberg had spread some British paratrooper seals and an explosives manual around. He took his machine gun and kicked it near one of the heavy water cells. To anyone looking into what they'd done, it would seem that British soldiers were responsible. He looked around one last time. "Ready?"

Jens glanced at the watchman. "What about him?"

"Please, I won't tell. I'm no Nazi, I swear. I fought in the last war."

"We have to shoot him," Jens insisted. "He'll sound the alarm."

"The *explosion* will sound the alarm," Nordstrum said. He looked to Ronneberg and received a quick nod in return. "Get up to the top level," he said to Gustav. "Say you were taking a pee."

"Of course, of course. I'm already starting to feel the urge." The watchman headed toward the door.

Stromsheim packed the last of the unused explosives into his rucksack. "I'm all set."

"All right, then." Ronneberg nodded. He struck up a match. "Let's take it down."

"*Hold it!*" the watchman suddenly shouted. "My eyeglasses. I need them. They must be on the table."

"You must be joking, old man!" Jens looked at him with astonishment. "We've got no time for your glasses." Then to

Ronneberg: "Just light the fucking fuses and let's get the hell out of here."

"Please, I'm blind without them. They're almost impossible to replace," the watchman begged. "The Nazis have taken over everything."

Nordstrum had heard even bare necessities like optics had ground to a halt under the occupation. With a chortle of exasperation, Ronneberg extinguished the match and threw it on the floor. He turned to Jens. "Go see if you can find them, quick."

In frustration, Jens ran over to the table, shuffled quickly through whatever was strewn upon it, found the glasses on the log, and hurriedly brought them back to the grateful watchman. "Here! Now let's go."

"A thousand thanks." The watchman's face lit up with relief.

"*Now*." Ronneberg struck a second match. They'd all been inside for close to fifteen minutes now. One minute after one o'clock—a patrol was just leaving the hut. Ronneberg turned to Nordstrum and Jens. "Take the old man. We'll meet you at the door."

But as he bent to finally light the first fuse, suddenly the sounds of approaching footsteps could be heard from the outside corridor.

"Shit."

Nordstrum and Ronneberg exchanged a look of concern. Whoever it was, they had no more time to delay things now. In just four minutes someone might come out of the guard-house to check. Nordstrum slipped behind the door, pulling the bolt back on his weapon, prepared to drop whoever it was in his tracks, if the wrong person a little early on his watch came in.

"Don't you say a word," Ronneberg whispered to the watchman with a finger to his lips.

"Gustav . . . ?" The door opened and someone stepped into the room.

As the man came in, Nordstrum put the muzzle of his gun to the back of his head and said in Norwegian, "Not a move or you're dead."

The man froze, his eyes wide and straight ahead.

"*Gunnar!*" the old night watchman exclaimed.

It was the foreman, Norwegian as well. Younger than the watchman, in a rumpled sweater and soiled boots. He looked in disbelief at the sight of four British commandos brandishing automatic weapons and his Norwegian colleague with his hands in the air.

"Just what's going on here?" he asked, jaw slack.

"I'm afraid it's too late to explain," Ronneberg moved him by the collar, "but if you want to live, you'll get over by the door with your friend Gustav there and not utter a single word."

"Okay. Okay." Ashen, the man complied.

Everything set, Ronneberg lit a match for the third time now and hurried from fuse to fuse, the intertwined cords firing up with a loud hiss as soon as the flame made contact. All to the mounting horror of the foreman, now seeing the mounds of explosives molded to the eighteen high-concentration compressors.

"Do you have any idea what you're about to do?" His eyes bulged in horror.

"Get them out," Ronneberg said to Jens. "Now!"

"You can't. It'll bring the whole building down."

Jens pushed the two plant watchmen out into the hall to the concrete stairwell. "When I give you the signal, run. Up the stairs. You should be fine up there. And be sure and say you were taking a leak when it all happened."

"Yes, you can be sure I will." The old watchman nodded nervously. "And Gunnar, if you're smart, you too."

As Nordstrum and Stromsheim prepared to leave, Jens made the two count patiently to ten, as the first fuses burned down and Ronneberg readied to light the final one. That would leave them only thirty seconds to get outside.

"All right, run! *Now!*" Jens pushed the two watchmen toward the stairwell. "And be sure and tell them how British commandos would not take a Norwegian life. Now, get on!"

The two Norwegians took off, scrambling as fast as they could up the concrete stairs.

"It's time, boys . . ." Ronneberg took one last look around with a nod of accomplishment. He reached down and touched the match to the final thirty-second fuse. Nothing could stop it now. Nordstrum met his eyes, thinking that a month ago what had been mapped out on paper at such long odds against had indeed been achieved. And not by Brits, the best-trained commandos in the world. But by Norwegians. Tronstad would be smiling a little tonight.

The shortened fuse began to hiss. "Now, Kurt," Ronneberg flicked the match toward the canisters, "what do you say we get the hell out of this place!"

43

"What the hell could be taking so long?" The Yank looked out from behind their storage drums and whispered to Poulsson. "They've been in there for over twenty minutes now."

Watching over the German guard hut, their nerves were starting to fray. They could still spot Kjelstrup in the bushes, keeping an eye on the guards on the bridge. Never once had they broken off their rounds. Gutterson got Arne's attention and tapped his watch as if to say, *A lot of time has passed. I hope they're all right in there.*

Arne answered back with an anxious nod of his own, indicating he was feeling the same way.

"Stay calm, Eric." Poulsson placed his hand on Gutterson's shoulder. "If they'd been caught, the alarm would be sounded. We'd know."

Gutterson let out a breath and nodded. He just couldn't believe how long it was taking. It was the hardest thing he'd ever done, keeping his control with a hut full of Germans only ten yards away. He felt his heart thumping loudly in his chest.

Suddenly the steel door to the basement flung open. Poulsson pointed. "*Look!*"

Ronneberg, Nordstrum, Jens, and Stromsheim sprinted out of the building in the direction of the rear gate. Ronneberg stopped and looked back their way and waved for the rest of the team to withdraw as well.

"My God, they actually did it!" Poulsson couldn't help but break into a wide grin.

A second or two later a loud rumble emanated from inside the building. Not the deafening blast any of them had imagined, for they'd all talked about the force of it possibly bringing down the whole building. A yellow flash could be seen from inside. The glass from a basement window blew. Still, the sound was more of a thud than a real explosion, clearly muffled by the ongoing hum of the turbines as well as the factory's thick concrete walls.

"Was that it?" Gutterson remained there, waiting for something louder to occur. They'd all expected the guard hut to empty at the sound of it and to have to open fire on them.

No one had come out.

"I don't know." Poulsson shrugged. But Ronneberg was waving frantically for them to come his way as the demolition team scurried toward the gate. "It had to be."

He turned and signaled to Kjelstrup to withdraw as well. "Time to get the hell out of here!"

Just as they were about to leave, the door to the guard hut swung open.

Gutterson and Poulsson froze.

Kjelstrup dropped to his belly in the snow, bringing up his gun. Expecting a rush of Germans to exit the shed, Poulsson and Gutterson stayed behind the drums and pulled back the bolts on their tommies, taking aim.

But only a single, half-dressed guard emerged, with a rifle slung over his back and flashing a light around the yard. "*Ist jemand da?*" he called out.

Anyone there?

Ten yards away, Poulsson and Gutterson remained behind their storage drums, fingers on the triggers.

The guards on the suspension bridge seemed to look

toward the factory as if they'd heard some noise, but didn't leave their posts.

"Is anyone there?" the German guard said again, as if expecting someone to reply. There was nothing. Just one of the usual bangs and concussions caused by the machinery. Nothing to get alarmed about. He ran his light around the yard, seemingly without much concern, going as far as the ground floor of the factory, only steps away from the crouched demolition team, and pulled on the steel outer door.

It was locked.

"Who's there?" he called out again, flashing his light.

One beam went directly over Poulsson, ducking behind the storage cask.

Gutterson tensed his finger on the trigger. "Shall I shoot?" he whispered to Poulsson, the steady drone from the turbines drowning out his words.

"He doesn't seem to know we're here," Poulsson replied. Shooting him would only create an all-out confrontation, and even if they wiped out the guards and escaped, the alarm would be sounded. He placed a steadying hand on Gutterson's elbow. "Not unless he spots us for sure."

"*Jemand* . . . ?" the guard called out one more time. *Anyone?* He stepped over, barely ten feet from where Poulsson and Gutterson were crouched, and shined a light directly over their heads.

Gutterson sucked in a breath. *If that bastard lowers that light another foot, it'll be the last thing he ever does.*

"*Schiesse* . . ." the guard muttered to himself, and headed back to the hut.

"See anything . . . ?" someone asked him as the door opened.

"Who knows . . . ? Maybe the falling snow exploded a

land mine or something," the German muttered. "C'mon, let me back in. I'm not dressed for out here."

The door quickly shut behind him.

Barely believing their luck, Poulsson and Gutterson both blew out a breath of relief with a roll of their eyes. They waved Arne forward, who scurried over to them in a crouch.

"Let's get out of here."

The three picked up in the dark and ran silently past the factory in the direction of the rail tracks.

The demolition team, which had taken cover in the snow, preparing to come to their countrymen's aid, if needed, now saw three dark shapes hurrying toward them.

"Password?" someone called. It sounded like Jens.

"Fuck the password." Kjelstrup appeared out of the darkness. "Let's just keep moving."

"What's the point in having a password, if you don't use it?" Jens insisted.

"Leicester Fucking Square. There's the password. Does that make you feel good? Now can we go?"

"Are we sure it blew?" Poulsson looked at Nordstrum with uncertainty in his eyes.

Nordstrum shrugged. "You saw the flash."

"Yes, but it was more like a couple of cars crashing in Piccadilly Circus. Not exactly what I imagined."

"Me too, to be honest," Stromsheim agreed. "I thought the whole building would come down."

"It blew," Ronneberg said, ending the dispute. "The compressors are gone. I'm sure." The world's extant supply of heavy water. "It's all down the drain."

"I can't believe it." Gutterson shook his head, finally letting out his amazement. "We actually did it. I thought we'd all be dead."

"Well, we will be," Ronneberg said to him, "if we don't pick it up and get the hell down that ridge. We still have a lot of work to do before we can celebrate."

In a minute they were back at the wire gate they'd come in through only half an hour before. Advancing out of the shadows, this time they heard the word "Piccadilly" whispered loudly ahead of them. Helberg. And this time they answered, "Leicester Square."

Helberg stood up. "Is it done?"

Ronneberg nodded. "Yes."

"I didn't hear a thing. And you're all here?" he said in amazement, silently counting each of them to be sure. There was no big explosion, no sound of gunfire, no alarm. "The Germans don't even know?"

"Not yet, apparently," Ronneberg said. "But let's not hang around too much longer to find out."

Quickly, they edged themselves through the same gap in the gate they'd come through when they arrived, which Ronneberg did his best to fit back together so it would not be obvious how they had gotten in. Then they hurried back along the tracks. Nordstrum knew that the feeling of elation he had would be completely in vain unless they got back across the river and up the other side to safety. Inside the plant, the two watchmen likely would be running their mouths off about now. *Brits. Sabotage.* Every second was vital. At any moment, the sirens might sound. Nordstrum recalled what Tronstad had told him somewhat whimsically: "There's a pretty good chance you'll blow the compressors. But only a fifty-fifty chance you'll make it out alive."

Maybe the odds had tilted just a bit in their favor. Sixty-forty now. But they had to put as much distance between themselves and the plant as possible before the alarm was sounded.

The trip down the ledge proved to be far easier than the climb up. Helberg went ahead and found a more forgiving route, without the vegetation they used to hoist themselves up. The warm *foehn* wind that had blown in within the past hour had softened the ice and snow. They slid and lowered themselves down the rock face, all of them making it without incident.

But crossing back over the river was another matter. What had been a frozen trickle only two hours earlier had now become a rising current. The warming breeze they'd felt had melted away much of the ice, which had cracked into large, floating chucks, the current slicing through them. Jumping from loose chunk to chunk, they all leaped onto the far bank, helping each other over. Another hour, and it was likely that their route to cross back over would have been totally swept away.

The urgency now was to get back to their skis and rucksacks and get up to the vidda as fast as they could. By now, the Nazis had to have discovered what had taken place and, any second, the alarm would sound. If the searchlights on the factory's roof and the bridge fixed on them in the ravine, they'd be trapped there with no hope of escape. Even if they did somehow make it to the Ryes Road, there would be hundreds of troops on their tails. They headed along the bank until they found the rutted path they had used to slide their way down the slope two hours before.

Then they began to climb.

The snow, which had been packed on their descent, was now soft and deep, just what they didn't need. Their boots sank in up to their knees, making each step a grueling exertion. They knew that every second that delayed them could mean their lives. Grabbing at bushes and branches, reaching for whatever they could, they pulled themselves up, doing their best not to start a snow slide that would drag them or a teammate back down.

Six hundred feet.

Where are the searchlights? Nordstrum wondered. *Why haven't the Germans responded?*

Huffing and sucking for air, they finally saw the main road winding a hundred feet above them, where they had stored their skis and packs.

Nordstrum grinned at Jens. They were almost home.

That was the moment they heard the penetrating wail of sirens behind them.

44

In Rjukan, Dieter Lund shot up in bed. "Trudi, what is that?"

Out of his window, sirens were blaring. The clock read 1:20 A.M. He knew in an instant something wasn't right.

"It sounds like an air raid," his wife said. "Dieter, we should head to the basement!"

"No, wait!" Lund ran to the window.

It wasn't an air raid. There was huge commotion on the streets. The Germans were organizing. He could hear truck engines starting, commands shouted. The clop of heels and boots as troops were assembling. A line of trucks with soldiers in them, along with armored vehicles heading up the road at a fast clip.

The road to Vemork.

From that direction, there was a shifting glare in the sky. Searchlights, Lund realized. And the wail of sirens.

It could only mean one thing.

"My God, something's happened up at the factory," Lund said. The troops were being sent up there; the searchlights fanned over the entire valley.

Sabotage.

He ran to the closet and threw on his uniform, for once not worrying if it was neatly pressed.

Trudi leaped out of bed and went to the dresser. "Dieter, wait. Your cap."

"My cap? Trudi, there's no time. The plant's been attacked. I have to go."

45

Adrenaline surging, sirens wailing behind them, the saboteurs picked up their pace, grabbing at anything—rocks, vegetation—that would support them, propelling themselves up the other side.

They had to make it to the road before the searchlights fixed on them.

From the bridge and the factory's roof, the beams from searchlights crisscrossed the valley, once or twice missing them only by a matter of meters.

Panting, drenched with sweat, they finally made it up to the lip of the main road. Exhausted, they toppled over the edge and caught their breath. For a moment all seemed clear. Their skis and rucksacks were on the power line road just a few yards above them.

But as they went to cross, the rumble of fast-moving engine noise and the beams from headlights rapidly approaching sent them scurrying back to the ground.

Two trucks came around the bend fifty yards in front of them, chugging up the hill.

The first pushed along a large plow to clear the road, whose switchback turns made the drive up the mountain a treacherous one. As it passed by, barely six feet away, the group buried their faces in the drift the truck created. Twenty yards behind, the second truck motored toward them, the back crammed with German troops from Rjukan.

They pressed their bodies into the snow.

With a grinding shifting of gears, the troop truck roared past them as each heart stood still.

They remained there, their fingers on their triggers, until the two trucks continued on and did not stop. The next bend in the road took them out of sight.

One by one, everyone pulled themselves up to their feet and sprinted across the road, scrambling to the ledge above them—the power line road where they had stashed their gear. Quickly, they put on their suits and skis. Each had prepared packs with their civilian clothes, forged identity papers, local kroner, food and water.

Across the valley, lights could be seen running along the railway tracks behind the plant as the alarm continued to sound. The Germans had finally figured out their route. Seconds later, the giant search beams from the roof of the plant began to fan over the valley near where they had just crossed the Mann. Gradually, the lights ascended the very slope they had just climbed. As the light neared, they ducked for cover, the beam passing right above them.

Below, there was now a steady rumble of traffic coming up the road, a continuous line of trucks and official vehicles heading up to Vemork, filled, no doubt, with troops, brass, and Gestapo. It had been the right plan to climb. There was no way they could have continued along the road as they had on their way in. Above them, the cable car rose to the vidda, another two thousand feet up. To get there would involve an exhausting climb. And then the Ryes Road, with its treacherous, zigzagging bends in and out of the cable car trestles would prove even more demanding.

Nordstrum, who knew the way as well as anyone, looked up to pick out the best path through the trees to start. Then, with the sort of offhand smile that conveyed they had come through their share of danger, but the toughest part still lay ahead, he took in a breath and set off, saying, "I'll take the lead." Jens followed next, then Poulsson and Gutterson, who had pulled his weight every step of the way.

The rest of them fell in line.

The climb they now faced would have taxed the will and conditioning of even the most experienced of mountain men, without even factoring in all they had already done that night. For the next three hours they forged their way up the steep incline, one ski at a time, often sideways to the ridge, ignoring the biting pain in their lungs and the grueling strain on their thighs. They pushed on, knowing their only escape was to reach the top, which towered over them at almost four times the altitude as the factory had at the start of their earlier climb.

All the while three hundred German troops were fanning around the valley in a frantic attempt to find them.

After an hour's rigorous climb, they made it up to the starting point of the Ryes Road. The vidda was still another fifteen hundred feet towering above them. That's when the real climb began. The path switched back and forth across the sharply angled slope, cutting between the darkened trestles of the shut-down cable car. At a point, the snow had melted enough that rocks protruded and they could no longer use their skis, so they had to lug their skis over one shoulder, their weapons on the other, packs on their backs, one grueling step at a time. When they could go no further, they stopped and bent over, but only for a minute, and chugged down water or took a bite of dried fruit or beef. Nordstrum, who led, bent over, recalled his father's words, words that had stuck in his brain now more than ever before: "*A true man is a man who goes on till he can go no farther, and then goes twice as far.*" He waited until whoever was in the rear silently caught up to them. And then he continued on.

All the while, behind them, they heard the incessant rumble of trucks and military vehicles speeding up to Vemork. Every once in a while they had to come out from the cover of the bushes and trees, which put them in open terrain. Where were the dreaded searchlights that they feared would illuminate their escape? Scanning other parts of the valley because the Germans still must not have thought it possible they could have crossed the valley from the gorge.

Another worry was that the Germans would power up the cable car and send a detachment of troops to the top. This could have happened in a matter of minutes and would have put an end to their escape up the ridge. Yet as they reached each successive trestle and then went onward to the next, the summit now in sight, this fear never materialized.

At a brief rest stop, Joaquim Poulsson pointed up to a ridge. "My family lives about a mile over there. We could go knock on their door and ask for a cup of coffee."

"Yes, that sounds good about now," Nordstrum said, puffing air out his cheeks.

"A pity," Poulsson said, and sighed. He knew it would only put his loved ones at risk. "But what a nice surprise that would be." He looped his arm back through his pack. "Let's keep going."

At five in the morning, after three hours of exhausting climbing, as the sun rose majestically over the horizon—a sun none of them thought they'd ever see—they pulled themselves over the final ridge and fell, breathless, panting, onto the vidda. The wind up there was so strong it nearly blew them back over the ledge.

Across the valley, they could still hear the sounds of the Germans mobilizing their efforts to find them. They could be spotted from the air; in a few hours, the Germans would likely send up patrols. The mountains would be swarming with them. But they were finally on the vidda and knew the odds had now swung to their favor.

Everyone just lay there, sucking in precious air, too exhausted to even move. Then it seemed to hit them all at once.

They'd done it—done what everyone—their planners, Tronstad, even themselves—thought was nearly impossible. And amazingly, all ten had made it back.

For the first time, Ronneberg looked at his men and said in his way of understatement: "Well, that went pretty damn well now, didn't it, boys?"

"Yes, it did go pretty well." Jens laughed.

One by one, they all began to laugh as well. The laugh of a held-in joy that had kept quiet every step of the way after they'd done their jobs—because at each hurdle they'd cleared, the dangers they still faced were even more overwhelming—finally let loose, and echoing, like the applause of the gods (or the trolls, maybe), who, in infinite praise, looked down on them admiringly.

Yes, it had gone pretty damn well—they laughed until they fought back the pain.

"Who among us had ten?" Joaquim Poulsson looked around. He was speaking of how many each thought would, in the end, survive. The last day at the hut they had discussed it, without sharing their picks.

"I had only two." Arne Kjelstrup shook his head. "Not much of an optimist, I confess."

"It was two for me as well," Olf Pedersen said. "And, trust me, never for a moment did I think I'd be among them."

"I had three," said Jens. "And I *was* one of them."

"Four," said Claus Helberg.

"Four for me, too," said Stromsheim. "I felt sure the blast would take one or two."

"Five." Gutterson grinned. "But I was certain my lousy Norwegian would give us away."

"This might be the time to admit your Norwegian's not as bad as we've all made it out," Storhaug said. "Still, even I figured there'd be no more than six at best."

"I never had a number." Ronneberg, their leader, shrugged. "But I've never been so happy as to see all of you here."

"Kurt . . . ?" Helberg said, realizing Nordstrum hadn't answered.

Jens pushed up on his elbows. "Yes, come on, Kurt, why so quiet?"

"My number was always ten," Nordstrum said with a shrug. "I knew the odds, but in my heart, I always thought we would all make it. At least this far."

"*Ten?*" Jens shook his head in disbelief. "Come on."

"It's the truth. Though I admit that on that cliff, seeing Olf hanging there, I was revising my estimate."

"That makes two of us!" Olf Pedersen cackled.

"Well, that makes you the winner then, Kurt," Ronneberg said. "Here." He tossed Nordstrum his sack. "You get to carry the equipment."

After a short rest, it was essential they move on. Their destination was the Langsja hut, ten kilometers away, where Knut Haugland was waiting to radio back the news.

Once there, they would split up into groups. Ronneberg and the rest of Gunnerside, Nordstrum included, were to head across the vidda to Sweden. Two hundred and fifty kilometers

239

away. Poulsson and the Grouse team were to head to Oslo. Everyone had the clothes, identity papers, and the mannerisms of an everyday civilian.

Even up here, the Germans could easily be on top of them. Once they realized where they'd gone, they would surely throw everything they had at tracking them down. But for now they had to face another adversary, one they knew well—the weather. The wind was already howling. The sun had risen over the mountains, a gorgeous molten orange band, as if Nature herself was congratulating them, saying, *Job well done!* But behind it, they could see the clouds.

As soon as they started to walk again, a storm flared up, biting winds blistering in their faces, frozen ice balls splintering their eyes. It took six long hours traveling into the teeth of it to make their way back to the cabin. The only good news, of course, was that even if the Germans came up here, now they had no way to follow their tracks.

On the edge of exhaustion and collapse, they finally made it to the cabin. Knut Haugland was waiting for them with bated breath. Ecstatic to see his friends return, even more eager to hear how it had gone. He gaped and hugged each one in joy and disbelief when, to a man, all ten staggered in.

"Tell me," he said to anyone with the strength to talk to him.

Ronneberg groaned in exhaustion and collapsed on the floor, panting, his body on the edge of giving out. "The job's done," was all he said, in between breaths of agony.

"You got them? All the compressors? The heavy water too?"

"All." The leader nodded. "You can tell them all."

"*All?*" he said again, repeating the word in amazement.

"All."

It had been thirty-six hours since any of them had caught a wink of sleep. Fighting to stay awake and not submit to his body shutting down, Ronneberg went through the events, Haugland jotting them down as feverishly as a reporter taking down a story for the afternoon edition. Not a shot had been fired.

Then the ten of them simply shut their eyes. Their goal was to continue on to Skrykken, deeper into the vidda, but outside, the winds raged and the snow fell and the storm socked them in.

But they knew they were safe, as the Germans would be at the storm's mercy too, and would not venture up after them until it had cleared.

In a few minutes all of them gave themselves over to a well-earned rest. Amid the snores, Haugland settled down to his keys, and toward morning, when the storm broke for a short while, long enough to allow him to transmit, he tapped out a few words.

46

Back at STS 61, Jack Wilson burst into Tronstad's quarters with a cable, catching him in his shorts, trimming his mustache. "Read this!"

Both had been up all night.

Putting down the scissors, and scanning the text, Tronstad slowly allowed himself a grin, a subtle one at first, more of a warming swell of pride and amazement, until the two espionage officers looked at each other and could no longer hold themselves back from hugging each other in triumph and joy.

Shortly after, the news reached Winston Churchill, at 10 Downing Street. He read the cable not once but twice, and then sat back and closed his eyes. Maybe for the first time he could see a path to victory in this long, bloody ordeal. Then the old artillery officer pounded his fist against his night table with such force the report he'd been reading before bed flew onto the floor. When an aide ran in and asked if everything was all right, the prime minister answered, "Quite all right. Thomas, do we have a sherry at hand?"

"Sherry? Of course, sir. But it's six A.M."

"You're right, damn it. In that case make it a cognac. And something of quality, Thomas. One that we might toast Monty or FDR, if he was here."

Four thousand miles away, at the White House in Washington, D.C., Franklin Delano Roosevelt, still at work long into the night, received the cable, leaned his head back, and whispered to whatever Providence had guided these men. "Thank God." Maybe He had taken sides.

The cable they all read said simply:

Operation carried out with 100 percent success. High-concentration plant completely destroyed. Shots not exchanged since the Germans did not realize anything. The Germans do not appear to know whence they came or whither the party disappeared.

47

After the storm began to wane the next day, the eleven quickly split up the supplies and prepared to go their separate ways.

The plan was for Nordstrum to head with Ronneberg, Storhaug, Stromsheim, Pedersen, Jens, and Gutterson across the vidda to Sweden—two hundred and fifty kilometers away, which, with luck, they could make in ten days—while Grouse was to head to Oslo to be reassigned.

They knew the Germans would be throwing everything they had at them to stop them.

The storm that reared up had served them well, for it had covered their tracks up the Ryes Road, and as it continued into the second day, would conceal their escape routes as well. The group going to Sweden remained in their British uniforms, counting on the idea that if they were somehow caught, it would lessen the reprisals against the local population. The rest of their party buried theirs deep in the snow.

The mood in the group was soaring. To a man, there was the feeling they had done something few others could have even contemplated, much less dared. But now they had to get out. The winds were starting to die, the snow weakening, and the hut they had slept in, while safe, was still only ten kilometers from the factory. Once the storm stopped, the Germans would be on their tails.

The two groups prepared to bid farewell.

Jens caught sight of Nordstrum changing out of his uniform and into civilian clothes as well. He looked at him, perplexed. "Kurt, what's going on?"

"I won't be going with you," Nordstrum said to his friend.

Their leader, Ronneberg, was also taken by surprise. "What are you saying, Kurt?"

"I'm staying behind. Tronstad and Wilson asked me before we left. There's some work to be done here. I agreed."

"What work?" Jens asked.

"The recruitment of agents and radio operators. They need to build a network here."

"You realize by midday the place will be swarming with Germans." Jens looked at him, dismayed. "Where will you go? Every Heine who can limp will be on the hunt for us."

"I realize that. But I also know these mountains better than any of them. That's why they chose me. Now, go on. All of you. Look, it's snowing again. I told you, Jens, the trolls are with us."

Jens put down his skis and removed his rucksack defiantly. "Then I'll stay with you. We've been together a long time."

"I told Colonel Wilson you'd likely say just that. It's not a request, I'm afraid, Jens. It's an order. Remember, I still outrank you. What I have to do will only bring more attention to it if it's more than one man."

Jens stared at him with bitter disappointment. "We've fought together for three years."

"And we will again. But when I see you all next, hopefully we'll be on the side doing the routing."

Ronneberg stepped up to him and put out his hand. "When we see you again, I hope it'll be over a beer and herring. We'll have much to share." He gave Nordstrum a hug. "You be safe, Kurt. We could never have done this thing without you."

"And you. All of you," Nordstrum said, as they all came up and, one by one, embraced him.

"You helped me through," Gutterson said, taking off his cap. "I hate to leave you behind."

"You earned your place." Nordstrum gave him his hand. "As well as anyone here. Consider yourself a fucking Northman now. The rest of us do."

The young American grinned with pride and strapped his pack on his back. "I hope to see you again."

"We did something good," Nordstrum said. "All of us."

"Yes." Olf Pedersen nodded. "We did. I owe you my life up on that ridge."

Jens was the hardest to leave. His friend's boyish good looks and innocent blue eyes had weathered into the features of a hardened soldier now.

"When this is over, we'll meet at the Gunwale on Lake Tinnsjo," Nordstrum said. "Where we met with Einar, before we took the boat to England."

"It's a date. Just no Germans this time, if you can work that out. Or Hirden, for that matter."

"Yes, I make a solemn promise not to toss anyone overboard ever again." Nordstrum laughed. "That *is* what got us into this mess. And a little matter about reappropriating a coastal steamer. Yes, we've been through a lot." Nordstrum held out his hand.

Jens took it and looked at him with tears in his eyes. "I meant what I said last night. Before the raid. If anything happens to you, you do have those who would care. Like family. It would be a real loss for me."

"And the same for me, Jens. You take care." Nordstrum

pulled his friend close. "Now let's get on with it before we end up blubbering into our ski masks."

The rest had buckled into their skis. In a sign of providence, the snow had started up again, as Nordstrum had observed. Their tracks would be covered. Putting out his palm, Jens laughed. "And don't give me any business about the trolls. Though I admit, I'm maybe starting to come around just a bit. . . ." He skied over and joined the team.

"You all take care." Nordstrum put up his hand as they headed off in single file along the shore of the frozen lake. East. In the direction of Sweden. "Yes, we did do something good," he said to himself, when they were well out of earshot.

Maybe a hundred meters out, Jens stopped a last time and waved to him.

Within minutes, the men were merely specks against a vast sea of white, gliding and shushing around the perimeter of the frozen lake. Nordstrum knew there was no lonelier feeling than watching your comrades skiing off. Men you fought with side by side. Who did their jobs when called upon and held their nerve.

Men who had gone twice as far.

He pushed his arms through his own rucksack and clipped on his skis. Now it was just him and the mountains. The way he liked it. Yes, they had done something good. He looked back once and took off, heading away from the lake.

West.

Deeper into the sea of white and the valleys of the vidda. The wind picked up. Slanting snow knifed at his face. Soon his beard was covered with it.

Jens was right, in hours the place would be swarming with Germans, looking for the team who had dealt them a blow right under their noses. He'd better put as much distance between himself and them as he could.

There was much more to do.

He looked again toward the hut. His friends had disappeared.

And the fresh snow had covered his tracks.

PART TWO

TRACKS IN THE SNOW

48

General Wilhelm Rediess, Obergruppenfuhrer of all the Gestapo and SS battalions in Norway, stared in anger at the mangled heavy water compressors in the basement of the Norsk Hydro factory.

He was one of the few people in Norway who knew the true importance of the precious liquid being secreted there. He had sped to Vemork from Oslo that Sunday morning as soon as he'd received word of the raid. News he could not believe, since only three months before, he and General Falkenhorst, the supreme military commander in Norway, had upgraded the security measures for the plant after the failed glider attack.

And now they lay in ruin—twisted shards of metal, pipes, and valves. Canisters that once contained the most valued military secret in the Reich toppled like bowling pins, the trail of their irreplaceable contents a slow drip down the drain.

Before him, those responsible stood stiffly, awaiting his reaction.

"You are absolutely certain," Rediess grilled the night watchman, an aging fool named Gustav, clutching his cap, "that these four saboteurs were British?"

With the watchman was his foreman from the previous night, as well as the chief engineer of the plant, named Larsen. And the overall director of the Norsk Hydro facility himself, Nilsson, a heavyset, nervous businessman who saw this only in terms of profit and loss and not the strategic value to the Reich; also the military officer in charge at the plant that night, a Lieutenant Frisch, who stood sweating at attention but who in a matter of days would be freezing in the snow a thousand miles east of here. The local head of the Gestapo, Gruppenfuhrer Muggenthaler, stood by silently, as did Colonel Rausch, in charge of the local garrison in Rjukan, and the head of the local NS police in the region, a Captain Dieter Lund.

"They certainly appeared British." The watchman nodded nervously. It was as if he had a practised speech. "They wore green-gray uniforms; they spoke in English mostly. They even said they were British. You heard them, didn't you, Gunnar?" he said to his foreman. "They said, 'Tell them British officers wouldn't take a Norwegian life.' "

"I did hear them," the foreman said, but he was clearly not happy to be brought into the conversation in front of the senior Gestapo officer from Oslo.

"But they spoke Norwegian as well, I heard you say?" the Gestapo chief pressed further.

"Yes, a little," the watchman admitted. "When one has a gun trained on you it's not great for the ears."

"You can see the gun they left over there for yourself, Herr General . . ." The chief engineer, Larsen, pointed to the discarded Thompson submachine gun, doing his best to deflect the heat from his man. "And the explosives manual . . ." It had been charred in the blast but still had the British insignia on it and was written in English.

"I do see them." Rediess looked at the engineer. "And I've seen the gate near the railway tracks and the footprints in the snow leading to the gorge."

"With all due respect, Herr General . . ." The NS police captain, Lund, stepped forward. "I do not believe myself the people who committed this act were, in fact, British. Or at least, it had to have been accomplished with significant local support."

"I am listening, Captain," the Gestapo general said, surprised to hear a Norwegian who could think for himself. Usually, they did nothing in this country but back each other up to the bitter end.

"First, sir, to have gained access to the building through the pipe duct, they would have to have received inside knowledge. Former Chief Engineer Brun is the likely source. He is thought to be in England now, as you know, with the previous head of the plant, that traitor Leif Tronstad. Second, there are mines set throughout the plant's grounds. To make their way up here, not from the bridge or from down the cliffs, but from the gorge—only someone with a keen knowledge of the local terrain would even attempt such a feat."

"I agree with you completely, Captain Lund." The Gestapo chief stepped up to him. "Keep going."

Lund knew this was the only chance he had to turn disaster into opportunity, if he could play his cards right. "Thank you, sir. Third, the likelihood is the saboteurs came together from up on the vidda. Over the past week, there have been severe storms up there. In such conditions, familiarity with the terrain would not simply be an asset, Herr General, it would be essential. In my view, I am sad to say that only Northmen could have pulled this off. And only ones familiar with the region, down to the smallest detail."

Rediess betrayed a knowing smile, his suspicions confirmed. "Anything more?"

"Lastly, in spite of what the night watchman claims, Herr General, I believe we are looking for more than four saboteurs. Four, perhaps, to enter the plant and set the charges . . . But others would have to have been watching over the guard hut in the case the guards became alerted."

"Yes, I believe you are right on that." The Gestapo man nodded. Rediess knelt and picked up the charred British explosives manual and tapped it in his hand. "And on the supposition that you *are* right, if you were these people, where would you be headed now?"

"To the safety of the huts and cabins spread out over the vidda. And then to Sweden, I suspect. But it is also possible that some who helped them have remained behind. Or worse, they are part of the local community, right under our noses, and a threat to continued danger."

"I agree again, Captain. It's as I've been saying. And as such, you will order an immediate sweep of the entire area," Rediess declared. "Colonel Rausch . . ."

The officer in charge of the Rjukan garrison snapped to attention. "Yes, Herr General."

"We have three thousand men in the area. Planes. Armored vehicles. Wireless direction-finding locators. Why are they not mobilized yet? The Swedish border is roughly three hundred and fifty kilometers away. These criminals cannot go undetected forever. What is the delay?"

"Again, if I may, sir." Lund stepped forward. "I'm afraid we won't catch them on skis. In fact, if one of the persons involved is the man I am thinking of, we may never find them. And in camouflage suits, even a reconnaissance plane would not likely spot them against the snow from the air."

"Are you saying you have some idea who it is?"

"Only a hunch, sir. But a solid one, I believe."

Lund felt certain a man like Nordstrum had to have something to do with it. He knew the area as well as any local. He'd made it to England, that they knew—on the *Galtesund*—where Tronstad and Brun were known to be and the raid was likely planned. And if Lund had a sense of Nordstrum at all, the man would not be scampering like some frightened deer across the vidda to safety. He would remain here. This was only one job. An important one, perhaps, but there was other mischief to be done. "It is also possible he knew people on the inside of the plant who helped him pull this off."

Lund saw that Larsen, his fellow Norwegian, was regarding him with a look that bordered on contempt and shame. The word "treachery" blazed in his eyes. No matter, it was what he must do.

"That is precisely my suspicion as well." Rediess returned to the plant director, Nilsson. "As such, I want all department heads who were on duty last night placed in jail in Rjukan."

"*Herr General!*" Director Nilsson's jaw fell open in outrage. "These men have done nothing—"

"And since these people are civilians," Rediess turned to Lund, "I place the matter under your jurisdiction, Captain. I am sure you can carry this out?"

Lund bowed his head and nodded. "It would be my duty, General."

"And if we do not discover the name or names of whoever has provided aid to these provocateurs," the Obergruppenfuhrer pulled off his wire-rim glasses and began to clean them with a huff of breath, "then one of them will be shot each day, until the traitor or traitors' identity is confirmed. I will oversee the interrogations myself."

"General Rediess, I must strongly object!" The plant's director stepped forward, aghast. "This raid is clearly a military matter. Not a civilian one. These men are loyal employees.

Many have held jobs in the plant for years. It will disable the work."

"The *work* . . ." The Gestapo chief's eyes fell on him like a heavy weight. "There is no longer any work here, Herr Director, other than what we tell you to perform. The only work"—he pointed to the disabled compressors— "is restoring this equipment and resuming the production as swiftly as possible. The rest . . . Whatever chemical you create, or whatever it is you do here, is precisely what it is destined for—fertilizer. Shit. It is completely irrelevant. Do you understand?"

The director cast a hapless glance toward Chief Engineer Larsen.

"As such, you will get your best engineers on the task of fixing these compressors and getting them back up and running as soon as possible. That is all the work this plant is responsible for now. Any day that the effort slackens, even for an hour, in my estimation, another worker will be shot. Is that understood, Herr Director?" The Gestapo chief's gaze remained fixed on him. "Or would you prefer it would be you who will be shot instead?"

Nilsson released a breath of held-in anger through his clenched jaw and stepped back in line. "Perfectly understood, Herr General."

"In addition, there will be a state of emergency imposed in Rjukan, effective today. There will be a nightly curfew of six o'clock. Anyone on the streets after that will be deemed up to no good and shot. And there will be house-to-house searches in town. Anyone in possession of explosives or even a fuse will be immediately imprisoned. Captain Lund, I imagine you are capable of overseeing such measures. Does any of this present a problem in any way?"

"No problem at all, Herr General." Lund clicked his

heels and stood facing straight ahead, his chest expansive. In fact, one such farmer came to mind immediately. One he would love to toss into his cell. And for a farmer, dynamite and fuses would be a common possession, to blow up rocks and clear the land. Lund would only be upholding the law.

"Colonel Rausch, I am not sure why you are still standing here." The Gestapo chief turned to face him. "By day's end, I want five hundred men up in the mountains on the trail of these criminals. They cannot have gotten too far away. Surely German mountain divisions are every bit the equal of a few Brits and local mischief makers?"

"Indeed they are, sir." The colonel snapped his heels. "But, I'm told, we are hampered by severe storms up there today. Nothing will be visible until they clear. Besides, in this weather, any tracks they left will be swept away."

"Then I would dress warmly, Colonel. Indeed." The Gestapo general went up to him, his face only inches away. "Am I clear? And turn over every hut and cabin in the region so you do not need tracks. Burn each unoccupied one to the ground; that way anyone cannot double back. Captain Lund, I am certain you have men who know their way up there as well as any, do you not?"

"Yes, there are some." Lund nodded.

"Fit these men out and have them get after these intruders. And if I find out the people responsible for this are, in fact, Norwegian, and not British after all," his stare landed on Larsen and Director Nilsson, "there will be hell to pay in town. Do you understand? And I might be starting with you two as the first examples. Just so we fully understand each other."

With blanched faces, Larsen and Nilsson both looked back at the Gestapo man.

"So get on with it. I want those processors repaired, as quickly as possible, Herr Chief Engineer. That is your work now. I am certain there is an assistant chief engineer who would be happy to comply if his boss were to be lined up against a wall. " He nodded and dismissed everyone with a formal Heil Hitler. "That's all."

The group made for the exits. Rediess took out a notebook from his jacket and jotted something in it. Everyone hurried to get out of his sight.

"Oh, and Night Watchman Fredrickson . . ." the general muttered, still buried in his notebook.

Gustav stopped, a hand on the door. "Sir?"

"It was on your watch that this sabotage took place, was it not?" The Gestapo chief finally looked up. "You didn't honestly think that I had forgotten about you, did you now . . . ?" he said with a blank smile.

49

For the next two weeks, Nordstrum traveled from hut to hut, staying ahead of the German pursuit, which came onto the vidda in a presence larger than anyone had ever seen before.

The first few days, the storms in the mountains continued to rage; despite his blistered cheeks and ice-stung eyes, Nordstrum knew it only aided his advantage. His tracks would be concealed. The reconnaissance planes couldn't fly. After a week, he'd eaten the last of the food he'd brought with him, and from then on it was whatever he was able to find or catch in the wild. On the Songvaln he shot a deer, which lasted him for days. He hoped to get back to Rjukan to see about his father, but right now it was far too dangerous there. More German soldiers were flooding into the Telemark every day, and there was always the risk that someone in town might recognize him.

After a month, when he felt safe enough to show his face again, he got on with the work he was sent to do.

His assignment from Wilson and Tronstad was to recruit three agents who would be set up as radio transmitters. Things had become a little too heated for Einar, who had a family, an important job and, as such, couldn't easily disappear for days at a time. Not to mention Einar's brother Torstein had been picked up by the NS for questioning, which cast the glare of suspicion on the family. And as SOE intended to drop in more agents and plan further operations, it required a broader network on the ground.

The first recruit he found was a friend of his cousin,

named George Hansen. He was a bull of a man, with a thick red beard and a gap in his teeth, a farmer whose house had been burned to the ground by the Nazis and whose wife had been shot. He was now skinning hides in a slaughterhouse in Uvdal, the same town Kristiansen, the ill-fated hunter they'd had to shoot, had come from. He had a daughter somewhere.

The butcher wasn't hard to convince. Haugland's radio and codebook had been hidden before they left and Nordstrum knew enough about how to operate it. George was willing, though a little slow on the coding and decoding. "I'd much rather shoot the fuckers," he simply said. "Given a choice."

"You'll get your chance. I promise," Nordstrum assured him. "In the meantime you have to be careful." A working radio was a valuable commodity in occupied Norway. George still had his old stone barn and a cabin deep in the wilderness, which he could use as a transmitting site.

"You have to move from place to place," Nordstrum instructed him as they set up the transmitter in the remote cabin. "No two transmissions in a row from the same location. I'll meet you every other Tuesday. There'll be a stone in your mailbox if I have something for you. And you leave one on the post if you've something for me. We'll meet the next afternoon at the barn."

"Okay," George agreed, scratching his beard.

"You'll need a code name."

"How's Okse? That's what they called me back in school."

"Ox. That works. Welcome to the Free Norwegian Army, Ox." Nordstrum put out his hand.

The big man grinned and took it, almost burying Nordstrum's grip in his. "I'm happy to finally be doing something in this war."

The second possibility happened serendipitously, in the town of Rauland. From a ridge on the vidda, near where he was hiding out, Nordstrum had spotted German patrols, and thought, at some risk, that there would be better cover for him in the town, since no one knew him there. From the word he'd received, the Germans were not only looking for Brits, but for some locals as well, who might have assisted them. He skied in and found a hotel and presented the forged identity papers to the proprietor behind the desk. He said he was a hunter from up north, on his way to Oslo for a family funeral. "Watch out, they're rounding people up left and right here," the manager warned. "Some big sabotage raid down in Rjukan a few weeks ago. Everyone's gone crazy over it. If I were you I wouldn't go out after dark."

"Thanks for that," Nordstrum said appreciatively. He carried his pack up to his room. Who knew who he could trust, even among the staff? The main thing he had to be careful of was that no one found his Colt pistol, which was a sure sign he wasn't who he represented himself to be.

For the first time in weeks he took a bath and cleaned himself properly. The hot water washed away all the dirt and grime that had caked on him since he'd left England, and took the chill from his bones that had been there since he first landed on the vidda six weeks ago. He asked for a pair of scissors and trimmed his beard and dressed in the most suitable clothes he had. In case the room was searched while he stepped out, he used his belt to strap his gun to the bottom of the bed frame. Then he went downstairs to the restaurant for dinner.

As soon as he stepped in, he knew he'd made a mistake. The place was swarming with Germans. There was a large table set up for eight of them, high brass—he could see a major, a captain, and several others in civilian clothes. Gestapo, he assumed. Conversing loudly. Singing. Ordering lots of booze.

There were a few other tables filled, but the rest of the patrons were subdued with the Germans present. Nordstrum took a seat in the corner by himself.

His first instinct, if it wouldn't draw attention to him, was to get out of there. Ox had warned him that people were being randomly searched all over and the hotel proprietor had backed that up. In fact, at that point, he had no idea how things had gone for the rest of the team. If they had made it safely, or if any had been captured or killed. Or had to swallow their pills. Nordstrum kept his in his pocket at all times. In the end, though, he thought it better to remain at the table and have his meal, rather than draw unwanted attention to himself by leaving abruptly.

A waitress came up, plump and red-cheeked, likely the hotel manager's wife. He ordered fish in butter and dill, and picked at some bread. The noise at the table of Germans grew loud—ordering the harried waitress left and right, demanding more drinks and wine, laughing boisterously. As the liquor got to them, their actions began to spill over on the neighboring tables.

At one of those tables an attractive local woman was seated with four friends. She was nicely dressed, with long, dark hair folded neatly into a bun, and high cheekbones, in her mid- to late-thirties, Nordstrum reckoned, and had clearly drawn the interest of one of the German officers. He was an SS captain who kept leaning toward her, trying to gain her attention. The woman did her best to ignore him, burying herself in conversation with her friends and turning away from his advances.

"Madame, have you ever been to Germany?" The officer finally swung his chair around and spoke loudly enough for Nordstrum, who was across the room, to overhear.

"Please, if we can only continue our meal," the woman said politely, and went back to her own conversing.

"Maybe you'd like to come there with me someday," the officer continued, turning to his colleagues with a suggestive wink. Their group laughed.

"I should very much not like to do that," the woman finally replied, unable to ignore the officer's rudeness.

The rest of the Germans laughed at their rebuked colleague, which only urged him further on.

One of her party, an older woman in a black dress, took her by the arm and scolded her. "Hella, please."

But the boorish officer kept at it. "I see you wear a ring, madame. So where is your husband? To allow such a beautiful woman out at night, unescorted . . ."

"And that would be none of your business," the woman remarked defiantly. "And anyway, I *am* escorted, as you can see, quite happily." As she looked across the room, her gaze happened to land on Nordstrum's, who nodded back with just enough encouragement to convey his support for her bravery. Still, he knew she'd better not press her luck too far. Anything could happen with these bastards.

"Why so rude, madame?" The chastened officer now stood up with his drink and went over to their table with the slightest stumble. "Do you not know things are at a very sensitive time in this region? It doesn't take much to end up in a jail for questioning these days. Even a pretty thing like yourself. Never a fun experience, I can assure you. Of course, we could easily look the other way, don't you agree, gentlemen," he turned back to his party who chuckled at his efforts, "if perhaps you'd agree to meet us for a drink later. We Germans are very forgiving types. And we know how to show it, trust me."

At first the woman did not reply. Ignoring the slight would have been the best tack. But when he splashed a little of his drink on their table and stood there, drunken, seeming actually to be waiting for an answer, she finally looked at him.

"I would rather you put me in jail then," she said, unable to back down. "And if you really must know where my husband is, I'll tell you. He was a captain in the Free Norwegian Army. Sadly I have no idea where he is today. Captured or killed, I expect. Fighting the likes of you. So if you don't mind, leave a woman alone who is merely here with her friends, celebrating a birthday, and go back to your table. I've committed no offense against you but trying to eat my meal in private."

The rebuked captain stood there stiffly. Nordstrum saw his jaw tighten. "You should not be so bold, madame." The captain took another gulp of his drink. "People have been brought in for questioning for far less offense. And then no one knows what they will find. There is always something."

Every eye in the restaurant went to him.

"Come on, Hans . . ." His fellow officers waved their countryman back. "Leave the lady alone. She's not worth it. There are others, be sure. Come, have another drink."

The officer stared at her, granite-faced. No one knew what might happen. Then he merely bowed politely, gritting his teeth and saying, "My condolences, madame," and finally retook his seat.

If there was some great victory won by her courage, the woman didn't act it. She merely went back to her meal and her friends and resumed her conversation. Nordstrum gave her another smile and a nod at a point when their gazes happened to meet, to indicate he admired what she had done.

His fish arrived. The first real food he had had in weeks that wasn't rations or what he had killed on his own and put over a fire himself. He ate it as if it came from a Cordon Bleu kitchen. All the while, he kept an eye fixed on the table of Germans, hoping their interest wouldn't wander to him. And also wondering just what he would do should the drunken officer decide to renew his case with her.

Over coffee, the woman got up to go to the powder room in the small hotel's lobby.

The officer knocked over a glass in a drunken manner, and stumbled clumsily out of the dining room too.

When she didn't come back promptly, Nordstrum asked for the bill and got up to investigate. It wouldn't be a wise thing for him to make trouble, but after the courage the woman had displayed, he wasn't about to back down if the situation called for it.

To his relief, he spotted her outside smoking a cigarette, the German nowhere around.

He stepped outside.

"The air is a little thick in there for you as well?" she said, acknowledging she had recognized him.

"That was very brave," Nordstrum said. "Not exactly wise, but my compliments nonetheless."

"Wise hasn't gotten us very far, has it?" she replied. He could see why the German was so intrigued. She would turn any head with her thick brown hair pulled back, large almond-shaped hazel eyes, and full lips with just the right amount of color on them. "Norwegians are always wise when it comes to history. And look at where we are." She blew out a plume of smoke and looked at Nordstrum as if she was waiting for an answer. By any standards the woman was beautiful.

"Traveling . . . ?" Nordstrum asked.

She looked at him and slowly edged into an amused smile. "The drunken German captain got shot down. So now, you'll try your luck?"

"Not at all. I merely was thinking whether you had some-one to accompany you home. In case Romeo in there has a desire to press his luck further."

She looked at him and smiled, in apology now, and chuckled lightly at his remark. "I'm here with friends. My landlady's birthday. I actually live a short way away. They'll take me home. I work in town. Everyone knows me here."

"Everyone but me, then. I'm Knut," he said, using the name on his false papers.

"Hella," the woman acknowledged. "Amundson."

"Hella, the unwise. But certainly courageous."

"Hella, the fool, I suspect." She laughed derisively and blew out another plume of smoke. "But someone has to stand up to them."

"That was true?" Nordstrum lit up his own cigarette. "About your husband?"

"Almost two years. The last I heard he was in Tonneson." She shrugged. "I suppose there's not much hope I'll ever hear from him again."

"I knew an Amundson," Nordstrum said. "Tall, dimple on his chin. Spectacles. He fought in the Gudbrandsdalen Valley."

She looked up at him with surprise and a bit of hope. "You were there?"

"Yes. But I'm afraid I don't know what happened to him. We were all kind of on our own by that point."

"And now?"

"*Now . . . ?* Now the fight is much different, of course."

One of the Germans came out. A squat, heavyset man in a homburg and a thin mustache. Leather jacket. The look of the Gestapo. He nodded to her with a slight snicker, noticing them both as he passed.

Nordstrum said under his breath, "I may know how you can really do something, if that's what you want."

"How do you have any idea what I want?" she said with a bit of an edge.

"*If* that's what you want, of course. I'm sorry for my unkempt appearance, but I've been on the vidda for a time. Perhaps we could talk."

She looked at him, blew out a breath, and dropped her cigarette in the snow. "I think I'd better get back inside. I assume if I'm not already arrested they'll let me finish my dessert," she said, declining to pick up on his offer.

"Now *that* would be wise." Nordstrum stamped his out as well.

"Tomorrow, maybe," she said, surprising him. A look that was curious though not fully trusting. "Just a talk. I manage a small perfumery in town. On Princess Juliana Street. No one's buying these days, other than the Germans and their whores. There's a café next door. I always take my coffee there. Around ten."

"Tomorrow, then. Around ten." Nordstrum nodded.

"If I'm still around." She smiled and went inside.

"And make sure your friends walk you all the way home," he called after her.

267

50

The next morning, Nordstrum found Hella precisely where she said she would be. The café was more like a small indoor eating stand, with a counter, some local workers around, a few muffins and biscuits, the morning newspaper for sale, and three rickety-looking wooden tables.

Nordstrum caught her eye from the street. He went in, ordered a coffee at the counter, and pretended to borrow a sugar from her table. "Not here," he said.

"There's the lake. It's all frozen over. But we could walk along it."

"My fiancée is in need of a new scent. Perhaps you can pick one out for me."

She got up and took her coffee with her. "That would be my pleasure."

Inside her shop, which also sold soaps and some inexpensive but tasteful costume jewelry, Hella brought out various scents for him to sample—from France, Italy, even Denmark, and placed them on the counter. She had her hair in a braid today that fell across one shoulder, long and brown. She wore a typical Norwegian sweater with a long wool skirt, but she still made it look stylish with a belt around her waist, and her figure was one that would attract any man. No wonder the German had been so intrigued. Nordstrum figured she was perhaps ten years older than him.

She said, "I don't know her taste. Or how much you care to spend."

Nordstrum picked up the French scent—Eau de Elyse—inspected the box for a moment, then placed it back on the counter and looked at her. "I'm in need of someone."

"Would you like to smell the scent? I could put it on."

"Of course. Why not?"

She went to the shelf behind her and took a small bottle from it. "You may go on. I'm listening."

"Someone to operate a radio. It's dangerous work. As you know, transmitters are expressly not permitted now. If you're caught, there's no guarantee I could protect you."

"I don't look for anyone to protect me these days." She sprayed a quick dab on her wrist. "You've already seen that."

"I have. It would be good, though, if you had the freedom to come and go without people watching. And a place from which to send the transmissions. Not in town. Town is far too dangerous. They have their W/T trucks patrolling everywhere. If you're interested, of course."

She waited a moment and put her wrist out for Nordstrum to smell. "Do you like?" He drew close and inhaled. "Transmissions to where?"

"It's lovely. To England," he said, looking back at her.

"England . . ." She let the word out like she was languorously blowing out a plume of smoke, a new appreciation in her eyes. "My father has a farm. In the Songvaln. It's only twelve kilometers to the east. But twelve kilometers here might as well be the North Pole."

"I wouldn't want to put your father at any risk."

"You wouldn't be. He lives in Bergen now. With my aunt. He's not so well and she can take care of him better than me. Every week or so, I ski out and look in on the place. Otherwise, it's completely empty."

Nordstrum nodded. "You'll also need to learn code."

"That should be no problem," she said with a small smile that went straight to her brown eyes. "Math was always my strong suit."

"And we would need some sort of system. So I can contact you. And you, me. When something comes in."

She stared at him for a moment, in a loose, evaluating way. "So how do I know I can trust you? Knut, if that's even your real name. So far all you've done is smile at me from across a room. I've already spoken too much about myself. You might well be an informer for all I know. NS. They're all over. The Germans pay well."

"Or you?" Nordstrum shrugged, and looked back at her.

"That's true. But if I was, I certainly had an unusual way of displaying it last night. Not to mention . . ."

"Not to mention what?"

She placed the cap back on the perfume bottle. "That it was you who came out of the restaurant after *me*. Anyway, there's something about you. Your face is hard, but you have trusting eyes."

Nordstrum waited until she put the bottle back in the box, leaving it on the counter. "You've heard of a particular incident that took place a few weeks ago the Germans seem to be interested in?"

"You mean in Rjukan?" she said with a gleam of surprise. "It's why the Germans are all over us up here. People say they were making arms. In a factory."

"The Norsk Hydro factory," Nordstrum said.

Her almond eyes widened with surprise. "That was you?"

"Now I'm the one who is compromised." Nordstrum smiled. He picked up the perfume box again and tapped it on the counter while meeting her eyes. "Persimmon . . . ?"

"Why would you even tell me such a thing? A person could trade that information for a lot of money."

"It must be that you have something trusting about you as well."

She took the perfume box from him and placed it back in front of her. "Yes, persimmon. You have a good nose. But I suspect you're really not so interested in the gift after all . . . ?"

"Another time. I promise."

"Tell me . . ." She stacked the boxes back on the shelf. "Do you even have a fiancée?"

Nordstrum shrugged. "Sadly, no. Not any longer."

She nodded with kind of a knowing smile, leaning back against the shelves, facing him, her palms wide on the counter. "Say I agree. No one can know who I am."

"They won't. Not even in England. I promise you. But I want to repeat, this is dangerous work. You have to be very careful. Far more careful than you were last night. The Germans have mounted W/T vehicles. If you're discovered, it won't be about pushing a drunken officer away from your table. You'll be shot."

Hella let out a pensive breath. "What am I going to do, sit out the war in this shop? My husband didn't hesitate. It was a second marriage for me. It lasted only three years. The first . . ." She gave a scoffing laugh and shook her head, as if to say, *a real pig.* "Now . . . if the bastards win this, losing him, it will all be for nothing."

"They won't win," Nordstrum said.

"You sound sure?"

"More than ever."

"Maybe. But we're still in for a long fight."

"Then welcome to it, Hella Amundson." Nordstrum smiled.

51

Over the next weeks, Nordstrum put his team in place. He instructed them both in the skills of transmission and code. He went from hut to hut, finding several burned to the ground—sometimes having to spend the night in his sleeping bag in the bitter cold under whatever makeshift shelter he could find. More than once he came within a hundred meters of German patrols, which were still blanketing the vidda, or barely avoided the reconnaissance of a low-flying Fokker, keeping a watchful eye over the most remote valleys. He felt hunted, like some lone, prized stag locals knew had broken from the herd. The only benefit to the Germans' constant presence was that there were now so many tracks crisscrossing the wilderness, patrol after patrol, half-track after half-track, that his became impossible to follow.

He prayed that the rest of his mates were safely in Sweden by now.

He began to send a few trial messages back to SOE. About the increased German presence on the vidda. That martial law was continued in Rjukan. One reply came back through Ox. That his old friend Einar Skinnarland wanted to see him. He asked Nordstrum to meet him at the Swansu cabin near where his family had a farm in the mountains.

Einar's brother's family was there. Torstein was still detained, but his wife, Lise, had prepared a small meal for them.

Nordstrum and Einar exchanged happy hugs, as they hadn't set eyes on each other since before the raid.

"Any news on my father?" Nordstrum asked.

"Yes." Einar shrugged and looked away. "But bad, I'm afraid. I'm told he's been arrested."

"Arrested?"

"It's Lund. Who I spoke of to you last time. He was rounded up after the raid. It was hard to get word to you. He's in his jail."

"My father cares as much about politics as a mule. It's because of me, of course."

"Because of all of us, Kurt."

"Maybe." Nordstrum picked up a loose branch. He traced the edge in the snow, then cracked it in half and flung it into the field. "I wonder if there's a way to get him out?"

"*Out?* He's locked up in the basement of the NS head-quarters, Kurt. And in failing health. This Lund is not a man you can bribe."

"I wasn't speaking of bribing anyone, Einar."

Einar looked at him. "Where would you take him, even if we could?"

"I made an oath on my mother's deathbed to watch over him."

"I think that oath has long run out, Kurt. Your father's his own man. And the town is swarming with NS and Gestapo. Lund knows you. Don't do something stupid, Kurt. People back in England are counting on you."

"I won't." Nordstrum nodded. Still the urge rose inside him. "But my father's counting on me too, Einar."

52

On King Gustav Street in Rjukan, the birchwood-stave building that for fifty years had been home to the Seamen's Guild now served as Gestapo and NS headquarters.

Both the German swastika and the Nasjonal Samling shield hung over the wood-carved entrance.

Nordstrum pulled his wool cap low over his eyes and hunched his collar. He had on a pair of wire spectacles and his beard had grown out in a week. He went up to a young SS guard positioned on the front steps. "*Captain Lund, bitte?*"

"*Fragen innen.*" The soldier pointed to the desk. *Ask inside.*

"Danke."

The lobby was jammed, both with those in German uniforms and civilians, some seeking licenses that had to be approved by the German authorities, others petitioning about family members who were being detained there. On a bulletin board Nordstrum saw a poster with photos of those on the run. Of himself and Jens—both from far younger days and clean shaven, bold letters underneath. WANTED. FOR CRIMES AGAINST THE STATE. 5,000 KRONEN REWARD. But here it was clear that everyone was far too concerned about their own business to even be thinking of looking for a familiar face.

At the reception desk, a German clerk was doing his best, in broken Norwegian, to calm a woman who could not find a family member, a Hirden officer translating her rant as fast as he could. There was a broad, carpeted staircase that led to the higher floors—the building was only three stories, but still one of the most prominent in Rjukan. A red swastika banner hung boldly from the rafters. Up that staircase, Nordstrum knew, was where the real architects of all the reprisals and crimes against the state were: this Dieter Lund, whom Einar had spoken of, and whom Nordstrum recalled from his youth. And Muggenthaler, the chief of the local Gestapo.

Under the staircase, Nordstrum noticed a door that clearly led to a basement. As he watched, a burly sergeant stepped out from it, rolled down his sleeves as if he had been doing some grimy work, and headed upstairs.

He realized the man had come from the cells that contained his father.

He cased the room and quickly calculated that it wouldn't take that much to pull it off. Most things didn't take much more than the will and the daring to do it. At night, there would likely be only a few guards. He just needed a partner to help him take out whoever was in the lobby, silently if they could, and make their way downstairs. How many guards could there be? He'd need one more man in the car outside, waiting. He knew Ox would be happy to volunteer. He noticed a rear entrance down a hall, a single guard manning it, that led onto Kveg Street.

Still, he was building his network for the good of the Allied cause, not for personal vendettas.

And, as Einar said, his father was infirm. Even if he could get him out of the cell and away, where could he take him? On the vidda? His father would never be able to make the climb. Out of the region? After such a brazen act, the two roads in and out of town would be shut down within five minutes. Put him up in a friendly basement somewhere? For the duration of the war? That would be the same as jail to him. Cooping him up. Besides, they wouldn't get halfway to Vigne.

And then there would be reprisals, of course. Even if they did get away, many innocent people would surely pay. How many other Anna-Lisettes would there be on his conscience? Because of his will to free his father. And his hatred for those who had taken him.

Like Einar said, *Don't do something stupid, Kurt.* There was still work to do. *And you are needed.* His father was always his own man. He probably wouldn't even come along, knowing he would be a burden. Nordstrum could see him stubbornly remaining in his cell, refusing to leave. An ox to the end.

Best to just get out of here. *You'd be mad to risk it.*

As he turned to leave, Nordstrum's attention was grabbed by the sound of heavy footsteps coming down the stairs.

Dieter Lund headed from his office down to the lobby, set to inspect the new security procedures for the dam at Mosvatn, which, after the raid at Norsk Hydro, he and Gestapo chief Muggenthaler had mapped out personally. With him was his aide, Lieutenant Norberg of the NS, and, a step behind, the chief security engineer, Oren Karsten, an asthmatic sycophant pushed on him by Muggenthaler, who was always pratting around with his papers and charts. Lund's staff car was waiting outside.

While over the past weeks they had been unable to apprehend a single one of the saboteurs directly involved in the Norsk Hydro bombing, they had rounded up dozens of potential troublemakers in town. Their jail was overflowing with them. Also, there was word from the Gestapo of recent observed activity on the vidda. New signs of radio signals transmitted. Single tracks spotted, to and from certain huts. If someone was up there, sooner or later he'd make a mistake. They'd catch him. There were troop increases all over. It was only a matter of time before they ran into him.

Even if it *was* Kurt Nordstrum, who everyone claimed was so crafty, as Lund was certain it was.

"Captain, this diagram shows the new mine pattern at the dam . . ." Karsten, the engineer, said, following Lund as they went down the stairs. "Perhaps we can review it on the way?"

"Yes, yes." Lund waved the engineer off, coming down the last flight into the crowded lobby. The man had the breath of someone who had downed a tin of cat food for lunch, and was always so overbearingly obsequious with his pages of charts and diagrams.

The lobby was unusually crowded this morning. It would be pleasing to take a drive in the country to inspect the dam just to get away from this nest of influence seekers, even for a few hours.

"Please, make way, coming through." Lieutenant Norberg pushed through the crowd to create some space. Lund's eyes fell over those waiting in long lines to have their grievances heard, or who had been called here to act as a witness or make a deposition. Or those clamoring uselessly on and on about the disappearance of a loved one.

"Captain, please, I beg you . . ." someone said, spotting someone in command.

"Sorry. No time. Please put in your request." Lund brushed by them. The woman in an eiderdown coat. The tall man in a gray wool cap. Just cattle. He went past them toward the entrance where his car was waiting for him and—

He stopped.

He'd nearly gotten to the front door when the face he had just passed suddenly came clear in his mind. An image, like a frame spinning into focus in a film, a film from years ago. Spinning, then coming perfectly clear.

Lund spun around.

The man was gone.

"Norberg, that man in the hat," he said. "Did you see him?"

"What man, Captain?"

Lund looked back across the lobby. "In a navy seaman's jacket. Gray wool cap." He headed back through the crowd. "He was just there. A moment ago."

It had been many years, of course. Six, seven? But there was something. Something in the eyes he just saw. Something that transported Lund back through those years. *He was here?* Impossible, Lund thought. It would be an act of complete audacity. Only a fool would dare.

A fool, or someone plotting something.

He must have learned that his father was in the cells below.

"Lieutenant, there was a man with a navy coat and gray hat standing there just a moment ago. He must have gone out the back. Find him!"

"Yes, Captain." Norberg took out his gun and blew his whistle. Three sharp shrills.

The crowd in the lobby quickly parted. Lund and Norberg pushed their way through, elbowing by a woman in a long coat who was in the way. "Let us through."

Down a narrow hall there was a short set of stairs leading to the back entrance, which he had to have gone down.

They ran out into the street and scanned both directions.

Norberg had his gun out and the whistle in his mouth, prepared to call the alarm.

The street was empty.

A German guard stood at the door. "Hauptman, a man in a navy coat just left through here a moment ago. Did you see him?"

"I'm sorry, sir," the guard said. "I saw no such man."

"No such man . . . ?" Lund looked both ways. "Impossible, he only just came out a second—"

Before he could utter the word "ago," Lund bolted back inside the building. Down the narrow hall they had come through, there was a door just off the lobby. A janitorial closet. Lund stopped at it, removed his pistol, and wrapped his hand around the doorknob.

He stood aside, his gun readied against his chest, and yanked the door open.

Hanging on the handle of a mop in a pail was a navy scaman's coat and a gray wool hat.

Lund's eyes lit up and he smiled almost triumphantly. "Nordstrum.

"He's here!" he said, and sprinted to the end of the hallway, searching for a tall man with short light hair, exactly how he remembered him.

Nothing. Again.

"Lieutenant, come with me!" Lund pushed his way to the front entrance, hurrying past the guards, outside.

He raised his gun and spun, his finger tensed on the trigger, in both directions.

No one.

Still, it didn't stop his blood from racing like a swollen stream spilling over a dam in long, held-in validation.

From his first impulse, months ago, about who had killed

the Hirden on the ferry. And now, who was behind the sabotage at the Norsk Hydro. And he could be here, at Gestapo headquarters, where his father was being held, for no other reason than to try and free him, fool that he was.

"Captain, who was it?" Norberg finally caught up to him out on the street.

"An old friend."

"Old friend . . . ?" The lieutenant looked at him, puzzled.

"Kurt Nordstrum, Lieutenant. Sound the alarm. And circulate the photos we have of him through town. He can't be far."

53

Hurrying past the guards, pretending to recognize a woman on the street and running to catch up with her, Nordstrum turned at the corner and ducked through the stalls on Market Street, fishmongers and meat suppliers hawking their catches, until he wove his way to a cousin's bicycle warehouse on King Olaf Street, which had been shut down since the war. He ducked into the loading dock as the tramp of boots on pavement and the shrill of whistles could be heard piercing the streets nearby. Soldiers hurried by.

"Look down there!" a man's voice ordered in Norwegian. "You three, check these buildings."

He kept his gun close to his side and held his breath, waiting to see if he'd have to use it.

The footsteps passed.

After an hour or so, the sounds of pursuit diminished. Nordstrum found a yellow fisherman's slicker in the entrance and slipped away, taking the back streets past the cemetery out of the town.

It was three kilometers to his father's farm. Every once in a while he saw an NS police car speeding by, its siren wailing. He waited for darkness and hid in the shadows of the church, down from his father's home. He was in need of a warm jacket and skis. He noticed a car parked on the street not far away, two darkened shapes inside. Too risky, he decided. NS or Gestapo, they were watching.

Now they knew who he was and that he was nearby.

Deciding where he would go, he tramped through a field

knee-deep with snow and then hooked back onto the main road a mile west of town. He flagged down the public bus to Vigne and Mosvatn, which was about twenty kilometers away. The old driver, a man he recognized, merely nodded at Nordstrum as if he had seen him daily for the past three years. He went to the back and put himself across from the rear exit, near a bundled old woman doing her knitting and a girl of maybe sixteen or so, perhaps on the way home from work. At each stop he prepared to bolt out the back if the wrong people stepped on.

They didn't.

In Vigne, he ducked off the bus and, pulling up the collar of his jacket, walked about a mile to the Nils road. It began to snow. He found the pleasant stone house with an Opel in front at the end of a large field. He waited behind a tree until he made absolutely certain no one had followed him. When he was satisfied, he went up to the porch and knocked on the front door.

Einar Skinnarland answered, his eyes wide with surprise. "Kurt?" He looked past him to be sure no one was watching. "What the hell are you doing here?"

"Sorry to bother you, friend. But I need a jacket and some skis and I'll be out of your hair."

"Of course. Come in." Einar knew if Nordstrum had showed up at his door it was not an ordinary situation. "What the hell's going on? You really shouldn't be here, Kurt. Jesus, you look frozen."

"I'm sorry, but there was no other choice. I had to ditch my gear in Rjukan." He greeted Einar's wife, who he hadn't set eyes on since the war. "Marte." He took off his boots so as not to wet the rug. "Sorry to intrude."

"Kurt." He couldn't tell if she was angry that he had

shown up like this or merely concerned at his condition. She took a look at him dripping with snow. "Go and stand near the fire. Let me get you a blanket and some tea."

"That would be great. If you don't mind, I will."

When she left, Einar said to him, "It's too dangerous for all of us for you to be here, Kurt. My little one's upstairs. What possibly brought you into Rjukan?"

"I won't be here long. I promise." Then he looked at him. "I couldn't just let him rot there, Einar, without seeing it for myself."

"Your father?" Einar lowered his voice. "And seeing if you could what, Kurt, break him out? I told you not to do something stupid. So what did you find?"

"That it could be done." Nordstrum warmed his hands over the flames. "It would take three of us maybe. At night. Depending on what we encountered downstairs. A car could be pulled around the back."

"And then what? Even if you pulled off another miracle, your father's in no shape to be on the run. You'd get yourselves both killed. One thing you learn, Kurt, it just takes one stupid act to undo all the good you do in this war."

"I hear you." Nordstrum wiggled his fingers as the warmth slowly came back into them. "I saw him though, Einar."

"Your father . . . ? How?"

"Not him. Our old school mate. He walked right past me in his Hirden grays."

"*Lund?*"

"Yes. And he saw me as well."

"So that's what all the commotion was about. Now it's starting to make sense. Still, it was damn foolish, Kurt. People are counting on you. You're far too valuable to be caught up in a game of personal vengeance. Next time—"

"Next time I'll put a bullet in him, that's my promise." Marte came back in with a tray of biscuits and a mug of hot tea. "Marte, you're too kind. I didn't mean to trouble you."

"It's no trouble at all, Kurt." She hesitated. "But our son is upstairs. You can't stay long."

"I won't. Just let me drink my tea. It's been a long time since a woman made some for me."

They outfitted him in boots, skis, and a hunter's coat Einar found among some old things. Once warmed, Nordstrum left through the field at the back, and headed into the hills. Over the next few days he made his way to the Skinnarland family farm, where there was an unused meat-curing hut in the woods only the family knew about. Emma, Einar's sister-in-law, brought him food and a blanket. The days were lonely and cold with only a woodstove there, but he filled his heart and warmed his bones with the belief that what he was doing was right and necessary. He slept with his gun on his pillow and kept his eye on the fields in case the Germans tracked him to the farm. After four days, when he was sure the coast was clear, he made his way back up onto the vidda.

In Uvdal he found a stone in Ox's mailbox.

There were messages back and forth now between Ox and Sassy (Hella's code name, a word Nordstrum had learned in England that well described her) and SOE in England. A cache of supplies was being dropped on the vidda, which he and Ox went out and retrieved, including a new radio. They reported the new troop intensification on the vidda and heard back that there might be a few more agents dropped in the area soon. The exchanges of information were working perfectly now; both Ox and Hella were well suited to the job. Though he had to admit he found his thoughts drifting far more to her than to the broad-shouldered slaughterhouse hand in his heavy oilskin coats.

SOE appeared to be pleased.

The best news he received was that Gunnerside had successfully made it to Sweden. All but one, they said. They had separated from the Yank. They feared him lost.

Gutterson. He was a good lad who had earned his place with them, and Nordstrum felt genuinely sorry to learn that.

"What's Gunnerside?" Hella asked in her father's cabin after handing him the decoded message.

Nordstrum shrugged. "Just some friends of mine."

"Well, they must be good friends. I've never seen you smile so widely as a moment before. Or now so sad."

"You know there are things I have to keep from you. And I do smile every now and then. I just haven't had much to smile about in the past few years. So is there anything to drink in the house? We should have a toast."

"My father kept something somewhere." Hella found some whisky and an old bottle of aquavit in a cabinet and poured out two glasses and they toasted to his friends' safe return, and to the Yank, whose fate was unknown.

"It would be good to go to Sweden." Hella sat down at the table. "It would be good for one week to pretend this war wasn't happening. I was in Stockholm a couple of times. With Anders."

"Maybe one day I'll take you," Nordstrum said.

"You and me?" She tilted her glass toward him. "So you actually do have a heart in there. Anyway, I must be ten years older than you. I'm sure you can find some pretty young thing who doesn't have two marks against her."

"One thing I've learned: In war, there's no such thing as

age. Or one's past. We're all the same. Anyway, if your husband doesn't return, consider it a date."

"I'll mark my calendar." She laughed. "But I won't buy an outfit just yet."

"I'm a man of my word." Nordstrum put down his glass. "Don't be so sure we won't."

Einar knew of someone in Miland who might be interested in some work, so Nordstrum traveled there by ferry and bus with a bag of tools, posing as a carpenter. The man was a beer salesman, which was perfect, as he was always on the road, so he could transmit from anywhere. His name was Reinar.

If a man was smart and careful, he would always say no, of course, to Nordstrum's initial entreaty for this kind of "work." And with good reason to be wary of the Gestapo's reach and infiltration into the general population.

Which Reinar did, of course. Even with Einar's recommendation.

Nordstrum would then give them a small radio where they could pick up the BBC.

"That's illegal, isn't it?"

"Tell me your mother's name," Nordstrum said. "Then listen to the news Friday."

"Her name?" Reinar said, cautious. "Her name's Regina."

"Remember." Nordstrum got up. "Friday."

Three days later, the lead-in: "A special greeting to Regina," was played just before the *News of the Night*, convincing Reinar that Nordstrum indeed had a genuine connection to England.

"So what's your favorite beer?" he asked Nordstrum on

their second time together, showing him his catalogue, which these days included Lowenbrau and Hofbrau from Germany.

"Guinness, these days," Nordstrum replied.

Reinar closed his catalogue. "Mine too."

The deal was fixed.

"If they search your car, you'll be shot," Nordstrum instructed him.

"Then a lot of people will go thirsty." The beer salesman smiled.

They needed a radio. Nordstrum placed a pebble in Hella's mailbox and put his coded message in a bottle in a drainage culvert near her home. She picked it up on the way to work.

Two days later she shifted the OPEN sign on her storefront from the front door to the left window. Nordstrum bought a pack of cigarettes at the tobacconist across the street. He skied up to her cabin that afternoon.

"Give them a week, they say." Hella handed him the message. He leaned his skis up and kicked the snow off his boots. "They'll drop the radio near Mosvatn on Saturday. If you need help, I'll go with you."

"*You?*" Nordstrum smiled. "A nice thought. But I'm afraid not."

"Why not? I can ski. Anders and I always vacationed in the mountains. I can handle a gun too. Look . . ." She had a Czech-made pistol in the drawer where the radio was.

Nordstrum smiled again. "I bet you can. But you never know what you might run into on the way. And anyway, you've become far too valuable where you are."

"Well, I won't let up. I can do more. Let me make you a tea."

"A quick one." Nordstrum took a glance out the window.

"I don't like the looks of it out there." He looked over the message one more time and fed it into the fire. "I've got a long trek. I should be on my way."

He watched her while she went to the wood-burning stove and put on some water. She looked pretty today. She always did. Today she wore a long white sweater and tight black wool stretch pants that accented her shape. Her hair, brown and thick with streaks of henna, fell below one shoulder in a loose braid.

"Milk?" She turned back and caught him watching her, as the water boiled.

"Black, please," Nordstrum said.

They talked a bit, about rumors of the impending Allied invasion, which was said might take place in Norway. About her husband, a school principal before the war. And for the first time she told him she had a son. He allowed her to freshen his cup one more time. Finally Nordstrum went to the window. "It's starting to snow."

Hella came over next to him and looked out as well. He was sure he smelled the scent he had sampled in her store. Persimmon. "How far do you have to go?"

"A fair way." He never told her where he stayed, in this case a hut by Lake Maure, if the Germans hadn't burned it. A good fifteen kilometers. He was always careful about that. In case she was discovered. And not to involve her any deeper than she already was.

"Maybe it'll stop soon," Nordstrum said.

"It's coming from the north," she said. "Not the best sign."

Their eyes met, and there was a moment between them, her braid falling over her chest and a silence long enough to take their thoughts to a place they might never have thought of. She said, "If you want, there's an extra blanket in the closet . . ."

He looked at her. *Why not?* he heard the voice inside him asking. Anything could happen. Who knew if they'd be alive in a week. Or even tomorrow.

"Hella."

"Make no mistake, I love my husband. But who knows when he's coming back. Or *if* . . . ?"

It would be so easy, Nordstrum thought. Putting his hand on her. He already felt her breaths going in and out. And it's not like he hadn't thought of it. But giving in would only make them careless, he knew. And expose them both. And feelings—in this war there was no place for them. *After* . . . That was another thing.

"When we go to Sweden." He smiled, his eyes showing a tinge of regret. He put his hand on Hella's shoulder. "You can wait?"

"Don't flatter yourself." She pulled away and smoothed her sweater. "I can wait."

"Good. I ought to be going now. We both should. Those tracks outside might alert some uninvited guests. I'll help you hide the radio." They had made a false compartment in the bedroom closet that would be hard to find.

"Of course." He detected a tremor of disappointment in her. As there was inside him as well. She stood up and looked at him with her dark, stolid eyes. "I have to be at the shop early tomorrow myself." Still she smiled. "Until Sweden then."

54

It didn't take two years as thought for the Nazis to resume their heavy water production at Vemork.

It only took two months.

By May, with Nordstrum having successfully developed five agents now, Einar passed along the news that the high-concentration cells, which Nordstrum and his team had executed such a daring raid to eliminate, had been repaired enough that production of new deuterium oxide was already under way. Since the distillation of new heavy water required an existing supply of finished product, canisters of D_2O that had previously been shipped to Germany were sent back to Vemork to accelerate the process.

Even more disturbing, according to Skinnarland's source inside the plant, the mandate from Berlin was no longer the 1,000 pounds per month Norsk Hydro had previously been maintaining, but now 3,000. Word was that the recent collapse of the German Army in Stalingrad gave Hitler new urgency to develop a weapon that could tilt the war his way.

All of this had the Joint Command in London in a state of high alarm, more convinced than ever that the Nazis were getting close to something. And in Washington, General Leslie Groves, the military head of the Manhattan Project, as well. He urged the commanders in London that the heavy water production at Vemork must be stopped at any cost, and this time for good.

But the raid on the Norsk Hydro plant had convinced the Nazis to redouble security measures at the plant—tripling the detachment of guards and replacing the old ones with fresh, crack troops; ringing the plant with dozens of barbed-wire fences and additional layers of mines; stationing guards on the roof, who now manned searchlights full time; and bricking over all doors to the facility, save one, and covering all windows with iron bars, making it virtually impossible to gain access to the plant through forced entry.

Back in London, SOE planners came to the conclusion that another raid like Gunnerside was impossible. The contingent needed to carry it out would have to be of such size that merely landing them in Norway without notice would be a feat. The raid itself would need to be a full-out assault. The plant's defenses were far too advanced now. And then escaping, even if they proved successful, across the vidda to Sweden, was another matter entirely. After the loss of life on Freshman, no one in Whitehall was prepared to sign off on such a risk: to send in highly trained soldiers and operatives with such a slim likelihood of ever returning.

There was one last option that loomed over the discussions. An option no one at SOE was in favor of.

In recent months, the United States Air Force had shown in other theaters that precision bombing was indeed possible now. Factions in Washington, D.C., and even in the Joint Command in London were pushing for such an action in Norway.

General Ira Eaker, in charge of the U.S. Eighth Air Force, in Britain, was tasked with studying the mission. But he could give no assurance other than saying such a raid could be carried off with only a "relative" prospect of success. The gorge was far too narrow and the target too protected by the canyon's walls. The compressors lay in the basement of a heavily constructed seven-story concrete structure. And all the smoke and dust that would result from the first wave of bombers that dropped their payloads would make visibility practically nil for the ones to follow.

Not to mention the dozens of civilians living within a few hundred meters of the plant, Tronstad pointed out, and the town of Rjukan, with over five thousand people in it, only a kilometer away, if things truly went awry.

Nonetheless, in London and Washington, Churchill and Leslie Groves knew the costs of doing nothing would become a whole lot higher.

The summer passed. Nothing happened. Nordstrum thought maybe they had come to their senses.

In October, he received a cable through Ox: *Most important to obtain exact information and conditions and volume of present production at Vemork. When is final production expected to commence? How will the product be transported? STOP.*

He was assigned the task of finding someone of authority on the inside who could answer these questions.

Now that Jomar Brun was in London, that left only one person.

55

Twice a week, Chief Engineer Alf Larsen stopped off at the bakery in Rjukan and brought home a small box of chocolates for himself, his one vice.

Larsen wasn't a drinker or a gambler; he preferred a night of bridge to poker or dice. In truth, he was never very comfortable with women, and in spite of his steady nature and well-paying job, he had never attracted a wife. He had worked all his career for the job he now held, though his appointment had been made only after the hasty departure of his predecessor and his family in the middle of the night. As much as he detested and feared the Nazis—they had terrorized the workers and narrowed the plant's entire production to their single military concern—resisting them meant certain death. They had made that abundantly clear. He simply resigned himself to do the job for which he was tasked and ride out the war. Stay under the radar, take no large risks; leave the fighting to others. A night of bridge on Saturday. An occasional chocolate. One day it would be all right.

"Here you are, Chief Larsen." The woman behind the counter tied up his box of chocolates.

"Thank you, Astrid." Larsen poked through his change and laid out the precise amount.

"See you Friday, I'm sure." The clerk smiled. "Almond brittle."

"God willing, I'll be here."

He got back in his Opel, which he had left in the alley

bordering the shop. He placed the box of candy on the passenger seat next to his briefcase and put his key in the ignition.

"Don't turn around, Chief Larsen."

He felt something metallic and cold against the back of his neck. His heart came to a stop. His eyes shot to the mirror and he saw the man in a woolen cap and clipped, blond beard in the backseat, his fingers wrapped around a gun.

"Don't be alarmed. Just drive. I only want a word with you. I'm sure this won't be necessary." He removed the gun and silencer from the back of his neck.

"Whoever you are, this isn't the way to do this," the engineer said, his eyes furtively shifting to the mirror. "You may know I'm being watched. The Gestapo may even be watching now. There are ears everywhere in Rjukan."

"That's why this is the *only* way to do this," Nordstrum said. "Just put the car in gear and drive. Maybe you can make a stop at Rolf's Tavern for a beer."

"*Rolf's?* That's on the way to Vigne, isn't it?"

"That's the place."

"You know, I don't drink."

"Don't drink? What a pity in this war. Not to worry, just drive there nonetheless."

Nodding tremulously, Larsen turned the key in the ignition and did as he was told.

Nordstrum said, "I'm sorry for the jolt to your heart. I assure you, I would never have used it," he said, putting the gun away. "But we need a hand inside the plant. As you know, the situation there has recently changed."

"Changed?" Larsen wove the car out of the town onto the main road east. "What's changed?"

"The heavy water production has changed," Nordstrum said, and for the first time, sat up behind him.

Larsen didn't say anything for a while. Then he just nodded. "Who are you with?"

"What does it matter who I'm with? I'm with the king, that's all you need to know. I'm with anyone who sees that the Allies must prevail and the Nazis must be stopped. Who are you with?"

"I'm for staying alive." Larsen cast a glance behind him. "Look, of course, I try to help. Like I told your friend Skinnarland—he is your friend, I assume—you just can't ask too much. There are too many eyes. It's far too dangerous."

"I know you try, Chief Larsen. Just keep driving. Einar said you were a good man. We know you're no Nazi. There'll just be a time when we'll need you to prove it in a deeper way."

"A deeper way . . . ?" Nordstrum noticed the engineer break out in a sweat. He drove on the winding road past Nordstrum's family house, taking the turnoff toward Vigne. Out here, the traffic was light. "Look, I'm not Tronstad. Or even Brun. I'm no hero. I do what I can."

"I'm afraid doing what you *can* do is no longer sufficient, Chief Engineer. You can see that, can't you? You're a scientist. You can't pretend. You see exactly what they want from you. And you also know why."

"Yes." Larsen met Nordstrum's eyes in the mirror. A bead of sweat wormed down his collar. "I know why."

"At some point," Nordstrum put his hand on the man's shoulder, "even those who have the most to lose have to act."

The harried chief engineer swallowed. He drove on a bit farther. "Look, I'll try to help. Where I can. How's that? I'll get you information. I can't promise more. Even you must know it's important to have someone like me inside. I can't jeopardize that."

"No one's looking to jeopardize that. I'm simply here to tell you that one day soon we are going to need more. You'll have to choose. You can drop me off around that curve."

Larsen slowed the car. Around the bend was a bus stop. A bicycle leaned against a rock. He pulled the car over. He waited a second, looking straight ahead, and said, "I honestly don't know if I'm your man."

"Oh, you're our man, Larsen. I'm sure of it. You'll hear from me again." Nordstrum slid out the door. "Look in the mirror, Chief Engineer, I think you'll find the answer. Maybe next time, we'll share a game of bridge. In the meantime . . ." Nordstrum shut the door and leaned inside the window. "Enjoy your chocolates."

56

With October came the snows. Nordstrum spent much of it shifting from place to place, developing his team of agents.

In the past months the German sweeps across the vidda had finally pulled back and become far less organized. Their assumption, according to Einar, who'd heard it from his sources at the plant, was that the team of agents responsible for the sabotage at the plant had likely long since left the country, and even if one had been sighted and was still in the region, production at Norsk Hydro was back under way and they could no longer justify such heightened troop levels in the pursuit of a single man. The Germans' real effort now was poured into fortifying the plant's defenses. They still had their W/T vehicles on patrol. Whoever was out there would make a mistake, they reasoned, and then they'd have him. Sooner or later, he'd fall into their hands.

That summer, Nordstrum heard through the network that his father had been transferred to the concentration camp at Grini. A death sentence, he knew, to a man in his condition. And not long after that he found out through a message snuck out from the camp that indeed his father had died.

What could I have done? he asked himself. Taken him from his house. To where? England, maybe? *How?* Another town? The old man would never have come. Organized a raid to spring him from the jail? Einar was right, such things would have been mere stupidity and jeopardized the cause. War just took things, Nordstrum had learned. Ground them up in its indifferent jaw, like a tank running over friend and foe alike, spitting them back out as memories. Now was not the time to regret anything. If anyone, his father would have understood. What could you do, Nordstrum came to view it, except to do everything you could to make sure those jaws didn't clamp their teeth on you one day and chew you up as well. That was all.

In mid-November Nordstrum made his rounds to Uvdal and noticed the CLOSED sign in Hella's shop placed in the window, and not on the door.

It was only four in the afternoon. Her shop lights were off. She knew to take the strictest precautions about leaving early or drawing attention to herself.

Clearly something had come in for him.

More than once he had thought about the time at her cabin when he'd almost given in, and often wished that he had. Since that time the moment and the opportunity had not coincided. Besides, he had a strict rule, and to let things go any further, even once, or to become involved, would only expose them both to danger. For now it was about the war. *Afterward . . . ?* Still, what was there to stop them, he sometimes let himself think. Tomorrow they could both be dead. It would give him something pleasurable and life affirming to take his mind from all the death he'd seen. Even if only for a few hours.

But he did not.

There was adequate snow, so Nordstrum skied the hour-long trek from town to her cabin. He was always careful to avoid any travelers on the way, especially in the summer and fall when there were more people in the mountains. Today, he passed only two. He merely pulled up his mask to hide his face. "Good day!" He waved to them as he passed by. As he neared the valley where her cabin was located, he noticed a low-flying Storch in the sky, buzzing around. What was it looking for here? He took cover until it went away.

In another mile or so, the maze of public ski tracks ended and he picked up what he assumed was Hella's single track on the way to her cabin. At first he felt lifted that she would be there, though a stab of uneasiness picked up in him, as examining her trail, he began to feel the tracks were not fresh. Maybe even from the day before.

As he glided down the final ridge, still a kilometer or so away, any concern he had intensified into outright worry.

A second track seemed to have intercepted hers. A vehicle. It looked like that of a German half-track with its wide treads, the only thing that could get around in the mountains. It came from the west, from Haukeli maybe, a village known to be full of Germans.

A knot tightened in Nordstrum's chest.

The German W/T patrols were always a constant threat. Which was why they had to make their transmissions brief and infrequent. And why a skilled operator was the only kind that survived.

And Hella was as smart and careful as they came.

A short distance away, he took out his binoculars and scanned the surrounding hills, worried the house might be under watch. He saw no sign of anyone. Still, what he saw on the snow was not a good sign. He increased his pace, finally coming around the lake and in sight of the cabin. A thin trail of smoke came out of the chimney, heartening him. Hopefully she was there and all was fine. The radio was well hidden behind the false wall in the bedroom. He only prayed Hella hadn't been in the act of transmitting when they showed up. But if anyone could hold herself together through such a visit, it was her.

Even more worrisome, the half-tracks led directly to her door.

Nordstrum skied up quietly and took off his skis. *Are they still here?* He pulled out his Colt. Before entering, he searched the perimeter of the cabin. No sign of anyone. But what he did see in the snow was the second set of vehicle tracks, the half-track, heading off to the west. And no sign of Hella having left—unless she'd been taken in and was now in custody.

He noticed her skis were stacked outside.

He went up to the door, cocked his Colt close to his chest, and called out, "*Hella . . . ?*"

There was no reply.

"*Hella!*" he shouted again. He waited. Nothing.

He pushed open the front door.

She was there, in a chair at the table where she did her transmissions, and he was about to relax and say, "Oh, good, you're here . . ." when he noticed her mouth parted slightly and her head crooked on her shoulder and her eyes staring blankly ahead.

Her white sweater was dotted with crimson holes.

"*My God, Hella!*"

Her gun was on the floor, the gun she boasted she could use so adroitly, which she clearly had gone for in the drawer, now hanging open loosely. The radio was on the floor, hammered into a dozen useless pieces, riddled with bullets. The door to the bedroom was ajar, and the false wall they had built in the closet ripped open.

Nordstrum sank into a chair next to her and shook his head sadly. "Hella, no . . ."

Sitting there, she looked as beautiful and as defiant as when he had first seen her from across the restaurant. He placed his hand against her cheek. It was cold, cold as a mossy rock in January, but still smooth. Smoother than there was a right to feel in such a war.

He detected a hint of persimmon on her. It made him smile.

He found a blanket folded over a chair and draped it over her. It was better to leave her as she was, he thought, painful as it was. She'd be missed. People in town must know about the farm. Someone would come to look soon enough. Her son would need to be told. She deserved a hero's burial, not just to lie here, exposed and alone. But that was best.

For a second he considered the possibility that they had been betrayed. Ox? Reinar? He had never spoken of her to anyone. Just as he had never spoken of them to her. No one would connect them. "*There are others, I assume . . . ?*" she had once asked him, with that smart smile of hers and bright, almond eyes.

Others, yes, but not like you.

No one like you.

Maybe all she'd been was simply unlucky. Maybe the Germans were just patrolling the hills nearby when they caught her signal. Anyone knew, luck trumped all the courage and preparation in the world any day. They would have definitely taken her in, perhaps forced her to give him up— *maybe even threatened her son*—had she not gone for her gun, and—

A stab of dread knifed through him.

He looked to the open drawer and pawed around inside. It wasn't there. Then he remembered, she usually kept it with the equipment. In a sweat, he ran into the bedroom closet, got on his knees, and frantically searched in all the corners of the false compartment.

Nothing there either.

His heart began to race. If he didn't find it, it was more of a loss than the radio. More of a loss than any of their lives. A sweat broke out on his neck. SOE would have to know.

His gaze traveled to the hearth, which was still smoldering, and he saw the shredded embers of the black notepad amid the coals.

The codebook.

He let out a relieved breath.

When they had come, knowing she had no time to hide the radio, that she was likely done, she still had the presence of mind to toss it into the flames before going for her gun. She could have traded it for something, he knew. *Her life? Her son's?* But she did what he would have done. He reached in and picked it out of the fire, the crisp, charred pages that were still warm shredding in his hands.

She hadn't given him up.

"*Someone's got to do something,*" she'd once said to him. And she had. She'd done her job.

Nordstrum stoked the flame, throwing on another log, tossed the charred codebook back on the fire, and waited until it broke up into ashes. Then he went back and draped the blanket over her face. "You can rejoin your Anders now," he said, recalling the officer he had once seen in the Gudbrandsdalen. It was as good as any blessing he knew.

Then he went back outside and put on his skis. He left, heading east. Toward Rauland. The thought went through him that he had been foolish to allow any attachments in this war. Attachments could only cause regret and death and there was already enough of both without adding to the flame.

A day later, that feeling would grow far, far stronger.

57

Dieter Lund was at his desk in Rjukan when he heard the first rumbles.

It was just after noon. He was contemplating heading home and taking his lunch with Trudi when the building, then the entire valley, began to shake. At first it sounded like thunder in the far-off sky. Then all of a sudden the ground began to tremble. He ran to the window. The sky was perfectly blue. It wasn't thunder. Certainly not an earthquake. Maybe a landslide somewhere, above the gorge. Such a thing had happened years before. But then Lund realized it was only November and there was not nearly enough snow for such a thing to—

Then he heard the first deafening blasts and the sirens start to sound. He felt the ground shake beneath him and he knew precisely what was taking place.

They were bombs.

The Allies were bombing Norsk Hydro.

In a flash the sky became dark with a sea of planes. Dozens. Hundreds, maybe. American planes. Through the mist and smoke, the Stars and Stripes could be plainly seen on their fuselages. Suddenly the ground exploded all around. He should hit the floor, he knew, or take cover under his desk; it was a heavy one and would keep him safe if the building came down around him. But Lund remained at the window, staring. Incredulous. The streets of Rjukan lit up with fire. People on the street were screaming, running for cover, their hands over their heads.

They were bombing the fucking factory, the fools, and wayward bombs were landing here.

The concussion from distant explosions shook the town. Every once in a while, a bomb exploded closer to home. One street away, a building collapsed in a ball of flame, debris hurtling into the street. Wood flying, roofs crumbling. Fires springing up all around.

Were they mad? No air force on earth could be so precise, or bombs so powerful, as to bring down the Norsk Hydro factory. It was simply protected too well by the narrow gorge in which it stood. Lund knew what they were after. The compressors, in the basement. Underneath a building of solid concrete, sturdier than any other structure in Rjukan. In all of Norway, perhaps.

The valley shook as wave after wave of planes came in. The skies were opaque with an umbrella of gray dust.

Corporal Holquvist ran into his office. "Captain, please, you must get down! You can't stay there!"

Lund ignored him. He remained, eyes fixed on the rain of bombs leveling the town, wooden structures bursting into flame, concrete buildings crumbling.

"Damn you!" he screamed at the sky.

Not from any sympathy for what he saw. Or about the destruction to his own town. Still, it was almost as if his own heart was being torn apart. His future. What was in the basement of that plant was as important to him as it was to any physicist or party leader in Berlin.

"Corporal, get my car."

"Your car . . . ?" Dust came down from the roof after a close hit. The corporal looked at Lund as if he were mad. "Captain, I'm sorry, but we have to wait this out. No one can possibly drive in this."

"Order my car!" Lund turned and said. "Or so help me, Corporal, I'll strap you to that plant myself and find someone who will."

58

Nordstrum heard of the raid while in Rauland with Reinar, and rushed back to witness the bombing runs on the second and third days, a feeling of both hope and sadness in his heart.

Hope—quickly dashed—that the raid would prove successful, as each new bomber dropped its payload against the seemingly impregnable factory. Nordstrum was one of very few who knew the true reason for the attack.

And sadness, as he watched his own town come under attack. The cratered buildings, the fires all around, the horror of innocent townspeople who had no idea why they were being attacked. Streets reduced to rubble. If the Allies claimed they knew how to conduct a raid of such precise bombing, what Nordstrum witnessed in anger showed they had a long way to go.

Over those three days, three hundred U.S. Air Force B-17 Flying Fortresses and Liberator bombers pounded the Norsk Hydro facility with over seven hundred five-hundred-pound bombs. They also targeted the Saaheim plant in Rjukan, where it was thought some of the finished heavy water stock was being stored. According to the *Rjukan Daily Times*, which continued publishing, even the very next day, twenty-one civilians were killed in town and in the houses that ringed the plant, and sixteen in a bomb shelter, where women and children had gathered, and which took a direct hit.

When at last the smoke subsided, the Norsk Hydro factory still stood unscathed with barely a mark.

Over the next week, England radioed Nordstrum over and over:

"*Please send earliest possible information on success of American air attack.*"

"*Urgent. Need information on current IMI status.*" IMI was the code name SOE used for heavy water.

Gradually, information leaked from the plant. One of Einar's sources secretly met with him at the market in Vigne. He told him the stocks of heavy water in the high-concentration room had suffered no damage at all. The processors and the canisters of finished inventory were untouched. However, he told him, the hydroelectric power station *had* been struck, incapacitating the massive turbines that produced the power for the D_2O electrolysis process to take place. Given the vast amount of power needed to run the processors and the Allies' ongoing effort to destroy them, the engineers ultimately decided that further repairs and construction to continue the operations would be pointless.

"*By all accounts, heavy water production put on hold,*" Nordstrum radioed back to England. Further distillation was now stopped. Still, there was adequate finished inventory already stored there that continued to pose a real problem. And by draining the cells, Einar's source told him, the Germans were able to almost double the amount of "juice" in their possession, even though not all of it was fully concentrated, giving them close to eleven thousand pounds.

Nordstrum traveled to the town of Porgrum at the end of January and met with a representative from Milorg, the Norwegian underground, which his own small network of agents was now a part of.

"It's possible they will try to move what they have," he told the Milorg man, whose name was Rolf and who was from Oslo. "Once it leaves the area, it will have to be put on trains and ships. Perhaps you have contacts on the docks?"

"Contacts, yes, but trained agents . . . ? That's a whole other thing. Plus, the docks and train station are closely watched by the Germans. How large a shipment are we talking?"

"Twenty to thirty drums. Maybe more. Several truckloads. They'll have everyone protecting it. And they won't exactly be telegraphing the time and place when they move it. Or how."

"Maybe the Brits can bomb it from the air?" Rolf suggested. "Or attack the ship."

"We've already seen the wisdom of that. We can likely let you know when it's on the move." Nordstrum got up. "The rest . . . ?" He shrugged, helpless. "It would be wise to get your men on the docks alerted."

"So what the hell is this stuff anyway?" Rolf asked as he put out his cigarette. "Heavy water?"

"All I know is, we lost thirty-six lives trying to eliminate it. Ask London if you want to know, but they won't tell you any more."

59

On his way back to Rjukan, Nordstrum took the ferry up the Heddasvat to Nottogen. He was dressed in a calfskin jacket and thick wool sweater. His hair had grown out a bit and these days he sported a light beard and fake wire-rim glasses.

The day was clear and the trip calm, the mountains reflecting off the water's ice-blue surface. Nordstrum leaned on the railing in the stern deck with a smoke. He had seen a few Hirden on board, but it was worth the risk, he decided, for a few moments simply to enjoy the view. It had been a year since the Norsk Hydro sabotage, and his face was no longer on most people's minds.

A woman came out to stand near him to take in the view from the deck. She was pretty, in her early twenties, he thought, in a stylish purple wool shawl. A woman of some means, he assumed, and taste. Her brown hair was blown by the breeze, and she grabbed at her brimmed hat to keep it from being swept into the lake. Taste perhaps, but not wisdom, he chuckled to himself. A Norwegian woman would have known better.

She let out a cry as without warning her hat fell out of her grasp and blew toward the railing. Nordstrum took a quick step to his left and blocked it with his foot at the railing.

"Madame," he said in Norwegian, as he picked it up, brushed it off, and presented it back to her.

"*Tussen tak*," the woman said with an appreciative smile, in what Nordstrum perceived as a Germanic accent. She went to pin it back on and Nordstrum gave her a slight shake of his head, to suggest, given the breezy conditions, perhaps it wasn't the smartest idea. "*Bist du Deutscher?*" he enquired.

"*Nein. Oustereichsch,*" she replied. Austrian. "*Sprechen sie Deutsch?*"

"*Nein,* I'm afraid." Nordstrum shook his head again.

"*Français?*"

"*Juste un peu.*" He shook his head again. "English, perhaps?"

"Yes, English, a little," she said, nodding. "I guess it was clear I am not Norwegian," she admitted, a glimmer of embarrassment in her pretty brown eyes.

"Well, yes, a Norwegian woman would never step out on deck without a firm grasp on her hat, that's true. A clear giveaway," Nordstrum said.

"Ah . . ." She smiled. "Next time I shall be in the know."

"And if you are trying to appear Norwegian," Nordstrum looked down, "I'm sorry, but such shoes, though stylish, will not do you much good in the snow, which can come up at the snap of your fingers," he said with a smile of his own.

"Yes." She looked down too. Her short black leather boots might be comfortable for a long journey, but . . . "Even in Austria, you are right on that. But I took a chance on the day."

"You are a long way from home," Nordstrum shrugged, "so it's forgivable. Where are you heading?"

"Nottogen," she said, pronouncing it with a hard *g*, in the German manner.

"Nottogen," he corrected her gently.

"Nottogen . . ." she said again.

"Spoken like a true Norwegian. And what's in Nottogen,

if I may ask? There's not much there but a whaling museum and lots and lots of lutefisk."

"I am accompanying my grandfather, who's inside. He's a cellist. His name is August Ritter. Perhaps you know of him? We're here for a series of concerts in Norway. Do you know music?"

"I played the clarinet as a boy. Terribly, I should say. Finally they simply barred me from continuing."

"You clearly moved on to football goalie then, I see. You showed great skill in saving my poor hat."

"I merely put out my foot and it stuck." Nordstrum shrugged modestly. "A lucky grab."

"Well, it impressed me. Actually my grandfather is quite well known. He's played with the Vienna Philharmonic. Nottogen," she pronounced it correctly now, "is our third stop of the tour. We've already been to Oslo and Sognefjord."

"And how long will you be in Nottogen?" Nordstrum asked. "I don't think of it as a center of music in Norway."

"Actually, the German Army sponsors his tour. We'll be there three days only. And from there we go on to Rjukan."

"Rjukan . . ." Nordstrum replied with curiosity.

"Do you know it? I hear it is very chilly there."

"It's chilly everywhere in Norway. But Rjukan has a climate of its own, you're right. I'm afraid you'll have to retire those pretty shoes for good, if you'll be there for any time."

"I have boots with me as well. And we'll stay a week. He performs two concerts there. One for the army. The other for the townspeople. He insisted on that."

"At the King Edvard Hall?"

"So you know the place?" She looked at him with curiosity.

"Yes. A bit." *I'm heading there myself,* he was about to

divulge, then thought better of it. He took out a cigarette. "Do you smoke?"

"Thank you, no. My grandfather says it makes the cello out of tune." She turned and rested her arms on the railing and looked out. Nordstrum found he could not take his eyes away from her. "It's so very beautiful here."

"When the storms come, it's quite another thing. And they come frequently."

"Well today we seem to be in luck. In fact, so far we have only been blessed with sunny days in Norway."

"Then you must stay for a bit longer. You'll see. So look, do you see that mountain? All the way out there . . ." Nordstrum pointed across the lake to the highest snowcapped peak. "That's called the Odinskjegg. Legend has it Odin himself would go there to trim his beard, as he could see himself in the lake."

"The Odinskjegg," she repeated.

"Yes. A hard 'g' this time."

"Odinskjegg. And people say German is a difficult language."

"We Vikings know how to build ships, but don't talk so much, so that's what we ended up with."

She laughed. "So do you really believe that?"

"About the Vikings? It's true, I'm afraid."

"I meant about the legend you spoke of."

"The Odinskjegg?" He shrugged. "In times like these, it's not so bad to believe in something. Even a folk tale."

"Or a Beethoven concerto."

"Or a Beethoven concerto, why not? Though here, we prefer Sibelius and Grieg."

"My grandfather plays Sibelius as well," she said. "And Grieg's Holberg Suite."

"Is that so?" He watched her as she stared out at the snowcapped peaks, leaning on her toes. They remained silent for a while. The ferry cut through the breeze on the silvery lake, and she shielded her eyes from the bright sun. He knew it was silly to feel anything but a moment's diversion. In Nottogen their paths would diverge and likely never cross again.

"No," he said, out of the blue. "To your question, I never did believe much of that. The trolls and all . . . But at the very least, it makes a nice story."

He finished his smoke and tossed the butt into the lake.

She looked at him. "My grandfather will be wondering where I am. He's probably thinking I fell overboard. He cautioned me not to talk too much to the people here. He said German speakers are not so well liked here."

"No more than the Vikings would be if we rode down the streets of Vienna in tanks and trucks. However, in your case we'll make an exception. Your command of English has saved you."

"Thank you for my hat, Herr . . . ?"

"Holgersen," he said, after a moment's pause, giving her the name on his forged identity papers. "I was glad to help, Fraulein Ritter. Perhaps I will see you again when we disembark."

"I'll wear this hat." She turned as she headed back toward the first-class compartment. "That way, you'll be sure to distinguish me from all the Norwegians."

The rest of the trip Nordstrum didn't think on much else, going back over their conversation. He thought he could have been wittier, and maybe not so dour when it came to the Occupation or the weather. Even in war, he thought, did people not laugh, smile, drink, even fall in love? Even with a pretty Austrian gal who would be out of Norway in a week and he would never see again.

Still . . . The fates of Hella and Anna-Lisette were never far from his mind. When you let your guard down, he reminded himself, look what can happen.

He tossed another cigarette butt into the Heddasvat. The Odinskjegg had now ducked behind the clouds.

Still, as the ferry docked in Nottogen, he searched for her amid the crowd. Her grandfather was in a dark coat and full suit, maybe seventy, with a head of thinning white hair under a low knit cap. They walked slowly as the crowd filled in around them near the off-ramp, the musician clutching his instrument case. At the ramp a crewman brought their bags.

"May I help?" Nordstrum edged over to her from the crowd. "I saw the hat. I couldn't help but be drawn to it."

"Thank you," she said brightly. He could see she was happy he had found her again. "Grandfather, this is Herr Holgersen," she said in German. "He saved my hat from a watery grave. But in fact," she turned back, "I think we are being met by our hosts."

On the dock, next to a large Daimler with red flags with Nazi crosses on it, two German officers were waving to get their attention. One, a major, seemed to pick them out of the crowd on deck, and shouted above the throng. "Herr Ritter! Over here!"

"Ah, Natalie, *schau!*" Ritter pointed toward them, waving back.

"Please allow me anyway." Nordstrum took their two heavy suitcases across the ramp and placed them on the wharf. The German officers hurried up to them and warmly shook hands. Nordstrum didn't want to get too close, though the officers were far too excited to greet their famous guest to have even the remotest interest in him. He said with a shrug, "If all is well, then, I think I'll leave you to your hosts."

"Thank you again," Natalie Ritter said. He detected a touch of disappointment, as this was where their paths would diverge. Were life different, he would have surely found a way to ask her to a drink or to dinner.

"Perhaps we shall see you in Rjukan? At the King Edvard Hall?" she said.

"You never know. Life takes you where you least expect." He shrugged. But the place would be crowded with Germans, and who knew where he'd have to be. "I wish you the very best. For your hat, and for your concerts, Fraulein Ritter."

"Natalie," her grandfather cut them off. The officers had placed their bags in the car.

"I'll say good-bye then." Nordstrum stepped back.

She nodded, showing disappointment too. "Good-bye."

With a glance at the German officers, Nordstrum edged his way into the safety of the crowd. When he turned back, he watched Natalie and her grandfather step into the car and, with a beep of the horn to clear the way, drive off.

Stupid, he told himself again, to even think of it. Still he whispered her name out loud. "*Natalie.*"

60

Nordstrum spent the week on business trying to assess what the Germans' intentions were with the plant, and it was only when Einar contacted him, saying it was urgent they speak the following morning, that Nordstrum ventured into town. Natalie had crossed his mind many times in the past few days, but just as quickly he'd pushed the thought away, as something that might have had hope if he was not in the midst of a war, but now had no prospect. Not to mention she was an Austrian citizen who would be gone in a week, and in the meantime, was surrounded by a company of Germans.

Still, he did come down into town the night of the concert from the hut at Swansu to wait in the shadows of the Mercantile League building across from King Edvard Hall. He did not dare go in, of course. It was far too risky. He was still a hunted man, though it had been a year since the raid and his face was no longer on every door. But from across the street he did hear the pleasing sound of a cello from within, punctuated by peals of enthusiastic applause.

He had no real intention to meet her—there were far too many Germans around. Still, he was here, even if inside he couldn't fully answer why.

After what he was sure was the final applause, the doors of the hall opened and spectators streamed out—mostly Germans of all ranks and a few Hirden, some with women on their arms, which made the bile in Nordstrum's gut rise. There were collaborators in every crowd.

He waited across the street from the side entrance, the

performers' door. Several German officers and a few town dignitaries congregated there. A voice inside him told him to go. Go. He had no business here. But after a few minutes, the doors opened and Ritter and Natalie came out, to much attention. She was beautiful, dressed in a tasteful red dress with a brooch on her breast, her hair pinned up, a black wool coat covering her against the cold, and this time, to his amusement, she wore real boots. Still, her smile was as radiant as her dress as she greeted and shook the hands of the well-wishers, German and Norwegian alike, tied to her grandfather's arm.

At a lull, her gaze drifted to the street, in some disappointment perhaps, as if expecting someone who did not show.

Nordstrum stepped out of the shadows.

She saw him. Her face lit up. There was no way to hide it. She waited for him to come over, but he motioned her over to him. After she shook another hand or two, she whispered something in her grandfather's ear and, buttoning her coat, came across the street.

"I'm happy to see you," she said brightly.

"Me, as well," he said. "I found myself here after all. Would you mind stepping over here?" Out of the glare of the street, a few feet down the alley. The congratulations were ongoing. No one seemed to have noticed her departure.

"Were you at the concert?" she asked.

"I'm sorry," Nordstrum lied, "music is not my passion. But I see you are now in the height of Norwegian fashion." He acknowledged her laced boots.

"Yes, after your lesson I'm trying hard to fit in. We are going to have dinner back at the hotel with some of our hosts. Are you available to join us?"

"I'm afraid not," he declined. His eye shot across the

street to the crowd of officers and Hirden. "And I'm afraid I'm not dressed for the occasion."

"I understand," she said. "I told Papa I had a headache and would meet him back at the hotel. At the very least you can walk me there." It still wasn't the smartest idea, but Nordstrum didn't want to give her any cause to suspect him. Or disappoint her. The crowd had now dispersed. "It would be my pleasure."

It was only two or three blocks. And while Rjukan was a tiny town, he led her to the side of the street. A couple of Germans went by, tipping their caps to Natalie. "Fraulein." Maybe they had been inside.

Nordstrum averted his gaze as they went by.

"You don't seem to be at home in the company of Germans," Natalie observed.

"As I told you, they are occupiers of my country," Nordstrum said. "I feel like a lot of the people do."

"You know, to some, Austria is an occupied country as well. The *Anschluss* that merged our countries is not how all of us feel."

"Still, your grandfather plays Beethoven and Bach, serenading the Nazis."

"Yes, the Germans come to hear," Natalie said. "A musician plays to his audience. So who is your audience, Mr. Holgersen? Besides saving ladies' hats, what is it you do?"

"I was studying to be an engineer before the war."

"An engineer. Buildings? Ships?"

"More like bridges and dams."

"And whose bridges or dams would *you* be building these days, if you had the chance? Norway's or the Reich's?" She stopped. "In war, we all do things that are not a matter of choice. I'm sure you understand."

"Of course I understand," he said. "The answer is, if directed to, I would not be building bridges or dams right now."

He looked at her. Her eyes glistened in the lamplight. As bold as it would have been, if he wasn't in public, with a hundred Germans only paces away, he might have kissed her right there.

"How long will you be staying?" he asked instead, taking her arm and continuing down the hill.

"We have another performance scheduled for the sixteenth. Next Sunday. Then we are off to Oslo and Copenhagen on the morning ferry on Monday, and back home. Are you around in Rjukan during that time?"

He didn't answer right away. He had a job to do. Even to be here now was a risk. Her hotel was just ahead. As they approached, he noticed too many Hirden and Germans for him to go any farther. He led her to the side under a shop's canopy. "I think it's best I leave you here."

"If I told my grandfather my headache would cause me to miss supper, would you be able to dine with me?"

"I can't." Though nothing would have pleased him more. "I'm sorry."

She took his arm. "Well, anyway, I'm very pleased you showed up. I was wondering if you would. Perhaps I will see you again before we leave."

"That would be my wish."

"My wish as well." She stood on her tiptoes and gave him a kiss on the cheek. She said with a wry smile, "I'm not sure you could be building any bridges these days, Mr. Holgersen, given how you seem to keep to yourself."

He squeezed her hand as she went into the lobby. She turned back once with a smile, and then he saw her being greeted by the throng of fawning German officers. "Ah, Fraulein Ritter . . ."

Averting his face, Nordstrum headed back up the hill. He wished this war would be over at last. He was tired of having to live life in the shadows.

61

Dieter Lund heard August Ritter's performance at the concert hall, seated in the third row, next to Trudi, who was bulging a bit out of some new bright red dress she had ordered from Copenhagen, and Major Ficht, newly in charge of the security team at Vemork.

The old cellist held the house spellbound, playing Brahms, Mozart, and Beethoven, and finishing with a Grieg concerto.

At the end, the hall stood and erupted in applause.

It was true Lund knew little about classical music. It had never been something that had interested him much in his youth. Or that he'd had the time or the inclination for since then. And now that he served the Germans, he tried to stay out of those conversations when they turned to culture or the arts.

But one thing he did know was that he had never seen anyone quite as beautiful as the cellist's granddaughter who had accompanied him to Norway. During the concert, he could not take his eyes off her, seated in the balcony above them. He had met her as part of the delegation upon her arrival in Rjukan and offered to make her and her grandfather's stay as pleasant as possible. Perhaps even a private tour of their beautiful region, he proposed.

Staring up at her, his eyes flitting between Ritter and the occasional, perfunctory smile at his wife, he couldn't believe the wild thoughts that were dancing through his head.

Later, he was among those invited to dine with August Ritter and his granddaughter at the Prinzregent Hotel. It was an honor, he knew, to even be included. Among the dignitar ies were Gestapo chief Muggenthaler and Josef Terboven, the German civilian attaché in Norway, and the heads of the German cultural legation. Trudi was not asked to attend, as none of the other officers had their wives, which was fine with Lund. And when he saw Natalie Ritter come down the street from the concert hall at the hotel, he felt goose bumps on his arms in the greeting line. He thought and thought about what he would say. She had several days to fill here. He chastised himself that he had let such an unlikely fantasy interfere with his thoughts of the real work that needed to be done.

As she arrived he noticed a man, maybe twenty yards up the street, heading back up the hill. There was a momentary familiarity about him and then he was gone. And she was here, radiant as ever, distracting his attention.

"Fraulein Ritter . . ." Lund took her hand. Then just as quickly the dignitaries swallowed her up and escorted her to the dining room for dinner.

After dinner, the thought still nagging him, he took her aside. "If I might ask, Fraulein, who was that man I saw you with as you arrived at the hotel?"

"Merely a friend," Natalie Ritter replied. "I met him on our journey here."

"And does your friend have a name?" Lund pushed, traversing the delicate boundary between politeness and insistence that was his learned terrain. "Perhaps we can invite him along for our ride."

"Do the police always enquire so boldly of personal things here in Norway, Captain . . . ?" she said back.

"Lund." He bowed again as he reminded her.

"Yes. Captain Lund. Leave it that he is simply a friend.

I met him in my travels. If the police require more, I'm sure my grandfather would be happy to accompany me to your headquarters."

Lund smiled. This girl had a resiliency beyond her young looks. "That will hardly be necessary." He took a step back. "I merely thought he looked familiar. My apologies, Fraulein, if in any way I have—"

An SS major stepped up, his gushing captivation diverting her attention, and then Lund was left standing by himself, a familiar hole of feeling ignored expanding in his chest, and then a face coming into his mind, like a dark cloud sweeping over the mountains, foretelling rain on even the brightest of days. *Someone I met on my travels.* A face he pushed back, distracted by the toast taking place now, and he looked at her surrounded by fawning officers, convincing himself that no, of course, it could not be.

62

Having agreed to meet Einar the next day, Nordstrum spent the night in the custodian's room at a warehouse in Rjukan. In the morning, he got on the bus to Vigne, which was filled with people on their way to work. Einar met him in his car on his way to work in Mosvatn.

They hadn't seen each other for months, since the day Nordstrum had tried to free his father. "How have you been, Kurt?" his friend asked. "The work must be appealing, you look a little different than I've seen you."

"Different?" Nordstrum was groomed. His beard was trimmed a bit.

"I don't know . . ." His friend took a long look at him. "Happy, somehow."

"Who knows? Must be all the good weather lately."

"Well, I'm afraid what I have to tell you will make you anything but happy. I've heard from inside the plant that the Germans are planning on moving their stocks of heavy water back to Germany."

"To Germany?" Clearly that meant they'd made enough to do the job. "When?"

"Soon. A week, maybe. My man wasn't sure."

"A week? You're sure of this?" In such a short time, it was virtually impossible to organize anything with England to stop it.

"He said they've shut down the compressors and are in the process of draining the cells. So far, it seems they've built up an inventory of around eleven thousand pounds."

"The people at SOE won't be very happy to hear this," Nordstrum said.

"They should have thought of that possibility when they recklessly bombed the plant. What other option was there for the Germans to do? We forced their hand."

Nordstrum nodded and blew a blast of air out his cheeks. "The place is overflowing with SS. The new security measures make it almost impossible to get a team back inside. Even if we could get one together . . ."

"Yes, I advised them of that," Einar said.

"And what was the reply?"

"Here . . ." Einar reached in his pocket and handed Nordstrum the handwritten message, from Tronstad himself.

It read, *Under no circumstance must the shipment be allowed to leave. Organize a local team and carry it out. All good luck.*

"All good luck . . ." Nordstrum gave a cynical chuckle and handed it back to Einar.

"You're the only trained operative in the area, Kurt. Who else is there? I've never pulled a trigger in my life."

A *week*? A team of thirty to forty trained commandos might be able to fight their way into the high-concentration room now. Two or three, they'd be cut down before they even got inside. Of course, there was the route back to Germany. There could be many points along the way that were vulnerable. "Do we have any idea how it's being shipped?"

"That's all a big secret, as is the exact date. But we both know there is one person inside we can go to who would have to know those things."

Einar stopped the car in front of the bus stop that headed back to Rjukan. Nordstrum knew precisely whom he meant.

It was Tuesday. Tomorrow was chocolate day.

"I think it's time to see just how far the good engineer's loyalties are prepared to go."

63

In the late afternoon that day, the phone rang at Alf Larsen's desk at the plant. With all the preparations under way to transfer the heavy water stocks, he'd barely left it in the past two days.

"Chief Larsen . . . ?"

"Who is this?"

"I'm wondering if you are up for a night of bridge? I told you I'd be calling soon if I found the right game. There's one planned for tonight."

"Tonight? Tonight, I'll be working," the engineer replied, his heart leaping up with nerves. He knew precisely who it was. His Gestapo overseer, Captain Stauber, peered up from his desk across the room.

"This one I strongly advise you to make," the caller said. "All the best players in town will be there."

Larsen hesitated as long as he could. Even he didn't know just how he would answer. Finally he drew in a short breath and asked under his breath, "Where?"

"Usual place. How does eight o'clock sound?"

"Eight o'clock," Larsen muttered, pretending to scribble it down.

"So can we count on you, Chief Larsen? Seats are filling quickly."

Larsen gave an eye to the captain and turned a page in his report. "I'll do my best to be there."

"Your best, Chief Engineer . . . ?"

"Yes, I'll be there." He hung up.

"What was that, Herr Larsen?" Stauber, a short, pasty-faced policeman from Dresden, so chubby he looked out of place in his black Gestapo uniform, looked up from his workstation. "You're looking a little pale."

"Just bridge, Herr Major." The engineer cleared his throat, wiping the film of sweat off his forehead.

"Bridge . . . ?" the German questioned.

"Yes, Herr Captain, bridge. Do you play?"

"No, Chief Engineer. I'm afraid I don't."

"It is quite a welcome distraction from all the work. You should learn sometime."

That evening, Larsen remained at his desk until a quarter to eight, a few minutes after his Gestapo watchdog finally grew so bored or hungry he called it a night. Larsen, checking the time that seemed to move at a snail's pace at least a dozen times, was not sure, until the very moment he cleaned his desk and packed up his briefcase, what he would do.

He could easily not attend. They had no leverage to make him. Surely that would be the far safer course.

In the end he filed his reports away and slipped a paper from a folder marked PRIVATE BUSINESS into his jacket pocket. He said good-bye to the night manager as he always did, and drove to the Kjellssons', home of a chemical engineer on his staff, a short distance from the plant, where they held a regular game each Saturday night.

He pulled his Opel up to the stone house, checking that no one had followed, and cut the ignition. He had a throbbing in his chest that said he was crossing a line, his heart readily stepping over, but his body unwilling to move.

That was when the passenger door opened and the man

he had met with two weeks before slipped into the seat across from him.

"Sorry to disappoint, Chief Engineer, but I'm afraid tonight's game has been canceled."

"You're playing with fire to contact me that way. You know I'm being watched?"

Nordstrum said, "We're all being watched these days, Chief Larsen. And yet you are here."

"I came merely to tell you to back off from contacting me at the office. Security is far too tight."

"Did you now? I believe you came because you know precisely what it is we need to know from you. The stocks of deuterium oxide are being transferred back to Germany. And I believe you know how? And when?"

Larsen blew out air from his nose and rested his head back on the seat.

"Time is short, Chief Larsen, and there's no point in misplaced loyalties to people who may well shoot you after it's gone for as much as you know."

"Yes." He finally blew out a breath. "It is leaving. On Saturday, I think."

"You cannot think, Chief Engineer. We must be sure. "

"On Saturday," he said again, firmer.

Four days.

"Is there enough of it for them to do the job?" Nordstrum pressed.

"You mean build a weapon?" Larsen looked at him and shrugged. "I'm a chemical engineer," he said, "not an atomic scientist. You'll have to ask that question to your friend Tronstad in England. But they have a hundred and fifty-seven canisters of the juice. Some, the highest level of concentration, others in more diluted form, which needs to be further refined. They'll be moving them from the factory by train in large chemical drums marked POTASH LYE, so as not to attract attention. Then put on the ferry to Tinnoset."

By train. Heavily guarded no doubt. It would be tough for a small team to destroy it. "Can we get to them beforehand?"

"You mean at the plant?" Larsen shook his head. "Not a chance. That time has passed. Security is way too high. They've brought in crack SS units to oversee things, not those misfits like before. Everyone has someone watching them, even me. You can't even get near the high-concentration room these days without a permit. You'd need an army to get explosives in."

"Then we need to know the route. You say it will leave by train. Train to where?"

"I told you the last time. . . ." The chief engineer brushed the hair off his forehead, sweat running down his neck. "I'm not the hero you're looking for."

"No one's looking for a hero, Chief Larsen. Only for someone who is not afraid to stand up and do what needs to be done. The train to *where*, I asked?"

Larsen took off his glasses and let a long breath escape from his cheeks. He snorted almost wistfully. "You know, all I ever wanted to do was sit behind a desk with my numbers. I like numbers. How things fit together. They're fixed and patently without an outside agenda. My whole life, only they've been my real friends. I never even wanted this job."

"I'm sorry for how fate puts us where we least intend to be." Nordstrum waited impatiently.

Larsen remained silent for a while, his eyes focused straight ahead. Then he finally reached into his jacket with a kind of philosophical smile. "I'll probably be shot for this . . ." He handed Nordstrum a paper.

Nordstrum scanned it quickly. It had a swastika on the top, and was marked FOR THE EYES OF RESTRICTED PERSONNEL ONLY. STRICTLY CONFIDENTIAL. He only read the first few lines, folded it back up, and handed it back to Larsen.

"Keep it. I made a copy."

Nordstrum smiled. "You may not yet be a hero," he put his hand on the chief engineer's shoulder, "but you're getting commendably close."

"Now let me go. Shame, I could use a night of bridge. But we can't just sit out here all night."

"Before you do, I'm letting you know, we may still need more."

"I've given you what you need. There is no more." He looked at Nordstrum testily. "Now it's up to you to do what you have to."

"You more than anyone know the importance of this, should this cargo find its way back to Germany."

Larsen looked at him, blood exiting his face. He nodded. "I honestly don't know if I'm capable of doing more."

"In the end, you may surprise yourself, Chief Larsen. We go as far as we think we can—and when the situation demands it, we go just a bit farther. That's all it is."

"Sounds so easy." The plant engineer sniffed. "Living up to it is another matter. Now please get out. I won't be any help to anyone if the Nazis find you here."

Nordstrum cracked open the door. "We'll be in touch again. You know that, right?"

The chief engineer's tie was askew, his hair a little moist from sweat, his neck as thin as one of his drafting pencils. As unlikely a man to count on as Nordstrum had ever called upon. "I think you've made that abundantly clear."

Nordstrum folded the paper in his jacket and climbed out of the car. "I'm sorry, but you're not looking so well, chief engineer."

"I know. Everyone's telling me that today."

64

Once Nordstrum and Einar sent over the content of Larsen's top-secret memo, it took only three hours for SOE's reply to come back: *The matter has been considered at the highest levels with great consideration of the possibility of reprisals, but it is thought vital that the heavy water should be destroyed in transit. Hope it can be done without too disastrous results. We send our best wishes for success in the attack.*

Einar handed Nordstrum the message. Nordstrum chuckled cynically. There was no time to organize a new crew or a raid from the outside. There were no new military options. No support. Only a cheery slap on the back: *Best wishes for success in the attack.* The fate of the one thing that kept Churchill and Roosevelt awake at night had fallen on the backs of the two of them.

Nordstrum took out his lighter and watched the edge of the paper take the flame. "Four days," he said. "That's not much time."

He never gave a moment's thought to backing off or turning it down.

And any thoughts he had of Natalie drifted away in the embers.

Wednesday and Thursday, they met after work. Larsen had agreed to be fully part of it now. SOE ruled that Einar had to sit this one out since he would be the only radio link remaining in the Rjukan area and because of his position at the Mosvatn Dam, which they thought one day might have to be blown. But he was involved in the planning.

In transit. Now that they knew the route—by train from Vemork to Mael, then across the lake by ferry to Tinnoset, then a second train to Nottogen (two trains actually, to keep the real one with the cargo concealed), and finally on to Skien, and across the North Sea by freighter, surely with a naval convoy, to Hamburg—they could try to find a breakdown somewhere. A weak link.

One option was to blow up the transport train en route between Vemork and Rjukan. Larsen mentioned that the train would go past Norsk Hydro's explosives dump, where 4,500 pounds of dynamite were stored. The dump was generally lightly guarded, but the Germans were taking every precaution on Saturday, Larsen noted, so who knew how many might be assigned to it that day. To ensure the canisters' destruction, Nordstrum said the explosion would have to come at precisely the moment the heavy water drums were passing by. Which could easily be accomplished, he explained, by a detonator placed on the tracks, but there was always the risk the Germans would send a trial engine down ahead of the train and detonate the charges prematurely.

The more likely option was to attack the train farther along its journey, between Tinnoset and Nottogen. But Nordstrum knew a direct attack like that would have to be done by a team large in number and highly organized. And Larsen said the transport train would also be carrying the plant's usual cargo of ammonia products, which, if exploded, would pose a serious hazard to the population of Nottogen if it happened too close.

Attacking the ship by air or submarine as it crossed the North Sea was a last resort if all else failed, but there was sure to be a naval convoy protecting it, and anyway, that was completely out of their control.

"There's still one option we haven't discussed," Nordstrum said, when the mood was at its gloomiest.

"And that is . . . ?" Larsen asked.

"Blowing up the ferry once the heavy water is loaded on, and sending it to the bottom of Lake Tinnsjo."

"The ferry . . ." Einar reacted with equal parts resistance and interest. "To do that would require sneaking onto it the night before and setting the charges. The morning of, there would be far too much commotion and too many people about. Not to mention there would be guards, no doubt."

"Guards can be diverted." Nordstrum shrugged. "Or silenced. What's tricky is that it would have to be a time-delayed fuse, as, yes, we'd need to set the charges the night before and ensure it would explode at precisely the right spot. In the middle of the lake, so that the cargo could not be salvaged."

"Explosives? Fuses? Where would you even get your hands on such materials here?" Larsen stared back in disbelief.

"That's not the problem," Nordstrum said. In fact, they had all the explosives they needed; the same adhesive, putty-like plastic that was left from the first raid on Norsk Hydro, which now lay buried on the vidda.

"Here's another problem. You said the shipment is set for Saturday?" Einar turned to Larsen. "There are always two ferry trips scheduled on Saturdays. With two different boats. We'd have to be sure precisely which one the cargo would be loaded on. And what if that particular ferry spent the night on the Tinnoset side and then crossed over that morning? We wouldn't be able to get to it."

"That's so." Nordstrum nodded in thought. "But I'm

335

pretty sure there's only one trip on Sunday. Not to mention a lot fewer civilians on board." He looked at Larsen. "Do you think you could arrange to delay the shipment another day?"

"Why don't I just ask Gestapo Chief Muggenthaler? He's overseeing the transit himself. I'm sure he'd be pleased to accommodate you," Larsen said.

"Alf." Nordstrum tried to steady the man.

"I'm sorry, but I'm not exactly cut out for this work," the engineer said, taking out his handkerchief and wiping a film of sweat off his brow.

"Do you think you could do it, Alf?" Nordstrum asked again.

After some thought, Larsen blew his cheeks out in exasperation, shrugging. "We're still draining the cells. The finished product must be tested for its concentration level and then placed in the appropriate drums. It's possible we could slow down the pace. It would be hard for anyone to know it was deliberate. Sunday, you say?"

"That would help immeasurably." Nordstrum patted the chief engineer on the shoulder.

"You realize what we're even suggesting . . . ?" Einar pushed back his chair. "Sunday or Saturday, there will still be dozens of civilians onboard. We're talking about sending the ship to the bottom of the lake. It's clear many of those people will not survive. We're talking women and children, Kurt."

"And if we don't stop it," Nordstrum said, "you know better than anyone that tens of thousands of innocent people could die."

"Yes, but not Norwegian."

"But still, just as innocent. Einar, look, you know no one wants to spare innocent lives more than me. Perhaps we can rig the explosion so that the boat would sink at a slower pace.

Maybe set the charges in the bow, where the rail cars with the heavy water would be situated. Once the hull takes on water, the ship would pitch forward and the rail cars would plunge into the lake. That would leave more time until the boat fully sank. If we time it correctly, it's over four hundred meters to the bottom. They'll never be able to bring them back up."

"Yes, in theory deuterium oxide is heavier than regular water," Larsen confirmed. "It should definitely sink."

"It would minimize the casualties. The hard part will be constructing the charges to go off at just the right moment. We have only short fuses. We'll need a real timer. Maybe an alarm clock," Nordstrum said. "Or two."

"Okay." Einar nodded. "But we still have to make our way on the night before."

"You mean *my* way on," Nordstrum corrected him. "As per orders, you won't be anywhere near. But yes, we may need someone to divert the guards. If I have to, I know what to do."

"You know if this actually takes place," the color drained from Larsen's face, "they're going to know in about one second I must have had a hand in it. Undoubtedly, I'll be put up against a wall the next day and shot."

"Yes, that's certainly a possibility," Nordstrum said.

"I can see that too," Einar said, nodding.

The chief engineer stared back wide-eyed. "Thank you both, for such inspiring concern."

"But you're right, it won't be safe here anymore," Nordstrum agreed. "I'll be heading to Sweden after it's done. Can you ski?"

"I'm not exactly a champion, but yes," the engineer said. "I've spent my time in the mountains."

"Then make sure you pack a bag that night, and make it a small one. You'll come with me."

"To Sweden?" Larsen looked out blankly. "I've lived my whole life here. I don't know any place else."

"And you may well again," Nordstrum said, "as a hero, if we're successful. If not, what does it even matter? All will be lost."

"So it's agreed then?" Einar looked at both of them. "It's the ferry. On Sunday . . . Alf, you'll look into slowing the transfer of heavy water and pushing it back a day?"

"Sunday." Larsen nodded. "I'll get it done. Listen to me, I'm talking like some kind of secret agent."

"We'll make one of you yet," Einar said. "All right, I'll inform England of our plan."

"One more thing," Nordstrum said. "I could use another hand. Preferably someone with a knowledge of explosives. And who knows his way around."

"You know I'd like to be that person," Einar said. "But they've tied my hands. And in truth, Kurt, I've never actually pulled a trigger in my life."

"Me neither," Larsen spoke up. Einar and Nordstrum stared at him. "Just in case you were wondering."

"I'm surprised to hear that, Agent Larsen. You came so highly recommended."

Larsen shrugged meekly. "I just thought I'd say."

Nordstrum said to Einar, "Ask England. They must have people. There has to be someone available."

"I'll ask."

A day later, via return message, SOE had approved their plan. And they informed Einar that yes, there was someone local around who fit the description of the person they needed.

It turned out to be someone Nordstrum already knew well.

PART THREE

THE FERRY

65

Nordstrum and Ox met at the Swansu cabin where the Gunnerside team spent their first night after the raid at Norsk Hydro. "You said you wanted to do more than just send messages," Nordstrum appealed to him.

"What do you have in mind?"

"Do you know how to use a gun?"

Ox's heavy beard parted into a grin. "Does ice melt in July?"

Together they dug up Stromsheim's pack, which contained the excess explosives and fuses they'd brought with them and buried near the cabin's cistern after the raid, a year ago.

Nordstrum knew they'd have to jerry-rig something more intricate, as the original fuses were only two minutes long.

They brought the explosives back into town and stored them at Alf Larsen's house. He was now a full-time member of the crew. "Can you find me an alarm clock from somewhere?" Nordstrum asked.

"I might have one somewhere," the engineer volunteered.

"I'll need two. And that violin case over there . . ." It was propped against the wall in a storage area where they hid the explosives.

The chief engineer shrugged sheepishly. "I used to play when I was a tyke."

"I can use that too."

"You played as well?" Larsen asked.

"No." Nordstrum eyed his Sten gun. "You can keep the violin."

The next day, Thursday, in old work clothes and with Larsen's violin case in hand, Nordstrum took the bus to Mael to the ferry landing.

There were three ferries that piloted the lake. Nordstrum checked the schedule posted outside the ticket counter and saw that the one on Sunday morning at 10 A.M. was the *Hydro*, an old screw-driven vessel with twin smokestacks that dated back to the 1920s. He had ridden it many times.

The *Hydro* was also scheduled to make the 3 P.M. crossing that day.

The flatcar that would bear the heavy water drums from Vemork would be offloaded from the train at the rail terminus adjacent to the wharf, shunted by a switch engine onto the bow of the *Hydro*, and then offloaded again in Tinnoset. Nordstrum had no idea, at this point, whether it would be brought down from Vemork that very morning or the night before. Either way, there was no doubt it would be heavily guarded.

"Ferry to Tinnoset," Nordstrum said to the ticket master, a man with a scruffy white beard and a navy cap who looked like he'd been manning the window for decades.

"One way?"

"No. Round trip."

"Four kroner."

Nordstrum pushed through four one-crown coins.

"*Nyt turen*," the agent said, stamping his ticket. *Enjoy your ride.*

The time was twenty to three and Nordstrum took his violin case and waited on the dock while some of the passengers

342

began to board. He was hungry, so he bought himself a bite from a vendor, a local sugar pastry filled with cream. It was a clear day and the crowd was large—families, workmen; even a party of four German officers who pulled up in a car and went on board, moving past the ticket collector with simply an entitled wave—a major, a captain, and two lieutenants.

At three minutes to, the ferry master sounded his horn three times and yelled, "All onboard!"

Nordstrum balled up the pastry wrapper and tossed it in a bin. He showed his ticket to the crewman at the gangplank and went on board.

It took about eight or nine minutes while some last-minute freight was loaded on and a few latecomers scrambled aboard. There was time, and then there was ferry time, it was known, and the two didn't often coincide. Nordstrum took a seat in the upper compartment as far away from the party of German officers as he could. He'd heard how people were being stopped lately for ID checks and for inspection of large bundles. All they had to do was ask what was in his case and he'd have no choice but to come out shooting.

Once away from the dock, it took about thirty-five minutes for the ferry to come about and chug its way to the middle of the lake. Here, and for the next ten minutes or so, it was over 1,300 feet to the bottom. He thought, if he could place the charges in the bow, once it blew and filled with water, the stern would rise out of the water, sending the railway cars on deck loaded with heavy water drums toppling into the lake. At this depth, there was no possible way they could ever be salvaged. He calculated he should set the timer for forty-five minutes after departure, in order to account for five or ten minutes of possible delay. That would be 10:45 A.M. Five minutes either way, it would still be deep enough. He also noted that the Tinnsjo was a long, narrow lake shaped like a finger, and even at its center point it was not more than a couple of hundred yards to either shore, ensuring that if he could somehow slow the sinking of the ship, the locals should have no trouble rescuing the majority of those onboard. Yet not too slow, he made a note to himself, that the Germans could salvage their precious cargo.

He took a look at the passengers onboard. People heading back from work or to families across the shore. Some keeping to themselves, smoking, reading. Others talking and laughing in groups. The crew just doing their job. They had no stake in any of this, other than on Sunday morning to be in the wrong place at the wrong time. They would be faces just as these. Panic would take hold. Clearly some would die. He'd seen a lot of innocent people die in this war already. Anna-Lisette. His father. Still, the stakes demanded this be done. Even Einar saw there was no choice. It was either ten or twenty, or ten or twenty thousand. A hundred thousand. One day, would he be looked at not as a patriot, as someone who had done his duty, but as a murderer? A killer of innocent civilians no better than the Nazis? He wondered, if there was a God, would ten thousand innocent lives, even a hundred thousand, be worth more than only ten or twenty? Or is one just the same as a thousand? Or ten thousand?

It was hard to calculate things like that. He was just a soldier. He was under orders to destroy the cargo. Who knew, perhaps the Germans would do him a favor and close the Sunday ferry to outside traffic. He could hope.

The ferry split the lake, heading closer to the Tinnoset side. Nordstrum checked the group of German officers who were chatting and laughing among themselves, oblivious to the rest, and got up. He took the stairs down, past the main deck, below. He made his way toward the bow. He heard the churning rumble of the engine room. He looked around. In the hold of the engine room he came across a water-tight compartment. If this would fill up with water, he calculated, the bow would dip and be brought under. It might take up to an hour for the ship to fully sink, but at some point, the pitch would send the train carriages of heavy water drums bursting through their bindings and plunging into the lake.

Yes, many might perish, but there would be time enough for the rescue efforts on shore to save most, he hoped.

"Excuse me, can I help you?" someone said from behind, startling him.

Nordstrum went rigid. He expected to find himself face-to-face with one of the Germans, and gripped the handle of his "violin" case, but it was merely an engine room worker.

"I must be in the wrong place," Nordstrum said apologetically. "I was searching for the loo. Someone said it was down here."

"There's toilets on the main deck. Near the gangplank. Nothing down here but the engine room."

"Sorry." He feigned embarrassment. "I should have seen."

"By the café," the crewman said again, pointing upward.

"Yes. I'll find it."

He went back upstairs, and just to cover his tracks, slipped inside the bathroom for a minute, in case the crewman happened to follow him. When he came back out, the ferry was almost at Tinnoset. The mountains gave way to flatter terrain. Here, the Nazis' cargo would be loaded off and hooked up to one of two transport trains that would take it to Skien—one fake, the other real—on its path to the North Sea.

Nordstrum stepped out on deck. Passengers had formed a queue, waiting to disembark. Travelers with suitcases; mothers and children holding hands. The ferry slowed as it approached the dock. People on the shore waved. A few German vehicles could be seen on the wharf. Tinnoset was a far larger town than Mael, with a commercial railway yard that linked it to the capital. Nordstrum's plan was to stay out of sight for an hour and go back on the 5 P.M. ferry.

He noticed that the group of German officers had come down and, as the ferry came about to dock, were edging their way to the front of the line.

With a smile, Nordstrum placed himself behind a woman and her boy of eight or nine as if to appear to be all together. A crewman threw a rope to a hand on the dock, who tied it to a post. A few people on the shore waved to those onboard.

Then one of the Germans, the major, with SS bars on his lapel, seemed to notice Nordstrum's case.

"*Die geige?*" He looked at Nordstrum curiously.

Nordstrum did his best to pretend he hadn't heard. "Sorry?"

"*De geige. Die violine.*" The officer pointed to the case and made a violin-playing motion with his hands.

"*Ah, ja.*" Nordstrum nodded, his gut tightening inside. The crew was readying the ship for arrival. If the officer asked to see it, Nordstrum knew he would have to shoot it out and run.

"I played myself," the German indicated, tapping his chest with his index finger. "*Zehn jahre.*" *Ten years.* He drew his hands like a bow, humming the opening of Beethoven's "Ode to Joy" with a laugh with to his fellow officers. "Bach, Beethoven. Handel. *Skalen . . .*" *Scales.* "*Drei stunden,* three hours, every day." He rolled his eyes, as if to say, *Such drudgery.*

Then he turned back to Nordstrum and smiled with curiosity. "May I see?"

Nordstrum froze, his heart jabbing tremulously against his ribs. Once he opened the case there would be no choice about what he would have to do. Besides the Germans, there were a lot of people waiting to disembark. Women, children. Smiling back, he looked to the dock, which he could now leap to if he had to, and went over what to do. There was only so much longer he could pretend he didn't understand. The officer beckoned again with his fingers. "May I see it, please?"

With a glance at the other officers, Nordstrum put the case on the ground. Each carried only a Luger in their belts. They'd be dead before they got them out of their holsters. He knelt and drew in a breath. He put his hands onto the clasps. "Of course, Herr Major, I'd be honored to—"

At that moment the ferry glanced against the dock, sending a few in the line back a step to regain their balance. The boy next to Nordstrum fell back into him and, pretending to bolster the lad, Nordstrum sent the boy back over his foot onto the deck, virtually falling at the German officer's feet.

His mother cried out, "Jan!"

"He's all right, madame." The German major bent down and helped the boy back up. "Just a little bump on his backside."

"I may have caused it, I fear," Nordstrum said. He helped the lad up and back in line. "Sorry, young man."

"I'm all right," said the boy, slightly embarrassed. "I just tripped."

One of the crewmen threw the gangplank to the dock and people began to move toward it.

"Say *danke*," the boy's mother prodded her son, and the boy meekly complied. "*Danke*, sir."

"You are welcome."

One of the major's fellow officers signaled to a fellow soldier on the dock. "We are disembarking, Major. Our driver is waiting."

"*Ja, ja*." The major took one more glance at Nordstrum's violin case and smiled. "Enjoy your play," he said with a nod.

"*Danke*," Nordstrum replied, his heart settling back into his chest. "I will."

They moved ahead and Nordstrum hung back in the line, putting as much distance as he could between them.

On the wharf, he immediately headed in the other direction, merging in with the crowd. Only then did he allow himself to blow out his cheeks in relief. There had been four of them. Even if he had been able to surprise them, he would have been hunted down in the town. He would likely be dead. There would have been reprisals. The heavy water shipment would likely have gone as scheduled. *All for a fucking glance at a violin*, he thought.

The ride back was uneventful.

66

Ox had a friend in Rjukan, John Diseth, a retired Norsk Hydro inspector, whose hobby now was repairing old clocks and watches. He kept a shop on the outskirts of town. Over a beer he said he would do what he could to help. By Wednesday, Ox had convinced him to supply the second alarm clock and to handle the complicated wiring.

Using Diseth's workshop, late the next night Nordstrum and Ox prepared the plastic explosives while the sixty-year-old repairman configured the two alarm clocks. They calculated just how large the hole should be in the ferry's exterior. Not so large that the ship would immediately sink and cause more people to die. But not so small, either, that the rail cars carrying the deuterium oxide wouldn't slide into the lake until after help arrived. Einar, the engineer, used the *Hydro*'s tonnage and estimated its displacement of water, and arrived at the figure of five feet across. Working together, Nordstrum and Ox kneaded the nineteen pounds of plastic explosives into a sausage some nine feet long and wrapped it in burlap for easier handling. The fuses would be inserted on the ship at the last minute, once the alarm clocks and detonators were set and wired.

Meanwhile, Diseth removed the bell, but not the bell hammer, from each clock. Determining the exact contact point of each hammer's swing, he attached an electric insulator from an old telephone receiver, a tiny strip of Bakelite, and ran a wire into it. When it all was correctly wired and the clocks set, the bell hammer, at the moment the "alarm"

349

rang, would strike the metal contact, complete the electric circuit, and activate the percussion caps in the detonators, which would set off the bomb. The repairman used four flashlight batteries to power the entire mechanism, soldering the terminals so that the wires would not come loose. The only worry was that the distance between the hammer and the contact point was so razor thin—merely a third of an inch—that an unsteady hand, or even a wayward movement of the ship, could set it off prematurely.

"Be very careful when you connect it to the plastic," Diseth instructed Nordstrum. "If your hands are unsteady and the contact points touch, then, boom!" He snapped his fingers. "You won't have to worry about if it works or not. You may want to take a gulp of whisky before you go."

"Not to worry," Nordstrum replied, extending his hands. "Why would anyone be nervous setting nineteen pounds of explosives with a hundred Germans close by outside? Still, good advice," he said with a smile. "We may want that drink anyway."

Nordstrum and Ox packed the equipment and, in the dead of night, climbed back up to the hut they'd been staying in atop the mountains. It was a three-hour trek in the dark, up a winding, icy path, and they arrived exhausted. To be absolutely sure that the clocks would work as planned, they set them for 10 A.M., later that morning. Then they went to sleep.

Six hours later two sharp cracks made them jump out of bed. Ox took his rifle and went to the window; Nordstrum grabbed his Sten and held it against the door, sure that the Germans had found their hiding spot.

They found no one there.

Suddenly the two men looked at themselves in embarrassment and began to laugh. It was the detonators—going off on schedule, the percussion caps sounding exactly like rifle shots.

Diseth had done his job well.

67

The next day they came back into town to go over a few more details and convey that the clocks had worked to perfection— almost too perfectly.

Larsen was at work at the factory. Einar took the afternoon off from his job at the dam. They met at Diseth's place. As Einar came through the door, he had someone with him. The person SOE had sent in to join the team.

"I believe you two already know each other," Einar said to Nordstrum.

As Nordstrum looked through the stubbly beard and the no-longer callow eyes, he lit up with surprise. It was the last person in the world he expected to see. In fact, he thought that person was dead.

"Yank!" His face split into a wide grin.

It was Eric Gutterson.

"I was told you didn't make it." Nordstrum went up and threw his arms around him.

"I almost didn't," the Yank admitted. "I got separated from the team. It's quite a tale."

"Well, let's hear it," Nordstrum said. "Here's a beer. There's no time like now."

"Two days after we left you on the vidda on our way to Sweden," Gutterson started in, "we stopped near the Skrykken hut where we had all taken refuge from the terrible blizzard we encountered after we parachuted into Norway.

"Ronneberg pushed us to move farther east. The Germans were known to be in pursuit. He wanted to put as much distance as he could between them and the Telemark region. But you remember we had buried that cache of arms, as well as sleeping bags and tents back at the cabin. Olf Pedersen and I volunteered to ski down and dig them up. The others continued on a few miles east to set up camp. It was far too risky to sleep in the huts at night.

"Upon digging up the equipment and getting ready to rejoin the boys, I spotted four skiers in white suits coming down the slope toward us," Gutterson said.

"'What do you think, Olf?' I asked. I admit I was pretty concerned.

"Olf nodded grimly. 'Germans.'

"He took his rifle off his back, knelt, and aimed at the first one in line. And fired. The German went down. The other three still bore down on us. Olf had his skis fastened, I was lugging some of the gear, and he took off up the slope, yelling, 'Eric, leave it all. Come on!' So as quickly as I could I affixed my skis and pulled out my Colt, the only weapon I had on me. I took a shot toward our pursuers, who were now only about a hundred yards away and closing fast. I saw I had no time to make it up to Olf, who was already half-way up the ridge and had now turned with his gun to cover me. 'C'mon,' he was yelling. 'Quick. I've got you covered.' I had to make a call. I decided my chances were better to put some distance between me and the people bearing down on us. I waved to Olf and took off down the slope in the other direction.

"Behind me, the Germans yelled, *'Halt. Halt!'* and I heard the crack of three quick rifle shots and tensed. At my feet, bullets thudded into the snow. I raced down the slope in a tuck as fast as my skis could take me.

"So the Germans decided to let Olf go and come after yours truly. To my surprise, they could all ski pretty damn well. I thought I'd quickly be done with them and find my way back to the boys, but they kept up the pace. I was fortunate we'd had those six months of heavy training, otherwise, Kurt, I swear they would have caught me. We pushed up ridges with everything we had and glided across long flats, I was giving it everything I had, glancing behind me every few strides. Still, the fucking Germans stayed within a hundred yards or so. They weren't giving up.

"After about an hour of going at it full out, I'd finally put a little distance between us. Two of the Germans started to fall behind and, exhausted, seemed to give up. But this one guy continued on. He was tall and athletic and clearly as powerful on his skis as any of us. I'd been on the run for two days by then and my skis weren't waxed for shit. Plus, I had my rucksack on my back, all of which slowed me down."

"Yeah, yeah." Nordstrum shook his head. "And I thought we had taught you how to ski."

"I know how to ski, Kurt. But this guy . . . Anyway, the German was almost in range, and gaining . . . I hurried up a slope, digging my poles in with everything I had, my lungs on the edge of giving out. It became clear that while the German seemed to gain on the straightaways with fresh skis, on the hills, I was in better condition than him and built my lead back up. For another hour we continued the same way—gaining, falling back; it would almost have been a game, if I knew the outcome wasn't life or death—until each new slope became excruciating and on each flat, gliding and working my poles at full speed, my legs began to tire. Still, the fucking German seemed unwilling to give up. He had a

Luger, and once or twice as he closed on me he got into a firing position and took a shot.

"Each time I could hear the bullet whistle wide.

"Finally, at the crest of a long and particularly brutal climb, my thighs were about to give out. My lungs could barely draw in the next breath. I knew I was done. As we went down the next ridge, the German would gain on me, enough that he would likely come into range. His next shot might not miss. So I just said, the hell with it, and pulled up. Fifty yards behind me, the German stopped as well. For a moment, we both just looked at each other, both of us too exhausted to even move. The fading light was flat and uneven and the distance between us was hard to gauge. Maybe fifty yards. Neither of us seemed like we wanted to take another step. Maybe it was better to just let it play out here, I thought. So I took out my Colt. Like the OK Corral."

"What is that?" Nordstrum asked.

"A Western. Never mind. Anyway, the German shouted, '*Hande hoch.*' Hands up. And aimed his Luger.

"I didn't comply, knowing the guy had already shot four times, and that whoever emptied his gun first would be the loser, as from this distance and in the uneven light, you'd have to be a marksman to strike home.

"He took his shot, his hand shaking from exhaustion. I heard four more cracks. I crouched, waiting for one of the bullets to strike. And prayed.

"But they all whined harmlessly by.

"When there was nothing left in his chamber but empty clicks, the German turned to take flight.

"Now it was my turn. My hands were steady. I aimed and squeezed the trigger, just like we learned. The German arched upright and stopped dead in his tracks. He slumped over his poles. For a while, he didn't move an inch. I wasn't sure if I'd killed him or not. Part of me wanted to go find out, out of respect for the man's pursuit. Instead I decided to get the hell out of there."

"A good choice. Well done, Eric." Nordstrum slapped him on the arm.

"I'm not done. By now, I was way too far away to simply retrace my steps and rejoin the group. And I had no fucking idea where I was. And no guarantee, of course, I wouldn't run straight into a larger party of this guy's bunkmates. So I continued down the vidda—southward. The plan was for us all to head east in the direction of Vegli, so I thought they might wait up for me there. Gradually it became dark. At some point, I was unable to see more than a few feet in front of me. I skied over what I thought was a rise but what turned out to be a sheer drop. I tumbled, it must have been fifty, sixty feet, coming to rest on my shoulder in a hard snow bank. I could barely move; I tried to lift my arm. I've never felt that kind of pain.

"My left shoulder was broken.

"Luckily, my skis were still intact, so I continued on, shaken and in pain, and took cover at a farm I finally came upon. And using my vast command of your mother tongue," the Yank winked, "I found out from the sympathetic owner that a Hirden patrol was literally at the next farm, only a few hundred meters away. I was so beat and shaken I couldn't take another step. I thought maybe the best plan was to head to Oslo now. We had resistance contacts there. But first I had to get my shoulder repaired. They let me stay a couple of days; I was far too exhausted to ski. After a few days I changed into civilian garb and continued on, ending up in Rauland, where the farmer said there might be help."

"I've been in Rauland many times," Nordstrum said. "What a shame."

"Yes, but this was in the days right after the raid and the town was overflowing with Germans. One patrol stopped me on the street, and demanded to see my ID. Using the papers I was given in England and my Norwegian—you would have been proud of me—I told them I was a hunter and had witnessed a chase in the mountains. The soldiers brought over their captain and I pointed up to the hills, all the while my shoulder exploding with pain. The soldiers organized a patrol to make a sweep.

"At some point, though, my luck ran out. I was checking out this local hospital, knowing I had to have my shoulder attended to, when I gave out a few squares of my chocolate to a group of children who had gathered around. That was dumb. Minutes later, a German sergeant demanded to know where they had gotten it. Chocolate was clearly in low supply around there. 'The man over there gave it to us,' they pointed.

"So I was questioned again, but this time I was told to come along. My shoulder hung limply in my jacket and I had a Colt tucked into my belt, which, if they discovered it, would have given me away. I also had my cyanide pill. Still have it. A sergeant questioned me about the chocolate. I said I had met someone up in the hills who gave it to me; 'Someone in a white ski suit.' I just played dumb. They checked my rucksack and found only food and extra clothes, and this whole time, my pistol was here. . . ." He patted his belt. "Totally undetected.

"So they put me in a cell for a day—I wasn't sure what was going to happen—then I was placed in a line of locals and loaded onto this bus filled with other civilians who had been rounded up as well. I figure the Germans clearly had to show some results from their sweeps. We were told we were all being sent to be interrogated at the concentration camp at Grini."

"Grini!" Nordstrum glanced at Einar. "That's where my father was."

"Well, I knew it would be death for me to even get near the place. The bus was an old-fashioned school bus with only one door, which the driver operated with a handle. Like we have in the States. There was one heavyset SS sergeant on the bus and three more on motorcycles that followed behind. Everyone was told that anyone who tried to escape would be shot.

"I realized I wouldn't last a minute under a real interrogation. My only options were to escape. Or take my pill.

"I figured since it was all the same, I chose escape.

"As the bus sped along on narrow, winding roads, I sucked in the pain in my shoulder, which was killing me, and looked for the proper moment: a steep drop of woods on the right side, where I could avoid the aim of the motorcycle guards, who were only a few yards behind. I honestly said to myself, what would Kurt Nordstrum do? The guard in the front of the bus was an obstacle. I figured I'd have to shoot him and run. I put myself next to this gal. She was prettier than pretty, Kurt, and I started talking to her. At some point I shared that I couldn't make it to Grini and needed to get off the bus. She played along, and called the guard back, kind of a jovial fellow who immediately started to flirt with her, and at some point I asked if he wanted to swap seats. Happily, the guard agreed, cautioning me no monkey business or else. . . . So I took his place in the front.

The bus motored on, winding on the narrow road, the cyclists forming a tight triangle a few yards behind. I kept my eyes peeled for just the right moment. Then, coming up on the right-hand side, there was a sweeping turn on the side of a dense wood that fell sharply from the road. I knew this had to be it. The bus driver downshifted into the turn. I waited until the vehicle was halfway into the curve and saw a break in the trees. With a glance back to the SS guard, who seemed happily diverted, I leaped forward and yanked on the door handle and hurled myself out of the bus.

"I landed heavily," the Yank said, "my shoulder crippling me with pain. I rolled off the road into the trees. The bus and motorcycles screeched to a stop. '*Stop. Now! Halt,*' the guards yelled. I threw myself into the woods as shots rang out from behind me. I felt a sharp pain in my ribs, but tumbled down the slope in the thick snow and rolled to a stop. I didn't even breathe. The Germans chased me about twenty yards in, then lobbed grenades toward me. One landed about five yards away. I hurled myself behind a tree as the grenade detonated, shrapnel tearing through my leg. See . . ." Gutterson pulled up his trouser leg and showed off a line of ugly red scars. "I'm lucky to still have it. Two more grenades were thrown at me, exploding harmlessly not too far away. I dragged myself deeper into the woods. The Germans went in a few more steps and sprayed bullets my way, but the dense trees shielded me. At some point they were only ten yards behind me. I lay there, exhaling, bleeding, not moving an inch. *This is it*, I thought. I actually reached inside my jacket for my pill. They fired another volley toward me, then I overheard one say that I was probably dead. Either that or I'd surely freeze in the night.

"'The major will have our asses,' I heard one say.

"'Just tell him we shot the bastard,' his cohort replied. 'Who'll know?' They gave up the chase and went back to their cycles and the bus. I heard the convoy go on. One day I'd like to find that major and show him I'm alive!

"Anyway, completely bloody now and my leg a mess, I stumbled around for a day through the woods until I came upon the grounds of a hospital in the town of Lier. Turned out it was a mental hospital. A doctor on staff took one look at me and said I likely wouldn't make it through the night. The next day, barely breathing, I was driven to a hospital in Drammen, where I was shielded from the Nazis by a sympathetic doctor and spent the next eighteen days recovering. The doctor had some friends in the resistance and contacted them. I was taken in a meat truck all the way to Oslo. When I had fully recovered, instead of finding my way back I joined a Milorg unit there. I've had chances to make my way to Sweden, but SOE said they could use every man they had in Oslo, now that the manhunt for the Norsk Hydro saboteurs was over, and put me to work. That part's another story. Nine months later a tall, bald man in a gray coat from Milorg met me at a café in St. Olaf's Square in Oslo and told me I was needed in Rjukan.

"'You'll find a man named Nordstrum there,' he said. That was all I had to hear."

"That's quite a tale," Nordstrum said with amazement. "Though I would have thought you'd be back in England by now. With a medal."

"Who needs a medal?" the Yank said. "Besides, why waste all the training when there's still work to do?"

"Spoken like a true Norwegian. And speaking of which,

I see your Norwegian has dramatically improved. Einar, when I met this boy, he didn't know how to say *ur* from *er*."

"When you're being questioned by SS, you learn the difference fast," he said. "And you, Kurt, what have you been up to?"

"Me? Just the same. You know me."

"'The same' means he should have been captured a dozen times himself," Einar said, "but here he is."

"It's true. I've had my share of run-ins as well. But now we're here. You said there was more work to do. Have they told you why you're here?"

"All I was told was to show up. When they mentioned your name I knew it was worthwhile."

"I'm afraid it's the heavy water again, Eric," Nordstrum said, switching to English. "They're back in business, bigger than ever."

The Yank nodded disappointedly. "Yes, I'd heard they'd bombed the plant before Christmas, so I suspected we hadn't completely finished the job. You're not planning on sneaking your way inside the factory again?" He glanced at Diseth, with his white hair, a little suspect. And Ox, with his heavy waistline and who was well over 250 pounds.

"No. Security is far too tight. Anyway, as of Sunday, it will all be on the move. It's being shipped back to Germany. In metal drums marked POTASH LYE. Tell me, how did you get here from Oslo?"

"I took the train from Nottogen to Tinnoset. Then the ferry to Mael." He grinned. "Just a bit easier than the last time we arrived here."

"That's the truth. Anyway, that's pretty much how they're planning on getting it out."

"We're going to attack the train?" Gutterson lit up, seemingly up for the challenge.

"Not the train. The ferry you just came on. We're going to sink the ship and send their precious cargo to the bottom of Lake Tinnsjo."

68

There were a few more details that needed to be gone over the next day, specifically what each person would do after the operation took place. No one wanted to be around to face a possible interrogation by the Gestapo.

Ox planned on going back to Uvdal and officially joining the resistance. Einar, who was forbidden from taking part in the operation, came up with the idea of checking himself into a hospital in Oslo on Saturday for an appendix operation Monday morning.

"My doctor's been telling me for months it has to come out." He clutched his side.

"Just be fucking careful what you say under anesthesia," Nordstrum said, only partially in jest.

Nordstrum, Gutterson, and Larsen would make their way across the vidda to Sweden.

They also had to be sure the shipment would be boarded on the ferry as planned and not further delayed. They needed to know for certain that the drums were on the train and in motion before placing the charges, otherwise the ferry would blow and casualties would result for no good end.

That night, Larsen called Einar and said, cryptically, "Fried fish tonight for dinner, please," confirming that his Nazi watchdog was close at hand, but that the loading of the drums onto the rail cars had begun.

The train would leave for Rjukan the next morning.

And they needed a car to get from Rjukan to Mael Saturday night. Ox knew someone who was in the country illegally who maintained one. He arranged that they could borrow it at ten o'clock Saturday night. A bunch of party-goers, he explained. They'd have it back the next morning.

"Hopefully, in one piece," the man said.

"Safe and sound," Ox assured him. "You have my word." If all went well, of course.

And they went over and over the plan, this time clueing in the Yank. He, Ox, and Nordstrum would be the ones going on board. If there was a guard, Ox would try to distract them. He had a routine of someone who had drunk just a bit too much aquavit that they hoped would do the job. Once onboard, they'd sneak below and set the charges. Twenty minutes max should account for it. If anyone had to be subdued all they could do was make sure the bodies were hidden well and hope for the best.

Word had come back from Larsen that the Germans were on heightened alert that their plans had gotten out. There were now, it seemed, more Germans than Norwegians in the area, and rumors were buzzing that something was afoot. The saboteurs dared not trust anyone now. They spent that night in Diseth's workroom above his shop. For the first time all week, Nordstrum felt his mind wander to a place he'd kept it from going recently. To Natalie. She and her grandfather had a concert that Sunday and then they would be off the next day. Back home. Of course, by that time, the *Hydro* would be at the bottom of Lake Tinnsjo and Nordstrum on his way to Sweden. There was a part of him that felt the need to explain this to her—who he was, what he was doing—though he had only known her a few days. That in another life, another time, perhaps, things might have been different. Inside, he felt there was a part of him buried deep in his core that longed to feel attached to someone again, to love again. One day. It was a part of him that the hole in his heart over Anna-Lisette hadn't killed, that had suddenly surfaced again, like a whale breaching the thawing ice in spring and majestically showing its face. Lying there, awake, Ox snoring, Gutterson drifting in and out of sleep, it made Nordstrum angry that he had met her at this time and not some other. That they had not somehow passed on the street a year from now, or two, say at the Karl Johans gate in Oslo, when there was no longer the smell of smoke in the air or the sound of boots on the pavement. And that their eyes had met each other's and they both suddenly stopped. Maybe her hat would fly off, just as it had on the ferry, and Nordstrum would sprint after it and pick it up, as fate had bound them. Instead, they met when there was no hope of a future. When it was all just another dream. After tomorrow their lives would part and never intersect again. She would be gone. And he might well be dead, or on the way to Sweden, and weeks later, back in the war.

He wanted to tell her these things—things he had never had the chance to say to Anna-Lisette or even Hella—though he knew it was foolish and far too risky. And though he felt he knew what was in her heart as well, he also knew she and her grandfather were still the guests of the SS.

Still . . . A beat of doubt persisted inside him. He realized he wanted to tell her what he felt almost as much as he wanted the mission to succeed.

"Eric," he whispered, hearing the Yank turn. "Are you awake?"

"This wooden floor isn't exactly meant for sleeping. I'm embarrassed to say I've gotten used to mattresses over the past months."

"Tomorrow I have to go into town. Before our work. There's someone I have to see."

"Who?" Gutterson pushed up on an elbow. Ox snored.

"A friend."

"A *friend* . . . ?"

"Yes."

By his inflection, it was almost as if the Yank instinctively knew what sort of friend he meant. "Do you think that's wise?"

"You know me. I'll be careful."

"If you have to, I suppose. But just remember what's at stake."

"Yes," Nordstrum agreed, vaguely.

"Yes, there's a lot at stake . . . ?" the American asked after a pause.

Nordstrum put his head back down. He wrapped himself in his blanket. "Yes, I have to."

69

Friday night, in the glare of the klieglights, Dieter Lund walked the length of the train that would carry the heavy water down to Rjukan the next morning.

Thirty-nine metal drums marked POTASH LYE, loaded onto two flatcars pulled by an engine. There, they would spend the day garrisoned in Rjukan under heavy guard. The following morning at eight o'clock they would proceed to the ferry landing at Mael where they would be put aboard the *Hydro* for the final journey across the lake.

Lund's handprint was on every aspect of the security. By any scrutiny, it was tight as a drum. Still, rumors were flying that something was afoot. An Allied bombing raid in Rjukan. A commando sabotage of the train. He and Gestapo chief Muggenthaler had gone over every step in great detail, shoring up every possible point of vulnerability. Once the shipment left the region, Lund knew his own importance would be diminished. The "golden goose," as his Gestapo colleague liked to call it, would be gone. Rjukan would go back to being the remote, sleepy village it had always been, without its vital treasure. His Nazi overseer had promised that if all went well, a promotion would be in the works. Perhaps to major. Perhaps over the entire Telemark region. With that kind of title there was influence to peddle no matter who won the war. That was why it was vital no mistakes were made at the end. If this was the last point where the "golden goose" could shape his destiny, Lund would make sure it got to where it was going without a single drop being lost.

There were one hundred elite SS troops who would line the railcars and, to much fanfare, accompany the heavy water drums on their trip down to Rjukan. Lund had pointed out that the tracks went right past the Norsk Hydro explosives bin, where two tons of dynamite were stored. They stationed ten men to stand guard over it for the next day and night.

They also decided to send a trial train, a single engine, down the track an hour before the heavy water shipment, just to be certain no explosives had been laid. Fieseler Storch reconnaissance planes would patrol the skies above them, scanning for suspicious activity on the ground, and coastal watchers along the North Sea were on high alert for the first sign of Allied bombers. In Rjukan, where the cargo would be garrisoned Saturday night, the exact location of where it would rest had not been revealed—only Lund and Muggenthaler knew for sure—and it would be guarded by the full detachment of a hundred SS troops. To try something there would be suicide, for not only would it take a substantial force to even get close to their target, but individual charges would need to be set to destroy each of the drums—thirty-nine in total. The next morning, the procession would make the journey to the ferry port of Mael, where it would be quickly loaded onto the ferry. Even the ferry dock had guards stationed on it that night.

Lund had also decided that he and five of his most trusted men would accompany the cargo across the lake. It was important to make a show that he was fully in control. What happened after, he could not vouch for, but nothing would interfere with the shipment while it was entrusted in his hands.

Yet there were always rumors, rumors that something might be happening. In the plant, there were workers, scared of reprisals, who said there was an attempt in the works to sabotage the shipment. He couldn't prove it, of course. The work had slowed a bit and the entire transfer process had been delayed a day to Sunday. Lund didn't like that. And he didn't trust that wormy chief engineer a bit. He'd had the man watched twenty-four hours a day. And if something was up, he knew who it was who *was* likely behind it. Though it had been months since he had actually seen him, Lund knew he was still here somewhere.

Nordstrum.

The man's face was like a picture indelibly etched in Lund's mind. If he was there, he would be spotted. There would be no risk acceptable, no margin for error tolerable, until the shipment crossed the lake to Tinnoset. Every base was covered.

To this day, Lund still had no idea of the exact importance this "golden goose" bore. Only that it had the highest military value to the Germans. And that his own future had now become inextricably tied to it. *Major*. He imagined how it would feel. The rank suited him. He thought of the leaves on his jacket. Trudi would be pleased. He would show all the gossiping housewives and petty civil servants his schoolmates had become just who had made the right choices and who held the true power now.

On Sunday, he would be on the train and the ferry himself.

If Nordstrum showed his face, Lund would be there.

70

Saturday afternoon, Nordstrum asked a boy in town to drop a note at the front desk at the King Olaf Hotel in Rjukan, addressed to Fraulein N. Ritter. *Natalie, if you are free, please meet me at the Mintzner Café on Prinzregent Street for coffee at 3:00 P.M. It is important that I see you.* He signed it, *One who maintains a keen interest in your hats.*

The Mintzner was a small, Austrian style café on a narrow street near the stock pens, where Germans were not known to go. Nordstrum prayed the letter had made it into her hands and that the time was all right for her. Just before three, he waited across the street, in the entrance of a small curio shop that closed Saturday afternoons. In case of any problem, he had his Colt tucked into his belt. It had begun to snow. By three, Natalie hadn't arrived, and every passing minute convinced Nordstrum all the more she would not come. Why would she? Why would she even think of him? He had not contacted her all week.

Yet at 3:09, just as he had begun to lose hope, he saw her come up the street and his heart brightened. She was dressed in her hooded wool shawl, a long skirt, and her boots in the snow, and she stood in front of the café to make sure it was the right place and then opened the door and went inside. Nordstrum waited two or three more minutes to be certain she had not been followed. When he was convinced everything was all right, he crossed the street, and after another look up and down, went in also.

He saw her at a table in the corner. Her shawl was off,

her hood down; she wore a pretty red sweater and her hair was in a bun. If she was angry at all at him for not being in touch, she did not show it. Her face grew pleased as she saw him come in. It was clear she felt the same as him. A few other tables were occupied, mostly couples talking. Coffee was a luxury in Norway these days, so what they served was watered-down beans, brewed multiple times.

"Tea would be better," he said as he sat across from her. "The coffee's terrible. At least for us."

"I was happy to hear from you," she said, ignoring the inference that perhaps the coffee shared by the Germans was fresher. "I had hoped it would be a bit sooner. I wasn't sure."

"I'm sorry. I had to go away for a few days," he lied. "Some business matters. And the reason it was important I see you today is that I'm afraid I have to go away again tonight as well. I am sorry to have to miss your concert again."

"Tonight? *Again?*" She seemed disappointed. "Just that sudden?"

"Yes, very sudden, I'm afraid."

"Where do you go?"

"Up north," he lied again. "Trondheim."

"Trondheim? You have a building project up there?" she asked. But something in her eyes said she was just being coy with him.

"In a way."

"You're always rushing somewhere, Knut. And always so secretively. Here we are . . . having to meet in such an out-of-the-way place when the café at the hotel would have been fine. Not that I mind. I'm happy to see you under any setting. But you are very wary, if you do not mind me saying it."

"Wary?"

She lowered her voice. "Of Germans, it appears. The way you rushed away last time from the hotel and declined to have dinner. The way you shied away on the dock when we left the ferry. How we are meeting now. There is a part of me that doubts very much you are even an engineer, if you don't mind me saying it."

"Then why do you even meet me," he asked, "if you believe I am not being truthful with you?"

She looked at him a while. He was sure his feelings were transparent, that she could see right through him. "And why do you keep waiting in the shadows to see *me*?" she answered with a question of her own. "Do you think I don't notice?"

He didn't reply.

She smiled. "Perhaps it's that in spite of your actions you have trusting eyes."

"I do, do I?" He laughed. "Someone else once told me that."

"I suppose all that intrigue to avoid attention has made me curious about you. You've managed to pique a lot of interest from one ill-advised hat."

Inside, he was filled with desire for her. It was only a spark of something, something that might grow, that if the situation were only different might easily turn into some-thing, something he wanted, but now was fated to yield only longing and sadness.

She reached across and took his hand. His knuckles were rough. "You do not have the hands of someone who spends his day with pencils and rulers."

"I'm a structural engineer," he said. "I'm generally in the field."

"The field . . ." She raised an eye to him, doubtful. "Ah, that explains it. But sadly I have unpleasant news for you also. My grandfather and I, we have to leave abruptly as well. My aunt has taken ill. My grandfather's sister. It came up only this morning. We've actually had to cancel the concert tomorrow night. A plane has been arranged. From Oslo. For tomorrow afternoon."

"Tomorrow . . . ?" Nordstrum said, eyes wide. The route to Oslo was clear.

"Yes." She let his hand go. "We are taking the first ferry back in the morning."

The words hit him like a brick hurled through the pane of glass that was his heart, shattering. "The *Hydro* . . . ?"

"Yes, I think that is the one. The German cultural legation has handled all the details. Are you all right? You've lost color."

"I'm fine," he lied, though inside, dread and indecision took hold of him, as cold as a slab of ice. "Your aunt," he said, doing his best to regain his composure, "I hope she will be all right. But there are faster ways to get to Oslo if you are in a hurry. The ferry is actually indirect and sometimes unreliable. I'm afraid you've only seen it at its very best. Perhaps I could arrange something privately. Some other means of transit?"

"Thank you, Knut, but it has already been arranged. We would have left today if they could have located a plane for us this afternoon. I'm afraid it would be impossible to change it now."

"Yes, of course," he said, his heart racing inside like a timer on the fastest setting. He asked, "You're sure that it's the *Hydro* . . . ?" Knowing of course it was the *Hydro*. He knew better than anyone it was the only ferry leaving tomorrow. At 10 A.M. A throbbing beat at his chest. He knew, if he pulled off what he was set to do, what he was committed to do and must follow through on, the boat would never make it to the other shore. It would sink. There would be many casualties. Her grandfather was an elderly man. He could easily be one of them. Likely. And he could see, as he looked at her, her sweetness and devotion, how she would never abandon him. Even at the risk of her own life.

It was suddenly clear to him he had put in jeopardy the one thing in this war he felt the chance to love.

"You mustn't go." He took her hand again. This time squeezing it purposefully.

"We have to, Knut," she said, allowing him to keep hold of it. "My grandfather and his sister are very close. Besides, if you are leaving tonight as you say, what is the difference? By tomorrow, we will both be gone."

"Yes. Of course, you're right."

Under his collar, a sweat broke out on his neck. Inside, he was riddled with fear. A fear he had not felt even the many times when his own life had been on the line. He knew, as surely as he knew anything, he could not divulge his plans. Even if he fully trusted her, her grandfather was an Austrian, and a guest of the German Army. Who knew where his loyalties lay? In a million years he could never tell her what was ahead. Or worse, abandon it. His orders came direct from London. Destroying that cargo was one of the most crucial missions of the war. There was no way back, not now. The stakes of altering anything were too high. Einar, the Yank, they would never allow it anyway.

"I'm sorry," she said, placing her hand over his. "You seem sad."

"It's just it's likely I will never see you again."

"I know. I feel the same. But this war will not last forever."

"Who knows how long the war will last. Or who will win."

"And what you are feeling—I can see it in your eyes, Knut—feel it too. Here, I want you to have this. . . ." She dug into her purse and handed him her card. *Fraulein N. Ritter. Konigstrasse 17. Vienna.* Fancy, raised lettering. He took the card and stared at her name, not knowing what to do. "When it is over, there is always a way to contact me. You never know, Knut. In a world that is upside-down like ours, anything is possible."

"You are right." He looked at the card and forced a smile. "Anything is possible."

He wanted desperately to tell her. Just blurt it out: *You cannot go. This ship is not safe.* But he could not. Instead he just tightly squeezed her hand. There were thousands of lives on the line. Not just theirs. Tears bit at his eyes. "Promise me something then."

"What?"

"That you'll sit in the stern."

"The stern . . . ?"

"The view is the best there. I've ridden it many times. You'll be pleased, Natalie."

"All right." She nodded agreeably. "The stern."

"You *and* your grandfather."

"Yes, both of us. I promise." She looked closely at him, as if she was sensing what was inside him. "Is everything all right?"

"Yes, fine." He nodded. He checked his watch. It was going on four. Einar was to meet them at Diseth's shop. They still had to pick up their car. "I'm afraid I have to leave now."

"So soon, again?" Disappointment crossed her face. "You are always running off somewhere."

A torrent of doubt knotted in his gut, a wave of feelings he was helpless to control. It was foolish, he knew, but he was prepared to take the risk. He had to.

"Natalie, there's something I have to tell you."

"What?"

He looked at her. "My real name isn't Knut. It's Kurt, actually. And my family name isn't Holgersen. It's Nordstrum."

"*Kurt* . . . ?" Her eyes dimmed, not understanding. "Why would you let me believe it was—"

"Listen to me, it's important to me that you know that. And you're right, I'm not an engineer. Though I did study to be one before the war. I can't tell you any more. So please don't ask. Just . . . just know that if we should ever be lucky enough to really meet in Vienna, *after* . . . in a different way, just know I would feel it had all been worth it."

"That *what* would all be worth it, Kurt . . . ?" She saw the turmoil etched onto his face and reached for his hand. "I'm not sure I understand what you're talking about."

He shook his head. He couldn't explain any more. "Just the war. Things I've had to do. Everything."

"What have you done? I don't understand."

"I know you don't. Just forgive me for having been deceptive with you. It was not my intent. But now I have to go."

He drank in the sight of her face, the liquid shimmer in her eye, the dapple of color on her cheeks. He slowly leaned toward her. He placed a kiss on her lips. Softly. With everything he felt in his heart. He lingered for a second or two, squeezing her hand.

When he pulled back there was not pleasure in her eyes, but worry. "Kurt, you're scaring me a little with how you sound . . ."

He got up and threw a few bills on the table. "Remember, Natalie—the stern. It's very important to me." He smiled. "One day when we see each other again, in Vienna, you can tell me about the view. Remember how we met, your hat; this will make us even."

"Even . . . ?" She looked up at him with a question in her eyes.

"Well, not quite even. You'll see."

He got up, before his heart broke in two and he changed his mind. At the door, he took a last look at her that would have to stay in his mind forever, and went outside.

71

An hour later, Einar stopped the car and looked at Nord-strum with a cast of concern. "There is no way you can tell her, Kurt."

On the short drive back to Diseth's with the car they'd managed to procure, an old Volvo sedan with a stubborn engine, Nordstrum shared with his friend what was in his heart. He'd been sullen since leaving Natalie so abruptly an hour ago, knowing he was putting her life at risk. Einar had seen that something was clearly troubling him.

"You know that, don't you? Her grandfather is a guest of the Nazis. There is no telling where his loyalties lie. Or hers, for that matter. You may trust her, but do you know, for sure? And do you entirely trust him?"

"I trust that I do not believe she would betray me, Einar."

"Maybe so. But would she understand? Without telling her everything behind it. A few days ago she may have been a card-carrying Nazi for all you know. Diseth has a friend too, who's scheduled to be on the ferry. He asked me whether he could warn him and I told him no. He can't. He vouched for his friend as well, but the problem isn't simply that friend, it's who knows what friends *he* might tell, and then those people . . . If word gets out, where does it go from there?"

"I understand all that, Einar. As long as you understand I may well be sending her to her death."

"You're not sending her, Kurt. Life is sending her. And even if you are . . . ?" The engine was running and a man with a cart of fish wobbled by. "Look, I see you have feelings for her. And I know you've been wounded in your heart a long time. But hers is only one life. One life measured against thousands. Possibly hundreds of thousands. I know what it is you're feeling. I have people I love too. And I don't know what I would do, if it was Marte, or her sister. But I do know what you would tell me. Which is exactly what I'm saying to you. You simply cannot jeopardize this for a person you may never see again. Who you've only known for what, two days . . . ?"

Nordstrum let a long blast of air out of his nostrils. It didn't seem like there was any more to say. He knew Einar was right. There was no telling how Natalie or her grandfather would react. And even if she kept his secret, there was no guarantee her grandfather would as well. Or how she might react to having to be part of a secret that would likely result in the loss of dozens of lives.

Still, he felt he loved her.

Yes, he'd had to do the hard thing many times. It had cost him Anna-Lisette. And his father, who had been rounded up by this Lund simply because of the path Nordstrum himself had taken. And even Hella. He'd grown used to it.

Reluctantly, he gave his friend a nod.

It was dark now. They continued on in the car and pulled to a stop in front of Diseth's shop. He was a soldier. Those were the choices he had had to make. It was war and he had let a random person dig her way inside him. He knew it was foolish. Afterward, there would always be time for life. But for now . . .

They sat for a moment.

For now, he had to forget they'd ever met.

"There are lifeboats, Kurt." Einar looked at him. "People

will come from the shore. You calculated that in how you prepared the charges. I only mean to say there's hope. You're not just putting her up against a wall like the Nazis did Anna-Lisette. Besides . . ." Einar opened the driver's door and cast his friend a smile, "you probably won't survive planting the explosives anyway."

Nordstrum gave him a laugh back. "You're right. I told her to sit in the stern. That the view was best there."

"Then you've done what you can. The rest is just war, Kurt. It's in God's hands. Not ours."

"God hasn't always been so kind to me," Nordstrum said, bringing Anna-Lisette and his father to mind.

"Well, he's kept you alive, hasn't he?" Einar looked at his watch. "Now let's relax. It's five fifteen. You have only a few hours to prepare. And I, I'm afraid, have to catch the six-thirty train to Oslo for my aching appendix. Trust me, I wish I could stay with you."

Nordstrum nodded. "I feel better knowing you're far away. Marte too."

"Thanks." Einar squeezed his shoulder. "I wish you luck, my friend." He put out his hand. "We've said that many times now."

"Yes, we have. I wish you luck too," Nordstrum said. "And whatever you do, remember, make sure you watch what the hell you say when they put you under anesthesia."

Larsen arrived around 9 P.M. with his rucksack and his skis. He seemed a wreck. "I had to sneak out into the woods behind my house," he said. "They've put a car in front."

"Are you sure you weren't followed?" Nordstrum pressed.

"As far as they're concerned I'm soundly asleep after being up all last night loading the rail cars. But what I do regret is I'm missing my bridge evening. I haven't missed my Saturday night bridge game in over three years."

"I'm afraid they're going to have to find a new fourth," Nordstrum said.

"Yes. And bridge players are not so easy to come by here in Rjukan."

They wrapped the explosives in a burlap blanket and stuffed the detonators and clock in a small bag. They took a Sten, two Colt pistols, and a couple of grenades. The sight of the weapons made Larsen look almost sickly, as if the life-and-death stakes of what they were doing finally kicked in. They went outside to the car. It was a ten-year-old Volvo and the engine coughed and coughed before it finally started up, making them concerned for a moment they wouldn't be going anywhere.

"God, I'd forgotten just how cold it was up here," Gutterson said in the backseat. The temperature read minus thirty centigrade.

"Happy to make you feel right at home." Nordstrum looked at Ox, Gutterson, and Larsen. "Ready?"

"As we'll ever be," Ox grunted.

"Like old times, huh, Yank?" Nordstrum elbowed his friend.

"Aye." Gutterson shoved his Sten beneath his parka. "Old times."

Before he climbed in, Nordstrum excused himself and went up to the toilet above Diseth's shop. With the door shut he dug through his ID case and took out Natalie's card. *N. Ritter. Konigstrasse 17.* It still carried her scent on it. *If we were lucky to meet in Vienna . . .* Even if she survived tomorrow, she would always know it was he who brought down the ship. Who had kept this from her and almost sent her to her death. Or her grandfather. Would he even survive?

Promise me you'll sit in the stern . . .

She would never understand.

Sadness stabbing at him, he tried to harden himself. He tore the card into several pieces and dropped them from his fingers into the lavatory, like dried petals falling out of a book. Then he flushed the drain.

In another time . . .

And as Einar had said, he quickly reminded himself, it was unlikely he would even survive the night.

72

They left just before midnight, and were able to drive past the train station in the center of Mael, where twenty or thirty soldiers milled about, to a spot on the road above the wharf, within three quarters of a mile of the ferry station. The streets were completely empty this time of night; there were no lights, except theirs, but amazingly, they were not stopped. They left the car on a small rise above the dock, behind a snowdrift to hide it from view.

They told Larsen to wait for them there.

"Two hours," Nordstrum instructed him. "If we're not back by then, leave. Drive the car to Kongsberg and take the early train to Oslo. Put this in your pocket. It's the name of a contact there. If you hear gunfire, the same arrangements apply. Don't wait for us in either circumstance, do you understand?"

Larsen nervously wiped the film off his glasses and nodded. "Yes, two hours."

"Here." Nordstrum took out a gun and handed it to him.

The engineer took it like it was something he had never seen before. "What do I do with that?"

"Point it at someone in a gray uniform if they give you any trouble and squeeze the trigger," Nordstrum said.

Larsen held it in his palm like a glove two sizes too large for him. "I don't know if I can."

"For your own sake, you'd better. Now, are we all set?" Nordstrum turned to Gutterson and Ox.

The American had the satchel of weapons and the

detonators. Nordstrum took the plastic explosives wrapped in burlap and tucked the package underneath his parka.

"All set."

Nordstrum said to Ox, "If there are any guards on the dock, make your way down the road a bit and let off a blast from your tommy. That will draw them. Then get the hell out of there. We'll go it alone."

"Okay, but I would hate to leave you." The big man nodded dutifully.

"That's the best job you can do for us. Remember," Nordstrum turned to Larsen again, "two hours, Alf. Not a minute more. If we're not back, go."

"Just get back." Larsen exhaled. He checked his wristwatch with a nod.

It was now a quarter to one.

They made their way to the end of the road, a fifteen-minute walk in the moonless night, then wound through the snow and brush down a small embankment to within sight of the ferry.

Nordstrum's heart picked up.

The *Hydro* rested calmly at the end of the long dock, a few dim lights coming from inside. There was an armored car and a wooden restraining barrier set up at the foot of the long dock about a hundred meters away. Five or six guards were posted, who didn't seem overly concerned. Another two, in long wool coats, rifles on their shoulders, could be seen patrolling up and back along the dock.

It was bitterly cold as Nordstrum, Ox, and Gutterson crept down from the embankment, the ice cracking and popping like champagne corks under their feet, so loudly it sounded like an entire company of men were approaching.

Nordstrum held his breath. There was a wire fence separating them from the dock. They took cover behind a large bush.

There was no one to be seen on the ferry, no guard or watchman. Just lights coming from below.

"I'll go first," Nordstrum said, stuffing his Colt in his belt. "If it's clear, I'll wave you both across. Watch for my signal. If they spot me, wait until they come up to get me and then come take care of them," he said to Gutterson, who nodded back. "Quietly, if possible, Yank." Nordstrum winked.

The American patted the knife in his belt. "I'll be there."

Yards away, they could hear the boot steps of the closest guard patrolling the wooden deck. A minute later he turned and went back the other way.

Nordstrum said to Ox, "If they don't give us some distance, go back up the hill like I said and let out a short burst with your tommy. That should distract them. Then get the hell out of there."

"What about you?"

"Don't worry. The Yank and I will go on alone."

"If I have to," Ox said. "But you're robbing me of all the fun."

The three of them crouched there until the guard was all the way back at the foot of the wharf and stopped to chat with his comrades near the barrier. He remained there long enough that the second guard turned and started his way back, facing away from Nordstrum and his crew. They waited until the guard was about forty meters away.

"See you on board," Nordstrum said, with a thumbs-up to Gutterson and Ox. With the tube of plastic explosives under the burlap wrapped around his neck, Nordstrum came out of the bushes and made his way over the fence. Taking a quick look down the dock, he sprinted in a crouch across the dock to the gangway.

He slipped quietly onto the ferry without being seen.

He didn't see any sign of a guard or a watchman on board, but there were loud voices coming from the forward compartments.

It sounded like a card game.

He waited, as the guard heading down the dock had turned and began to make his way back up the wharf in their direction. Gutterson and Ox knelt across from him in the brush. About a third of the way toward them, a military vehicle pulled up at the foot of the dock near the barricades. Perhaps an officer checking the final arrangements. The patrolling guard was called over. As soon as he reached them, Nordstrum waved Gutterson and Ox across. In a crouch, they both climbed over the fence, Ox struggling to make it over. Then they darted across to the gangway, as close to a scamper as Ox was able to pull off. In his fur jacket he looked like a large bear.

They snuck onto the boat.

"There are people on board." Nordstrum pointed below, raising his index finger to his lips for them to be quiet. They heard shouting and cursing coming from the forward compartments. Twenty minutes had elapsed since they'd left Larsen in the car. Nordstrum signaled toward the bow. "Let's go."

With as little noise as possible they went inside, snaked past the open door that led to the crew's galley, where what looked to be four or five men sitting around a table were engrossed at cards. Silently they made their way down the stairs to the third-class compartments. Nordstrum had scouted the ship just three days before. On the lower level, he found the airtight hatchway that led to the bilge, which he had judged to be the perfect place to plant the charges.

"Quick. In here."

They went to undo the hatch.

That was when they heard the sound of footsteps coming down the stairs.

Ox and Gutterson put themselves against the wall and instinctively reached beneath their parkas for their weapons. A man came down the steps. He was large, with wiry, dark hair, a crew's cap, and a thick mustache. He looked at them with suspicion. "What are you people doing down here?" He eyed their hands underneath their parkas as if he had some idea what was there.

"Relax, friend," Ox spoke up. "We mean no harm. It's just that the fucking Hirden are on my friends' tails. A matter of some forged ration cards, if you know what I mean. They just need a place to hide out a few minutes. Until it passes over. You know these bastards, they never call it a night. We thought we'd find somewhere suitable down here."

"Hide, you say?" The crewman looked at them questioningly.

"Just until things pass over. Any trouble, you can go back up and say you never even knew they were here. In the name of the king, we beg you."

"The king? You're Jossings, then?" the watchman said. Good Norwegians.

They stood there for a moment, not sure what would happen next; if the man was going to agree to Ox's request or blow the whistle and turn them in.

"Yes, Jossings," Ox said. Nordstrum reached inside and wrapped his fingers around the knife he had hidden there.

"Well, there are places." The watchman finally relaxed.

"You wouldn't be the first who needed to escape those bastards. Or had a piece of contraband that needed to be on the other side."

With palpable relief, Nordstrum and Gutterson took their hands from underneath their parkas.

"Go right ahead." He opened the hatch for the bilge pumps, just as they had hoped. "In there. That should be fine. But don't make a night of it. I'll come back in twenty minutes and it's best that the three of you were gone."

"We will be," Ox assured the man. "Thanks."

"Yes, thanks, friend," Nordstrom and Gutterson agreed.

"And there's water up to your knees, so watch yourselves," the watchman added. "Never know what you'll find in there. But the good news is, no one else will want to go in and find out, even if they come aboard."

"That's great. Twenty minutes, and we'll be gone."

"I'll keep a watch out for them on deck, if it's okay," Ox said, with an eye to Nordstrom.

Nordstrum nodded. "Yes, that might be best."

The man went back upstairs and Nordstrum and Gutterson crawled inside the hatch. Ox remained outside and went back upstairs to keep an eye out for any Germans and keep the watchman occupied.

Inside, the oily water was indeed up to Nordstrum's and Gutterson's knees. It was completely dark and, making sure the fuses and the explosives remained dry, they edged their way forward in the smelly tide. Who knew what had made its way into the bilge? The chamber was so low, there were only about four feet from the water to the compartment's roof and they had to keep the explosives and the fuses above it.

"Quickly, Eric. Over here."

They made their way to the front of the bow. An explosion here should rip open the boat's exterior. It was one thirty. They opened their bags and began their work.

Time was of the essence now.

In the Volvo, Larsen was beginning to sweat. An hour had elapsed. He was an engineer, a scientist. Not someone trained for these situations. He looked at the gun on the seat next to him. Gingerly, he wrapped his hand around the handle. What if he had to use it? What if Nordstrum, Gutterson, and Ox never came back? He'd have to steel his nerves and do what Nordstrum had instructed. He prayed he had made the right decision. If he hadn't let his guard down, if he hadn't been so open to their recruitment, he could be playing bridge at Kjellsson's right now.

He looked at his watch again. An hour and five minutes now.

One way or another, he knew he would never be playing bridge with them again.

Then from down the street, he heard voices. Larsen's heart stopped. *Who would be out and about now, other than . . . ?* Confirming his alarm, two soldiers came into view. Heading down the street. Toward him. If they found him there with a gun he was sure to be interrogated. *Show some nerve, Alf, please.* He pulled the Colt to his side. His car lights were off. He was hidden behind the large mound of frozen snow. The two Germans carried lanterns. They were checking the street.

Larsen's blood froze. He could hear their voices growing louder now. He took the gun, not knowing what to do. Would he shoot? Then what, put the car in gear and run off, as Nordstrum had insisted? To where? And what if they came out soon, expecting to see him here? He looked at the gun again. He felt his breaths start to get tight. No, he knew he wouldn't use it. It wasn't him. He'd never pulled a trigger in his life. He would sit here in the dark and pray they didn't see him. The soldiers' voices grew louder as they approached him. He would wait for them to find him and then try to explain himself. Why the chief engineer of Norsk Hydro was sitting in a car above the boat on which the shipment of heavy water was planned to be shipped. He had come here to kill himself, he would say. Yes, that might make sense. But with an American gun? Where would he have gotten it? Larsen thought of rolling down the window and tossing it into the snow. But he was too scared it would hit the ground, not the snow, and they'd hear.

Sweat inched down his temple. He was trapped.

He slumped as low as he could so that his eyes were the height of the dashboard. The two soldiers were now about halfway down the street. Larsen cracked the window. He was suffocating. His undershirt was soaked with sweat. They swung their lanterns, trying to see down the block. Thank God the car they'd borrowed was black.

"Anything down there?" he heard one of them ask the other. Over the past two years he'd become fluent in German.

Larsen's throat went dry and he didn't move a muscle.

The Germans just stood there, following the trail of light.

"Nothing I can see," the other said.

"Fuck it," the first said. "We've got a dozen more streets to clear and it's cold as shit out here. Let's go on."

"Your call." His partner seemed to agree.

Larsen's heart leaped with hope.

He heard their boots on the snow and pavement retreating, suddenly heading away from him. Larsen slowly let out an exhale. His neck was covered in sweat. He looked at the gun and put it back on the seat.

An hour and ten minutes now. He knew he couldn't take much more of this. He wasn't meant for this type of work. He rolled the window down, letting much-needed cold air into the car, then threw his head back and took a big gulp into his lungs. Gradually, his heart regained its normal rhythm.

He checked his watch again. *How much longer?*

Inside the bilge, Nordstrum and Gutterson taped the alarm clocks and batteries to the hull. They found a spot above the water line that was dry and where the tape would stick and nestled them inside one of the wooden girders.

Then Nordstrum unwrapped the nine-foot sausage of plastic and molded it to the ship's skin in the form of a circle just above the waterline. Working quickly, but still as carefully as possible, Gutterson handed him the four detonator fuses one by one—tubes filled with gunpowder—and Nordstrum tied two to each end of the mound of plastic. The loose ends of the fuses he let rest for a moment on the tops of the alarm clocks. Then he set each clock to the prescribed time they had determined was best, when the ferry would be over the deepest part of the lake:

Allowing for a few minutes' delay on the dock—10:45 A.M.

Twenty minutes had passed since they came aboard. Nordstrum wondered what the watchman must be thinking upstairs. They continued to hear voices above them from what Nordstrum remembered was the ship's bar. Hopefully Ox was keeping him occupied, either with whisky or some stories.

Now the more dangerous part began.

Diseth had warned him that this was a most delicate thing: wires, fuse ends, and battery terminals would break if too much pressure was applied, and here they were, in a bilge half full of water, mindful of a crew that would surely turn them in if they even had an inkling of what was going on, and only a limited time more to keep their suspicions at bay. Nordstrum's heart beat heavily; he felt a bead of sweat roll down his face.

Asking Gutterson to hold the detonators well away from the fuses, which were attached to the bomb, Nordstrum connected the battery terminals to one of the alarm clocks, doing his best to keep his breathing steady and ignore the rising drumbeat of his heart. In his mind he went over Diseth's warning of just what would result if the hammer of the clock's bell—merely a third of an inch away—came in contact with the live circuit once it was connected. It would all be over. Nordstrum had to pull away and take a deep breath.

"Steady, Kurt," Gutterson urged. "I'd like my grave to be in one place, not a hundred," he said with a crooked smile.

Nordstrum nodded back with a small smile of his own. "Yes, mine too."

He went back at it a second time. With steady hands this time, and a deep, calm exhale, he managed to connect the batteries.

It didn't blow.

They both looked at each other with a smile of relief. Hopefully, the only time it *would* ring would be 10:45 A.M., a little over eight hours from now.

Then there was the last, but most dangerous step in the process— connecting the electric detonators to the fuses.

Nordstrum calmed himself and drew in a few deep

breaths. His hands were steady yet he couldn't deny an inner nervousness. *Who wouldn't be?* A sudden jerk, the wrong movement, and they'd all be blown to kingdom come. Carefully, he wrapped the wire of the fuse to the terminal Diseth had made on the clock.

"Eric, above my right eye, please . . ." A bead of sweat had made its way there. Gutterson took the burlap and brushed it away. "Thanks."

His hands firm, Nordstrum made the final, delicate connection. Then he took his hands away. He looked at Eric with a relieved smile. Everything held. The clock was ticking. All the wires were in place. When the alarm rang and the hammer touched the fuse contact, the plastic charges would blow. By that time, they'd be on the vidda, miles away.

"I think that's it," Nordstrum said, exhaling.

Gutterson nodded resolutely. "Let's agree not to make any sudden movements on our way out."

"Fine with me."

With caution, they crawled aft and climbed out of the bilge compartment. Their shoes and trousers were soaked with oily water, their undershirts wet with perspiration. Once out, they hurried upstairs. The watchman and Ox were in a heated debate about politics.

"Thanks for allowing us a bit more time," Nordstrum said. "It would seem that things have passed now."

"Watch out when you get off," the crewman said. "The Germans are all over the wharf tonight."

"Thanks for the warning," Nordstrum said.

"So are you on watch for the night?" Ox asked the man. He'd taken a risk for them and the last thing they wanted for him was to be blown up or go down with the ferry. Yet they dared not tell him, as his bigger loyalty would be to his crew-mates.

"Yes, but I go off when the train arrives at eight A.M."

"Train . . . ?"

"Something important is coming down from Norsk Hydro, we've been told."

"Is that so?" The saboteurs looked at each other. It was comforting to know the watchman wouldn't be anywhere near the ship when the charges blew. Ox grinned. "Lucky man."

"I guess I am lucky," the watchman said with a conspiratorial wink, "what with the likes of guys like you around."

They all shook hands and then the three saboteurs headed back up on deck. It was two fifteen. An hour and a half had passed since they had left Larsen. The night was cold but moonless, which gave them cover. The closest guard was halfway down the dock, continuing his rounds. On the wharf, a switch engine was being turned into position, the engine that would likely load the disengaged rail cars carrying the heavy water onto the ferry. They waited, crouched by the gangway, until the guard turned around again. The switch engine made its share of noise, hissing steam and gears in motion.

"Go!" Nordstrum tapped Eric on the back. The American darted across the dock in a low crouch and deftly hurtled the fence. "Okay, Ox, you're next."

The commotion by the dock was covering any sound, so Ox lumbered across while the pacing guard watched the large switch engine being put into position. He waited by the fence, and Nordstrum, realizing the covering distraction was still in place, sprinted after him.

They still had twenty minutes to make their way back to Larsen in the car.

"Give me a hand over the fence," Ox said. "Never my sport, I'm afraid." The big man put his boot on a link half-way up the six-foot chain-link fence and tried to drag the other leg over.

Then, from his fur jacket pocket, a beer bottle tumbled out. It rolled around a bit, making a conspicuous rattling sound on the dock.

Just as the switch engine went silent.

"Shit." Ox exhaled under his breath, one leg straddling the fence.

The bottle rattled for a while and then came to a stop in plain view.

The guard turned around.

"Come on!" Nordstrum said under his breath. "Let's go!" He hurtled the fence and waited to lend Ox a hand. It was a steep embankment through the bushes back up the hill, and if they ran, they would certainly be heard. And anyway, his friend was in trouble.

"My jacket's caught," said Ox. It was snagged on the top link.

"Rip the fucking thing off," Nordstrum said. "Come quick. We have to hide. Let me help."

The guard came toward them. They stood still. He stood over the beer bottle, knelt and picked it up, then quickly looked toward the woods. "*Wer ist da?*" he yelled, his gun extended.

Who is there?

Ox remained as still as a church mouse in the range of a cat, concealed by the brush. But that would only aid him so long. He didn't want to jump. He couldn't. He'd be heard.

He just remained still, holding his breath, praying the guard would grow disinterested and go away.

"*Wer ist da, sage ich? Raus, raus!*" The German raised his weapon. "Come out, or I'll shoot."

Caught on the fence, Ox looked at Nordstrum. His face displayed a sinking look of resignation. *I'm afraid it's up for me.* If the guard came any further, they could all be caught. *Go on, go . . .* He motioned to Nordstrum with his chin. *Get out of here.* He gave him a helpless smile. "Damn, and I was really looking forward to that beer . . ."

"Whoever's there, come out now!" the German shouted.

We could kill him. Nordstrum ran through the wisdom in his head. They could wait for the guard to appear and do it silently with a knife. But any shout or gunfire would alert the rest. That would signal immediately that something was up and they would surely ask the crew and search the boat. Ox's expression as he hung there seemed to contain all that. Nordstrum met his friend's eyes.

"I'm coming! I'm coming!" Ox called out with resignation. "Don't shoot."

He extricated his coat and jumped down from the fence with his hands up and stepped out from the bushes.

"Why do you get so all excited for a fucking bottle of beer," he said to his captor in Norwegian with his hands in the air.

"*Unten! Unten!*" The guard screamed at him in German, and forced him down to his knees.

"Kurt, we have to get out of here." Gutterson tugged on Nordstrum's collar.

Nordstrum went through the ways he could possibly save his friend. One man, they might just believe him, that he snuck onboard to steal some beer. To save his own skin, the watchman might even vouch for him as a friend. Any more of them, the Germans would surely suspect something. And to shoot now would only bring a dozen guards on their tails.

If Ox could do one thing for sure he could talk himself out of a mess, maybe even this one.

"Kurt, now!" Gutterson said in a sharp whisper. "There's only fifteen minutes, or we'll all be left here. Ox is a capable man. He'll find a way out. We all faced that chance. We have to go!"

Reluctantly, Nordstrum let Gutterson pull him by the jacket back up the slope.

It ached in every bone and took every bit of restraint Nordstrum had to leave Ox. But to save him was to risk the whole mission. He would certainly be interrogated. But he could stand up to that with the best. He could play as innocent as an altar boy when he had to. An altar boy who had merely snuck aboard the ferry to pilfer a few beers. The two of them quietly climbed up the embankment, treading silently over the ice. They could hear Ox trying to talk his way out of it, the guard commanding him to move, pushing him along with his rifle. It was now only fifteen minutes until a quarter to two, when they'd told Larsen to leave. They hurried back along the road, quickly putting as much distance between themselves and the ferry as they could, jogging the last quarter mile.

Finally they came through the brush and saw their car.

Larsen looked at them with an expression of utter relief when they came out of the woods and opened the doors. "It's a quarter to," he said. "I was sure something had gone wrong. I was just about to leave. How did it go?"

"It went fine. Perfectly according to plan." Nordstrum climbed in the front.

"So where's Ox?" The engineer looked around, expecting him to climb into the backseat.

"Ox won't be coming."

"Won't be coming . . . ?" Larsen stared, not comprehending.

"No. Start the engine. It's just us now."

73

The rest of the night they spent watching the clock back at Diseth's. Gutterson and Larsen dozed. Nordstrum just sat with his eyes open. He went over who he was.

A soldier. A saboteur.

A killer—for however he had tried to limit the number of those he had hurt, through his actions many innocent people had died. Still, it was all in service of the king. Of that he had remained constant. After the charges blew on the ferry, he would head to Sweden. Perhaps the war would be over for him for a while. Perhaps he would be back. As the night ticked slowly away, he went through the faces of the losses he had borne. Anna-Lisette. Hella. His father. Maybe Ox now. Tomorrow, possibly Natalie and her grandfather too. He knew everyone had such lists. All compiled in the name of doing the right things. Still, they were dead and he went on, and each, in their own manner, he'd had the chance to save. "*I know you, Kurt, you won't be there. You'll stay and fight*," Anna-Lisette had told him. And he had.

How many more would be on that list tomorrow?

One day, he told himself, all anyone would remember was what they did—those who fought. Not the costs.

He was a saboteur.

He drifted in his half-awake state to the last conversation he'd had with Natalie. He was glad he was able to say the things he had to her. Tomorrow she would know exactly what he meant. "*In war, we all do things for which we have no choice*," she'd said.

Still, how could she understand?

In his heart he always knew there was only the most far-fetched hope for them. What would he do, go to Vienna after the war, if he was lucky enough to survive. And she would be there for him? They were not of the same class or station in life. She probably would not even remember his name. By tomorrow, life would have torn them apart anyway—one wind going east, the other west—for good. Whether he set off the charges on the *Hydro* or not. He closed his eyes and tried to drive her face from his mind. To other things.

He prayed that Ox would be all right.

When it was finally light they all put on their skis and headed up the mountain. After a two-hour climb, they made it to a perch that offered a wide vista of Mael and the lake. The sky was a deep blue, the sun shone brightly. The water reflected a beautiful opal light.

At 8:00 A.M., the blast of a whistle reached them and they saw the train with the heavy water on it chug down the narrow valley into the town. In his binoculars Nordstrum could see red Nazi flags waving on the front grille and soldiers standing guard and watching out on the cars. It steamed through the small town right to the lake's edge, where what looked like a division of soldiers was gathered along the wharf and in the square. The *Hydro* was preparing to depart, its cargo ramp down, people climbing aboard. A trail of smoke wafted from its fore smokestack as its coal engine fired up. Some early birds went down the pier and boarded.

He, the Yank, and Larsen watched as the train came to rest in front of the pier. Two open flatcars carrying the thirty-nine drums of heavy water marked POTASH LYE. Troops jumped off. The engine car was disengaged. A switch engine was wheeled in and attached to the two flatcars, which were swung around and into position in front of the open cargo ramp. High up where Nordstrum was, he could not hear, but there clearly was much commotion about. The ferry's cargo deck was emptied. The switch engine was positioned behind the two railway cars. Slowly, in a ritual the dock crew had likely performed a thousand times with other Norsk Hydro cargo, they loaded the flatcars up the ramp with at least two dozen soldiers onto the ferry. Who would have guessed the import of what the old ship was carrying? Passengers climbed aboard as well. Old folk, saying good-bye to family. Mothers holding the hands of their children.

By 9:00 A.M. it was all complete.

"We should get going," Gutterson said, digging the snow out from his skis with his poles. "We can watch from a higher perch. We're going to need all the head start we can get once the charges blow."

Their route had been worked out. Larsen would hold them back a little, but together Nordstrum knew he and the Yank would get him through. Even if they had to carry him half the way. It was February. Winter was in full force. The traveling would be tough. Still, the vidda was his friend. It always had been. He was sure they'd make it.

"Yes." Nordstrum finally put down the binoculars. "Let's go."

He gathered his poles and put his arms through the pack on his back. While Gutterson and Larsen readied their own gear, he allowed himself one last look—willing his heart into a dull, protected state; reminding himself again that it was war with whom blame lay, not him, and that such things happened, things you couldn't hope to control, things you must put out of your heart, as Einar had said, and not take the blame onto your shoulders —when he noticed a black sedan drive up on the wharf, red Nazi flags flying. His blood started to race. From the front, two Germans in black uniforms hopped out, snapping their fingers at nearby porters to assist with the luggage. Then from the rear, August Ritter emerged, and a moment later, Natalie—too far away to see her face, but . . .

A throbbing started to build in Nordstrum's chest.

Gutterson called out, "Kurt, we have to go. In two hours we can be in the mountains."

"Yes, I'll be there," Nordstrum answered, but continued to watch. Natalie and her grandfather made their way through the crowd toward the ferry, their bags on ahead, and exchanged good-byes with their fawning German hosts, likely senior officers in the cultural legation. The old man clutched his instrument case. They were escorted to the gangway and stepped aboard the ferry.

Gutterson and Larsen pulled their caps tightly over their ears and skied a few strides. When the Yank realized Nordstrum had not followed, he turned back to him. "*Kurt . . . ?*"

Something in Nordstrum kept him rooted there. A force, which, while it insisted to him where his true duty lay and that there were still battles ahead to fight, and this was merely one small frame in a film playing out whose ending had not yet been written, still tightened like a knot in his gut, even as he willed his legs to move, *Now, let's go*, to start the journey.

"*I know you, Kurt, you won't be there. You'll stay and fight.*"

They would not comply.

He took out his Colt and stuffed it in his belt.

"Kurt, in a couple of hours every Nazi in Norway will be

looking for us," Gutterson appealed to him. "You can't do anything for her. It's time to leave."

"Yes, Nordstrum, I don't want to be anywhere near when those charges go off," Larsen said, backing him up.

Nordstrum put down the binoculars. He looked at them. "You go on ahead," he said.

"Go on ahead?" The Yank looked back, bewildered. "What do you mean? We're all going."

"You know the Skrykken cabin, don't you, Eric?"

"Of course. Where we left from the last time. But—"

"Grab what there is to eat there. Ox and I stocked it well. Don't stay the night. It'll be far too risky. Unless there's a storm, of course. I'll try and meet you there tonight. If not there, farther up the slope, where we met the hunter. You recall it, right?"

"Of course I recall it, Kurt. But there's no chance. We all go together."

"No, Yank. Not this time. I can't."

Startled, Gutterson skied back to him. "C'mon, Kurt, we're leaving now. What do mean, you can't?"

Even Larsen, who was now a bit nervous, and not quite understanding what all the hesitation was about, said, "Yes, what's going on, Nordstrum? Let's go."

"If I'm not there, get yourselves to Miland. I'm sure you know it, Alf? It's a day's trek. But there's a man there. His name is Reinar. He's in the beer business. He knows what to do with you. I've already contacted him. He's a friend. You can trust him with your life."

"Kurt, what are you doing? You can't go back there now." Gutterson read Nordstrum's plans on his face. "You'll have no chance. The place is swarming with Germans. The boat is going to sink, Kurt. There's nothing you can do for her now,

403

no matter how badly you want to. We have to go. Otherwise we'll all be trapped here."

"You're a good soldier, Eric." Nordstrum cast him a sage smile, the same slightly prophetic smile he had seen on Ox's face only hours ago. That said they both knew what was truly in store ahead, but still were helpless to change the outcome. "Get Larsen out. With any luck, I'll see you on the vidda."

"You won't be there, you know," Gutterson said, almost with anger in his voice. "You'll be shot. Or worse, caught. And then interrogated. This was an order, Kurt. From Tronstad. I beg you to think hard on this. The war's not over. You're a soldier and they still need you."

You won't be there. Words he'd heard before. From Anna-Lisette.

But this time he would.

"The order was to blow up the shipment, Eric," Nordstrum said, "and nothing's changed on that. It will go down as planned." He dug his poles into the snow and pushed off a few yards. "And you should show some faith. I just might surprise you, Yank. And if not . . ." He tapped the pocket on his parka. "I still have my pill. Do you have yours?"

"Sorry, Alf." Nordstrum gave the chief engineer a contrite nod. "But you're in capable hands, I promise. At least, for a non-Northman, isn't that right?"

With a wave, he took off. His thighs pushing through the snow that whooshed beneath him. His heart racing ahead of him. Down the ridge.

Not toward Skrykken. And Sweden. Where safety lay.

But toward Mael.

Toward the one duty his heart would not let him abandon.

74

On the deck of the *Hydro*, Dieter Lund watched the flatcars of heavy water being loaded onto the ferry. It was a striking day, he observed—blue sky, Nazi flags waving, dozens of crack SS troops standing motionlessly at attention. He had ridden the train from Rjukan himself, looking out at every turn. But nothing out of the ordinary occurred. The track had been cleared ahead of time. Reconnaissance planes swept the air. At the ferry dock, a crowd had assembled. But he had his own men filtered among it, on the watch for anything suspicious. Groups of men traveling together. The lone man on the edge signaling another. There was word that some kind of sabotage was in the works. But it would not be here. On his watch. It would take an army to penetrate the web of security. The precious cargo was now onboard. In minutes, the ferry was scheduled to leave. Muggenthaler and Terboven would be pleased. Everything had gone precisely to his plan.

A Gestapo officer oversaw the IDs at the ferry's gangway. No one was let aboard who hadn't bought a ticket and who didn't have proper ID. Just to be safe he and his men would accompany the cargo to Tinnoset, and watch it loaded on the train to Skien. He was taking no chances. The Germans might know how to run a war, he thought, but in Norway, he knew every face, every sign that something wasn't right. He had staked his future on it.

A few minutes earlier, August Ritter and his granddaughter had boarded the ferry as well, the start of their journey home. It was a shame their visit had been cut short—he had looked forward to seeing her again—but, in truth, Fraulein Ritter had not been kind to him about his enquiries after the concert. Nor had she taken him up on his invitation to show her the sights. She was a bit of a bratty tart, if truth be told. Her nose stuck in the air. Hardly worthy of the attention he had devoted to her.

"*Guten morgen, Herr und Fraulein Ritter,*" Lund had greeted them as they came onboard. Their luggage was taken to the first-class hold. The old musician clutched his instrument case.

"*Guten morgen,* as well, Captain," his granddaughter replied politely. "I see you are making the trip as well?"

"Yes, we have a distinguished cargo on board, as you can see." He pointed to the tethered rail cars with thirty German troops standing guard. "In addition to yourselves, of course. It would be my privilege to escort you to your lounge."

"Actually, Captain, it is such a pleasant day, I think we will sit in the stern," Fraulein Ritter said coolly.

"The stern . . . but Fraulein, I believe your ticket is for first class."

"Yes, but it is all arranged. I am told it is best for the views there, if you don't mind."

"I don't mind at all, Fraulein Ritter. I was merely thinking of your comfort." Lund nodded formally and let them pass. No, he was no longer so fond of this impertinent girl. She had made him feel the way his own townspeople always had—small, insignificant, to be shooed away and swatted at like a fly. Still, it made him happy and he felt his chest expand that she could see him so clearly in charge.

"May I take your case, sir?" he said to the old man.

"No, no, thank you," he replied. "It's been with me for forty years. It never leaves my side."

"Then have a nice journey." Lund bowed. The matter was out of his hands.

Five minutes to ten. The cargo ramp was raised and the shipment now secure. Only a few last-minute arrivals were running toward the gangway. The ship's horn sounded. Three blaring blasts. People came out on deck to wave to those on the shore. The tie ropes to the dock were disengaged. Yes, everything seemed in perfect order. The crossing would be routine.

"Keep an eye on any late arrivals," Lund instructed his lieutenant, whose eye was peeled on the crowd.

In Tinnoset, his job would finally be done.

His job perhaps, but not his future.

Yes, Trudi would indeed be pleased.

75

Nordstrum skied down to the outskirts of Mael, leaving his skis aloft in the snow, and ran the rest of the way. As he reached the tiny lakeside town, he headed to the main square adjacent to the wharf and onto the pier.

9:55 A.M. Five minutes to departure. He heard the horn sound. He had to hurry. But not so much that he would stand out, for there were surely security agents watching everywhere. His antennae for such things were on full alert, just being around them. The ferry would be off in just minutes.

The switch engine that loaded the rail cars was still in front of the ferry, but the vessel's cargo ramp was raised and the rail cars of heavy water safely on board, German soldiers stationed on it. On the dock, a Gestapo officer was with a ticket clerk at the gangway, checking IDs.

Nordstrum hurried to the ticket counter. He heard a blast from a horn. It was literally three minutes to. "Tinnoset. One way," he said to the ticket master. "Quick, please. I know I'm late." He pushed across some coins.

"Yes, of course, everyone's always in a rush," the old ticket master grumbled. "Next time, leave a little more time. One way, you said?"

"Yes. Please, hurry."

"Here you go. Two kroner. I hope they hold it for you." Nordstrum took the ticket and rushed off.

"Hold it," the ticket master called after him, "that's way too much. Your change!"

Nordstrum sprinted onto the pier. The ferry's ties were

being disengaged. It was about forty meters to the boat, farther than it had seemed last night. He spied the place at the fence where they had crossed. Where Ox had been apprehended. A mother and her young daughter had just been let on board and the gangway was about to be reined in. He made it, just as the German officer made a signal that that was that.

"One more, please. Sorry."

"It's after ten." The Gestapo man looked at his watch. "The ferry is preparing to leave."

"It's ten precisely. And the streets are blocked up by all the military vehicles," Nordstrum protested. "Please, it's the only ferry today. I have to be in Oslo . . ."

The German looked at him with annoyance and put out his hand, his fingers beckoning. "ID."

Nordstrum pulled out his papers, the ones he had carried for the past year, which showed his name as Knut Holgersen, and that he was a construction laborer from Tromso.

"Tromso, that's a long way north of here." The German looked up, checking his face.

"Yes. I'm heading back to work. In Oslo. I was just seeing family here." Nordstrum's heart started to patter. All it would take was for the man to notice his gun bulging under his sweater and it would be over for him.

"Traveling light, I see?" the German commented, eyeing his rucksack. "From all the way in Tromso."

"Well, I was only gone for the weekend." It was now five minutes after ten. "Check." He held out the rucksack to him. "You can see."

"All right, get on, then. Quick!" The officer handed him back his papers. "But that's it! Pull the gangway," he ordered the crew.

"*Danke*, Major," Nordstrum said, and leaped aboard.

On the main deck, a considerable crowd had gathered. It was the only trip across that Sunday, and was now awaiting the cast-off. Nordstrum quickly melded in, avoiding direct eye contact with any of the soldiers standing guard, who seemed to be everywhere, as well as several gray-uniformed Hirden too. To anyone, Nordstrum looked like any other workman heading back after a weekend in the country. His eyes went to the two open railcars in the bow, some thirty SS standing rigidly on guard, their legs spread, their rifles at rest, their faces implacably staring ahead, almost daring anyone to make trouble, and the thirty-nine drums of heavy water they were guarding stamped POTASH LYE, situated precisely where Nordstrum hoped they would be.

The horn sounded again—three sharp blasts—and the ferry slowly disengaged from the dock. People on the shore waved. The boat drifted a short way into the water, its engines kicking in, and then the bow came around. In the sky, the sun was bright. The lake, clear and calm. A blessing, Nordstrum noted, thinking of the narrow space between the clock's hammer and the contact circuit. *Only a third of an inch. Even a choppy sea could connect them.* All on board were merely expecting a peaceful hour and a half's crossing. Whatever faces he fixed on—the grandfather in a cloth coat and floppy hat waving to his family back on the dock; the young boy tugging at his mother's coat asking for hot chocolate; the two young lovers excitedly pointing to the snowcapped peaks, who looked like they were commencing their journey in life—Nordstrum knew in barely forty minutes their lives were about to be torn apart. Any of them might die. The luckiest of them would be scarred by terror.

Maybe if there was a way to reverse time he would have

rethought it all and looked for another way. Each unsuspecting face reminded him of the choice he had made. The choice that was about to engulf them. But then he looked again at the steel drums in the bow on the railway cars and remembered why. Their contents were capable of tilting the balance of the war to Germany. Who would understand, one day, the significance of what had to be done here? Deep in his soul, Nordstrum felt certain once again he had done the right thing.

10:12 A.M. The charges were set to go off in just over thirty minutes.

His eyes ranged to the top deck, ready to search out Natalie and her grandfather, when he felt like something kicked him in the ribs. He saw the Hird, the one he had seen at the police station, looking down. The one who had imprisoned his father.

His throat went dry. Somehow in all the crowd their eyes seemed to find each other's.

It was Dieter Lund.

76

Lund fixed on Nordstrum too.

One second he was breathing easily, proudly, totally in command; the next, his breath seemed to wrap around his heart and squeeze like a clenched fist.

Nordstrum.

He was sure of it as he stared down at the man who had just boarded. He could not clearly see his face, as a workman's cap was pulled low on his forehead, but his size, his manner. Take away the stubbly beard and glasses. *It was him!* The face was as clear in Lund's mind as his own. But how? What was he doing here? There was no way, not one in a hundred, a thousand, that it could simply be a coincidence. That today of all days, with the most valuable cargo in the Reich on the deck, he would be making this crossing.

A jolt of both nerves and anticipation rushed through Lund's blood.

Whatever Nordstrum might be planning, he had him.

Lund looked away for a moment, his fingers tightly wrapped around the railing. There was sweat on his palms. He could stop him right here, of course. He had the men. All it would take was a snap of his fingers, one command. He could put an end to this game of cat and mouse for good.

But if he was here, Lund began to think, something had to be happening. There would be others involved. Nordstrum had already commandeered a boat once and made his way to England. Why not again? Maybe that was his plan now.

But commandeer it to *where* . . . ? If so, he would need men and arms. He seemed to be alone and carrying nothing. To attack the rail cars directly would be suicide. No matter how many others he had snuck onboard. Lund scanned around. Could they be coming from the shore? Was that his plan, hijack the ferry somehow and steer it to others in waiting? Lund looked away, but kept a watch on him out of the corner of his eye. If he arrested him too soon, whatever was afoot might still go on without him. For one resistance fighter, Lund would get barely more than a commendation and a pat on the back. Even one as highly sought as this one. But if he kept his eyes peeled and his men on alert, if he disrupted a raid, all the while making sure the ship was totally secure . . . If he saw who Nordstrum made contact with, a whole pack of them, rebels trying to sabotage the most valuable shipment in the Reich, well, that would earn him a whole lot more than praise. Lund could always arrest him. There was nowhere for him to go. He had the whole voyage. He had the men.

"Lieutenant, Sergeant . . ." Lund snapped his fingers for two of his men.

They appeared at his side. "Captain?"

"You see that man? The one with the beard. Who just came aboard?"

"In the ski cap, Captain . . . ?"

"Yes, that's the one. Lieutenant, take three men and make your way to the wheelhouse. Wait there. Keep your weapons ready. If you see that man, or any who come up there who look at all threatening, sound the alarm. And don't be afraid to use your weapons."

"Yes, sir," the lieutenant said, saluting.

"Sergeant, you take the bow, I'll drift aft. Together, we'll keep an eye on him. Take note of anyone he talks to. But don't arrest him just yet. Wait for my move."

"Yes, Captain." The officer snapped his heels.

Lund stepped away from the railing. His blood was soaring. He finally had him. The man he'd been sniffing after for a year.

And his senses told him that something big had to be happening.

77

It *was* Lund.

Nordstrum was certain of it. His throat grew dry and his blood came to a stop, though his heart continued to pound riotously.

And he felt equally certain Lund had spotted him too.

He let his gaze brush by the Hird as nonchalantly as he could, but inside, everything sped up. Had Lund recognized *him*? He couldn't be sure. No doubt the Hirden captain was here because of the shipment the ferry was carrying. But he was also the man who had thrown his father in a prison cell, and then sent him off to the Grini concentration camp, which the Quisling knew the old man could never survive.

Nordstrum turned his back to the top deck. If he'd been recognized it was already too late. There were dozens of Germans and Hirden onboard. He couldn't avoid them all if Lund had already signaled the alarm. Any second he expected to hear whistles sounded and the bustle of soldiers pushing through the crowd with their guns drawn, shouting, "On your knees!" What would he do? Shoot them? That would only signal to everyone that something was up. Break free and dive into the lake? When nothing else would follow they might well continue the journey. He reached into his pocket.

Was it time to finally take his pill?

But nothing came. He stood there waiting for the worst. Even if they did apprehend him, it was too late to stop it. The ferry was chugging across the lake, its engines building up to cruising speed. Nordstrum decided he would have to avoid the man at all costs. He checked his watch. Twenty minutes to go. He pulled his cap farther down over his eyes, racking his brain for what to do. He would not be captured. That he swore. Not before warning Natalie. That was why he was here. But he had to stay concealed. Lund had a dozen Hirden onboard—and no less than forty Germans. What if his presence made them suspicious and they directed the *Hydro* back to the dock? The charges would go off, but the ship would not sink in the shallow water. The heavy water would not be destroyed. And Natalie and her grandfather would still be on board.

No, the only answer was to continue the journey. He had to stay out of sight and delay as long as possible.

Then again, if Lund hadn't spotted him, the best thing was to remain in the crowd until a few minutes before the explosion. Showing himself to Natalie too soon would only attract attention, for he would have to explain why he was here and what was going on, which would surely start a panic.

Nordstrum took out a cigarette and lit it in the wind.

So if he had been spotted, why had they not arrested him? The answer, as he ratcheted through the possibilities, had to be because Lund wanted to see if Nordstrum was part of some larger plot. If he had friends onboard who had something planned. The most logical time to attack would be at their arrival in Tinnoset. Even Lund would not assume they had snuck aboard during the night and that charges were set. If so, why would he, Nordstrum, be back on board? Therefore he had to assume that every move he made now would be under observation. And he would have to make his escape in the confusion after the bomb exploded.

Calmly, he took a drag off his cigarette and cast a quick glance up toward the top deck.

Lund had disappeared.

78

Nordstrum's chest grew tight. Was this a good or bad sign? Perhaps they were on the way to arrest him now.

He glanced at his watch. Eighteen minutes.

He opened his ski jacket and loosened his gun inside. If it was Lund who came for him he would make sure he at least evened the score. He took a look at the mountains. The blue of the lake cast an opalescent brilliance against them. They were a beautiful sight. Not the worst way, if it ended here, he managed a smile, for him to go out. But there was still work to be done. He had risked it all for one purpose, so he flicked his cigarette into the Tinnsjo and edged his way through the throng of those who were still on deck. Many had now begun to head inside to their respective quarters. No one intercepted him. Perhaps he was in luck; he hadn't been spotted after all. He went to the first-class lounge.

"Ticket, please." An attendant in a navy crew uniform came up to him with a suspicious look at Nordstrum's attire.

Nordstrum showed him his slip.

"I'm sorry, sir, this is third class. Your lounge is down-stairs. You're not permitted in here."

"I'm only looking for someone," Nordstrum assured him. He peered through the glass door windows. "Herr and Fraulein Ritter? An old man and his granddaughter."

"Ritter . . . ? Well, I'm afraid you'll have to look below," the attendant said. "That's the way it is. Or out on deck. I don't think they're in here."

"All right. Thanks." Nordstrum couldn't make them out

inside the lounge. *Sit in the stern.* He hoped she had listened to him. Fifteen minutes now. Still too soon.

The *Hydro* was now streaming along at ten knots.

He ducked inside the men's toilet and locked the door. He would wait inside until 10:35, he decided. Then he would find Natalie on deck. He knew they were onboard. He pulled up his sweater and checked his Colt. He decided he was prepared to die, if that's what was in store; he had certainly been lucky to get this far. But to die onboard without seeing Natalie . . . ? Without alerting her? That would break his heart. Think with your head, Einar had warned him, not that silly heart you seem to be growing. What a laugh he would have now. Today Einar would check in to the hospital, grasping his side. Wouldn't it be funny, Nordstrum felt himself grin, if the doctor opened him up tomorrow and said, "I don't know what the problem is, sir. You don't even have an appendix!"

Suddenly there was a knock at the door.

"Yes. In a minute." Nordstrum ran the water.

It could be Lund with a gun on the other side.

If so, this was the way it would be. Did he have any better hope when he crawled through that drain duct to get to the high-concentration room at Vemork? He turned off the water, put a hand under his sweater around his gun, and flicked the lock.

He said a prayer to his father and mother as he opened the door. A man and his young son were standing there. "Sorry, emergency," the man said.

"Of course." Nordstrum smiled at the child. "I understand."

There were now eleven minutes to go until the charges were set to blow. Then pandemonium would reign across the ship. Nordstrum made his way back on deck. He looked around. He didn't see any sign of Lund or any of the Hirden, though he definitely had the feeling he was being watched. The ferry had now reached full speed, around thirteen knots, and was approaching the center of the lake, its two coal-fired engines chugging and chugging. On each side, the shore was less than a mile away, hopefully close enough for help to reach them. He walked toward the rear on the main deck. A few of the stouter souls were braving the breeze on deck. In the sun, and protected from the wind by the top deck and wheel-house, he saw Natalie and her grandfather on the benches, just as he had urged her to be. She sat bundled up in her purple wool wrap, a scarf around her hair. No hat this time. It made him smile.

It was 10:38. Seven minutes. He took a last look around. A lifeboat station was positioned directly across from them.

Now was the time.

He went up and sat himself in the vacant chair next to her. "Natalie, don't be alarmed."

"*Knut?*" Her eyes widened in surprise. "I mean, Kurt. What are you doing *here*? You said you had to be in—"

"Natalie, please, you and your grandfather must listen to me carefully." Nordstrum moved closer and spoke in a voice that was low, but direct, careful not to be overheard and start a panic. "You must remain by this lifeboat. In a minute or two there will be an explosion. I've come onboard to help you."

"*An explosion?*" She looked at him, disbelief written on her face. "What are you talking about, Kurt?"

"It doesn't matter. All that matters is that you remain precisely here. In a couple of minutes the ship will dramatically pitch forward."

"Pitch forward?" She stared at him, a mix of consternation and rising horror in her eyes. "How do you possibly know this? You . . . ? *You* are responsible for this? You put a bomb onboard? *Why* . . . ? Look around, people are going to be—"

"I know precisely what's going to happen, Natalie." He put his hand on her arm with a quick glance at his watch. "All that matters is when I give you the signal, you and your grandfather both hold on as tightly as you can to the seats in front of you. I'll help you to the boat. With any luck—"

"With any luck, what?" She cut him off. Her look sliced to his heart. "We must warn everyone. Who are you, Kurt . . . ?"

"Natalie—"

Suddenly he heard his name shouted from behind. "Nordstrum!"

It was Lund.

He looked at Natalie with a mixture of inevitability and regret and opened his jacket, placing his hand around his Colt. "I'm sorry," he said. "I only meant the best for you."

"My God!" Her eyes widened as she saw the gun.

He lifted his other hand from her and stood up.

The Hirden captain had his gun pointed at him from across the deck. A few people gasped. "Kurt Nordstrum. Nice to finally see you again. You must know I've looked forward to this moment for a long time. Since I first knew that you had come back. I believe I owe you something, for the death of Lieutenant Oleg Rand, a true patriot. Move away from Fraulein Ritter, if you please. I'm sure you wish her no harm. And don't do anything foolish. Put your hands in the air."

He did take a step away, out of the row of seats to near the gunwales. But he kept his hands by his sides.

"Why are you on this boat?" Lund kept his gun extended, stepping forward. "Something is planned, I know. Tell me what is going on. Tell me now, or you'll be with your father sooner than you think."

"He says there's some kind of bomb on board." August Ritter stood up. "He says it will explode. Any minute."

"Papa, no, be quiet!" Natalie stood up as well.

"A bomb!" Lund's face went ashen.

"It's too late," Nordstrum said to him. He gave a final glance to his watch. "Your precious cargo . . ." He smiled. "In a minute it will be at the bottom of the lake. There's nothing you can do."

Lund took out his whistle and blew four sharp peals of alarm. Gasps could be heard from the passengers nearby. Two of his fellow Hirden ran toward him.

"Natalie, hold tightly to your grandfather," Nordstrum said to her. His watch read 10:45. "*Now*." He lunged to grab hold of her.

Lund, believing his prey was trying to escape, squeezed off two rounds.

Just as the explosion rocked the ship.

It was muffled, more like a rumble from below. Toward the bow. But like an earthquake, it sent a ripple from fore to aft. The boat pitched forward with a violent wave. People were hurled about—one falling with a shout from the top deck into the icy water, others flung across the floorboards or into the walls. Or into the lake as well. The ship came to a sudden stop. There was shouting everywhere: wails of anguish, panic. People lunging to grasp hold of their loved ones. One of the Hirden was pitched into the water. The other, Nordstrum took care of with a blow to the body and a forearm to the side of his head.

422

Lund fell back against the gunwales, a crate toppling from the top deck and pinning him, likely snapping a leg, his gun slipping out of his hand.

Nordstrum took hold of Natalie, who yelled for her grandfather. The old man had fallen; he'd hit his head against the seats in front of him. He was dazed, but he seemed all right.

Pandemonium was everywhere. Alarms, horns, passengers screaming names. "Claus, where are you?" The ferry listed forward. "Inge, Inge, are you all right?" Several of the troops guarding the heavy water drums were either tossed into the freezing lake or crushed by the weight of the shifting rail cars.

"Wait over here." Nordstrum took Natalie by the hand and helped her and her grandfather to the lifeboat station across the deck. He put their hands on the railing. "Hold on. I promise I'll be back."

Then with a grinding, metallic roar that sounded more like solid metal being sheared apart, the two open rail cars carrying the heavy water drums broke free from their hooks and chains and crashed through the loading door, teetering over the front of the ship. One by one, the drums marked POTASH LYE—but which contained the most valuable cargo of the German war machine—toppled into the lake, soldiers who were still on the platform trying futilely to save them. Screaming, many were dragged into the water with them. A moment later, with a loud groan, the pitch of the ship increased a bit more now that the now-empty rail cars were gone, dragging the soldiers who only a minute before had stood guard over them so ceremoniously into the water screaming for their lives or crushing them under their weight.

A surge of validation soared through Nordstrum.

It was done.

The cargo was destroyed.

He ran across the deck to Lund, who was grabbing his leg, still stunned, but who had freed himself from under the crates that had fallen on him. He was on the wet, tilting deck clawing after his gun as it kept sliding away from him, farther and farther out of his grasp.

As he lunged for it, Nordstrum put his boot on Lund's grasping hand.

The Hird turned onto his back and looked up at him. Nordstrum noticed blood dripping onto the deck and for the first time felt a throbbing in his side. Lund's eyes traveled to Nordstrum's sweater.

The Hird smiled. "You're hit," he said, his eyes brightening at the sight.

Under Nordstrum's jacket, visible against his sweater, a pool of blood matted his side.

Lund met Nordstrum's gaze with an amused laugh. "It looks like you won't be going any farther than me. I owed you. For the death of Lieutenant Oleg Rand. On this very journey, it occurs to me."

"Yes, you did owe me." Nordstrum knelt down over him. He removed his gun from his belt. "And I owe you, for the death of Alois Nordstrum. My father." He pulled back the hammer and placed the muzzle against Lund's heart. "And for a hundred other Norwegians who will never have the chance."

In the chaos of the sinking ship, no one even heard the two quick shots that ended the Hird's life.

The ship was going down. Quickly. Along the sides, lifeboats were being lowered into the water. The more able were jumping into the lake and swimming to them, while those already inside pulled them aboard.

Nordstrum ran back to Natalie and her grandfather. A crewman was loading up the lifeboat. "Here, help them in," he said.

"In here, ma'am." The crewman reached for Natalie. He helped her aboard. Then they both tried to assist her grandfather into the lifeboat.

"Wait," he suddenly cried out, "my cello. It's on the seat. I must go back for it."

"Papa, no!" Natalie shouted, and reached after him. "You must get in the boat."

"I won't leave it!" Ritter pulled away from her grasp and headed like a man possessed to where he'd been sitting. But another sudden pitch of the boat, the stern elevating, hurled him to the deck and back toward them. From the boat, Natalie screamed. Nordstrum went over and lifted the old man up and carried him back to the lifeboat, which was ready to be lowered. He handed him across the gunwales to Natalie and another passenger and they helped him into the lifeboat.

"My cello . . . ," Ritter muttered brokenheartedly.

"Get in the boat," Nordstrum said. "I'll find it."

As he handed him over, Natalie saw the blood on Nordstrum's sweater for the first time. "Kurt." Her eyes went wide. "You're bleeding."

The stern of the ferry was now lifted out of the water. Everything that wasn't tied down—baggage, seats, loose equipment—slid as in a rockslide toward the bow. Something knocked Nordstrum into the rail. For the first time he felt weak. Legs rubbery, without power. He put his hand inside his sweater and removed it. It was covered in blood.

Lund's shots had hit home.

"Kurt, come now!" Natalie implored him from the lifeboat. The *Hydro* was taking on water. It was going down fast.

He'd have to leap for it.

There were about twenty people crammed into the boat, among them two other Hirden from Lund's brigade. Ritter too. How could he trust him? That the old Austrian wouldn't give him away. *There's the man who is responsible!* He already had said so once. Nordstrum would be at the mercy of the two Hirden in the boat. Even still, it was a broad distance to jump now. No, better odds to find something to grab on to, he decided, and swim to shore. He looked again at his side. Blood continued to seep out. He put a hand on it to stop the bleeding. He knew wounds, and this was bad. He looked at Natalie from the deck.

"I can't." He shook his head.

"Sir, you can jump. We have you," the crewman in charge of the lifeboat said. "But we've got to go. She's going under."

"Kurt, please!" Natalie begged. "Jump." Nordstrum could only look at her as the boat lowered away. "Please!"

He didn't move. Though he felt he had to sit down. His legs were without strength. The lifeboat fell away. He didn't want her to remember him this way—weak, unable to move. He only wanted her to remember him strong. Strong . . . if a bit undependable; he smiled inside. He shook his head again. "I'm sorry. I can't."

"Yes, you can, damn it," she said. "You can. Kurt, jump."

The ferry creaked and lifted forward. Nearing the water, the lifeboat swayed.

Natalie pushed her way to the front. All she could do now was hold on to his eyes. "I know it, Kurt. You only came back for me, didn't you? To save me."

He watched her from the deck as the lifeboat hit the water and slowly nodded. "Yes."

From the shore, witnessing what had happened, fishing boats and sail crafts, anything that could float, were on their way.

Nordstrum leaned back against the railing. Just for a second, he told himself. To collect his strength. His legs gave out. Then he was on the deck. He had to find something. Something that would keep him afloat. He had no strength left and it hurt too badly to swim. He'd float to shore; it wasn't that far. Then collect his skis in Mael and climb to the vidda. Tonight he could meet the Yank and Larsen. At Skrykken. He could do it. He could. *A true man goes as far as he can, and then . . .*

I know it, Nordstrum said, straining to lift himself.

No.

He coughed. Blood came out into his hand.

There was nothing more to give. Not this time.

The bow of the ferry was now completely underwater. The lake lapped toward him, encroaching up the deck. The drums of heavy water were on the bottom. London would like that, he thought. Tronstad, especially. That a Northman had done it. *We strongly advise you to destroy the heavy water*. And he'd done so.

All good luck, they'd written.

He smiled and spat up more blood. *Not this time.*

Something heavy went by him. A large case of some kind, and he grabbed on as the stern rose even higher. The damn thing would float, he reckoned. So he held on. *Time to get going*, he urged himself. *No, just a minute more . . .* His eyes fixed on a beautiful sight, the morning sun gleaming off the whitecapped mountains, and he put his head back. The vidda had always been the friendliest of places to him. Somewhere up there, the Yank and Larsen would be wondering how he was.

He wrapped his arms around the case. His legs would no longer move.

Yes, it was beautiful.

He'd better get going, he thought. The water was at his feet.

They'd be waiting for him. Waiting. For him.

"Anna-Lisette," Nordstrum said, as the water swallowed him.

79

High on the vidda, Gutterson and Larsen stopped on a ridge to catch their breath. The Yank looked at his watch. 10:49.

"It's blown," he said to Larsen. The charges would have gone off. "The heavy water drums should be at the bottom of the lake by now."

They exchanged a brief, congratulatory smile.

"You think he made it, don't you?" Larsen asked.

The Yank shrugged. "If anyone would, it would be him. You know that." But in his heart, he knew he wouldn't be seeing the Northman again. It was a whim for him to have gone back like he had. Everyone's luck runs out in the end.

"We'll go to the hut and wait?" the engineer said, holding out hope.

"Yes, of course, we'll wait."

They started off again. Climbing the ridge in a herring-bone pattern. Ahead, he saw clouds form in the distance. A storm, perhaps. A good sign. It would cover their tracks. It would be a long journey to Sweden.

Yes, they'd wait.

But in his heart, Gutterson knew what Nordstrum himself would say.

Yes, we'll wait—but not too long.

EPILOGUE

On February 20, 1944, thirty-nine drums of enriched heavy water on their way to Germany, over 162 gallons, enough to support all its atomic fissile experiments, sank to the bottom of Lake Tinnsjo, over a thousand feet below. Twenty-six passengers and crew aboard the ferry died in the sabotage, as well as many uncounted German soldiers.

Only a small trace of the Norsk Hydro heavy water was ever recovered. Four barrels did ultimately surface, containing eighty-seven kilograms, but of the lowest concentration, which explained why they did not fully sink. Gone as well were the German efforts to create an atomic weapon. After the war, speaking on the fate of the German *uranverein* research project and the sinking of the *Hydro*, Kurt Diebner, an atomic expert and head of the German Army Ordnance, said in an interview:

> When one considers that right up to the end of the war in 1945, there was virtually no increase in our heavy water stocks in Germany . . . it will be seen that it was the elimination of German heavy water production in Norway that was the main factor in our failure to achieve a self-sustaining atomic reactor before the war ended.

Nine months later, the high-concentration plant at Vemork was disassembled in secrecy and shipped to Germany. It was discovered in the village of Hechtingen in Bavaria by English and American intelligence officers. An atomic pile was found in nearby Haigerlock with uranium and heavy water that was on the brink of going critical.

All it lacked was about seven hundred liters of additional heavy water.

One could look no further than to the brave men of Freshman and Gunnerside for why those experiments came up short. It's been written: "Strong tough men who pushed themselves to the limits of human endurance and courage for the liberation of their country. During the hardest times, their focus was on the destruction of the heavy water plant. But they had another, even more important objective: they wanted their country back."*

And on the Tinnsjo, as their lifeboat filled with survivors waited for sailors and fishermen to come and rescue them amid the debris from the sunken *Hydro*, Natalie Ritter wept on her grandfather's shoulder. She wept with biting tears for all the horrible deaths she had just witnessed. And for the man she knew nothing about, who had saved them. Who she would never see again, but still felt something for, something so deep and aching she knew she would carry it the rest of her life.

If you could truly love someone, she thought, knowing nothing of him—who he was, only what was in his heart, and just for a brief moment—then she did love that person with every part of her being.

Boats were coming out to meet them. The crewman on their lifeboat rowed toward them. Everyone sat, silent. Until someone pointed to the lake and cried out, "*Look!*"

* Ray Mears, *The Real Heroes of Telemark* (London: Hodder and Stoughton, 2003), p. 230.

Bobbing on the surface a way away was a black case. An instrument case.

"Oh my God, Papa!" Natalie's heart suddenly lifted. "It's your cello!"

It was like a gift of life and hope amid all this carnage. They'd picked up whoever they could. Now there was only silence out there.

"My cello! You must get it, please," August Ritter begged the crewman. "It's been with me forty years."

"Leave it, old man," one of the Hirden scoffed. "It's just a fucking piece of wood."

"No, there might as well be some good that comes of this," the ferry crewman said, overruling him and picking up the oars.

They rowed toward it, maybe thirty meters away. It was just a black shape bobbing up and down on the black, oil-slick surface, not far away from the final eddy where the ferry had gone down. As they got close, the crewman leaned forward and attempted to fish it out, when, to his shock, he saw what he first thought was merely a piece of wood attached to it, but then, as he rowed closer, realized was an arm. An arm straining to hold on. And he turned to Natalie jubilantly, and shouted, "My God, miss, there's a man attached to it."

"A man?" Natalie stood up, feeling her heart quicken, hesitating a moment before allowing her faintest, deepest hopes to rise.

"Yes," the crewman said. "And he seems to be alive!"

Author's Note

This is a novel, of course, but a novel based on true events, and out of respect for the heroic men who participated in them, I have done my best to keep the two principal military events in the story—the raid on the heavy water facility at the Norsk Hydro factory and the sabotage of the *Hydro* ferry—as loyal as I could to what actually took place.

Kurt Nordstrum, as those familiar with this subject will know, is drawn from the real-life figure of Kurt Haukelid, an unassuming, yet courageous man, whose irrepressible will and sense of duty helped pull off the most important and improbable sabotage of WWII. Several others who appear in the book are also drawn from real-life figures as well: Einar Skinnarland, who in fact did make it to the UK by hijacking the *Galtesund* along with several others; Joachim Ronneberg and Joaquim (Jens-Anton) Poulsson, the leaders of their respective sabotage teams; Claus Helberg, Birger Stromsheim, Hans Storhaug, and Knut Haugland, all part of Grouse and Gunnerside. These men were brave and resourceful fighters who fought Nature as well as the Nazis and deserve their names to be remembered. Nordstrum's pal, Jens, and the American, Eric Gutterson, were characters invented by me—though Gutterson's remarkable escape after the raid described in chapter 67, did, in fact, take place, almost as written, but it was Claus Helberg who survived this harrowing ordeal and ultimately made it back to the UK after three months avoiding the Germans. The characters of Hella, Ox, and Reinar are all fictional as well, though are based on many who contributed to Norway's resistance in the war. And Natalie Ritter is also fictional, though a well-known German violinist visiting the area at the time and aboard the *Hydro* did manage to survive, and his instrument case later rose to the surface. And Kristian Kristiansen, the hunter encountered on the vidda by Gunnerside after they waited out the storm, turned out to be a bit luckier in real life, as, against the strong urging of the SOE command in their training, he was not executed but held captive by the men of Gunnerside in a hut and later released. Major Leif Tronstad finally convinced SOE command to let him go back to Norway in March of 1945, but sadly he was killed in a botched interrogation of a local collaborator in Rauland.

Real events as they unfold do have their undramatic sides (not always perfect for a thriller), and as the seconds ticked away before lighting the fuses in the high-concentration room of the plant, the bumbling watchman, Gustav Fredrickson, did, in fact, interrupt the countdown to locate his misplaced spectacles, not once but *twice*. (The first time his eyeglass case turned out to be empty.) And it is hard to fully believe that with such a vital cargo at stake, which the Nazis had gone to inexhaustible efforts to protect, they would not have stationed guards on the *Hydro* as it sat at the dock in Mael the night before its fateful journey, but they did not.

I came across this story while researching my previous novel, *The One Man*, and immediately thought it a tale of such extraordinary valor and survival that had not been adequately told. Two or three books and countless historical references were instrumental in the creation of this novel. First, Kurt Haukelid's own firsthand account: *Skis Against the Atom* (North American Heritage Press, 1989) as well as *The Real Heroes of Telemark*, by Ray Mears (Hodder and

436

Stoughton, 2003). Richard Rhodes's vast and iconic work, *The Making of the Atomic Bomb* (Simon and Schuster, 1986), was where I first read of it. Since I started the book, the subject of the heavy water sabotage has received much more attention: a November 26, 2016, *New York Times* article on Joachim Ronneberg, the last surviving member of the raid; a June 2016 article in *National Geographic*; and a 2016 BBC series, which to date I have not watched. The 1976 Kirk Douglas action classic, *The Heroes of Telemark*, on new viewing, remains fun, but dated, as only a forty-year-old, studio-made WWII action drama can be. What is inalterable is that the story of the Norsk Hydro raid and the sabotage of the *Hydro* ferry were two of the most selfless and stirring acts of the war, in which any sense of logic would have insisted there was almost zero chance of success, but where the stakes were so high and the determination of the participants to succeed so strong, that logic simply took a backseat to daring and courage. It is perhaps the ultimate, yet most pleasing irony of their acts that against such immeasurable odds, not a single member of either Grouse or Gunnerside was lost and each of them went on to survive the war.

Acknowledgements

Many people helped this book through various stages, some of whom I have already thanked in the Author's Note. But Roy Grossman and Lynn Gross, for their perspicacious early reads; my editor, Kelley Ragland, for truly hammering this story into shape (and removing words like perspicacious which conspicuously stood out); Andy Martin, Sally Richardson, Paul Hochman, Hector St. Jean, Maggie Callan, and the entire SMP team for their warmly felt support; Simon Lipskar and Celia Mobley Taylor of Writers House, for always getting it done for me; my wife Lynn, again, for all the other things beyond the book done daily, without which I would be just an unfinished mess; and as long as I'm at it, my kids who have grown into adults I am truly proud of; and last, my four-legged chorus of barking muses who sit with me for hours every day, Lily and Remy, whose ranks were sadly diminished by one this year, our little warrior, Tobey, who has left a hole here we struggle to fill every day just a bit, like by writing books like this.

If you enjoyed *The Saboteur*, then you'll love

THE ONE MAN

Auschwitz, 1944.

Alfred Mendl's days are numbered. But he has little left to live for—his family were torn away from him, his life's work burned in front of his eyes—until a glimmer of hope arises as he watches a game of chess. To the guards Mendl is just another prisoner, but in fact he holds knowledge that only two people in the world possess. The other is working hard for the Nazi war machine.

Four thousand miles away, in Washington, D.C., intelligence lieutenant Nathan Blum decodes messages from occupied Poland. After the Nazis murdered his family, Nathan escaped the Krakow ghetto and is determined to support his new country—and the US government knows exactly how he can. They want to send Nathan on a mission to rescue one man from a place no one can break in to—or out of.

Even if Nathan does make it in and finds him, can they escape the most heavily guarded place on earth?

'A brilliant tour de force'
Peter James